# The King of Stonewood

Book III of the Stonewood Trilogy

Jeremy Hayes

ISBN: 0991864247
ISBN-13: 978-0991864249

This book is for my sister Jackie and her late husband Mike (1960-2014). Thanks for all your help.

# The Stonewood Trilogy

## Book I: The Thieves of Stonewood

## Book II: The Demon of Stonewood

## Book III: The King of Stonewood

### Tales Most Strange
*Coming Soon*

### The Goblin Squad
*Coming Soon*

## Northlord Publishing

Visit us at: www.northlordpublishing.com for news about upcoming releases or to contact the author.

Copy Editor: Daphne Lavers, M.J.
Cover Art: Mike Kotsopoulos
Cover Design: Robert Przybylo
Website/Logo: Cody Kotsopoulos www.kotsysdesigns.com

# PROLOGUE

Evonne was shoved roughly along a cobblestone street in the lower east district and nearly fell for the tenth time. Her left arm throbbed with immense pain. She had worn a sling to support her broken arm but at the time of her arrest, the injured arm was torn from the sling in order to shackle her wrists together in front of her. Vrawg lay unmoving in a prison wagon pulled by two horses a short distance behind her.

A crowd had been gathering in the streets to watch the two prisoners being delivered to Castle Stonewood. There was no cheering from this crowd though, as was common when criminals were paraded through the streets. This day, the folk of Stonewood were silent. Many wore expressions of pity for the pair of unfortunate bounty hunters.

Following their escape from that ill-fated throne room battle on the King's birthday, Evonne and Vrawg had chosen to hide out in the cellar of the Emerald Clover Tavern to nurse their injuries. Evonne had suffered a broken left arm and Vrawg had received a terrible wound across his chest from the demon lord's flaming sword. The half-ogre's skin was already a greyish shade but his wound became infected and he now took on a sickly hue. The mighty bounty hunter was extremely weak and was unable to put up a fight when the Cult's guards had come to arrest them.

It would seem that the tavern's owner had turned them in out of fear, not wishing to be found as someone harboring wanted fugitives by the new ruler of Stonewood, Lucivenus. The demon had demanded that all those who stood against him in the throne room be found and brought to justice. Anyone found aiding these individuals would suffer the same fate.

With glazed eyes, Evonne looked back to her friend and partner lying inside the prison wagon. She figured if he had been himself, Vrawg could have torn the bars open. Instead, he lay there feverish and in pain, too weak to even raise his head. It broke her heart to see him in that state, since the sight was foreign to her. In all the years they had traveled together, she had never before seen him that injured.

The blonde bounty hunter owed him her life. Many years ago, Evonne was a grudgingly-accepted pirate aboard The Grinning Kraken, a well-known and feared pirate ship that terrorized parts of the western coast. Her brother was a crew member and one day she had snuck aboard and hid. Her presence had not been discovered until days later, out at sea. As a courtesy to her brother, her life was spared and she was put to work. She soon became an expert sailor and a fierce warrior, always having to prove herself to her fellow pirates.

The crew had begun to grumble about their current captain, who had been leading them on a series of unsuccessful missions and had executed a few good men for speaking out against him. Early one morning, in front of the entire crew, Evonne fought and killed the pirate captain and took command of the ship. Following that, the ship was battered by several severe storms. Men began to whisper that the sea gods were angry with them because they had allowed a woman aboard their ship and she was now their captain. One pirate in particular, who hated Evonne, predicted the next storm may be their last. Others began to agree.

Rather than killing her outright, the pirates left Evonne on a deserted island with almost no food or water. Even her brother was part of the group who had decided her fate. A week went by and the petite blonde figured her life was soon to end but that is when the sea gods introduced her to Vrawg.

Vrawg was a half-ogre; his mother had been a full-blooded ogre, his father, human. Vrawg had found no acceptance within either group. Full-blooded ogres shunned him and humans despised him as some kind of abomination. In great despair, the half-ogre had stolen a rowboat and decided to sail off the edge of the world. Instead, a great storm had raged and eventually carried his small boat to the island where Evonne had been abandoned. That was the beginning of a great friendship and bond that neither had ever experienced before. Each would be willing to trade their life to protect the other, if it came to that.

Now, though, it appeared that they were both going to lose their lives, with neither of them being able to aid the other. Evonne could imagine no other outcome after they were brought before Lucivenus and that wretched Sarvin. Stonewood was supposed to make them a fortune, not be their doom.

Another rough shove and this time Evonne did fall to the street, bloodying her knees.

"Get up, wench!" shouted one of the guards escorting the pair.

When the blonde bounty hunter did not immediately do as she was told, she took a hard kick to the ribs which stole her breath. The other guards chuckled while the crowd looked on silently.

"Now I am only going to count to three," the same nasty guard said, looming over the petite woman. "One….two…"

Three never came, as the guard choked on an arrow that lodged in his throat. The armored guard collapsed on top of Evonne, gasping for breath. She managed to squirm out from underneath him just in time to watch the next closest guard suffer the same fate. Shouts of alarm erupted from the crowd and Evonne noticed movement on a nearby roof. She watched as an archer, in a dark green cloak, drew back his bowstring and fired a third arrow into a guard who had his horn to his lips. He was on the verge of calling for backup but never got the chance to blow his horn.

Suddenly, it was chaos in the street as several cloaked individuals brandishing swords, struck out at the remaining guards. Evonne found one of the men a strange sight indeed. He was a tall, black-skinned warrior, wearing a steel mask like those of the gladiators in the south. He wielded his sword like a master, driving it through the belly of one guard, then removing the weapon-hand of another.

Evonne took note of the warrior closest to him, not quite as tall but more heavily-set. As he swung his sword at a guard, the hood of his cloak fell back revealing a head of salt-and-pepper hair, with a beard to match. She had seen this man before. He was a former guard captain, named Dornell and a friend to the thief Harcourt.

Dornell parried two attacks from the guard before felling him with a mighty counter-attack. Another guard attempted to rush in at the former captain's exposed back but ignoring her pain, Evonne kicked out a leg and tripped the man. Dornell drove his blade into the man's back as he sprawled onto the street, then shot a wink to the blonde bounty hunter.

Another cloaked individual, a sword in one hand, a dagger in the other, engaged two guards in a fierce battle. The man parried one blade with his dagger, then countered with his sword before skipping back and repeating the same moves with the other guard. Both guards suffered minor wounds without finding a way past the cloaked man's defense.

They spread out, hoping that one could draw his attention while leaving his back open to the other. The guard in front rushed in but had his attack parried, while the second guard swung but found only air as the man ducked and side-stepped out of reach.

The heavier of the two guards turned to face the man, then fell to his knees as a thrown dagger found his chest. The man sprinted forward to end the guard's life with his remaining sword but had his attack blocked by the second guard. Sparks flew off the pair's blades as they exchanged several quick strikes. The cloaked man was much faster and more determined. He found an opening and drove his blade through the mail shirt the guard wore.

The man then spotted a fleeing guard raising a horn to his mouth. "Barros! Quickly!" he shouted to the archer on the roof.

Barros had already taken aim at the guard and his shot was true. The guard was dead before he hit the ground. Dornell and Na'Jala, for that, in fact, was the dark-skinned gladiator, felled the last two guards before the former captain leaped upon one of the horses pulling the prison wagon and turned him around. Na'Jala lifted Evonne onto the wagon, then Dornell spurred the wagon team in the opposite direction it had been traveling.

There was a collective gasp from the crowd that remained at the scene of the battle as the cloaked man with the sword and dagger pulled back his hood.

"It's the King!" shouted one man from the crowd.

"King Stonewood lives!" shouted another.

King Stonewood smiled and nodded to the gathered group, then disappeared with Na'Jala and two others down an alley.

"God has not forsaken us! He has spared the King's life! King Stonewood shall save us!" shouted a tall, attractive woman with long brown hair, before she too disappeared into an alley.

# CHAPTER 1

"How is it possible that the King lives?" bellowed an enraged Lucivenus, who was seated upon his throne. "I killed him in this very room!"

The throne of Stonewood was inlaid with gold and jewels. It had been built much larger than the men who previously sat upon it, so it was the perfect size for the eight-foot demon lord.

"I witnessed the strike that felled the King, so this cannot be possible," added High Priest Sarvin, standing dutifully to the side of the throne.

"My lords," replied Captain Aaron, kneeling before the throne. "I have lived in this city for over twenty years. I have met the King on many occasions. I swear to you what I saw was him. He has led three separate attacks against us south of the river."

"A trick. That meddlesome Fezzdin has cast some sort of spell on everyone. The King could not have survived his injury," Sarvin said, unconvinced.

"How has he not been caught yet?" Lucivenus

growled. "Three separate attacks and each time he has escaped? Escaped to where?"

"My lord, they strike fast and without warning. They disappear just as fast. There are many places in this vast city to hide. Possibly, the sewers even," answered Captain Aaron.

Nearby, Gervas did his best to hide his smile. He was a frail and elderly man, who had been the closest advisor to the last King and his father before him. His life had been spared by the vile usurpers, for now. Gervas was the most knowledgeable about the city and its goings-on, as well as the day-to-day duties of running the castle. He was more useful alive and was not seen as a threat. The elderly man had prayed that the King was alive and well and now the rumors seemed to claim exactly that. Perhaps there was hope still.

Gervas then frowned as two figures marched into the throne room, blood splattered on their armor. The one on the right was an imposing individual, standing six-foot-six and wearing a full set of ebony plate mail armor. A great sword was strapped to his back. He was bald, with two small horns protruding from his forehead, his skin had a rosy tinge to it. Phyzantiss was a half-demon knight, some distant cousin to Lucivenus.

Next to him stood Gryndall, another half-demon. He too wore black armor but held an ebony scepter in place of a sword. The six-foot demonic warlock, sported various tattoos along his neck and all over his face and bald head. A gold ring hung from his nose much like the demon lord seated before him.

High Priest Sarvin also frowned at the arrival of the pair. He did not much care for either of them and they did not show him much respect. Lucivenus had opened a gate to the Abyss and summoned his old companions to join with him here. Demons were very territorial and jealous of one another. Lucivenus could have summoned any number of full-blooded demons to this world, where they could wreak utter havoc but it would not be long before they would become jealous of each other and attempt to kill one another. It was just their way. Half-demons were less powerful and less ambitious, easier to control. Lucivenus knew that neither of these two would ever dare raise a hand against him. He was a full-blooded demon and a lord among his own kind.

The demon lord also appeared to enjoy the company of his own kind as well and conversed more with these two than with the High Priest. Sarvin felt they saw him as inferior, just a weak human but that was not the case.

"You have just seen battle?" Lucivenus figured by the fresh blood splattered on their armor, he could even smell it.

"Yes, my lord," Phyzantiss replied in a deep voice. "This King has struck again in the lower east district. Gryndall and I arrived too late. The cowards were already fleeing. They slaughtered fourteen of our men before scattering into the streets. We killed only four."

"How do you know it was the King?" asked Lucivenus.

The demonic knight then looked to a portrait of King Stonewood that still hung from the throne room wall; nobody had yet bothered to tear it down. "That is who I saw my lord, it was exactly him."

The demon lord growled. "Impossible! He should be dead! How is that you saw him and yet he got away again?"

Gryndall spoke up. "The old wizard put up a force barrier between us. By the time I dispelled it, they were gone. These worms know the city well, they can blend in and disappear very easily."

"They will slip up soon. We are too many. They cannot fight us all," said Phyzantiss.

"There is still the matter of how the King survived. Do you suspect a trick, Gryndall?" asked the demon lord.

"I sensed a great deal of magic on the street, my lord. But then, the old wizard was there. He is no minor magician, this one. It could have been emanating from him," the warlock replied.

"If this is not a trick from Fezzdin, then it is possible the priests from the temple found a way to revive him," Sarvin cut in, wanting to be a part of the discussion.

"I thought you said the First Priest was killed?" Lucivenus inquired.

"He was, but many priests still reside within that temple. Perhaps one or more are powerful enough with spells of healing," Sarvin answered.

The demon lord turned his attention back to Captain Aaron, the Cult-promoted captain of the lower west district. "What is the status of the temple?"

"We have it surrounded, my lord. The priests have barricaded themselves inside. None may escape," the captain informed him.

"I do not wish them just held captive, I wish them destroyed. Phyzantiss, I want you to lead a force against the temple. Get inside and kill everyone you find. Leave none alive. Then torch the building," Lucivenus commanded.

"Yes, my lord," Phyzantiss said with a bow.

"I have been too lenient on this city thus far," the demon lord said, turning back to the High Priest. "We will root out this King and these rebels and we will make examples of them for all to see what happens to those who oppose Lucivenus. Perhaps we should begin bringing in wraggoth troops for increased patrols of the streets and a sweep of the sewers."

"I do not think the King, if it is indeed the King, would be hiding in the sewers. They are controlled for the most part by the Thieves Guild and there is no love between those two groups," Sarvin figured.

"After we have dealt with this temple, perhaps we should begin searching every building then, one by one. When we catch the King, I will make him wish he had stayed dead," Lucivenus promised.

Gervas hung his head; those poor priests and priestesses, he thought.

\*     \*     \*     \*

Sister Krestina said the words of a blessing and touched the blade of a sword with a silvery, glowing finger. She had been at this all evening long. The wizard Fezzdin had informed them that normal weapons could not harm demons and devils, which was part of what made them formidable enemies. Only magical weapons or those blessed by someone of strong faith could hurt the vile beasts. So Krestina had been tasked with blessing all of the weapons and armor available to her companions, since none of them possessed any magical blades. Eventually, they planned to meet Lucivenus in combat again but this time they would be better prepared.

The old wizard had been tirelessly seeking answers to how they could defeat the demon lord and banish him yet again from this world. The problem was that they simply did not have the magic and allies available to them that the first King of Stonewood had when they defeated Lucivenus three hundred years ago. Fezzdin was a powerful wizard but there were limits to his power and his knowledge of such things as battling demons. It was not a topic he chose to study at much length, never believing it would be necessary.

Krestina wished that First Priest Viktor was still alive. Surely he would have knowledge of such things. The elderly priest seemed to know a little bit about everything. He was wise and perhaps even older than Fezzdin, whose true age was not known. That disgusting Cult murdered the First Priest though and many other friends of Krestina. Her eyes glistened with tears at the memory of the temple massacre.

The beautiful, brown-haired priestess sat alone in the cellar of the Ogre's Den tavern where her companions had stock-piled weapons and armor. Three lanterns illuminated the dark and chilly room, causing strange shadows to dance upon the walls. The tavern had lain abandoned since the murder of its owner, the northern-born mercenary, Wulfred. So they had decided to use the building as one of their many hideouts.

Lucivenus had patrols of Cult-led guards scouring the city for the survivors of the throne room battle, searching especially for the King of Stonewood. A curfew was placed on the city and woe to those who were caught prowling the streets at night. Torture and death was also promised to anyone who aided this group.

Aside from that, Stonewood was to continue on as usual. The people were to go about their daily business and would not be harmed if they followed the rules set by the demon lord. He had told them that nothing had changed, only the one who sits on the throne was different. Most folk were disgusted by the demon and the Cult but were too afraid to speak up or act. They felt there was nothing that they could do, especially since the King was said to have been killed, the two princes gone missing and the royal wizard Fezzdin had fled.

Now though, there were whispers in the streets. People swore that they had seen the King of Stonewood with their own eyes, fighting back against the usurpers. Others claimed to have seen the wizard Fezzdin and even Prince Orval fighting alongside the King. Some folk just thought them rumors, spread by people needing something to believe in. But the sightings had become more frequent, with more and more eye-witnesses. Some group was taking up arms and fighting back, so hope had begun to spread.

The cellar door opened and gave the priestess a momentary start. A smile spread across her face as she watched the King of Stonewood descend the stairs to stand beside her. He wore black, studded-leather armor and was draped in a dark cloak that now hung in tatters. Blood flowed from a wound on his right forearm. He returned her smile with bright blue eyes.

"My lord, you are hurt?" she said with genuine concern.

"It's just a scratch," replied the King, who mumbled some words under his breath and peeled off his face.

His bright blue eyes were replaced with brown ones

and his blondish-grey hair and beard vanished, leaving behind the short dark hair and facial stubble of the thief she loved.

Krestina grabbed Harcourt's arm to examine the wound, then quickly began praying for a spell of healing. Her hands glowed with a silver radiance as the prayer was answered. A moment later, a faint scar was all that was left of the wound. The thief leaned over and kissed the priestess before sitting down on the floor and leaning against a barrel of ale.

"How do your spells differ from Fezzdin's?" the thief asked curiously.

"Well, Fezzdin studies his spells from books or scrolls. He memorizes the words then recalls them at the time he so chooses. His mind can only hold so many spells at one time, so he must choose which would be the most useful for different situations. Fezzdin was someone born with a natural ability to read magical texts and understand their workings," Krestina answered. "I pray for mine. If God so chooses, he grants me the ability to cast them. The more experienced you are and the stronger your faith, then the more powerful the spells. I study books too, but those increase my faith with more knowledge."

"If God is so powerful and is a goodly being, why does he suffer the existence of Lucivenus? Why does God not destroy the demon himself?"

The priestess thought on her answer before continuing. "Because this is our world. God has given us a place to live and it is ours to defend. God provides us all with the tools with which to defeat evil but it is up to us how we use them."

Harcourt held a razor-sharp dagger up before his face

and admired the workmanship. "I don't know. Wendall, the dwarven smithy, provides me with the tools to do what I have to do."

Krestina sat down next to the thief and playfully pushed him. "You know what I mean. I was not referring to physical tools."

"How do you know your god is the true god? There are so many gods. Are the others false? Are their followers a bunch of misguided fools?"

"No, there are other gods, lesser gods. And they do answer the prayers of their faithful. This Sarvin worships Xorbanzula, the god of demons and devils who watches over the Abyss."

"But if this demon god is only a lesser god, then surely they can be no match for you and the others that worship the true god," Harcourt reasoned.

"No. Remember I said that experience and faith play a large part. Sarvin is unwavering in his faith and devotion to this dark god, which makes him very powerful."

"You know you are very cute when you are talking about the gods," the thief teased, causing the priestess to blush.

Harcourt felt he was fortunate that Krestina had been so understanding about everything. Not long after her rescue from the castle, when she had enough rest, the thief had sat her down and explained everything to her starting from the night he met Warden and received the magical mask. She sat silently, like a child being read a favorite bedtime story and listened to the entire tale. She told him how devastated she was when he had been arrested for murder and given a life sentence, then completely heartbroken at the news of his death.

She was angry at first that he had not simply told her the truth from the beginning, when he had met her as Weldrick. But he convinced her that it was for her own safety that she not know it was him, and that he had been planning to tell her before being arrested and sent away again with Dornell. Krestina had told him of her visions and dreams and how she always felt there was a connection between him and Weldrick. She marveled at the magical mask and how it worked so amazingly. When Harcourt wore the face of the King, none could ever tell that it was the thief with a mask. It was a truly wondrous item.

Sounds of booted feet above drew the thief's attention. "They are back. Come on up," he said, standing and holding out a hand to pull the priestess to her feet.

"You go, I will join you shortly. I have only a few more weapons left to bless," she replied.

Krestina watched the thief ascend the stairs and disappear. She smiled. Never in her life had she been in more danger and yet never in her life had she been more happy. For most of her life she had dreamed of being with Harcourt, to hold him, to kiss him. And for most of her life he did not even realize she existed. Krestina was younger then and the thief loved another. The priestess always wished that she was in Jalanna's place and yet she never wished the woman any ill-will. She was jealous of her but not in a hateful way. Krestina was truly saddened by the news of Jalanna's murder. She also knew how devastated Harcourt must have been at that time and she wished she could have been there for him, to console him, but he was thrown in the dungeon, far out of reach.

It was hard for her to imagine ever loving another as

much as she had loved Harcourt. The man was ruggedly handsome and a kind soul. A criminal yes, but his heart was in the right place, she knew. Harcourt always did his best to look after the kids who needed help in the south district and was always first to lend a helping hand or chase off bullies. The thief had saved Krestina on countless occasions, though was too drunk at the time to remember them all.

Krestina was a woman now and not the little girl she was when she first met the thief. She had finally achieved her life-long goal of finding a way into the man's heart. After telling her his tale of the mask and his life leading up to this point, they embraced and kissed. She was fearful, then, that she would wake from one of her many vivid dreams, that Harcourt's story was but an illusion, only this time it was real. Their city was in peril, they were being hunted by an evil Cult, but she had the love of Harcourt that she had always sought. She knew that Jalanna still held a piece of his heart and always would. But she understood that and would never ask him to forget her completely. She was willing to share.

She thanked God for allowing him back into her life. With all the danger around them, she felt very safe knowing that he was here to protect her, as he had many times in the past. And now he was using his magical mask in a noble cause, to help protect the rest of the people in Stonewood and give them hope that this evil demon would be overthrown and defeated.

Long live the King of Stonewood, she thought with a smile, before returning to her task of blessing the last few weapons.

\*   \*   \*   \*

"Fezzdin, what were those two we saw at the end of that last battle, more demons?" Harcourt asked, as he joined his companions in the main taproom of the boarded-up Ogre's Den tavern.

Fezzdin had just arrived, along with Dornell and Na'Jala, cloaked and very careful not to have been seen or followed. Already in one corner of the room, lay Vrawg. The monstrous bounty hunter was still weak but feeling much better; his infection having been eliminated by Krestina's healing hands. His normal shade of grey had returned. Evonne was seated at an empty table hoisting a mug of ale with her previously broken arm, which had also been healed by Krestina.

"Not demons, but half-demons. But do not think them any less dangerous," replied the wizard.

Harcourt shook his head. Their situation went from bad to worse. So much of the world he thought he lived in had changed. The thief had grown up without ever leaving the confines of the city. He had never believed in magic or monsters. He thought they were all tales spun to amaze or strike fear into children. But oh, had he ever been wrong.

A demon now sat on the throne of Stonewood, half-demons roamed the streets looking for them and an army of subterranean beasts surrounded the entire city. On top of that, one of his closest friends now, was a wizard and his lover could cast spells granted to her from a god.

"One of them was a wizard, I think. He took down your magical barrier just as we got away," Dornell commented.

"A warlock, and yes he did. Very careful we must be

in the future. These are two formidable foes," Fezzdin said.

"Are we having any real effect?" Harcourt wondered.

"Of course we are, my boy!" the wizard replied, patting him on the shoulder. "Folk are whispering that the King is alive and well and is going to save the city. They are gaining some measure of hope. Some have already even struck back. There were some minor skirmishes earlier this morning."

"We still cannot win this city back without Stonewood's army," Dornell reasoned. "We are going to have to dispatch some riders to reach them and inform them of what is going on here. I believe they must still be oblivious. We should also get a rider out to Thelvius and his mercenaries, his help will also be greatly needed."

"Agreed," the wizard said. "It is just a matter of how to get them past the wraggoth, but I may have an idea."

Harcourt rubbed his chin in thought. "Why Stonewood? What does Lucivenus have against this city?"

Fezzdin sat down in a chair and leaned back. "This tale begins centuries ago with a foolish wizard, as stories such as these often begin. Del-Haro was a minor conjurer here in Stonewood, still an apprentice, and eager to prove himself. Many wizards are tempted, from time to time, to summon demons or other such creatures in order to gain more knowledge or to learn dark secrets. This is no easy task and the proper precautions must be taken. A summoning circle must be perfectly drawn and painstakingly warded, to prevent the summoned being from escaping. Del-Haro was a fool and not prepared to deal with the demon lord that he had summoned, Lucivenus. Fortunately for mankind, demons and devils have no way into our world from the Abyss, unless summoned. Once here though, they wish to stay, finding humans weak and easily defeated. Del-Haro's wards could not hold Lucivenus within the summoning circle; a massacre took place. When the demon lord was finished with Del-Haro and his master, along with all their house staff, he set his sights on the castle and the King. Stonewood was his first taste of our world and his first taste of defeat. Revenge is always a strong motivator."

"Fezzdin, can we expect no help from other cities and territories?" Harcourt asked.

"Yes, what about Cardinal's Gate?" Dornell added, referring to the Holy City and main temple to the One True God. "Surely they would be outraged by our situation here. They have a massive army of holy warriors and warrior-priests."

Cardinal's Gate was the site of the oldest and largest temple dedicated to the One True God. Over hundreds and hundreds of years a city was built around the temple, a city that rivaled the size of Stonewood. It was governed by the priests and did possess a very large army.

"Surely they would be outraged," Fezzdin agreed. "But the Holy City is four weeks of hard riding away. That is four weeks for a rider to get there, then another four weeks or more for help to arrive. Time is not on our side here. The longer Lucivenus is allowed to sit on that throne, the tighter his grip will be on this city."

"Then we will keep fighting them, lessening their numbers and weakening them little by little," Na'Jala said, adding to the conversation.

Harcourt truly admired this man. This was not Na'Jala's city or his fight. He had spent many years as a slave and gladiator after being torn from his family by pirates. He was a free man now, free to leave any time he wished and return to his family. Harcourt had already offered him enough gold to get to a southern port and pay for passage on a ship to carry him home. But the man had refused. He considered Harcourt and Dornell his friends. Now, his friends needed help and a lot of it. He would do everything in his power to help his friends save their city. And not one of them could say they did not appreciate having him around; his swordsmanship was astounding.

A scratching sound at the back door to the Den had everyone in the room reaching for weapons. Fezzdin motioned for them all to calm down, then opened the door just enough so that an orange cat could slip into the room. Lex trotted in and dropped a dead pigeon onto the floor; a pigeon with a message attached to its leg. Fezzdin picked up the dead bird and detached the rolled-up piece of parchment.

"Now Lex," the wizard scolded, "you are not supposed to kill the messenger birds."

The cat responded with a series of meowing noises. As silly as it made the thief feel, Harcourt asked anyway. "What did he say?"

"He said 'what did I expect, he is a cat'," Fezzdin replied, scanning the contents of the message. His face paled, then he looked up. "It's from Gervas at the castle. Lucivenus means to destroy the temple and everyone in it."

Harcourt looked to the cellar door. Krestina was not going to take this news well.

# CHAPTER 2

The battering ram crashed into the great double doors for the third time with a thunderous *BOOM*. Wood splintered but still the doors held. The doors to the temple were thick and strong and barricaded from the inside. Windows had also been boarded up and barricaded. The faithful inside were under siege.

"Captain Aaron, the doors still hold," reported one of the Cult's warriors. "Perhaps there is an easier way in?"

"Keep battering them, they cannot stay standing forever," the captain ordered.

Once again a crowd of spectators had gathered at each end of the street, their expressions reflecting their shock. The Cult had a considerable force assembled for this task, so they were not so worried about any surprise attack from the King and his little band of rebels. But just in case, the two half-demons were present to oversee the destruction of the temple.

After watching several more failed attempts with the battering ram, Gryndall had seen enough. The demonic warlock approached the doors and waived away the men with the ram. He closed his eyes and fell into deep concentration. Hands held out in front of him, he began chanting the words of a spell. A moment later, a great ball of fire erupted from his hands and sped towards the temple's doors. It exploded with tremendous heat, incinerating the thick double doors, leaving nothing but a pile of ash in its wake.

Captain Aaron turned to Phyzantiss and received a nod from the demonic knight. "Into the temple! Spread out and kill everyone you find," he shouted to his men.

Cultists swarmed into the temple, screaming with weapons drawn. The assembled spectators looked on with sad faces.

"Captain, I don't think this is right," said a city guard, who now stood next to Captain Aaron outside the temple.

"Since when did you become a holy man, Len?" the captain replied.

"I am not, but those are still innocent people in there. Why do they all have to be killed? They barricaded themselves inside, they were not planning to attack anyone."

"Innocent? Innocent, you say? They were plotting against our new lord, Lucivenus. And for that, they must be destroyed. Now get in there and do your duties," Aaron commanded.

"No sir, I won't," Len replied defiantly.

"Christoph, Samm, arrest this man for disobeying orders. Drag him back to the castle dungeon. We will deal with him later," ordered Captain Aaron.

Len grabbed the hilt of his sword but the other two guards were on top of him quickly, forcing him to the ground and shackling his wrists behind his back. With shouts of protest, he was dragged away from the temple.

Brother Larz, a Cult priest, entered the temple with two guards directly behind him, charged with ensuring his safety. He watched as other cultists ran every which way in search of those accursed priests and priestesses. Thus far, there had been no screams for mercy or sounds of battle of any kind. Each corridor he walked down, each room he passed, were all empty. Quite strange, he thought, unless they were smart and holed up in one place to make a final stand.

He decided to seek the main prayer hall. If they were to be hiding anywhere, it would make sense that they would be there. The priest had a good idea of where it was located and soon found himself at the doorway where several cultists stood guard.

"We have found them, Brother," one of the men said as the priest approached.

Larz peered over the shoulders of the men and found a group of eight people, all wearing the brown robes of their order, huddled together in the hall, deep in prayer. Praying for their lives, the evil priest thought with a smile. Well, it would do them no good now.

"Where is your god now? Abandoned you has he?" Larz shouted, walking confidently into the prayer hall. "Pray all you want, he cannot help you now."

"No, but I certainly can," said one petite priestess, standing up to face the Cult priest.

As Larz sneered, the priestess threw off her robe to reveal a set of mismatched pieces of armor she wore underneath. The petite blonde raised a crossbow and fired a bolt directly into the chest of the shocked priest.

Speechless, Larz fell to the ground clutching his chest, while Evonne smiled ear to ear. With a roar, the cultists charged in.

The group in the center of the room all threw off their robes to reveal that they were not the members of the temple that the cultists had thought - well, all save one. A tall, slender woman, with long brown hair kept her robe on and her hands began to glow with a silvery-light. Sister Krestina spoke a single word; a ray of silver energy flew from her hand to blast a hole into the chest of a charging cultist. The two groups clashed in the center of the room. Sparks flew as steel met steel in a fury of motion. More cultists began to swarm the hall. Now finally, the sounds of battle rang out through the temple.

*     *     *     *

"That's our cue, it's begun," whispered Fezzdin, standing on the street amidst the crowd, concealed by his deep blue robe.

From within the hood of his dark cloak, King Stonewood nodded and drew his sword. He glanced up to a nearby rooftop and noted that Barros, an expert archer, was in place. They had waited for the bulk of this force to move into the temple so there were only a small number left on the street, although the demonic warlock was one of them.

Harcourt, wearing the face of the King, waited until the half-demon was rocked back by the blast of a lightning bolt, before charging the closest guards. Captain Aaron turned just in time to draw his sword and deflect the first strike from what appeared to be the King himself.

Smoke rose from Gryndall's black armor but he was otherwise unharmed. Lightning had very little effect on demons and half-demons but the audacity of the attack enraged him. He quickly found the source, as a crowd of spectators put as much distance between themselves and the blue-robed wizard as they could.

The warlock raised his scepter and pointed it at the old wizard. Before he could speak a command word, an arrow skipped off his ebony breastplate startling him. He noticed the archer on the rooftop pulling back his bowstring for a second shot. Gryndall smiled. The fools must not have realized that normal weapons could not harm him.

The archer let fly his arrow and with amazing accuracy, the shaft found an opening in the warlock's armor at the top of his left thigh. The arrow bit deep and the half-demon howled in pain as the wound burned with an intense sensation. The cursed arrow had been blessed, Gryndall assumed. He did not have time to ponder that issue as a blast of razor-sharp ice pellets assaulted him. Some bounced off his armor, some found openings and penetrated his skin.

With a growl, the warlock erected an invisible wall of force which protected him from the continuing rain of ice pellets, then hobbled for the doors of the temple seeking cover from the archer. A third arrow snapped in half as it struck his armored back before he ducked for cover within the walls of the temple.

Folk nearby watched in awe as the King of Stonewood battled with the guard captain of the lower west district. Three of the captain's guards were kept busy battling five other cloaked men who had rushed them from the crowd. A cheer went up as the King drew first blood, his sword slicing through to the captain's shoulder.

Captain Aaron grimaced as the wound stung. He was caught completely off-guard by the speed of the King's attacks. The captain knew that the King had been a great warrior but he should not have possessed the speed that he did for his age. Aaron was an accomplished warrior himself, one had to be to achieve the level of captain. He was thirty-one years old and youth, speed and strength were supposed to be on his side. Yet he found himself outmatched and it was all that he could do to keep the King's blade at bay.

The King led with a series of three quick attacks, only two of which Aaron could block. The third dug into his forearm just below the elbow and he nearly dropped his blade. The captain stepped back out of reach and from the corner of an eye watched the last of his men fall with an arrow in his neck.

As he turned his full attention back to the King, he watched the man's blade find his belly and slip through his mail shirt. Again, the speed of the King had caught him off-guard and it was now the last mistake he ever made.

A blast of frost flew forth from the tip of Fezzdin's staff, until the front doorway to the temple was completely covered in a sheet of thick ice, effectively trapping the warlock inside, for the time being.

Another cheer erupted from the crowd.

\*　　\*　　\*　　\*

Caught by surprise, the first wave of cultists were dispatched fairly quickly and without major injury to the group disguised as members of the temple. Harcourt had told his companions about a secret tunnel leading into the temple from the sewers below and about Brother Pitor, who was not actually named, which had drawn a disappointed head-shake from Krestina. The thief had never used the tunnel before, so navigating their way through the sewers to find the temple entrance had not been easy.

The priests and priestesses of the temple had been trapped inside the building, never aware that an escape route was available to them. Not wanting to leave these innocent folk to the fate that Lucivenus had in store for them, King Stonewood came to the rescue, liberating them. Then, disguised as members of the temple, a small task force lay in wait for the Cult to make their move, while others were positioned outside.

Harcourt had wanted to be inside the temple with Dornell, where the fighting would be the fiercest but Fezzdin had reminded the thief that the people of Stonewood needed to see that it was the King himself who was coming to the rescue of the temple. He needed to be visible on the street.

So it was Dornell who led the group inside the temple and it was Dornell who just removed the head of a screaming cultist who rounded the corner into the prayer hall.

"We have made our statement, I think now it is time we go," commented Evonne.

The petite bounty hunter did not wish to linger long within the temple since there was only a small number of them here. And Vrawg was not one of them. Evonne always felt safe when her hulking partner was close by but the group did not feel he was well enough to participate in this battle. It was not easy convincing the half-ogre to stay behind but eventually Evonne had won that argument. She knew that Dornell and Na'Jala were capable warriors but they would not have her back the way Vrawg would.

"I agree with the bounty hunter," Na'Jala said, impaling a second cultist who had just run into the room. "They are too many."

"No!" cried Krestina. "We cannot just leave. They are going to destroy the temple!"

Dornell placed a gentle hand on the shoulder of the priestess. "There is nothing more we can do, sister. We are too few. We have rescued your brothers and sisters and that was our main goal. The fate of the temple is out of our hands. We must retreat back to the sewers before we find ourselves overwhelmed in here. I trust that the King and Fezzdin have done their part outside."

Tears formed in Krestina's eyes. She could not stand the thought of her beloved home being destroyed by the evil Cult. She was supposed to be beyond the feelings of hatred and revenge but at this moment she did hate the Cult and wanted them to pay for all that they had done. She knew that Dornell spoke true but found her feet rooted to the floor, not wishing to leave.

It took Evonne, who was not as gentle as Dornell, to convince her. "Come on, you want to be Sarvin's guest in the dungeon again? Or a plaything for that demon?"

The bounty hunter grabbed the priestess by her robe and pulled her from her spot. Krestina reluctantly followed.

There was a small cloak room located in the far corner of the prayer hall. Inside the room there were several large closets. One particular closet was always locked to most members of the temple and that was where Brother Pitor and other thieves came and went. Dornell reopened the closet door and ushered Krestina into the dark stairwell first with Evonne in tow.

Cries of alarm, followed by a shriek of pain, brought Dornell running back into the prayer hall. One of their men, a former guard by the name of Koswell, lay on the floor nearly cleaved in half. A second man, Heinrick, then lost his head and joined the other body on the floor. Standing over both men, was the imposing figure of the half-demon knight.

Dornell's stomach was in knots. For much of his life he had been the captain of the guard in Stonewood's most dangerous district. In that time he had fought countless thieves and murderers. But those had been men. The figure standing across the great hall was no man.

"Na'Jala, Rolph, Drayden, get down into the sewers, I will cover the rear," Dornell commanded.

"We will cover the rear," Na'Jala corrected, having no intention of leaving his friend behind.

"We shall all stay. Surely that monster cannot fight all four of us," Rolph said confidently.

"Someone should get down there with the women in the sewers, that is no safe haven down there," implored Dornell.

"Those women are more than capable of taking care of themselves me thinks," Drayden said. "And besides, it will greatly aid our cause to rid ourselves of this one," the man said, pointing his sword at the demonic knight and charging forward. "For King Stonewood!"

The fact that King Stonewood truly was dead and

that Harcourt was playing at being the King was not
known amongst all their men. That information stayed
within their small circle of companions. It was good for
morale that everyone believed Harcourt really was the
King of Stonewood. In fact, it almost worked too well.

Phyzantiss raised his great sword and smiled at the
charging former guard. The three other men fanned out
doing their best to surround the demonic knight and he
did not care. Dornell did not relish this fight, even though
it was currently four on one. Drayden had a point though,
it would be a huge blow to the Cult if they could kill this
half-demon here and now while the opportunity presented
itself.

Drayden, who was no small man himself, swung at
the half-demon with a downwards, over-hand chop.
Phyzantiss held his sword out, effectively blocking the
attack as if it had come from a mere child. With a twirl of
his wrist, Phyzantiss, sent the former guard's sword
spinning across the room, then penetrated his mail shirt
and split open his stomach with a mighty chop of his own.

The demonic knight did not even wait for the man's
body to hit the floor before he maneuvered himself to his
next target and swung at the strangely-armored, black-
skinned warrior to his right. Na'Jala blocked the attack but
the sheer strength of the blow caused him to take a few
steps back. The former gladiator came back with a counter
of his own but was out of range and found only air, the
half-demon's much longer sword keeping him just out of
reach.

Na'Jala spent years fighting for his life in the arenas
of Gladenfar. The man who was once a peaceful fisherman
had been transformed into a master-warrior, a professional

killer. He had fought and killed more men than he could ever keep track of. On one occasion, after angering a lord of the great southern port-city, he was thrown into the arena against three opponents, which was supposed to have been the end of him. Na'Jala had prevailed. But never during his life as a gladiator had he ever faced-off against an opponent like this one. He did not fear death. To be a gladiator was to accept that death waited nearby during every battle, looking to clamp a bony hand down and claim you for the underworld. So Na'Jala returned the icy-stare of the demonic knight and stepped forward, looking for an opening to get into reach.

Dornell took advantage of the knight's attention on Na'Jala and lunged in striking the half-demon's left side with his sword but the ebony armor repelled the attack. The former captain barely ducked underneath a back-handed counter from the knight and retreated back out of reach.

Just as Rolph was about to attempt an attack of his own, a crossbow bolt found his chest and sat him on the floor in a sitting position. Three cultists entered the prayer hall from the main door, one reloading his crossbow.

"Stay back!" shouted Phyzantiss in his deep voice. "These two are mine!"

Not wishing to anger the half-demon any further, the cultists remained near the doorway to watch the battle from a distance.

Dornell and Na'Jala exchanged glances of concern. They had just gone from four on one, to two on one, very quickly, with more cultists held in reserve. They should have just fled to the sewers when they had the chance. Phyzantiss lunged at Dornell with an impaling-attack but the former captain was able to parry. Not missing a beat, the demonic knight spun and swung for Na'Jala with a decapitating strike which just missed. Even being outnumbered, the half-demon kept pressure on his two opponents which forced them both to remain on the defensive.

Na'Jala finally landed a counter-attack but was off-balance and his blade could not penetrate the knight's strong armor. Phyzantiss countered that counter and drew a line of blood across the former gladiator's shoulder before spinning back to parry an attack by Dornell. A gauntleted left hand shot out and struck Dornell solidly on the jaw with a crunch, staggering him. Seizing advantage of his stunned opponent, Phyzantiss, sliced Dornell's sword-arm causing him to drop his weapon and recoil with a gasp.

Na'Jala charged forward, more so to shift the half-demon's attention away and buy Dornell some time to recover. Phyzantiss blocked two attacks with a rain of sparks, before countering with two of his own. The second swing drew more blood from the former gladiator's neck.

The demonic knight was a formidable warrior, Na'Jala knew, but it was his size, strength and reach that truly gave him the advantage. For one of the only times in his life, Na'Jala, felt this opponent was too much for him alone and did not know what he could possibly do to defeat him.

At that moment, there was a blinding light, then an explosion which sent the half-demon flying through the hall's main doorway, taking the three cultists with him. When Na'Jala's sight returned, he found himself on the floor looking up at the ceiling. With a shake of his head, he sat up, noticing Dornell a short distance away wearing the same perplexed look. A voice drew both of their attention.

"Quickly, let's go. That will only have stunned him for a moment," said Krestina.

\*    \*    \*    \*

A loud explosion could be heard from within the temple and Fezzdin turned to the King. "We have lingered long enough, time to disappear."

As the wizard finished his sentence, horns began to blast about a block away. A quick glance up to Barros, who was still perched on the rooftop, confirmed that reinforcements were quickly approaching. The archer gave hand signals which told his companions below that ten men were on their way and then vanished from sight.

King Stonewood gave a salute to the gathered crowd before pulling his hood back up over his face. Fezzdin mumbled the words to a spell, then blew a handful of dust in front of him. The dust particles became fog, then grew in mass so that soon the entire street in front of the temple was enveloped in a thick cloud of fog.

The Cult's reinforcements arrived on horseback but when the fog eventually cleared, the King and his troublesome companions had all but disappeared.

\*    \*    \*    \*

As the fog on the street cleared completely, a large cloaked man, standing amidst the crowd, decided it was time to leave as well. He had watched the battle in front of the temple with extreme interest.

High Priest Sarvin had to see with his own eyes whether it was indeed King Stonewood fighting back against their forces. He was now convinced that the King lived. Surprisingly though, the King's reflexes were much quicker than Sarvin would have expected from a man his age. But that unexpected agility might also solve the mystery of Sarvin's missing elixir, the one that made you younger. Meddlesome thieves had broken into his private quarters that night of the King's birthday; one of them must have stolen it and it somehow found its way into the King's hands.

*They will all pay for this*, Sarvin thought to himself. Perhaps it was time he sent a message to his old acquaintance, Nestor Nightsbridge, if the man still existed. When rats were needed to be found, Nestor was the man to find them.

"Long live the King of Stonewood!" shouted a grey-bearded man in the crowd to Sarvin's left.

The man suddenly shrieked in pain as a magical blast of acid splashed against his chest and began to eat a hole through his skin.

Scowling, a cloaked Sarvin turned back for the castle.

# CHAPTER 3

The four companions came to a stop when they reached the second fork in the sewer tunnel. Dornell held his lantern aloft but did not recognize either of the two tunnels. Some city guards did patrol the tunnels from time to time but Dornell had never been one of them. The former captain looked to the others but they held the same expression.

"None of you remember if we came this way or not?" Dornell asked.

"It's as though we are a bunch of amateurs. We should have left some kind of markers along the way," commented Evonne, who was very disgusted at the thought of how filthy the water was that had filled her boots. She turned to the priestess. "Can't God just tell you the way out of here?"

"It doesn't work that way," replied Krestina.

Splashing sounds could be heard from the tunnel behind them. "We are being followed," Na'Jala said.

"Quick then, pick a tunnel," implored Evonne.

"Perhaps we should split up, two of us go left, two of us go right," suggested Dornell. "If it's that half-demon, he can only follow one group. We must do our best to find a way out of here and regroup back at the Ogre's Den."

"Ok, bounty hunter girl, let's go right," Na'Jala said, who had the only other lantern.

"Be careful and we will see you soon," Dornell nodded to the pair, before turning down the left tunnel with Krestina following closely behind.

"Let me see your arm," Krestina asked, finally noticing the wound that the former captain suffered.

"No time," he replied. "Let's get out of here first."

"Well see that you don't get any of this disgusting water into that wound," the priestess urged.

Most of the time, the water was only ankle-deep but in some places it rose to knee-deep. Surprisingly, the smell was tolerable, though at times they would pass the droppings of some unknown animal and Krestina truly did not wish to meet whatever left it behind. The tunnels were tall enough so that Dornell could stand without having to stoop.

"Thank you for saving my life up there," Dornell said, after a few twists and turns in silence.

"You and Na'Jala are both great warriors. I believe…"

Dornell cut her off in mid-sentence. "No, that demonic knight would have been the end of me, I have no delusions. Once he disarmed me, I knew it was over. Humans, I can deal with. I fear these creatures of the Abyss are beyond my capabilities."

"Captain, I have lived my entire life in the south district," Krestina said, keeping her voice as low as possible. "I have seen many men faced with certain death, or great harm and very, very few show no fear at those moments. When I ran back into the prayer hall, your expression never wavered, you never took your eyes off that monster. You are very brave."

"Brave? Or foolish?" the former captain actually chuckled.

"I think it is bravery to stare death in the face and not be afraid," the priestess replied.

"It's not that I am not afraid. I would be a liar to tell you that I do not ever feel fear," Dornell said. "But sometimes, I wonder, if I were to die, maybe I would see Zelna again. I am not looking to die but I am comforted by the thought that Zelna waits for me on the other side when I do."

"Was Zelna your wife?"

"No, but she would have been, as soon as we bought the house we were always dreaming about. A couple of street thugs ended that dream though, when they killed her."

"I am so sorry," Krestina said, placing a hand on the man's arm. "But you are right, Zelna's spirit awaits you on the other side. She must have been a good person, a kind soul, for you to have loved her. So rest assured, she will be there to greet you, someday. Just not this day, or any other day soon. We need your help, Captain. Stonewood needs your help still. So you better not go doing anything foolish to endanger yourself. Time has no meaning in the afterlife. Do not fear that Zelna will tire or become restless waiting for you. God looks after her and keeps her busy. When your time comes, then it comes. Do not ever go looking for it. Zelna knows you still have your life to live and I am sure she would be very upset to see you throw it away. Life is precious and we must do everything we can to hang onto it while we can."

Dornell opened his mouth, then just nodded instead. He scolded himself for his thoughts in the prayer hall. When his sword left his grasp, he immediately thought of Zelna and was ready to see her again. The fight had left his body and that was not good. The priestess was right, he was still needed here. He could not let Krommel, or Sarvin, get away with all he had done. He had to keep fighting with every ounce of his life to see this goal to the end. Zelna would want that. And he owed it to his friends. After Zelna died, Dornell did not really have any friends. He was too focused on his work. Captain Flannis was the closest friend that he had had and Flannis died in the throne room battle because of his loyalty to Dornell; another reason to make Sarvin and Lucivenus pay.

Dornell now counted Harcourt as his closest friend and could not abandon the thief. The thought forced another chuckle, albeit a silent one. The man never ceased to amaze him. Harcourt owed Stonewood nothing. Not so long ago, he was a homeless drunk. A common thief, a criminal, Harcourt was even given a life sentence in the dungeon. The city had done nothing for him but bring him misery and yet here he was now, its biggest savior. He was doing more to save this city than anyone else and he asks for nothing in return. The thief feels it is the right thing to do, so he is doing it, Dornell thought with a smile. Stonewood needs more Harcourts.

Krestina caught a slight smile from Dornell and smiled herself. She was hoping whatever demons may have been haunting the man were now gone. She did not plan on stopping until Lucivenus and Sarvin were destroyed and she knew that Dornell was an invaluable member of their group. She also knew that he meant a lot to Harcourt, so he meant a lot to her as well.

A high-pitched shriek erupted from Dornell's lips as he drew the sword he had retrieved earlier and Krestina's heart nearly stopped beating in her chest. She was momentarily paralyzed with fear until she could see no immediate threat, save for a large rat wandering around on a dry spot on the tunnel floor.

"What do you see?" she hazarded to ask.
Dornell merely pointed at the rat with the tip of his sword, his face now pale white.

"What? The rat? Is that all?" the priestess asked. Dornell nodded and jumped back a step when the rat looked up in their direction.

Despite their predicament, Krestina laughed. "Oh, this is priceless. You stare defiantly into the faces of thieves and demons but a rat makes you quiver in your boots?"

"It's not funny, I hate them," Dornell managed to say.

Krestina shook her head. She was worried about coming across snakes, or lizards, or worse. Rats she could deal with. Rats were all over the orphanage, they had almost become like pets. She walked towards the rat, which scurried away through a crack in the tunnel wall before she could get too close.

"Not a word of this to Harcourt," Dornell said without any hint of humor.

"My lips are sealed," Krestina replied.

Voices down another fork in the tunnel drew both

their attention. "Maybe it's Evonne and Na'Jala?" the priestess wondered.

Dornell was not so sure and kept his sword in hand. "Stay behind me."

They crept as silently as possible in the ankle-deep water until they found a small chamber that branched off from their current tunnel and the source of the voices. Two men were whispering but it was difficult to make out the details of their conversation. Dornell risked stepping into the chambers' entrance, Krestina right behind.

The two men jumped and reached for weapons that hung from their belts. "Oy! Who are you creeping about in the dark?" shouted the man on the right, recovering from his initial shock.

The two men were thieves, Dornell was sure of it. He could tell from their grubby appearance and from the coins and trinkets spread across a small table behind them. They had probably just stolen them and had come down here to divide the loot.

Dornell's first instinct was to arrest the two men, whom he believed he could handle without too much trouble but he had to remind himself that times had changed and he was no longer a captain of the guard.

"It's none of your business who I am. I was looking for a quiet place to bring the girl here. Wasn't expecting to find the two of you," Dornell lied.

"Who's the lass, then?" the other thief asked hungrily, licking his lips, eyeing the beautiful priestess.

Dornell held his sword up, blood dripped down his arm from his earlier wound. "She's mine," he barked. "I fought too hard to get her to share her with the likes of you two."

"Alright, alright, just asking was all," the man said.

If this stranger with the sword knew about this hidden chamber, then he must have been a member of the Thieves Guild, the two men figured. He was armed with a long sword and armored, and almost twice their size. They did not wish to anger this man.

"Just let us gather our belongings and the chamber is all yours," one of them said.

"Don't bother, I will find another," Dornell replied, pulling Krestina along roughly for show.

A few more turns in the labyrinthine tunnels and the pair spotted light a short distance away, sunlight.

\*     \*     \*     \*

Na'Jala stood a few inches taller than Dornell, so his head almost scraped the roof of the sewer tunnels. He took the lead, sword in his right hand, the lantern in his left. Evonne followed closely behind, her loaded crossbow held in front of her. She kept glancing backwards, hearing something that remained out of sight.

"You were a pirate, no?" Na'Jala asked in a hushed tone.

Evonne hesitated before answering, having a feeling as to where this conversation was headed. "I was."

"You ever take slaves?" he asked.

"No, not slaves like you think. We took prisoners from battle, yes, other pirates or sailors. Most of the time we ransomed them off," Evonne responded, telling the truth.

"Most of the time?" the former gladiator inquired.

"Yes, most of the time. Other times they were

executed if we could not get the coin we wanted for them. Or they were sold to others in port."

"Sold to slavers?"

"Perhaps. I do not know what happened to them after that. That changed after I took command, though I did not command our ship for very long."

"Did you sail the southern seas?"

"No," she answered, again truthfully. "We stuck to the western coast. Truth be told, there was not much to plunder in your southern isles, at least nothing we knew about. And most of the southern port cities are well fortified, with many ships."

"There is actually much gold and gemstones in the southern isles but they are found deep in the jungles, not a safe place for outsiders. Pirates find it easier to take people to sell."

"Yes, some do. Most pirates have no morals, I agree with you, a wicked lot. I would have been different, if I had been given my chance. But you men, always fearful of a woman in charge."

Na'Jala chuckled. "Not where I am from. Women are strong and cunning. Each village is headed by a matriarch and she is the most respected member of the tribe."

"You were a warrior then? A commander perhaps?" Evonne figured.

"We had no need of armies, no. I was a fisherman."

"But the pirates?"

"They did not appear often, where I lived. We did not see them as a major threat. One or two people would go missing at a time but that was not uncommon. As I mentioned, the jungles can be a dangerous place."

"Times are changing, your people should have had

armed warriors. Many pirates are not interested in attacking people who will put up a fierce resistance. They want easy pickings."

"Agreed, we should have thought of that. But we are a peaceful people and hoped the pirates would leave us be."

"Big mistake," Evonne stated matter-of-factly.

"Why are you no longer a pirate?" Na'Jala asked curiously.

"Let's just say, the sea gods decided another line of work would be best for me," she replied, not wishing to go into detail about being abandoned on a deserted island by her crew and own brother.

"What will your sea gods do for you now, I wonder?" said a deep, booming voice from behind the pair.

Evonne spun and spotted two dots of crimson light in the pitch darkness of the tunnel behind, the eyes of the half-demon knight. Without a second thought, she fired her crossbow but the bolt skipped harmlessly off the warrior's ebony plate armor.

Phyzantiss was hunched over uncomfortably, unable to stand to his full height in the tunnel but even then was an imposing sight. His eyes glowed eerily in the dark. In place of his great sword, the demonic knight held a wicked-looking, crimson-bladed dagger, a more practical weapon for the cramped-quarters of the sewers. It was a dagger to him but was the equivalent of a short sword to anyone else.

Na'Jala turned to Evonne. "Run," was all he said.

Evonne did not need to be told twice. She took off sprinting as fast as she was able in the shin-deep, murky sewer water, fumbling with her crossbow as she attempted to reload. She was a faster runner than Na'Jala but could not allow herself to get too far ahead since he carried the only light source. The former gladiator was right on her heels though.

Laughter echoed off the tunnel walls behind them. "Run, foolish humans. Make a sport of this," Phyzantiss taunted.

"Pay him no heed. He is hampered by the height of the tunnels, he cannot keep up," Na'Jala said, trying to reassure the blonde bounty hunter ahead of him.

The former gladiator was not so sure himself though. He had no idea how the demonic knight even got that close to them in the first place without them hearing his approach. Na'Jala had always known about the existence of monsters and super-natural beasts. The jungles of his homeland held many things that should not be seen through the eyes of men, horrors that crept out of ancient temples built by an unknown race. But he had no knowledge of how best to combat them. This knight was unlike any man he had ever faced in the arena. He felt no shame in fleeing, he was no good to his friends dead.

Evonne was in the lead, so made the decisions of where to go. They took a left when the tunnel forked next, then another left, then a right. All sense of direction was now lost to the pair, they could have been going in circles at this point for all they knew. They were relieved to find an intersection that branched off four different ways; it at least meant they had not been here before. The two companions risked a moments' pause, while they caught their breath and decided which direction to take.

A moment was all they were going to get. Without warning, a ball of fire exploded into Na'Jala's back, followed by that same booming laughter. The armor that was grafted to the former gladiator's skin protected him from the bulk of the blast but still sent him flying forward and bloodying his forehead against the tunnel wall. His pants had ignited and flames licked at his skin.

Evonne fired her last bolt before slinging her crossbow over her back. This time she missed completely. Noticing that Na'Jala was dazed, she swept out his legs tripping him into the disgusting water but extinguishing the flames from his pants. Seconds later, he regained his senses and nodded a silent thanks to the petite blonde before rising.

Again, Phyzantiss had not advanced. Just his crimson eyes shone in the dark, just outside the reach of the lantern's light, while he taunted them. Hearing strange sounds from one of the tunnels, Evonne decided to sprint down that one out of curiosity, Na'Jala right behind. A short distance ahead, the bounty hunter finally realized what it was that she was hearing and her heart sank at the sight before them. The water from the tunnel floor rushed off of a ledge in a waterfall into a large chamber. The pair skidded to a stop, peering over the ledge into the gloom below. They could not see the bottom, nor the chamber's walls, through the pitch darkness.

Na'Jala shoved Evonne into the tunnel wall as he flattened himself against the opposite side. A fireball whistled between them and exploded against the chamber wall, some twenty feet or so away.

Hunched over, Phyzantiss, stalked forward. "Nowhere to run now, fools," he teased.

Evonne swallowed hard and drew her curved sword. Noticing a hook in the wall near the ledge, Na'Jala hung the lantern and gripped his sword tight with both hands.

"We cannot fight side by side, the tunnel is too narrow. Stay behind me," Na'Jala said. "If I fall, aim for his neck and head, it's your best bet."

Evonne was no coward but paled at the thought of her companion falling and being left alone with that monster in this lonely, dark tunnel. She never imagined she would meet her end alone, in a filthy sewer. Who would look after Vrawg? She glanced back over the ledge and considered jumping if it came to that. At least then, she would not give the demonic knight the satisfaction of the kill.

Sparks flew as blades met and drew the bounty hunter's attention to the battle in front of her. Na'Jala went on the offensive but Phyzantiss parried each attack with ease. The former gladiator remembered the feel of that red-bladed dagger too well, during his captivity in the mountain stronghold. The evil priest Jaspar owned one just like it and he had no desire to feel its bite again.

Evonne winced, as a counter-attack just missed her companion's throat. She was amazed by Na'Jala's reflexes which had just saved his life, or at least prolonged it. She was also amazed by the half-demon's ability to fight effectively in a tunnel that was obviously too small for the tall knight. Several times sparks would fly as both blades scraped against the tunnel walls.

The red-bladed dagger finally found Na'Jala's shoulder and Evonne watched a strange expression of panic cross his face as he recoiled from the weapon, nearly tripping over the bounty hunter. They were running out of space.

A glint of something metallic in the darkness of the

tunnel, had Evonne squinting in curiosity. A familiar growl had her tackling Na'Jala, attempting to drag him to the filthy floor. "Get down!" she shouted.

Without thinking, Na'Jala did as instructed, diving into the shallow but rotten water. Just as he did, there was a crashing sound above and a grunt from the half-demon. Phyzantiss, flew over the prone pair and without slowing, went out over the ledge and plunged into the darkness below.

Evonne and Na'Jala glanced over to find the hulking-form of Vrawg, kneeling in the cramped tunnel clutching his chest, after knocking the demonic knight over the ledge. The half-ogre bounty hunter had been ordered to remain at the Ogre's Den and heal but Evonne could have kissed the ugly oaf for disobeying.

# CHAPTER 4

Ruggard Bloodaxe, the huge, red-bearded sellsword from the icy north, joined the lineup of people waiting to exit Stonewood through the east gate. Since the throne room battle on the King's birthday, Ruggard had laid low, hiding out at a seedy inn located in the south district. The northman was now weary of hiding and figured since weeks had gone by, it was now time to leave Stonewood behind and find work elsewhere.

The lineup was moving dreadfully slowly and not many people were being allowed to leave. Ruggard saw no reason for them to hold him here, he was not a citizen of the city and his work here was done.

"What is the hold up? And why are they denying so many people?" asked a merchant with a bushy, black moustache and rosy cheeks, who stood directly in front of Ruggard. "Why can we just not leave if we want to leave?"

"They are worried about folk running for help," Ruggard replied matter-of-factly.

"Who would want to cross that demon? Not me, that

is for certain. My lips are sealed. I just need to find a new city to sell my wares," said the merchant.

"Stonewood is the richest city in this region by far. Just stay here," the northman suggested.

The merchant shook his head. "Demons and half-demons and cults are not good for business. It is as though this city is under siege. Merchants and goods are no longer coming into the city, folk are fearful. And now the citizens of Stonewood are hoarding their coin with their future uncertain. I do not believe the King will be successful with his little rebellion. This is no place for me."

Ruggard had heard the rumors surrounding the King of Stonewood and his attempt to retake the city, little by little. The northman did not know what to make of it. As he fled the throne room battle, with his last glance back over his shoulder, Ruggard witnessed the King suffer a mortal wound. The sellsword had been in countless battles and witnessed all kinds of injuries; he would have wagered anything that the King could not survive his wound. Either the priests of this city were very powerful indeed or that white-bearded wizard had some trick up his sleeve. Regardless, Ruggard wanted no further part in the goings-on within this city. It was not good for ones' health, to oppose a demon.

It was not too long before the merchant in front of Ruggard shouted protests as he was refused permission to leave the city. The guards explained that the roads around Stonewood were unsafe for travelling merchants, that there was much unrest in the region. It would be safer for him to remain, for awhile longer at least.

Ruggard stepped towards the group of guards at the gate and motioned to the battle axe he wore strapped to his back. "Do ye plan on givin' me the same speech, that it's too dangerous for me out on the road?"

The guard who seemed to be in charge sized up the northman, who was much larger than any of the men guarding the east gate. "No, I don't suppose it would be as dangerous for the likes of you, northerner. What was your business here in the city?"

"I am a bounty hunter and sellsword. Did a few jobs while I was here and now I have a few appointments elsewhere that I intend to keep," Ruggard replied.

A flash of recognition crossed one of the guards face. "Bloodaxe, you are that Bloodaxe fella aren't you?" the guard asked.

Ruggard hesitated but knew he could not hide his identity. "Aye, 'tis me."

The first guard spoke up again. "Well, Mister Bloodaxe, Lord Sarvin wishes to speak with you. We have been instructed to keep an eye out for you."

"Ye can tell Lord Sarvin I will speak with him when I return, but first I have some appointments I need to keep," the northman stated.

"Lord Sarvin waits for nobody. You will come with us now," the guard commanded.

"And if I refuse?" Ruggard dared ask.

Two guards standing closely by, raised loaded crossbows to aim at the large northman, the others resting hands on the hilts of their swords.

"Then let's not keep the good Lord waitin," Ruggard said with a defeated tone.

\*    \*    \*    \*

Harcourt embraced Krestina in a tight hug, so

relieved was he that she had made it back to the Ogre's Den safely, along with the others. Only thing was, Vrawg was missing.

"What happened to Vrawg?" the thief asked, wearing his own face.

"The stubborn oaf followed us into the sewers," Evonne replied. "But I thank all the gods above that he did. He is at our hideout behind the smithies, with the priests and priestesses we rescued. Too dangerous for him to roam the streets back here, he kinda stands out."

"How is he doing?" Harcourt inquired, concerned about the half-orgre's health.

"Oh he is recovering just fine. Now he won't shut up," Evonne replied, approaching the bar to pour herself a drink.

Dornell and Na'Jala exchanged curious glances at her reply, as neither of the men had heard the monstrous bounty hunter speak a word.

Each shook Harcourt's hand in turn. "Glad you all made it back safely, my friends," the thief said.

"That half-demon knight is going to present us with a major problem," Na'Jala said to Harcourt.

"What progress has the wizard made in finding us a way to deal with them?" Dornell asked, easing his sore body into a chair at an empty table.

"Not much progress at all I am afraid, not yet anyways," Fezzdin replied, ascending the stairs from the cellar. "The Cult has my tower surrounded and there is some sort of protective, magical barrier preventing me from using any spells to enter. I do not have access to my library which would aid us greatly. The library within the temple has now been destroyed, unfortunately. I have bought every book of any value from Shashi's Books but alas, none have helped."

Harcourt rubbed his chin in thought. "You know, Fezzdin, while I was inside Krommel's office, I found an old tome, which seemed to outline how one could free Lucivenus from his prison. Had diagrams and everything. I'd be willing to bet somewhere in there would be clues on how to defeat him or send him back."

"Does us no good sitting in his office within the castle," Dornell said somberly.

It was then that a series of knocks at the back door to the Den had everyone startled and standing at the ready. Harcourt donned his mask and now wore the face of the King again.

Sword in hand, Na'Jala opened the door then relaxed when a cloaked man entered and pulled back his hood. It was Prince Orval Stonewood. A pained expression crossed his face when he looked to Harcourt and the thief quickly removed the mask. The Prince could not get used to seeing his father's face, the hurt of his loss still very fresh in his mind.

The prince, who was in his thirties, stood as tall as Na'Jala and had a lean, muscular frame. Normally, his face was clean-shaven, his dark hair reaching his shoulders. Nowadays, his hair was much shorter and his face covered with a dark beard. Most, who did not know him personally, would find it very difficult to recognize him.

Orval had been the most affected by the events at his father's birthday. His beloved father and King had been murdered by a foul demon, his younger brother was still missing and presumed dead, and he was forced from his home, to skulk and hide about in the slums of his city. The prince had visited the south district, albeit rarely, but was always accompanied by several armed guards. Now, however, because of the great need to not attract attention, he moved about Stonewood alone, doing his best to blend in with the common folk.

On his way back to the Ogre's Den, he had drawn some stares from a few local thugs, Guild members most likely, who viewed him as a stranger. Luckily, though, they decided to let him pass. Despite a few nervous misgivings, Orval always walked with confidence. He was a more than capable warrior, having been tutored by some of the city's finest swordsmen. Orval never went anywhere without his sword by his side, though now he was forced to forego his customary royal armor, wearing a simple mail shirt instead.

Fezzdin allowed the prince a moment to hang his cloak and get seated at a table with a mug of ale before he asked, "Have you been successful?"

"Fairly," Orval replied. "Five of the noble families I have visited are completely with us. The Kanes and the Denwolds have pledged coin and men, approximately one hundred men-at-arms."

Dornell just shook his head. "One hundred men does not make an army."

"It is better than none," Fezzdin shot back. "Every man helps."

Prince Orval had been dying to soak his blade with the blood of cultists. He was angry that he had to sit out these battles that the 'King' was waging. Fezzdin had given him another mission though, one of great importance. He was to secretly meet with noble families and merchants, that had always been loyal to his father and the city, and gain their support. Many of these families were very wealthy and many employed soldiers to protect their homes and villas. He promised these families great rewards, after he and his 'father' reclaimed the city.

Everyone needed to believe that the King still lived. As much as it pained Orval, he realized the importance of that. When this ordeal was over, he would become the new King of Stonewood but until that time, his father had to live in the minds of the citizens.

The prince glanced over to the thief known as Harcourt, the one who was impersonating his father. Orval recalled hearing his name before, sometime ago. It had something to do with a corrupt city guard and the Thieves Guild, plus something about being imprisoned for the murder of a tavern girl. The man was a criminal, or had been anyway, though the prince could not deny the great help this man was now, when the city needed it the most.

When Harcourt donned that strange mask, he became the King. So much so that at times, for the briefest of moments, Orval believed he was staring at his father, still alive and well. That thought though, brought the pain of reality, that his father was gone and was never coming back. He prayed that his younger brother Denniz, was being held somewhere alive in the castle, awaiting rescue. He had no other immediate family, as his mother had died when they were only young.

Evonne passed mugs of ale around to her companions, though Krestina and Fezzdin waved it away. "I still do not understand how is it that so many of the city and castle guard are loyal to this Cult?" the petite bounty hunter mused aloud.

"As I was in Krommel's office, I also found a ledger that he kept with years and years worth of records and notes," Harcourt said. "The Chief Magistrate is much older than you would believe him to be. He has spent at least fifty years replacing guards and guard commanders with Cult members. I imagine those that are not loyal to the Cult are being advised by their 'trusted' commanders, that they not oppose the demon lord and just accept the new changes to the city's ruler."

"I cannot believe this had been going on right under our noses and we had no clue," Prince Orval said, slamming a fist into the table.

"Do not feel so bad, my young prince, for I had no idea either. I should have been much more vigilant and paid more attention to this Cult problem than I did," Fezzdin confessed. "This Sarvin is very clever and very patient. He was content to spend many years subtly executing his plan."

"I always knew there was something odd about him, I always sensed something. I just didn't quite know what it was," Orval said in frustration.

Fezzdin nodded in agreement, remembering well the many times that the prince and the Chief Magistrate had butted heads and disputed over various topics. But none of them could have guessed the nefarious and all-encompassing schemes brewing inside the Magistrate's head.

"What about the horses? Did you manage to secure us any?" the old wizard asked the prince.

"Yes, we have six horses, courtesy of the Fiskyn family," Orval replied.

"What good are six horses to us?" Dornell asked Fezzdin. "Is that going to be our cavalry unit? Six mounted men riding out against thousands of wraggoth?"

"Do not be so silly, my good captain. These six horses are going to be very valuable to us, as there is going to be much fog tomorrow night," Fezzdin said, turning to descend back into the cellar.

Dornell turned to the others for an explanation to the wizard's cryptic reply but they had none. Evonne gave her best Vrawg impression and shrugged her shoulders.

\* \* \* \*

"Ah, the great Ruggard Bloodaxe. So nice of you to join us," High Priest Sarvin said, clapping his hands together.

The huge northman was led into the throne room of the castle, the very same room of that ill-fated battle. Walking close on his right, was the demonic knight, Phyzantiss. The half-demon had survived his plunge in the sewers; only his ego had been damaged.

Beads of sweat formed on Ruggard's brow as he approached the throne. The Demon Lord Lucivenus lounged on the chair, watching him curiously, with Sarvin standing to the left of the demon. Three-on-one odds was never something the sellsword had ever shied away from but these were not normal adversaries. Ruggard remembered well what Lucivenus was capable of. He made short work of the King and his personal guards, as well as Evonne's monstrous, half-ogre partner. The northman was unused to holding his tongue but deemed it wise at this time.

"Where have you been, Ruggard? We have been looking for you," Sarvin asked. "You never returned for the rest of your payment for your work on the night of the King's birthday."

"Been doing odd jobs here and there, keeping meself busy," the northman replied.

"And you were about to leave us without even saying good-bye and collecting the rest of your gold?"

"Well, there was so much chaos in this room that night, I wasn't sure we did a good enough job for collecting the rest of the gold."

"Oh, you are right about that. You certainly did not do a good enough job. In fact, I believe you killed four men that were loyal to me."

Lucivenus watched the exchange with an amused look upon his face.

"The room was chaotic. Those men attacked me."

Sarvin shook his head. "I doubt that. All men loyal to me were informed that you and the other bounty hunters were hired to protect me. They would not have attacked you."

Sweat dripped off the northman's head and it was not only from the heat emanating from the demon lord seated nearby.

"All the guards looked alike to me. All the uniforms were the same. I chose to attack those that appeared to be threatening you."

"Where are the others?" Sarvin shouted suddenly, his tone abruptly changed.

"Others?" Ruggard asked.

"Where is the King hiding? Where are those other two troublesome bounty hunters, the woman and the ugly ogre? Tell us, now!"

"I have not seen any of them since that night here," the northman answered truthfully.

"A pity. That was not the answer I sought. You must

have some idea where they could be hiding. Do yourself a favor and tell me where that might be."

"I don't have the slightest clue."

"Then you are no longer of any use to us, Ruggard."

Ruggard knew his fate was sealed. He was no coward and would not go down without a fight. He grabbed his battle axe off his back and gripped it tightly with both hands. Next to him, Phyzantiss stepped back and drew his great sword.

High Priest Sarvin though, made the first move. He spoke some words in an unfamiliar language and the floor beneath Ruggard began to shift and bubble. Confused, the sellsword looked to the floor, watching it liquefy and become like a thick mud beneath him.

Ruggard immediately began to sink into the floor. He struggled to pull his legs free but they were firmly stuck. The more he struggled, the quicker he sank. He roared with rage and spat curses at the high priest and the demon lord. Lucivenus laughed with amusement.

When the northman had sunk neck-deep, the floor seemed to solidify, holding him firmly in place. As he glanced up at the evil priest, Sarvin now held a strange black mace in his hands. It appeared to be made of swirling black mist. Sarvin smiled and swung the mace at Ruggard's head. The northman knew no more.

# CHAPTER 5

The single horse-drawn wagon slowly approached the western gates leading out of Stonewood. Tethered together and following behind the wagon, were five other horses. The guards posted at the gate watched the wagon approach with curiosity.

"Where are you going with those?" shouted the man in charge to a fellow guard seated upon the wagon.

"I have orders from Lord Lucivenus himself to deliver these horses to Hizzlack," the guard replied, referring to the leader of the wraggoth army that had the city surrounded.

"What do the wraggoth want with horses? They do not ride," the gate guard inquired.

"Well, ahhhh," the man on the wagon struggled with the words, "I believe they......eat them."

A second guard leaning against the gatehouse door screwed up his face in disgust. "What a waste of good horses."

"If any of you wish to relay that sentiment to Lord

Lucivenus, you are surely welcome to," said the guard on the wagon.

Without further conversation, the guards opened the city gates and allowed the wagon and the horses to pass. It was early morning but the sky was dark, with thick grey clouds. The wind had picked up and the promise of a storm loomed over the region.

The city guard drove the wagon along the western road, passing tent after tent of the wraggoth army. Wraggoth did not like sunlight, being a subterranean race, but with the grey skies overhead, many were out and about and eyed the wagon hungrily.

Harcourt had not been sure whether the creatures actually ate horses but it seemed to have been a good guess by the looks on their faces as he passed them by. With the aid of his magical mask, the thief wore the face of a guard who had frequently made trips to liaise with the wraggoth. It was good enough to fool the guards at the gate, allowing the thief to slip through.

Harcourt rode for what felt like an hour before the sight of the horrendous army was far behind. The thief spent the entire rest of the day dropping off horses in strategic locations, tying them to trees and hoping that no wolves or hungry wraggoth stumbled upon them. He was thoroughly soaked, as it had rained for much of the day and now a thick fog enveloped the region around the city.

As Harcourt left the fifth horse behind, he turned his wagon south. Earlier, a frustrated Fezzdin had taken an hour to teach the thief how to tell directions, by looking at the stars above and using landmarks around the city. Outside the city, Harcourt was completely out of his element. He felt uncomfortable in the wide open space, much preferring the crowded streets of Stonewood.

He managed to figure out which way was south though and set off in hopes of finding the camp of Thelvius the Great and his mercenary army.

\*     \*     \*     \*

The hidden door to a smuggling tunnel that led outside the city from The Last Stop tavern flipped open and Fezzdin stuck his head out for a look.

The fog was indeed thick, as he had predicted. The wizard climbed out and motioned for five men to follow him out of the tunnel. He cast a spell and fog seem to swirl around the men, loyal to the King, and made them even more difficult to see in the darkness.

"Go now," the wizard whispered to the five. "Seek out your horses and get word to our army and allies. Go with all haste. Avoid any confrontations. The King has chosen you all for your loyalty. The fate of Stonewood now rests in your hands. Go."

Swelling with pride and purpose, the five men scattered into the dense fog on their very important missions.

\*     \*     \*     \*

High Priest Sarvin strode into the council chambers for a meeting of the city's magistrates. The twelve men had already assembled for the evening meeting and had been waiting a half hour for the arrival of the Chief Magistrate. All conversations ceased as Sarvin entered and took a seat at the circular table.

Magistrate Tuullen was the first to speak. "Chief Magistrate Krommel, you have gone too far. Allying with demons?"

Sarvin turned to the man with an icy stare. "You will address me as Lord Sarvin from now on, and you had also better watch your tone with me."

Tuullen paled slightly; he was one of the few magistrates that had not been appointed by Sarvin over the years.

"I apologize for not calling this meeting much earlier but there has been a lot on my plate, as of late," Sarvin said, addressing the gathered men. "The tyrannical rule of King Stonewood has ended. For too long, his family has ruined this great city of ours. The Thieves Guild has forever been a blight upon Stonewood, terrorizing our citizens. The Guild is now in shambles and Lord Lucivenus will lead Stonewood into an era of immense prosperity. Those of you loyal to us will also prosper. Business in Stonewood will continue."

"But Lord Sarvin, what of the talk that the King is not dead? He has been seen by many, fighting to reclaim his throne," asked Magistrate Raelus.

"The King has no army and no castle to hide in. He will be dealt with and trouble us no further, of that I can assure you," the High Priest stated. "You will all receive an increase in your wages and I expect you all to speak with your peers, your co-workers, and talk sense into them. Life in Stonewood will not differ much, if everyone complies. Lord Lucivenus and I, do not suffer traitors. Magistrate Matteus, I now appoint you to the position of Chief Magistrate. I no longer have the time to deal with such duties."

With that, High Priest Sarvin stood and turned toward the door. Magistrate Pavlo, surely no warrior, would never have been considered a brave man. The middle-aged magistrate was skinny and was picked on at a young age. He was, however, a smart man and a loyal man, forever grateful for being trusted enough to be appointed the role of a magistrate. Pavlo was very fond of the King and the whole Stonewood family. They were good people, not the tyrants this evil Cult made them out to be. He could not just stand by while an evil priest and a demon, lorded over his beloved city. The magistrate decided his life was a worthy trade to see his city safe and ensure his name was never forgotten.

Pavlo produced a knife from under his robes and dove for the High Priest. Sarvin whirled around and caught the magistrate by the wrist. The High Priest was a much stronger man and easily held the weapon away from his body, despite Pavlo's best efforts.

Sarvin smiled and spoke the words of a spell. His hand began to glow a bright red, fueled by the heat from the Abyss itself. Pavlo shrieked as his wrist melted, his hand, still holding the knife, fell to the floor. The magistrate dropped to the floor and rolled about in agony.

Magistrate Tuullen's jaw hung open in shock. The spectacle effectively eliminated any thoughts he may have harbored of doing something similar.

Sarvin opened the door to the council chambers and addressed two guards that had been posted outside. "Remove this filth and have him hung for all to see."

\*     \*     \*     \*

Krestina rolled about in her bed within the Crimson Crab Inn, covered in an icy cold sweat. A cry of distress escaped her lips, then a loud clap of thunder from outside jolted her awake from her nightmare. She sat up and then relaxed as she oriented herself on her whereabouts.

The priestess had had trouble falling asleep as the city was enveloped in a thick fog, with thunder still booming overhead, left over from the afternoon storm. She hated being alone in a storm, they unnerved her, and worse still was that the man she loved, Harcourt, was out there somewhere, all by himself, surrounded with danger.

She tried her best to shake away the thoughts of the dream she had just been having. She had envisioned Harcourt prostrate and unmoving, at the foot of a headstone. A dark figure loomed above him, laughing, with blood dripping from his mouth. The priestess shivered and tried her best to think of something different, something joyful.

She mused that in the morning she just might risk a trip to the orphanage to see Dahleene and the children, see to it that they were faring alright. It had been too long and they were probably worried about her too.

\* \* \* \*

High Priest Sarvin had planned to retire to his private quarters for the rest of the evening when he was intercepted by Gervas, after leaving the meeting. The elderly man was always visibly nervous. Sarvin despised cowards.

"My lord," Gervas said with a bow, "there is a…..well, someone is here to see you. A Mister

Nightsbridge awaits you down the hall, the first chamber on the left."

Sarvin set off for the room without even acknowledging the elderly advisor. Gervas preferred it that way.

The High Priest was short on capable associates of late. He had been very distressed when one of his men found the body of Brother Jaspar, lying near the cells under the east wing of the castle, a knife buried in his heart. Jaspar had served Sarvin for many years and proved himself a powerful and valuable priest of their order.

He also found he missed the company of Devi-Lynn. She was the most loyal and a powerful priestess as well. His attractive assistant handled much within their order, duties which now fell to the High Priest. Her death was necessary though. They required a devoted heart as the heart to release Lucivenus from his prison. The time was right and Sarvin could not let the opportunity escape him. Since the priestess captured for that sacrifice had escaped, he was left with no other choice as Devi-Lynn stood before him. He knew that she was destined for great things and she had not let him down.

Now, though, he was pressed to find expert help. Syrena the Sorceress was a valuable member of the order but Sarvin had no delusions about her devotion. He knew the beautiful sorceress craved power and magical knowledge which he had promised her if she was willing to join with them. She did not seem to particularly care for their overall goals.

Brother Veral was clever and ambitious, but still young and not as powerful as the High Priest would have liked. There were other priests and warriors within their order, spread out across Stonewood, but none had yet been able to replace Jaspar and Devi. Sarvin wished to prove his worth to Lucivenus, to show him how valuable he was. So far, the two half-demons had been unsuccessful in finding and killing King Stonewood. Sarvin meant to succeed where the others had failed.

The High Priest entered the room that Gervas had directed him to and found one person standing within, facing an opened window and watching lightning illuminate the foggy night sky.

Nestor Nightsbridge turned to face High Priest Sarvin, tipping his black, wide-brimmed hat so that they could see eye to eye. He stood about an inch taller than six feet, and even though he appeared thin, there was an aura of strength and confidence about him. Dressed in a long black coat which touched the floor and a frilly-collared blue shirt underneath, he had the appearance of a swashbuckler. His skin was pale white, even paler than Jaspar, if that was possible, and his eyes had a red tinge to them.

"High Priest," Nestor said, with a slight bow. "What has it been, thirty years? Forty? You actually look…..younger than I recall."

"It has been at least that, and you look, well, you look exactly the same," Sarvin replied.

"I see you have acquired yourself a castle, since last I was in Stonewood. You have been a busy man."

"Busy indeed, my old friend. My problem now is that the former owner of this castle does not wish to give it up so easily."

"So you have sought me out, to help you with your problem then?"

"Yes, I would like to enlist your aid."

"Kings make for powerful foes, generally not a job I would take."

"King Stonewood has no army, nor a castle to hide behind. He is a fugitive now, in hiding and surrounded with insignificant rabble. Find him for me. Bring me his head and I will make you a very wealthy man."

"I am already a wealthy man, High Priest."

"What do you want then? Name it."

Nestor paused for a moment in thought. "I want a villa, in the north district. And a title in Stonewood."

"Deal," Sarvin said, smiling. "I trust you know what the King looks like? His portraits litter this castle."

"I do," Nestor replied as his body transformed into that of a large bat. Then the century-old vampire flew out through the window into the foggy night beyond.

\*　　\*　　\*　　\*

Jag, the giant, armored war-dog, gave a low growl as a stranger was led into his master's tent. "Easy boy, this man is a guest," said Thelvius the Great, leader of the mercenary army and former undefeated gladiator.

Thelvius lounged in his chair, similar to a throne but only slightly less extravagant. He wore only half of his gleaming bronze armor, his breastplate on the floor not far away. It was the middle of the night when the mercenary leader was roused from his sleep and informed that a man with a wagon had entered their camp.

"Harcourt, isn't it?" Thelvius asked, rubbing the sleep from his eyes.

"Yes, good memory," the thief answered, who wore

his own face, his mask carefully tucked away. "I was most pleased to find you still camped in the region, though your army looks about half the size."

"I have men searching the area for our next water source. It is not easy keeping two thousand men camped out in the field. I was considering leaving this region altogether in a few days since I had not heard a word from within Stonewood. So, what news?"

"Not good, I am afraid. Stonewood's army is still away and most likely oblivious to the current state of the city. A foul demon now sits on the throne, with the Cult doing his every bidding. The King still lives, as does his eldest son and they are fighting back, but slowly. They remain hidden and strike when the opportunity presents itself."

"So, twenty thousand armored wraggoth still surround the city and Stonewood has no army to deal with them? My men still only number two thousand, so there is no amount of gold you can offer me to risk any engagement."

"We have just dispatched some riders to carry word to the army and some other allies. With luck, we should have fifteen thousand men marching back, within a week's time. The King has promised to pay you handsomely, if you will lend your swords to the fight when the time is right."

Thelvius rubbed his chin in thought. "What of the cavalry unit we have spotted near the city. Who has their allegiance?"

"As far as we know, they are loyal to the Cult. They number a thousand," Harcourt said, not sure if that would scare off the mercenary and his men, since they did not possess as many horses.

"We don't worry much about cavalry here. That's what Jag and the other dogs are for."

Harcourt did not quite get the meaning of that statement. Sure, Jag was the largest dog the thief had ever seen but was still nowhere near the size of a horse.

Reading the confused look on the thief's face, the mercenary leader elaborated. "You see, our dogs are outfitted with spiked armor. The dogs are small enough that a mounted rider cannot strike at them. The dogs run underneath the horses, their spikes tearing open the underbelly of the mounts, bringing them down along with their riders. We hate to kill horses, but when presented with the choice of us or them, well, it's too bad for the horses. Jag and his brothers and sisters can decimate cavalry in no time."

The dog barked, knowing they had been talking about him.

"So, we can count on your aid?" Harcourt asked.

"Our services are not cheap," Thelvius answered. "And seeing as how there is a demon involved, those prices just went up."

"The King will pay, you have our promise."

"So a fugitive thief speaks for the King of Stonewood?" Thelvius said with a laugh.

"As strange as it sounds, I am close to the King, you might say. In my wagon is an advanced payment that I was bid to present to you," Harcourt said.

"As long as we are not in this fight alone, you will have our swords," the mercenary leader declared.

"Our thanks. We will get word to you again when the time is right."

The thief and the former gladiator shook on it. Before Harcourt could leave the tent, Thelvius had one last question. "It is one thing to battle this army outside the city but you have a demon to deal with. How do you plan on removing him from the throne?"

The thief had no answer for that, so he just shook his head and walked away. He was hoping Fezzdin would find the answer to that question, and soon.

# CHAPTER 6

The young Cult priest, Brother Veral, strolled into the small dark shop, leaving his two escorts to wait outside. The sign on the front of the south district shop read *Syrena's Fortunes*. The Cult sorceress, Syrena, read people's fortunes for a small fee, though none knew of her affiliation with the Cult of demon-worshippers. She found it was a great way to gather information and fill her pockets with a few easily-earned coins. There were spells she could cast that could give her an idea of someone's future but she never bothered. She had realized long ago, that when you just tell people what they want to hear, they are happy and always return with more coins.

Brother Veral was young, a man in his early twenties with messy, chestnut brown hair and an average build. For quite some time, he was known in the streets as a thief named Norvil. He had infiltrated the notorious Thieves Guild and orchestrated the killing of many senior members, sending the Guild into hiding. That gained him much praise from High Priest Sarvin and many others among their order except one whom he strongly wished to impress, Syrena. He could not keep his eyes off the sorceress, as she had many eye-catching attributes.

Syrena sat behind a small table that was littered with candles, playing cards and a pile of small bones, the smell of insence filled the air. She wore her customary, tight-fitting, low-cut black dress that gave her the appearance of a witch, a beautiful, seductive witch. She had long dark hair with a tanned complexion, having been born far to the south of Stonewood. She rolled her eyes at the sight of the young priest.

The front of the shop consisted of this small room; a beaded curtain hung behind the sorceress which led to her private chamber. Two candles on the table were the only sources of light in the tiny shop. Veral, who now proudly wore the dark robes of a Cult priest in the streets, took a seat at the table opposite Syrena, grinning all the while.

"Have you heard? Well of course you must have, you are a fortune teller. You must have known this was coming," Veral said with his foolish grin.

Syrena sighed. "Heard what, exactly? I see a lot of things, so to which one do you refer? Oh, and my eyes are up here," she said, pointedly indicating her face.

Veral blushed. "Heard that I have been given the south district, of course. I discovered that the last representative for the district was also a Guild member, so Lord Sarvin had him executed. I think Lucivenus even ate him." The priest could not contain a laugh at that thought. "So I have been given the entire district to govern, it's mine!"

"Oh, how lucky for you, you get to govern thieves, murderers and the homeless. And I wonder what the

Guild is going to think of that?"

"The Guild? Bah! They are scattered and cowering like children. They have seen what I am capable of," Veral said, puffing out his chest.

"Don't you mean, what Brother Jaspar was capable of? Wasn't he sent with you to dispatch the Guild's senior leaders?"

"He came with me, yes, but that was all my doing! I infiltrated the Guild, I gathered all the intelligence, I was their downfall. That fool Randar knows never to show his face near me again."

Syrena rolled her eyes again, she was so uninterested in this conversation. Not only was the young priest very annoying and arrogant, but he was also a fanatical follower of Lucivenus and so very devoted to the Cult. Syrena was not. The sorceress used the Cult to her advantage, gaining magical knowledge from High Priest Sarvin in exchange for her services. In truth, she never thought they were going to succeed in releasing the demon lord from his extra-planar prison. She had been just as shocked as everyone else in that throne room. As long as Sarvin kept providing her with ancient tomes to study, she would stick around.

"We need to celebrate," Veral suggested, his foolish grin returning.

"Celebrate what?" Syrena asked, as if she had not heard a word the young priest had been saying.

"Come on, Syrena. I will buy you a drink tonight and we can celebrate my taking over the south district. Every powerful man needs a powerful woman. You could be that woman," Veral gave a sly wink.

"I could? So who would the powerful man be then?"

"Ugh!" Veral blurted out, standing up and waving his arms in the air. "You can be so frustrating!"

"Do you want your fortune read or not? Because I am busy," Syrena said, noticing someone standing outside the shop door, waiting for their turn. "But I am getting the feeling that you are not going to have a good day. See the card of the crow here? The crow is always a bad omen."

"You have the heart of a troll, do you know that? One of these days you will come to your senses and see what you are missing and then it will be too late. I will have moved on," Veral said, exiting the shop.

Syrena laughed to herself. She did not like the priest's company but she sure enjoyed getting him all riled up. She quickly composed herself as another man now entered her shop. He was tall, wearing a dark cloak. The man had handsome features from what she could see within his hood and wore a dark beard. A warrior too, she knew, from the sword and mail vest that he wore.

Syrena gave her best, welcoming smile and invited the man to take a seat.

*   *   *   *

Brother Veral stormed out of Syrena's shop, nearly colliding with the tall man who was waiting to enter next. Why couldn't she see his potential? he thought to himself. He planned to stand with High Priest Sarvin, much like Brother Jaspar had done when he was alive. The sorceress would be sorry when he became a man of immense power and influence, and she was still reading fortunes to beggars in the slums.

The young priest looked about for his two escorts but

they no longer stood near Syrena's shop. This particular street was not that crowded and neither of the men were in sight.

"Brother Veral, over here," the priest heard come from the closest alleyway.

"What is it?" Veral asked, walking to the mouth of the alley. "We don't have time to fool around, I have much to do today."

Strong hands grabbed the priest by the front of his robes and roughly dragged him into the alley, throwing him up against a wall. "Is it Brother Veral? Or is it Norvil?" a man asked.

Veral paled at the sight of the short, powerfully-built, man. A patchwork of scars dominated his shaved head and face.

"Remember me?" Randar asked, pulling a knife from his belt. "These are my streets."

Before Veral could say a word, he gasped as the knife was driven into his belly. He died without a sound as the Guild enforcer then opened his throat.

\* \* \* \*

"It was the King himself, I tell ya, right there in the street fighting against those monsters working for the demon. I saw it with my own two eyes," said an elderly man with a green cloak, seated near the center of the bar at the Whistling Weasel Tavern.

A crowd had begun to gather around in the lower east district tavern to partake in the mid-afternoon discussion.

"My brother saw him too, fighting beside that wizard outside the big temple. Saw him clear as day," said another man, who was missing several teeth.

"How do ya'll know it was really da King?" asked a skeptical man, holding his mug of ale lovingly.

The elderly man with the green cloak spoke up. "I have lived in this city for eighty-three years, I would certainly recognize the King any day. I was there the day his father's crown was placed on his head. Walked right by me that day, he did. Coulda reached right out and touched him, I coulda."

"Why is the King cowering then? Hiding in the shadows like a thief?" inquired another man, a merchant whose business had been suffering since the overthrow of the King.

"There are many traitors in the castle," replied the elderly man. "The King does not know who to trust. But he has men and women loyal to him. Mark my words, they will take back that castle, they will."

"I heard the demon eats people," commented a serving girl.

Again, it was the elderly gentleman who spoke up. "Indeed he does lass. And what happens when he runs out of prisoners in the castle to eat, eh? Then he starts on the citizens, he will."

More than a few patrons in the tavern visibly paled at that remark. Most folk feared the demon lord and the cultists who followed him but felt powerless to do anything about it. The King was believed dead at first but then it was rumored instead that he was injured and chased from the castle, his two sons, missing. Strange monsters had the city surrounded and Stonewood's army was nowhere to be found. These were dark times indeed.

"We must all do our part and help the King. He was a

good King and you all know that."

There was several "ayes" spoken around the room in agreement.

"But what can we do to help the King? Most of us here are not warriors, we cannot fight the demon's men," asked a tiny man seated at the bar.

"Not all wars are won with soldiers," the elderly man replied. "We can each do our part. When we see the King and his men, alert them of coming danger. Shout out how many you see and from which direction. Form a crowd in the street to slow the demon's soldiers down, distract them when you can. Every little bit of help we can offer will go a long way. This demon is very evil, my friends, do not let them fool you into thinking Stonewood will prosper under his rule. We are already noticing that there has been no trade coming into the city. Those beasts outside and news of the demon usurper is frightening off merchants and traders. Even the farmers. Things are only going to get worse unless the King can reclaim his throne."

"I would love to drive my sword into one of those Cult members. I have not forgotten the atrocities they have committed," commented a smithy with giant arms.

"As would I," said another tall man, sipping his ale. "My friend disappeared a year ago, then he was found missing his heart a few days later by the river."

The elderly man bobbed his head. "Yes, yes, very evil they are. This is our city, not theirs. Everyone should do their part."

A man with a very long, brown beard then stood up from the bar and walked over to a window to observe a large crowd that had begun to gather in the market square outside.

"What do you see, Olgar? What's goin' on out there?" asked one of his friends.

"I don't rightly know, it's hard to see from here. But looks like something in the market has got everyone's attention alright," Olgar shouted back.

Everyone within the tavern made their way over to the front of the room to look out the windows for themselves. The elderly man in the green cloak left the tavern immediately for a closer look.

Some folk wore expressions of shock, others of disgust. Some mothers covered their children's faces and pulled them away from the gathered crowd.

Curious, the elderly man shoved his way through the crowd until he found what he sought. Near the center of the market square stood three long spears dug into the ground around a small tree. All three spears had a decapitated head mounted on top. The center spear, the longest of the three, sported a head that Harcourt, disguised with the aid of his mask as the elderly man, recognized, the traitorous thief Norvil. This would not have been the work of Fezzdin or any of the men fighting with the King. This was a message sent by the Thieves Guild and one specifically sent by Randar, if Harcourt had to guess.

Harcourt rubbed his chin. Maybe it was time he paid a visit to the Guild and see if he could recruit their aid. He had his mask once again. Perhaps Weldrick, the last leader of the Guild, should make his return.

\*　　\*　　\*　　\*

"I have never visited a place like this before," said the

bearded, cloaked man, sitting across from Syrena. "But my mother believed in this sort of thing. With all the madness going on within this city, I suppose anything is possible."

Syrena gave a warm smile. "What is it that you wish to know?"

"I have not seen my brother in some time, I am worried for him. I am hoping he is alive and well. I do not know whether that is just a fool's hope," the man said.

"Let's see what the cards tell me," Syrena said, flipping the top card of her deck over to reveal the card of the crow.

"Is that bad?"

"No, no, not at all. The card of the crow always foretells good fortune. Your brother is not within Stonewood, but I can see that he is close and he is well."

"Are you sure?" the man asked, leaning forward with a look of hope upon his face. "Are you reading the card correctly?"

"Yes, of course. The cards do not lie. You may not see your brother anytime soon but he is well and you will be reunited in the future. I just cannot say when, the future is cloudy."

The man breathed a sigh of relief. "And my friends. They face a difficult task tomorrow and I would know if they will be safe and successful?"

As Syrena was about to reveal the next card, she spotted it was card of the skull, so with some sleight-of-hand, she switched it for the card of the sun. "Oh yes, we have the card of the sun, always a good omen. Your friends will be fine, have no worry."

The man nodded, clearly pleased with what he had heard. "How much do I owe you?"

Syrena was a good judge of people, it came with the job. Prices varied depending on what she figured the person could afford. While this man was not dressed overly well, there was an aura about him and he walked with confidence. "Two readings, one gold piece," she said.

The man dropped a ten-piece coin on the table. "Take that, with my thanks," then he stood.

"Good sir, that is a lot of coin for two simple readings."

"Please accept it. The sight of you alone was worth the extra coins. It has been some time since I have beheld a woman of your beauty. It was a pleasure to share this company with you, no matter how brief."

Syrena genuinely blushed from the comment. He appeared quite handsome and had kept his eyes on her eyes the entire time, quite impressive. "Well, come back anytime," she said, "you know where to find me."

"I think I will do just that. Farewell Syrena, 'til I see your lovely face again," the man said, taking his leave.

Prince Orval could not believe that such beauty could exist in the south district of the city. In fact, he found that many of the ideas he had had were not true. While there was a large criminal presence here, he found most folk to be extremely kind and friendly, friendlier than those of any of the other districts and these folk were the poorest. He felt his father may have erred in not giving these people the attention and the aid they may deserve.

He took a glance back at the shop and decided he would be paying Syrena another visit very soon. Within the shop, Syrena found herself hoping the man would be back for another visit very soon.

# CHAPTER 7

Alexander Frock was the second-in-command of Stonewood's northern army, which numbered ten thousand men. Captain Frock had been a soldier for most of his life and fiercely loyal to the King. He strolled through the camp rubbing his black-bearded chin in deep thought, listening to the grumbling of the troops around him. They were hungry and they were tired. A week of training manoeuvers had turned into several weeks and now provisions were becoming dangerously low.

Frock found General Zayne, lounging in his tent as usual, enjoying an afternoon drink. The captain saluted as he entered. "General, have we not been gone long enough? Food is beginning to run low. The men are grumbling."

"Let them grumble," said the larger man, who also sported long black hair and a bushy black beard. "They have sat around getting lazy for years. It's about time they earned their wages and did a little work."

"Yes, that's fine but we have not prepared enough

provisions to stay away for this long. And we still have a long march back to the city," remarked Captain Frock.

"What if we were at war?" asked the general. "What if we were involved in a siege? These men should be prepared for anything. Instead, they are just spoiled."

"Understandable, sir. So am I to assume we will be out here awhile longer?"

General Zayne took another sip from his goblet, savoring the flavor of the southern liquor. "Yes, I believe we shall stay out here, for a little longer at least."

Frock gave a salute and left the general's tent. He was not sure what the general really hoped to accomplish, keeping the army out here, so far north from the city. The captain found him to be an odd man. Zayne was promoted to the position of general a few months back, a relative unknown, and bypassed several other capable men, Frock included. Frock found the decision strange but never questioned it. He always followed his orders no matter his personal opinions.

General Zayne emptied his goblet, then rose for a refill. He was hoping he would receive a message from High Priest Sarvin soon, before he ran out of excuses to tell his men.

\*　　\*　　\*　　\*

Harcourt, wearing the face of King Stonewood, parried a thrust with his sword, then countered by removing the cultists arm. Beside him, Dornell and Na'Jala made short work of their three opponents. From a rooftop, Barros downed two more with his bow. This group of the demon's men had been searching an inn for anyone harboring the King and his associates. They had dragged the inn's owner out into the street to torture him in front of a crowd, to make an example of him. That was when the King and some of his men had appeared and come to the rescue.

The fight in the street was fierce but brief. Harcourt made a point of keeping the hood of his cloak around his shoulders, keeping his face visible for all to see.

"My King! More men approach!" shouted a man from the crowd.

Harcourt glanced upwards to Barros and a nod from the archer confirmed it was true, before he disappeared. Harcourt saluted the crowd, then turned to his companions. "Split up, I will see you later."

The thief sprinted down the street, hearing behind him curses from cultists, ordering people to move out of the way and let them pass. The delay was enough for Harcourt and his companions to scatter down different alleys, without being seen.

The sun had set about an hour earlier and soon there would be nobody walking the streets, save for those who served the demon lord. Anyone caught outside would be dragged to the castle and most never returned. Harcourt was in the lower east district and had to make it back to the south. He knew the streets and alleys very well and now that it was dark, he saw no problem eluding any patrols or men in pursuit.

He was thankful for the crowd of citizens that had alerted them of the approaching men and delayed them. It seemed Harcourt's frequent visits to the taverns, wearing various faces, were helping rally support and give hope to the people. News that the King was alive and well and fighting back, had spread throughout the city. Sadly, it had inspired some less-capable folk to try their own hand at fighting back, which had not turned out well. But Harcourt admired their bravery.

All this work though, would be for naught if Fezzdin could not find a way to defeat the demon lord and if they could not get word to Stonewood's armies to return. Their group was not a large one and there was only so much they could do.

Harcourt turned down a wide street that would lead him to the dusty roads of the south district and stopped at the sight of five men on patrol. He turned and ran, the men now running after him. The thief made a right, then another right, returning back to his desired direction. His pursuers were more heavily-armored and were now falling further behind.

Foolishly, Harcourt stopped and turned, thinking to childishly taunt the men, when a crossbow bolt grazed his neck, drawing blood. Cursing, he made for the next alley and was soon back in the south district where he was sure he had lost the patrol. He leaned against the wall of an alley, panting, trying to get his breath back, blood dripping from his neck.

There were fewer patrols in the south district. As with the real King, the Cult was finding it difficult to keep the district under control. There were too many thieves and thugs, and just plain folk who loved to fight. Harcourt was thinking that with the help of the Guild, perhaps they could take back the entire district and make it easier for them to move about and organize their attacks. It would be a good start in reclaiming the city; they could do it district by district if need be.

Harcourt did not wish to continue sneaking about with the King's face and willed his magical mask to change to that of Weldrick's. At least if he ran into any undesirables, Weldrick's face was known among the underworld and feared.

The thief peered down the next street and found it empty. He quickly sped off heading for the Ogre's Den, where Krestina and the others would be waiting.

As the thief vanished down another alley, the shadows in the alley he had just left, began to move and take on a humanoid form. Nestor Nightsbridge wore a perplexed expression upon his ghostly-pale face. He had been about to move on the King of Stonewood, when the man's face had changed right before his eyes, giving him pause. What was he? the vampire thought to himself. Nestor had heard tales of doppelgangers, strange creatures that dwelled in the far east and were said to be able to change their appearances at will. He was positive that that was not the real King Stonewood.

The vampire bent down and ran his finger through the drops of blood on the ground, that had been dripping from the King's neck. He closed his eyes and licked his finger clean. Tasted human enough, he thought. And delicious.

*   *   *   *

"You want to what??" Dornell asked, incredulously.

"You heard me correctly, I want to seek out the Guild," Harcourt repeated himself.

The thief and his small group of companions sat at two tables in the Ogre's Den tavern. Harcourt and Evonne shared a pitcher of ale. Na'Jala crunched away on an apple and Fezzdin was lost in the pages of a book. Krestina nibbled on a stick of bread, happy that Harcourt had returned safely. Vrawg was still not present, as they felt it was too dangerous for the monstrous half-ogre to move about without drawing attention. He watched over the priests and priestesses who escaped the temple and were hidden in another safe location in the lower west district. Prince Orval had gone to meet with more noble families.

"I will not ally with that lot. I refuse!" Dornell said, slamming his fist into the table.

"Haven't you ever heard the saying, 'the enemy of my enemy is my friend'?" Harcourt asked.

"You are mad, they are no less evil than Lucivenus and the Cult," Dornell replied.

"I agree," Krestina spoke up. "And besides, they cannot be trusted."

"Some can be, believe it or not. There is some honor among thieves," Harcourt said. "I can use the face of Weldrick and return as their leader, possibly. We need their help. We need to take back the entire south district so that we can use this area as our base and move about freely. We do not have enough men to do this on our own. Fezzdin?"

The old wizard looked up from his book. "Harcourt has a point. In dark times, sometimes we must do things we do not agree with. We are at war, Captain Dornell, and we require more soldiers."

Evonne also nodded in agreement. "Who best knows these streets, than the Guild, right? Though Dornell and I will not be readily accepted by that lot, considering the trouble we have caused them."

"I will have to negotiate a truce. The Guild has no

love for the Cult. They wish an end to them just as much as we do," Harcourt said.

Dornell stood up in a huff and began pacing the room. "It's too dangerous. There may already be a new leader and you might not be accepted back. They will kill you."

"I do not think so. I had the respect of the senior members. I will tell them I have escaped the mines and returned," Harcourt countered.

Krestina put a hand on his shoulder. "I don't like this idea. Dornell is right."

The priestess was about to tell Harcourt about her dream, where he was in peril, but held back.

"I can go with you," Na'Jala said to the thief.

"It's ok my friend, I will be fine as Weldrick. The Guild won't take kindly to an outsider," Harcourt replied.

"Fezzdin, what about the demon?" Dornell asked, turning to the wizard. "Have you found anything in those books?"

Fezzdin frowned. "Nothing yet, I am afraid, nothing yet."

\*   \*   \*   \*

Harcourt, wearing the face of Weldrick, dropped down into the sewer tunnel and ignited a small lantern. He had decided to pay a visit to the Guild's headquarters, located beneath the streets of the lower east district. He figured in these troubled times most senior members, whoever was left, would be staying there as it was the most secret of their locations. He did not believe that the traitor Norvil would have known about the place. Still though, he had to proceed with the utmost caution. Dornell did have a point; if there was a new leader, Weldrick might not be a welcome sight, especially if that new leader was Randar. But Harcourt had to try. They needed help in a bad way and the Guild was better than actual soldiers when it came to battles in the streets.

Harcourt was not familiar with most of the city's sewer system and it would be easy to get lost in the labyrinthine tunnels. For the most part, he had memorized this route but still kept an eye out for the hidden signs that pointed the way, signs that only a senior member would know how to spot.

Whispered voices ahead stopped the thief in his tracks; he extinguished the lantern and placed it on a dry spot on the floor. He did not draw any weapons and silently strolled around the bend.

Two men, who Harcourt recognized as Syd and Coren, immediately ceased their conversation and drew swords. Both men were startled by the unexpected visitor. A lantern hung from the tunnel ceiling, so Harcourt stepped closer into the light to reveal his face to the two thugs. Both jaws dropped in awe.

"Weldrick? Is that you? How is this possible?" questioned Syd.

"Your eyes do not deceive," Weldrick replied, "I have managed to escape the mines. Not an easy task, I assure you."

"Incredible. Nobody has ever escaped the mines," commented Coren.

"I am no ordinary thief," Weldrick stated.

Harcourt did not even have to ask, before Syd was knocking on the wall, and a door, where none appeared to exist, opened. Both men gave a nod of respect and allowed their former leader to pass before closing the door and resuming their guard duty.

Weldrick nodded to the thug who stood inside the door and he too stared with his mouth wide open. The thief strolled down a narrow hall that would lead him to a large room where senior members hung out. They drank, they gambled, or just relaxed. This place was a virtual compound, built approximately a hundred years ago, by Guild members long gone. It housed living quarters, vaults with the Guild's treasury and rooms filled with maps and books, detailing all of the Guild's activities. The Kings of Stonewood would have given almost anything to have found this location but it had remained a mystery to them. Only the most senior and most trusted members of the Guild knew of its existence. To betray that trust would be a death sentence to the rat and anyone the rat held dear. In all the years the Guild existed, not one senior member had betrayed that trust.

It seemed that Harcourt could not have chosen a better time to arrive, as he walked in on what appeared to be a meeting of some of the senior members. All conversation ceased as all turned and stared at the man who had just entered.

Feylane, her hair a bright blonde, leaned against a wall, a glass of wine in her hand. Patch and Zenod were seated at a small table across from each other, a map laid out before them. Vordollan, an illusionist, sat in a comfy chair shuffling a deck of cards and Randar, who had been pacing back and forth, now stood motionless, eyes locked on Weldrick.

Randar was the first to speak. "You! How did you

escape?"

"That's a long story," Weldrick answered, locking stares with the infamous enforcer.

"Then why don't you enlighten us?" Randar countered, a nasty edge in his voice. "Nobody has escaped the mines. I wonder if you were let go and followed here. Or struck a deal to lead them here." The Guild enforcer's hand crept closer to the hilt of his sword.

"You can relax," Weldrick replied, matching Randar's threatening tone. "I can assure you I was not followed, nor am I in league with the Cult. Shame on you for your accusations."

Randar growled and took a step closer, then Zenod spoke up. "We can trust Weldrick, Randar, never has he given us cause not to."

The weasely-looking master thief, could not have been more happy to see Weldrick alive and here now. He had figured the Guild leader was lost to the world, never to be seen until his time to hang. Zenod liked the way the man had led the Guild, he had not one single complaint. With the arrival of the demon and the changes that had gone on in the city, Randar had not had the right opportunity to take over the Guild as he intended as he was kept very busy. Now, perhaps, Weldrick could return some stability to the Guild.

"Well, one does not just simply walk out of the mines," the enforcer said.

"I did not just simply walk out. Believe me, I left a trail of bodies behind. I am not claiming it was easy, but here I am standing before you all."

"I am impressed," Feylane said, walking over and smiling at Weldrick. She too, accorded the man much respect, which was rare for her.

Randar knew that Weldrick was a valuable ally, especially since they were currently short on capable allies and needed them the most. But he still fumed inside, realizing that the other Guild members would welcome the man back as their leader, the position Randar had planned to claim himself.

Patch, too, respected Weldrick, and he rose to shake the man's hand. "Welcome back, my friend. We can surely use your sword in these times."

"Not only do I return to you now with my sword, but I come with the prospect of many more, if you will hear me out," Weldrick said.

"What do you mean?" asked Zenod. "Did you escape with others?"

"One other, yes."

"Captain Dornell, eh?" Randar said with a raised eyebrow. "What were you doing with him when you were both arrested?"

"I had met with the captain to try and convince him to investigate Krommel. Dornell had already caught Krommel's eye, so he was set up and the captain and I were both arrested. All thanks to that traitor, Norvil."

"Norvil hangs out in the market square now," Patch said with a chuckle.

"So I noticed," Weldrick nodded.

"And what are you getting at then? You want this Captain Dornell to join with us?" Randar could not believe what he was hearing.

"Look, Dornell was set up by Krommel. He hates the man just as much as we do, possibly even more. The enemy of my enemy is my friend, right? We have a common goal at the moment and we could use all the help we can get," Harcourt reasoned.

Randar just laughed and shook his head. "Do you have any idea how many of our members have been locked up and even killed by that man?"

"And many more of our members will most assuredly die if we do not stop Krommel and this demon, us included," replied Weldrick.

"Dornell is just one sword, you said there were many?" Feylane inquired.

Weldrick gave a long dramatic pause, trying to find the right way to say, "I have met with the King."

For the second time, all the assembled Guild members stood slack-jawed and again, Randar just laughed at the madness of it all.

"You?" the enforcer said. "You have met with the King of Stonewood?"

"Yes and I have brokered a truce if you would just listen. Dornell and I escaped the mines and managed to sneak back into the city. The former captain took us to meet with some people that he knew he could trust. I have met with the King and some of his loyal followers. We all want the same thing at the moment and we are all short of allies. The King is willing to work with us, for now, to fight back against the demon and the Cult."

"It's a set up, it has to be. The King despises us. He plans to eliminate us and the Cult at the same time. I am sure of it," Randar said, angrily waving his arms in the air.

"It might be legit," Zenod said thoughtfully. "Think about it. The King has lost more than we have. He is desperate to reclaim his city. Who better to turn to in times of dire need?"

"Exactly," Weldrick agreed.

"What happened to Stonewood's army?" Patch asked, finding it odd that the army had disappeared.

"Krommel spent years promoting Cult members to positions of power, within the city and the army," Weldrick explained. "He had the armies sent away on training manoeuvers while he positioned his wraggoth army around the city. The King has dispatched riders to get word to the armies of what has happened and to return with all haste."

Feylane found the whole thing amusing. "So the King has told you that he is willing to ally with us, to what, storm the castle?"

"Small steps," Weldrick replied. "Right now, the King is in hiding, as are we, as usual. The King would like to take the south district from the hands of the Cult first. Use the district as a base of operations, allowing us all to move about freely as we plan what comes next. When the armies arrive back, then they will have to consider the castle."

Zenod nodded. "That is a fine idea. The Cult already has only limited patrols in the south. With some proper planning, we may just be able to run them out and hold the district. Provided of course, they do not send in a few thousand wraggoth."

"So let's say the King is successful and takes back the city. What then?" Randar wondered.

Weldrick shrugged. "We can deal with that at the time. Obviously we are not going to be divulging any of our secret hideouts to them. Our dealings with the King and his men will be limited."

"We will need to meet with him," Randar then said. "I want to see the King face to face and have him ask for our aid himself, before we agree."

"He already has, with me," Weldrick replied.

"Not good enough. If we are all going to be risking our lives, we should all meet the King ourselves. This will be an historic event. Just think of it!" laughed the enforcer.

Feylane had to agree with the thug, this time. "I believe Randar is right, but we meet in neutral territory, of course."

Weldrick sighed silently. "I might be able to arrange that."

It was then that another Guild member strolled in, entering through the door that led from the living quarters section of their headquarters.

"Hey Andil, look who came back," Patch said to the skeletal thief.

Harcourt froze where he stood, his heart rate increasing at the sight of his old *friend*. "Keep him away from me," the Guild leader growled, before he had a chance to think about what he was saying.

The other members held quizzical looks, especially Andil himself. It was Harcourt that hated Andil, not Weldrick. He was not sure how to explain his comment.

"Weldrick, it's me, remember?" Andil said, not understanding why the Guild leader had said what he said.

Harcourt could not think fast enough; he decided to just turn and leave. "I will seek out the King and try to arrange a meeting."

The Guild leader left quickly, entering the sewer tunnel once again and exhaled a deep breath. He found he had been sweating as well. The sight of the skinny thief just brought back too many emotions that Harcourt was not ready to deal with. He nodded to the two thugs, then scooped up his lantern and set off down the tunnel.

The thief finally reached the spot where he would climb back out onto the city street and decided to wear his own face for the trek back to the Den. He spoke the command words, then removed his mask. As he did, he was startled by a loud gasp and drew a dagger. Behind him, in the shadows, stood Feylane, her face turned pale.

"What are you doing, creeping about?" shouted the thief.

It took a moment for the beautiful assassin to find her voice. "I had wanted to ask you about your friend.......Harcourt......"

# CHAPTER 8

Lord Evan Dandelbaum climbed to the second floor of the upper west district inn. The wealthy nobleman made his fortune by exporting a liquor that generations of his family had been making for over a century. Traders from all over the world came to Stonewood to buy crates of the liquor to sell in cities elsewhere. Since the demon lord had taken the throne, traders had stopped coming. But that was about to change.

He found room two-thirteen and motioned for his three guards to stand close by while he knocked. The door opened a crack and a cloaked figure within peered out.

"Come in," the man bid, "but just you."

The lord nodded to his men, then entered the room, the door closing behind him. The room was dark, lit only with two candles, and quite tidy as if the room was not being used.

"Straight to the point then, as I have another appointment across town," Lord Dandelbaum began. "So, your message said you were interested in a considerable amount of my finest liquor. How many bottles were you thinking?"

The tall man pulled back his hood revealing his brown hair and beard. "I know you and my father have had your differences over the years, Lord Dandelbaum, but I have always known you to be a fair man."

"Eh? Your father? How in the world would I know who your father is? Have we met somewhere before?" the lord asked.

The man stepped closer to the lord and locked stares, recognition slowly crossing Dandelbaum's face. "Prince Orval?"

"It is I."

"By all the gods, it is good to see you alive and well! And your father? Are the rumors true then?"

"Yes, he lives," Orval replied, though it pained him to lie, wishing it was the truth. "He is fighting to reclaim the city but we have limited resources at the moment. We are calling on all of the cities' lords and ladies for assistance."

"But of course," the lord said with a bow. "How can I help?"

Lord Dandelbaum had not always seen eye to eye with King Stonewood on several issues, mostly those that revolved around trade. But his business was going to suffer with this demon sitting on the throne. Helping the King now was good for business, along with being the right thing to do.

"How many men-at-arms do you employ?" the prince asked.

"About fifty."

"Hmmm, I thought you might have had more than that?"

"It might appear that way, but many times I employ mercenaries to guard shipments to other lands."

"Fifty is still good. Would you be willing to lend some men to our cause? When this city is ours again, you will be greatly compensated and we will forever remember your contribution."

"Absolutely, my prince. My men are your men."

"I thank you, Lord Dandelbaum. I will be in touch. And please, not a word of this to anyone, not even the men you have outside. Only when your men are needed will they find out they are helping the King."

"As you wish. And please send your father my regards. May the gods be with you." And with that, Lord Dandelbaum took his leave.

Prince Orval took a seat and let out an exhausted sigh. That was four more nobles he had enlisted to their cause this day. He was praying these men could be trusted. Perhaps he would visit Syrena, to find out what the cards had to say about it.

\*　　\*　　\*　　\*

Dornell quickened his pace, constantly glancing over his shoulder. He had managed to elude the group of pursuing cultists, even with his wounded leg. The King had made another attack in the streets and they scattered as Cult reinforcements arrived. Now he was to rendezvous with the others in a lower west district warehouse where many of the King's loyal warriors hid. The large warehouse was owned by Lord Stockbarrow, who used it to store much of his shop's merchandise. The King's men now wore the emblem of House Stockbarrow and appeared to be the usual guards, hired to protect the warehouse so as to draw no unwanted attention.

Dornell lowered his head and did his best to walk without a limp as he passed a patrol of five cultists. He had wrapped his leg with a fresh strip of material torn from his cloak and luckily the blood had not yet seeped through.

Satisfied that he had not been followed, the former captain ducked down an alley and made a series of knocks on the back door of the warehouse. As the door opened, he rushed in quickly, closing it behind him. He soon found Harcourt, wearing the face of the King, and Fezzdin, conversing in a small room. All the men hiding here in the warehouse believed Harcourt to be the real King Stonewood, so here he had to maintain his deception.

"You're hurt," Harcourt said, noticing the way Dornell entered the room, favoring his right leg.

"It is not too bad," Dornell replied.

"I can fetch Krestina," the thief offered.

"No, it can wait. But I am getting too old for this, you know. I thought joining the Investigations Unit was going to get me away from fighting in the streets. I was supposed to be taking it easy. So, why did you want me to meet you here?"

"How well do you know Captain Gregor?" Fezzdin asked Dornell. "He was captain of the castle guard."

"Yes, I know who he is. We have spoken on occasion but I cannot say I know the man well. If I had to hazard a guess, I would guess the man is loyal to the King. He spotted us fleeing the castle during the night of the King's birthday, and if he had not led some men away in another direction, we might have never escaped."

"That is what I was thinking," Fezzdin said. "The

captain is here now, blindfolded in another room and under guard. He showed up in the south district, asking around about where he could find the King. Willis overheard him, then led him here blindfolded with the help of several others. We just wanted another opinion about the man."

"We need someone like him," Harcourt added. "We need someone who is very familiar with the layout of the castle."

"Why?" Dornell wondered. "We are not ready for an assault on the castle."

"So far my research has revealed nothing of value to help us defeat the demon lord," Fezzdin said. "Now Sarvin has a book in his office, a book Harcourt has seen. By the sounds of it, this could be exactly what we need and might have the answers we seek."

"Still, we cannot send men into the castle, that is far too risky," Dornell reasoned.

"Not men, captain, man," the wizard replied.

Harcourt cleared his throat, drawing Dornell's attention. "Are you mad? You are going into the castle alone? How would you get in? How would you get out?"

"I know exactly where Sarvin's office is and I know where he keeps the book," Harcourt answered. "How I will get in has not been decided yet. But I am sure with my mask, I can manage it somehow. I just need to find the right person to imitate."

Dornell shook his head in disbelief. "You might be some master thief but this is ludicrous. So after you steal the book, you think you will just walk out the same way you came in?"

"No, leaving is the easy part," Fezzdin said, holding

up a gold ring, with a bluish gemstone. "I have this handy little magical ring. It will allow one person to teleport to a location of their choosing. But it only works once. When Harcourt secures the book, he twists the gemstone on top of the ring and will immediately appear back at the Ogre's Den. After that, the ring becomes useless. I have been saving this particular item for just such an emergency."

Dornell looked to Harcourt, still with disbelief. The thief shrugged. "I was just as skeptical as you but Fezzdin assures me it will work, so I trust that it will."

"Have you told Krestina yet about this foolish plan?" Dornell wondered.

"Ahhh, no, not yet," Harcourt said with a pause. "We were still working out some details."

"Yes, well, you let me know how that goes."

"Well, let us go speak with Captain Gregor," Fezzdin suggested.

As the trio walked through the warehouse towards the room where the captain was held, Harcourt had to consider Dornell's words. Krestina was not going to like this idea, not one bit. It was not going to be a simple task to convince her that this was their best course of action. He would, however, have that talk with her. He had come to care about the priestess very much and valued her opinion. Not only was Krestina beautiful and kind, but she was a familiar face from his past, a link to a simpler time, when demons did not roam the streets. They had grown up in similar conditions and had faced similar hardships. They were kindred spirits that understood each others life struggles. She had always bore strong feelings towards him, but of course, she was much too young when they had first met, and Harcourt's heart belonged to another.

Krestina had grown into a fine woman; someone the thief could be proud to spend a life with. Harcourt hoped he could get her blessing for this mission.

The thief followed Fezzdin into a room where a tall muscular man, dressed in plate armor, sat on a chair with a hood over his head. The wizard pulled the hood off, revealing the man's dark hair and beard, and a long jagged scar which ran down the left side of his face. The man's eyes widened at the sight of the King standing before him.

Captain Gregor immediately knelt and bowed his head. "My King, I am overjoyed to have finally found you."

To keep up his charade as the King, Harcourt rarely spoke. He was not confident enough to imitate the King's voice well enough to fool anyone that had been close to the man. Part of Harcourt's illusion as the King was a scar across his throat. The story was that he was badly injured during his battle with Lucivenus and his voice had suffered as a result. So, Fezzdin did most of the talking for the King. Harcourt would just add a nod, or salute, or whispered commands at times.

Harcourt motioned for the man to stand and Fezzdin spoke. "We are all happy to see you alive and well, Captain, especially the King. Sadly, he has not regained much of his voice but is pleased to see you. What is your current status among the castle guard?"

"I am no longer with them, as I left the castle two days ago to come in search of you all," Gregor replied. "I attempted to keep up appearances that I had accepted the new ruler of Stonewood, hoping to aid you from the inside. But alas, I could stand it no longer. The half-demon knight, Phyzantiss, commands most of the men now and

Lucivenus has taken to eating prisoners and suspected traitors. My King, I am afraid your once majestic home is now nothing but a house of horrors."

"Gervas?" the wizard inquired.

"Alive and well," Gregor answered. "The man is too important in running the castle and not viewed as a threat. The High Priest, though, keeps a close eye on him at all times."

"You just up and left?" Dornell then asked.

Gregor gave a nod of respect to the former captain whom he had met on occasion. "I did. I made an excuse of some errands I had to see to, outside the castle and I have not returned. I asked about the King in taverns, hoping word would reach your ears and I was rewarded."

Fezzdin had cast a subtle spell the moment before entering the room, which would give him an idea if the man before them spoke untruth. He appeared to be telling the truth, so the wizard gave a signal to his companions that all was ok.

"I am happy to have you serving by my side once again, my old friend," Harcourt said to the man, in a raspy whisper.

Gregor bowed. "You have my sword and I will gladly lay down my life in service to Stonewood."

"Let's hope that will not be necessary, Captain," Fezzdin said. "Now, you must know the castle better than anyone else. Are there any secret ways in? Maybe somewhere not guarded, somewhere that Sarvin is not aware of?"

"Well, yes, there is one escape tunnel through the sewers that only a handful of people are aware of. But my King, you would know of that one already," Gregor replied.

"Sadly, some of the King's memories suffered as well as his voice, from his injuries. Only through the miracle of a brave priestess were the King's injuries mostly healed," Fezzdin said. "Can you guide us to this tunnel?"

Gregor lowered his head. "I am afraid I cannot. I know where it is from the inside of the castle, but I am not familiar enough with the sewer system to locate it from the other side. Also, it is well hidden from view so as not to appear as an entrance at all. It could be near-impossible to locate. I am so sorry."

Fezzdin sighed. "Fair enough, Captain. Go now, grab some food and drink, and speak with Barros. He can fill you in on our next plans. Make a right outside this door, to the main area of this warehouse."

Gregor nodded to Fezzdin and Dornell, then bowed again to the King before exiting the room.

"So a way in exists but there is nobody who can find it from the sewer side," Dornell commented. "Perhaps Prince Orval?"

"No," Fezzdin replied. "I have already spoken to the prince and he also has no knowledge of the sewers."

"Well, if anyone knows the sewers, it's the rats of the Thieves Guild," Dornell reasoned.

Harcourt shook his head. "None of them know the way into the castle. But I believe I know someone who might."

"Who?" Fezzdin asked.

"Have either of you ever heard of the game, *kick the kan*?"

*   *   *   *

"I have recently met with some old acquaintances of mine and I am curious to know if I can trust them," asked Prince Orval, who was seated across from Syrena at her small table within her shop.

"Business partners, are they?" the sorceress inquired.

"Something like that," he replied.

Syrena picked up her deck of cards and flipped over the card of the fool. She cursed inwardly, as she was supposed to place a more favorable card on top and had forgotten. She had been distracted by the mysterious man's smile.

"That's bad, isn't it?" Orval immediately said. "I am the fool?"

"No, no. This card says that you would be a fool not to trust your instincts. You are wise to have doubts but you trusted these people for a reason. You have shown good judgment, do not worry."

Orval relaxed then. He found he could not stop staring into the fortune teller's hazel-colored eyes. Syrena matched his stare for a moment, before blushing and looking away.

"Do you have any other questions?" she asked.

"Yes, one."

"Then ask and we shall see what the cards tell us."

"Is there a man in your life?"

The sorceress was taken aback, not expecting the direct question from the man with the charming smile. She stumbled over her words before she managed to answer, "no."

The prince placed a strong hand over hers, resting on the table. Syrena was powerless to pull away. She found the aura of strength and confidence in this man intoxicating. When he locked eyes with her, she could feel butterflies in her stomach.

"Walk with me? We could get something to eat perhaps?"

Syrena nodded and allowed the man to gently pull her up to her feet. She placed a sign by the door that read, *Be Back Soon*, and followed the man outside.

\*      \*      \*      \*

Harcourt wore his own face, concealed by the hood of his cloak, as he wove his way through the south district streets. There were not too many patrols to avoid, but enough that the thief had to stay alert and quickly change direction when need arose. Soon, he would set up the meeting between the King and the Thieves Guild so that they could begin to take back the streets of the poorest district.

Hopefully, Feylane would not see through his deception. He had been forced to share his secret dual identity, as Weldrick, with the beautiful assassin. She had witnessed him remove the mask and change his face. There was no way of denying what she had seen. She had been shocked by the mask and its abilities, but strangely, was not angry about his deception as Guild leader. The assassin respected him as both Harcourt and Weldrick, and gaining Feylane's respect was no easy task. She had promised to keep his secret safe and the thief hoped he could trust her. For all the time that Harcourt had known the assassin, he had learned that she was a woman of her word.

Harcourt turned quickly, appearing to admire some

wares in a shop window as several guards, loyal to the demon lord, passed him by. For the most part, they left folk alone during the day. They tended to stop suspicious-looking people, but in the south district, everyone looked suspicious.

When the men were out of sight, Harcourt continued on his way. He had left Fezzdin and Dornell back at the warehouse, leaving them to wonder what plan he had in mind. But until he was sure this would work, he had left his companions in the dark.

A few more twists and turns and the thief found the alley he sought and the man he sought seated therein. Old Kan, the one-legged beggar, sat up against a shop wall, his tin cup, empty, placed on the ground next to him. The years had not been kind to the old man and he looked worse than ever. His long white hair and beard were filthy and unkempt, his clothes were in no better shape. Harcourt had done his best over the years to always fill his cup with coins but Kan seemed to drink away the coins faster than Harcourt could give them.

The thief recalled the night of the King's birthday, when he had been inside the Chief Magistrate's office. He had found a ledger, kept by Krommel, with many interesting notes made inside. One in particular which caught the thief's attention, was a note about a Captain Kanalandiros, a war-hero, who had lost his leg in a battle defending Stonewood. It was said that the captain led troops through the sewers to come out behind enemy lines. The battle was then won.

Old Kan had always rambled on about being a soldier in Stonewood's army, though most people dismissed him as being mad. The crueler kids in the neighborhood, had invented a game they called *kick the kan,* kicking the old beggar then running, while he shouted curses, unable to pursue them. Life had not be kind to Kan.

Harcourt crouched down next to the beggar. "Kan? Hey Kan, you awake?"

"Eh? Who's there?" the old man said. He opened his eyes but his vision had been failing over the last few years.

"It's your old friend, Harcourt, you remember me?"

Kan was silent for a moment before he replied. "Harcourt? Harcourt is dead."

"No, it's me. I still live. I can explain all that later. I have something here I want you to try. It's a special liquor you cannot get anywhere in Stonewood," the thief said, producing a flask filled with a sparkling, gold-colored liquid.

# CHAPTER 9

Gervas nervously entered the throne room and cleared his throat. "Ah, Sarvin sir?"

"My lord!" the High Priest barked.

"Ah, yes, sorry, my lord," the elderly man corrected himself.

"What do you want?"

Gervas was pleased to find the High Priest alone in the throne room, it was a rare occasion. He loathed being in the presence of the demon lord and those other half-demons who served him. Gervas never knew when he would be the next person on the monster's dinner plate.

"The city is suffering, my lord. You planned for things to run just as they did before but they are not."

"Get to the point."

"Well, my lord, businesses will be forced to close. You have imposed a curfew at night and as you know, most of the taverns do their best business at night. They are struggling. There are also merchants who rely on traders who visit the city but these traders are no longer coming. And some merchants export their goods, but most are not being allowed to leave the city. If the people of Stonewood are not bringing in coins, then how do you propose we can collect taxes from them?"

Sarvin growled. He knew the old fool was right but at the moment, it was necessary. They could not allow the King to escape the city and join his armies. They also could not afford to have him and his men running about the city at night, wreaking havoc. But the High Priest was hoping that this little problem was soon to be rectified. He figured it would not be much longer, before Nestor Nightsbridge lived up to his reputation.

"Yes, yes, I know all this," Sarvin replied, annoyingly. "This little uprising will soon be over and Stonewood can then return to normal. A minor inconvenience is all. Now, if that's all you have to say, leave."

"Ah, yes, my lord," Gervas said with a bow, then hurried off.

High Priest Sarvin clenched his fists in anger. The King was supposed to have been dealt with the night of his birthday, to avoid all this mess afterwards. Somehow, the wretch survived his injuries, to torment Sarvin for a little longer.

He cursed the King for killing Brother Norvil. The priest had been young but showed great promise. The man's head was displayed in the market square, a tactic normally reserved for the Thieves Guild. A clever ruse by the King, Sarvin thought, for he knew that the Guild was crippled and would bother him no longer.

\* \* \* \*

Randar paced back and forth within the subterranean chamber. Torches lined the walls, giving the normally pitch-dark chamber some light. Water flowed from a hole in the ceiling, into a foul-smelling cesspool in the center of the room. This chamber was the deepest underground of any other under Stonewood and rarely visited by any, aside from Guild members.

"Where is Weldrick? And where is this King?" the impatient Guild enforcer hissed.

"Weldrick said he may be delayed but that the meeting was still set," Feylane answered, her dark hair straight, with streaks of red.

"This had better not be a trap," Patch muttered, nervously.

"Precisely why I chose this location to meet. The King needs our help, so he will play by our rules," Randar answered. "We know these tunnels well and I have men hidden all over."

Zenod leaned against a wall in a dark corner, virtually invisible to anyone who did not already know he was there. Vordollen also paced about nervously. He was a middle-aged illusionist, not a warrior, and very much hoped this meeting would not turn sour. His companions had all dressed for battle and were armed to the teeth, ready for anything.

The Guild members did not have to wait much longer, before booted feet could be heard approaching from a tunnel across the room, lanterns bobbing about in the darkness of the tunnel. First to enter the chamber, cautiously, was a tall black-skinned warrior, his hair worn in long braids, his face mostly hidden with a strange metal mask. He was followed by the famous Captain Dornell, decked out in chain mail armor, his sword in hand at the ready.

Randar's heart skipped a beat, as he watched the King, King Stonewood himself, enter the chamber. The thug never imagined a day when he would be this close to the King and for the even more unlikely reason of striking an alliance. Behind the King was the elderly wizard, Fezzdin, wearing his foolish-looking, blue conical hat. Last to enter was a petite blonde woman, her crossbow held loosely in front of her. Evonne's reputation had grown tremendously within Stonewood and the enforcer recognized her immediately. He wondered where her giant partner might be hiding.

Five on five, Randar mused to himself, well-matched unless you counted the ten other men he had spread out in the tunnels surrounding the chamber. Curse Weldrick for being late, the enforcer thought. Randar hated people who could not be on time. A meeting as historic as this and the Guild leader himself could not make it? Pathetic.

Harcourt, wearing the King's face, of course, glanced about the room, knowing that Randar would have prepared everything to his advantage. The circular cesspool sat in the center of the room, but a wide run-off split the room in half and disappeared into a hole in the wall. The two groups stood on either side of the run-off and one would need a running start to leap across.

Randar was the first to speak. "Well, well, well. Welcome to our domain, King Stonewood. You will have to excuse me if I do not bow, I have a bad back."

The King looked about the chamber before replying in a raspy voice. "A domain of filth, by the look of it. You are welcome to it."

Randar's smug smile disappeared. Harcourt knew that none of the Guild members would be familiar with the King's voice, so elected to do the speaking himself. He also knew that to gain the respect of the thug, he could not show weakness or appear desperate. Randar despised cowards, so the King must not back down, or succumb to threats.

"It may be a domain of filth, and yet here you are, hiding among us, seeking the help of thieves," Randar countered.

"I am sorry, who are you?" the King asked. "I was under the impression that the Guild was led by a different man. Am I to assume that you are to do the speaking in his absence?"

The Guild enforcer clenched his teeth tight, holding back the words he wished he could say. "My name is not important. And yes, in the absence of our leader, you will speak with me."

"Do not mistake my presence here as a sign of desperation, thief," the King said. "This is the city you all call home, as it is mine, and we all seek a similar goal."

"Indeed. But we have remained hidden, as always, and will endure, as always," the thug said. "No matter who sits on the throne."

"And how long do you think it will be before Lucivenus swarms the south district and these sewers, to root you out? This High Priest Sarvin seems to bear a hatred for you lot, almost as strong as that which you bear towards them. Where is your army, that you plan to fight back with?"

"Where is yours?" Randar spat back.

"Mine is on the way back to the city, as we speak."

"Then what are you doing here, your majesty?"

"I need to get a foothold within the city. I would like to start with the south district. It would be to your own benefit, keeping you free from Cult patrols. We take back the south, you don't bother us and we don't bother you."

"Take back? I was not aware the south district was yours to begin with," Randar dared.

"This entire city is mine! Everyone within this city is mine! You would do well to remember this," the King did his best to shout.

The exchange had everyone inching their hands towards their weapons. Evonne raised her crossbow, placing the thug in her sights.

"What does the Guild gain from allying with you, in the long run? You certainly are no fan of ours and will most likely turn on us, if you are successful."

"We should not even be negotiating with these scum," Dornell could hold his tongue no longer.

"Ah, the disgraced *ex*-captain," Randar taunted. "It seems that you did not mind dealing with the Guild, before your arrest."

Before Dornell could reply - and he was about to - the King cut him off. "I will reward you all, with gold, for your cooperation. You will then be allowed to leave Stonewood unharmed, but never to return."

"This is our home, just as much as it is yours," Randar said.

"You will be given gold and a chance to leave the city," the King repeated himself. "Choose to stay and we will become enemies once more. Old alliances will be forgotten. There will be no compromise."

"Allow me a moment to talk with my peers?" the

enforcer asked.

The King nodded. Randar stepped back into the shadows near the entrance closest to the Guild members. Zenod and Feylane had hung back in the darkness, not wishing their faces to be clearly seen by the King and his entourage.

"A fine deal," Zenod said. "Though we would not admit it, we need their help just as much as they need ours."

"We have remained hidden from the King for all these years, we would do the same with this Cult. It is they who need us the most," Randar replied.

"I agree with Zenod," Feylane whispered. "We won't get any more out of the King."

Vordollen nodded his agreement.

"We can always take the King's gold and stay here anyways, business as usual," Patch reasoned. "Life would continue on for us as it always has and our pockets would be a little heavier for it."

Randar was thinking along the same lines as Patch. Stonewood was his city, he liked it here. He had no intention of leaving but, would not mind letting the King believe that he would.

The Guild enforcer abruptly broke away from the group and strode directly towards the King. Randar walked right through the cesspool run-off as if it did not exist, until he stood directly in front of King Stonewood, his hand extended. "We have a deal."

Harcourt then realized that the water that appeared to separate the two groups was merely an illusion, created by Vordollen. Clever.

The King grabbed Randar's hand and the two locked

eyes in an intense stare down. "Deal."

As the King turned to leave, he added. "Think to betray us, thief, and I will see to it that it is the last mistake you ever make."

"Same goes for you," Randar called after him, as the group was leaving.

Feylane rubbed her chin in deep thought as she watched the King of Stonewood exit the chamber. She found it strange that Harcourt would miss a meeting as important as this. She found it stranger still that the King had a knife strapped above his boot that looked exactly like the one the thief wore above his.

\*     \*     \*     \*

Not long after the meeting, Harcourt donned the armor and clothing of the Guild leader and with Weldrick's face, doubled back through the tunnels to find his Guild associates. Harcourt was finding it increasingly difficult to play so many roles and remember who he was supposed to be at different times. He looked forward to a day when he could just be Harcourt - and only Harcourt - again.

The thief was too deep in thought and only noticed the movement in the shadows once it was too late. A figure dove out from the darkness to his left and tackled him around the waist. Strong arms threw him to the mucky floor of the sewer tunnel causing him to drop his lantern. There was still enough light to see that Randar stood over him, his sword now in hand.

"A pitiful leader you are," the enforcer spat. "Not even present for an historic meeting as that. I had to do all your talking for you. There is no excuse for that."

"You forget who arranged that meeting?" Weldrick answered.

"Well, we just made a deal with the King. We now have his sword, along with the swords of all his loyal followers on our side. That makes me think that maybe, one less sword fighting for us might not be missed."

"You dare threaten me?" Weldrick asked with a growl.

"Oh, I plan on doing more than just threatening you. Get up, draw your sword. Never let it be known that I am not a fair man," Randar said, finally issuing his challenge. "I think the Guild needs a new leader, a strong leader."

"You are more a fool than I ever thought," Weldrick said, getting to his feet and drawing his sword.

Randar rushed in immediately with three quick attacks. Weldrick was caught off guard by the suddenness but managed to parry each one, even countering with an attack of his own. Randar easily ducked under and stepped back out of reach. The pair circled each other, each searching for the right opening.

The shorter thug led with a feint, which Weldrick had fell for, then reversed his attack drawing blood from the Guild leader's sword arm. Furious, Weldrick pressed the attack. Sparks flew from their blades as they clashed over and over, before Weldrick's relentlessness was rewarded with a line of blood across the thug's cheek.

The two men backed off for only a moment, before clashing again, anger driving them both. This time, it ended with a boot to Weldrick's chest. The Guild leader stumbled back, then slipped on a slick part of the sewer floor. His sword fell from his grasp as his elbow hit the stone floor first, breaking his fall.

Randar was on him in a split second. The thug raised his sword until the sharp sting of a blade, pressed into the back of his neck, stayed his attack. On the ground, Weldrick suddenly had a dagger in each hand.

"Kill him and I kill you," Feylane threatened, her knife to Randar's neck.

"Are you mad, woman? You would side with him over me?" the enforcer asked, in shock.

"He is our leader! Voted in by senior members. Guild members do not kill Guild members. Not without the vote of other senior members," she replied, angrily. "Or are you not so familiar with the rules that you forever enforced?"

"He is a pathetic leader," Randar said, his sword still poised to strike.

"In your opinion only," Feylane countered. "The rest of us do not feel the same as you."

Weldrick got to his feet and pointed a dagger at the thug's face. "Let us win back the south district and rid the city of the Cult first and then we will deal with each other. This, I promise you."

"Until then," Randar reluctantly agreed. He sheathed his sword and disappeared down the tunnel, not even glancing back once.

"I had that under control," Harcourt said, removing his mask, no longer needing the deception with the beautiful assassin.

"I am sure you did," she replied with a raised eyebrow.

"Why did you side with me over him?" the thief wondered.

"You saved my life many years ago. That is not

something I will ever forget. So if I have a chance to return that favor, I will, even it means killing Randar."

Feylane referred to a time when Harcourt had seemingly rescued her from the clutches of an evil Cult member, Lord Mornay. Of course, Harcourt had also been Mornay, with the use of his mask. The assassin was never in any real danger at all but it certainly worked to the thief's advantage that she had believed she was.

Harcourt gave her a nod of respect. But her next words froze him place.

"There is no more King Stonewood, is there?"

The thief opened his mouth to speak but nothing came out.

"I know that was you back there as the King, using your little toy mask. And I thought I had secrets." The assassin then took on another tone, a softer tone, one that Harcourt was not used to hearing from the woman. It was almost as if she was….frightened. "Is there any hope of us winning at all, Harcourt?"

The thief gave her a warm smile. "Of course there is. We have Fezzdin, the great wizard, working on a way to defeat Lucivenus. Stonewood's troops should be heading back home soon. And now we have an alliance between the Guild and the King's followers. We can do this, Feylane."

The assassin stepped in close to the thief. He could feel her breath on his face, smell her intoxicating perfume. "And then what will you do? They will not let you play King forever. What will happen to Harcourt, when this is over?"

"I know not," he replied, startled by her sudden closeness. "I do not like to think that far ahead. One step at a time."

"You are one of the bravest men I have ever known. And the most honorable," Feylane said, kissing the thief softly on the lips, allowing hers to linger for a moment before turning away and walking into the darkness.

# CHAPTER 10

Prince Orval and Syrena strolled casually down a path through Stonewood's cemetery on the south side of the river. They found a bench that faced the river and took a seat, listening to the fast-flowing water rushing by. They had spent several days enjoying each other's company, neither truly knowing who the other was.

"It will be dark soon," the sorceress said. "It will not be safe for us to be out."

"You fear the dead in this graveyard?" Orval asked.

"No, I was referring to the demon's soldiers, the curfew."

"Bah. I do not wish to rush this wonderful time I am having with you."

Syrena blushed. She was truly flattered. "You do not fear the Cult? And the demon lord?" she wondered.

"Should I?"

"Yes, I believe so. They are dangerous and they do not play games. If you run afoul of them, you do not live to make another mistake."

"I believe their rule here will be short," the prince commented.

"Oh? You do, huh?" Syrena asked, curiously.

"Yes, the King is also dangerous and does not play games."

"Dangerous, you say? And yet he is without his throne. Forced to hide in the bowels of the city, like a common thief."

"For now," Orval said, "for now. Do not underestimate the King and his allies."

Syrena was becoming quite fond of this strange man and that line of thinking would get him into much trouble. There would be no defeating Lucivenus. She had witnessed with her own eyes how quickly the demon lord had dispatched the King and his men during their first meeting. A second encounter could not go any differently, especially now that Lucivenus had his two half-demon lackeys by his side. Along with High Priest Sarvin, there would be no stopping them.

"What is your name?" Syrena asked. "You still have not told me."

"I thought you would have guessed it by now. You are a fortune teller, are you not?" Orval answered with a chuckle.

Syrena pinched the man's arm and smiled. "Cheeky, huh? I do not like to use my powers for my own benefit. I prefer the old-fashioned way, where you just tell me."

"Minas, my name is Minas," the prince lied.

"And what do you do, in Stonewood, Minas? You already know that I read fortunes."

"I am a merchant," Orval replied, taking one of Syrena's hands in his. "Though business is not good for me right now."

Her heart raced, as his strong hand squeezed hers. "Umm, what, ummm, business are you in?" she stammered.

"That's not too important right now," he said, leaning in to kiss the sorceress, passionately.

Syrena did not resist and returned the kiss with equal passion.

\*     \*     \*     \*

"Dammit! Hold still, would ya?" Evonne said in frustration.

Old Kan, who did not appear that old anymore, leaned against a wall in the Ogre's Den tavern, trying his best to stand still while the petite bounty hunter put the finishing touches on his new leg.

His snow-white hair was now mostly brown, as it had been in his younger years. The wrinkles on his face had disappeared. The elderly beggar now looked to be a man somewhere in his fifties. In fact, any who were familiar with the one-legged man would not recognize him now.

Earlier, with the help of Krestina, Evonne had attached a broom handle to the stump of the man's right leg. She put a boot at the base of the broom and was now sewing it to his brand new pants. Now it appeared that Kan had two legs, with one injured which explained his limp.

"Where did you get that idea from?" Dornell asked, seated at a table, watching the bounty hunter at work.

"When I was a pirate, our first mate lost his leg in a battle once. One of the crewmen gave him this fake leg, which seemed to work quite well, though it will never be the same as a real leg. We all called him 'peg-leg' after that but he couldn't have been happier," Evonne said.

A tear ran down Old Kan's cheek. He was beside himself with joy but could not help but wonder if this was all just some amazing dream. It was certainly possible, since the man had polluted his mind with alcohol just about every single day for half a century. Had he finally cracked?

He had been sitting in his usual spot when he was awoken by a man he had been told was dead. Kan was fairly sure that he even attended the man's funeral. But there stood this same man, Harcourt. He gave Kan something to drink and the old man immediately felt a strange tingling sensation throughout his body, a better buzz than any drink that had ever before graced his lips. Within moments, his body was filled with vigor, strength returned to his weary limbs, his mind became clearer.

The man named Harcourt assured him that this was not a dream and bade him follow the thief to an abandoned tavern. At the Ogre's Den, he was introduced to Harcourt's friends and informed of all the goings-on within Stonewood. For the first time in his life, Kan sat in a tavern and refused anything to drink, even though it was free. He did not know how it was possible to be young again but he vowed not to waste away his memories with drink any longer. And now, this lovely little woman had even given him the ability to walk again.

Also seated in this tavern, watching intently, was the old wizard Fezzdin. Kan remembered that the man was the royal magician, even back in the days when he served as a soldier. Strangely, the wizard looked exactly the same as he did all those years before.

Fezzdin shook his head in amazement, for the hundredth time. This Harcourt was full of surprises. "So tell me, Captain Kanalandiros, you are still familiar with the sewer systems then? And the secret entrance into the castle?" the wizard asked.

"Yes sir, Mister Fezzdin, sir," Old Kan replied. "I was an accomplished engineer, you know. I helped design some of the tunnels under the castle, to be used for escape in times of dire need."

"Then why become a soldier?" Dornell wondered.

"Stonewood was under attack then," Kan remembered. "The barbarian king had led his hordes to our very doorstep. As a citizen of Stonewood, it was my duty to help protect this city, my home. I was honored to be allowed a spot in the army."

"Not just a spot, you became a captain as well?" Dornell mentioned.

"I was an expert marksman, the best shot in Stonewood," Kan declared proudly. "And my intelligence and understanding of battle strategies did not go unnoticed."

"Then how did you end up on the streets?" Evonne asked, looking up at the man she now had a new respect for.

"I lost my right leg, during the final battle on the fields outside of the city where King Stonewood killed the barbarian king in single combat. Weeks later, I lay in a temple, healing. I remember being approached by a strange man. He told me that the King did not care about wounded soldiers and that we would soon all be forgotten and cast aside. He told me of a group of people who planned to bring forth a new era to Stonewood, where men like me would be honored and hailed as heroes. The King was evil, he said, and some Lucivenus was going to right all the wrongs in the city. Naturally, I told the fool where he and his group could go. Shortly thereafter, a young magistrate dug up some shady behavior I was said to be involved with. All lies! I was dishonorably discharged and was then homeless and broke, forced to live on the streets."

"This young magistrate," Fezzdin inquired, curiously, "was his name Krommel?"

Kan scratched his head in thought; it was a very, very long time ago. But, the name did sound familiar. "Yes, yes, I believe it was a Krommel, now that you mention it. Why do you ask? He is somehow involved with this mess our city is in now?"

\*　　\*　　\*　　\*

Harcourt leaped over the fence into the cemetery, before helping Krestina over to join him. A bright, full moon was high in the sky, and an eerie silence surrounded the graveyard, as it usually did at night. It was the perfect place for a night-time walk, since citizens and city guards alike avoided the place after sunset.

The thief and the priestess had been hiding out in one of their secret locations waiting for night to fall, before slipping away to walk the graveyard, south of the river. Harcourt needed to have a talk with Krestina about his upcoming plan to slip into the castle and steal the High Priest's book. He wanted some privacy for this conversation. The cemetery was as private as it got and they would not have to worry about cultists on patrol.

Krestina looked about nervously. "Are you sure it is safe in here? I have never been in here after dark."

"Do not worry," Harcourt reassured her. "I have spent many a night in here, hiding out. No spooks have ever come after me."

"Yes, but you are a King, now," the priestess teased. "That might make you more appealing to a hungry ghoul. And I am apparently made of sugar. Dahleene always said so."

"You sure are," the thief said, reaching for Krestina's arm and taking a gentle bite.

She laughed and managed to wiggle her arm free from the thief's strong grasp. When was the last time I laughed? she wondered to herself. And as frightening as the graveyard looked at night, she did feel safe next to Harcourt. He was her guardian-angel, she thought. The man she loved could even save her from a prison cell, hidden within Castle Stonewood itself.

The two held hands and walked in silence for some time, enjoying the cool, refreshing breeze and looking to the twinkling stars. After many twists and turns, following one of the many paths, Krestina came to a halt and the thief felt a change come over her. When he looked about at their surroundings, he suddenly realized why.

"It is…beautiful," Krestina said, admiring the craftsmanship of the headstone, which marked the spot where Jalanna was buried.

Harcourt had purchased the tallest grave marker in all of Stonewood for Jalanna. It was carved in the likeness of an angel, her wings spread wide. Jalanna had believed in such things, so Harcourt thought it appropriate to have an angel watch over her. Also, she herself had been an angel in life.

"Ah, yes it is," Harcourt stumbled to say, feeling suddenly uncomfortable. He had come to love Krestina, very much, but there would always be a spot for Jalanna in his heart that would never go away. "I am sorry, I did not mean for us to come this way."

"Never-the-less, here we are," Krestina replied. "You love her still, don't you?"

Harcourt thought about the appropriate reply for a moment and decided honesty was the best course. "Yes, I do. And I always will, most likely. But that doesn't change anything about you or I, just so you know. She was…"

Krestina held a finger to his lips and cut him off. "You do not have to explain, I understand. I would never ask you to stop loving her, ever. I am fine with sharing your heart with her," she smiled. "Besides, I am just happy you remember my name now and know that I exist."

Harcourt chuckled at the playful jab. "You have to understand, I lived much of my life in darkness. I found that drinking chased all my problems away, for the short-term at least. I am sure there is much that I have done that I cannot recall. I have probably said and done many things which I would regret, if I could only remember them."

"Well, you were always kind to me. A true gentleman, even when you were drunk and even when you did not know who I was."

"I don't know what you and Jalanna ever saw in me but I am glad for it, whatever it was."

Krestina shook her head at the silly comment. "You are a kind and honorable man, which cannot be said about most people, especially among thieves. Look at where you came from, Harcourt, and look at where you are now. You, a homeless thief at one time, are now the savior of Stonewood."

"I would not go that far. There is still Fezzdin and Prince Orval and…"

The priestess cut him off again. "You are the one playing King Stonewood, the most wanted man in the entire city. And you are the one inspiring hope in the citizens that the King will overthrow this demon and his Cult and save the city. Do not downplay your role here."

"Yes, well, about that," the thief said, figuring this was the time to have their talk.

"Yes?"

"There is a book that Sarvin possesses, I have seen it within his office at the castle. It goes into much detail about demons and outlined the process of how the Cult was able to release Lucivenus from his prison."

"Yes?"

"Well, Fezzdin has had no luck in finding a way for us to defeat the demon lord and send him back to this magical prison."

"Yes?"

"So, we need that book. That should have all the answers that we seek."

"And?"

"And," the thief paused for a moment," and I am going into the castle to steal it."

"Harcourt, no!" the priestess said, wrapping him in a tight embrace. "That is too dangerous."

"Krestina, we need that book. We are not going to be able to defeat Lucivenus without it."

"Let Fezzdin do it," she pleaded. "He is a powerful

wizard, surely he can get it."

"Yes, Fezzdin is powerful. Lucivenus and Sarvin may have a way to detect his presence. Also, he would not be able to move about the castle freely, to reach the office. I can use my mask to move about."

"How would you even get in? How would you get out?"

"There is a secret entrance to the castle from the sewers - that's where Old Kan comes into this. He knows where it is. As for escaping, Fezzdin gave me a magical ring that can bring me back to the Den, anytime I choose to use it."

"I still do not like this," she admitted, with tearful eyes. "This is way too dangerous. They cannot ask this of you."

"Nobody has asked, this is my idea."

There was that charming quality again that she fell in love with, Krestina thought to herself. "There has to be another way, another book."

"There could be another book, somewhere, but we have not the time to search for it. If our plan works, and Stonewood's armies return, then it will all be for nothing if we cannot actually defeat Lucivenus."

Krestina understood, she really did. But she had lost Harcourt once, or at least thought she did, and she did not want to go through that again. From a young age, her dream was to be together with the handsome rogue and now she finally was. She supposed she would have to trust in God to keep him safe for her.

"I just love you, is all. I worry for you," she said.

"Awwww, how touching," said a voice from behind the pair.

They whirled about in surprise, Harcourt drawing his sword. Before them stood a strange man, wearing a long dark coat, with a wide-brimmed hat. A slender sabre hung at his hip and even in the dark night, they could tell how pale his skin looked, with a peculiar rosy tinge to his eyes. Oddly, there was now a different chill in the air, one that reminded Harcourt of the undead wizard of Morgaldrun.

"Who are you? Speak now!" the thief shouted, pulling Krestina to stand behind him.

"I am Nestor Nightsbridge," the man said, with a slight bow. "The more important question here, I feel, is who are you? Are you Harcourt? Or are you Weldrick? Or are you King Stonewood?"

"What do you want?" Krestina asked, her heart racing.

"I want......the King's head. I am going to be greatly rewarded for bringing his head to Lord Sarvin. So, if you would not mind, please use your little magic trick to turn your face back into the King's, so it will be worth more to me when I remove it."

"A bold threat," Harcourt growled.

"And one that I mean to act on," Nestor replied, his voice so very calm.

"Get out of here," Harcourt whispered to Krestina. "Run. I will deal with this pompous fool."

"Running will do you no good, I am afraid, my dear. I will find you when I am done here. I cannot let you go, since you look so positively delicious," Nestor said, licking his lips.

"Draw your sword then," the thief demanded.

"As you wish," Nestor replied, drawing his thin-bladed, curved sword. "Let us get this unpleasantness over with."

Krestina ran to stand behind a nearby tree as the two men slowly circled each other. Harcourt looked bigger and stronger than the strange man, who appeared to be quite thin beneath his long coat. She knew the man she loved was a capable fighter, so she had confidence in him to win this battle.

Harcourt smiled, as his mysterious opponent made exaggerated movements with his sword and posed in ridiculous-looking stances. *Showing off does not win you a fight.*

Nestor suddenly darted towards the thief in a blur of movement. As he danced back out of reach, Harcourt bled from two cuts, one on each cheek. The thief's smile faded.

In life, Nestor had been a swashbuckler and was already an accomplished swordsman at the age of thirty. He hired out his skills to ships that required added protection from pirates, while delivering valuable goods or persons. On one fateful night, during a stopover in the port city of Bayswater, Nestor ran afoul of the vampire, Edmund Kirkov, his life forever changed.

Shortly thereafter, his master, Edmund, had been slain by a vampire hunter. Nestor was now free to roam the world, the bond to his master severed. Once he was finally accustomed to living as an undead creature of the night, Nestor continued to hire himself out to those who required his unique services. He did it more out of boredom than a need to make a living. For him, it was fun, it was sport. So the swashbuckling vampire had spent the last century improving his swordsmanship. Harcourt was now getting a taste of those skills.

Nestor danced in again and Harcourt found he could

not parry the attacks. The man's sword moved with blinding speed and now the thief bled from two more minor wounds on his sword arm. It appeared the strange man was toying with him.

Harcourt decided to take the offensive and moved forward with two deadly slashes of his sword. Both met with air, as Nestor ducked under the first and side-stepped the second. The thief felt a sting on his left side as the man suddenly positioned himself behind him. Harcourt whirled around and thrust his blade towards Nestor's stomach. The vampire twisted his body at the last possible second, narrowly avoiding the attack, then countered by drawing blood from Harcourt's neck.

As the blood dripped from this thief's neck, Nestor licked his lips, his hunger now growing stronger. He enjoyed the game though and did his best to keep his urges in check.

Krestina found herself trembling with nervousness. This strange man had turned out to be a master swordsman and it was becoming clear to the priestess that he was playing with Harcourt. The fact that the man knew about Harcourt's various identities was extremely troubling. Krestina did not like taking someone's life but at the same time, she realized they could not let this man go. She stepped around from behind the tree and considered her options.

In one swift movement, Harcourt grabbed a boot knife with his free hand and launched it at Nestor, catching the man square in the chest. The thief's jaw dropped open, as the man pulled it out, like it was nothing, and tossed it aside. There was no blood, not even a wound was left behind, where the knife had been embedded a moment before. That particular knife had not yet been blessed by the priestess and had no effect on the undead creature.

Nestor laughed, then danced in again. Harcourt decided to change tactics. The thief gritted his teeth and accepted a slash to his shoulder in order to get in close to the thin man. With his free hand, Harcourt grabbed the man by the front of his coat and pulled him, while slamming his forehead into Nestor's nose. Nestor grunted and appeared momentarily stunned.

The vampire reached for a dagger with his free hand, a movement that caught the thief's eye. Harcourt planted a boot into his chest and kicked him back several feet. Nestor glanced downwards and growled with disgust at the mud that now dirtied his coat. "Now I am angry," he said.

"STOP!" Krestina shouted, attempting to enact a spell that would immobilize the mysterious man.

Nestor began to stride towards the thief with a scowl, when he froze in place, like a statue.

Harcourt walked over to inspect Krestina's handiwork. "He cannot move? How long will that hold him?"

"It's different for everyone," the priestess replied. "It all depends on how strong of will they are."

"Thankfully, my will is strong," Nestor said, breaking the spell and gaining full control of his body.

Harcourt raised his sword in defense but Nestor slashed him across the hand, disarming the thief. Now, it was the vampire who grabbed Harcourt with his free hand and threw him with amazing strength. The thief flew head first into a tombstone, then lay still.

Nestor sheathed his sword and hissed, sharp fangs

now visible in his mouth. It was then that Krestina made the horrible realization of Nestor's true nature.

"Vampire!" she shouted, the fear evident in her voice, but Harcourt did not move.

With other-worldly speed, Nestor pounced on the thief and sunk his fangs into Harcourt's neck. Krestina screamed, as she realized her last vision had come true. Nestor laughed as blood dripped from his mouth.

The priestess prayed for the use of the silver energy she had witnessed other members of the temple use and her prayer was answered. A beam of the silvery, holy light, shot forth from her extended hand and blasted the vampire off Harcourt. Nestor landed a short distance away, his back smoking, a hole burned through his coat.

"Whoa," he said, sitting up. "You are young, girl. How do you wield holy magic as powerful as that?"

"You'll find I am full of surprises," the priestess said grimly, but did not quite believe her own claim.

She always had trouble casting spells and it usually took years of study and devotion before a priest or priestess could wield such magic. Lately, though, she had been able to use spells far beyond her experience. Other members of the temple were beginning to think she was chosen by God to be a savior. There was no other explanation.

Nestor ran straight for the priestess with inhuman speed. Krestina had only enough time to raise her hand again but was unable to get off a spell before the vampire was on her. He grabbed hold of her with surprising strength, for such a thin man, and lifted her into the air.

"Let's see if you are as delicious as you look," he said, with a wicked grin.

Thinking fast, Krestina grabbed the cross she wore from around her neck and pressed it against the vampire's forehead. Nestor howled as smoke rose from his skin where the cross touched him. Krestina fell to the ground as the vampire stumbled back, an imprint of the cross burned into his forehead.

Her heart pounded as she nervously held her cross out in front of her, thinking that would keep the monster at bay. She said a silent prayer to God to let her and Harcourt survive this encounter, so they could continue with their mission to save Stonewood.

Nestor hissed at her. "I had planned to make you a plaything and keep you alive. Now, you have gone and made me angry, girl. Very, very, angry."

The vampire advanced towards her, seemingly unimpressed by the cross she held out. Then he stopped and tilted his head, as if listening to something in the distance. Nestor drew his sword, then smiled, as another man emerged from the shadows.

"Move away from her," Prince Orval demanded, his sword held in front of him.

The prince and Syrena had been walking and talking long after nightfall when they heard the sounds of battle. Against Syrena's insistence, that they leave the graveyard, Orval had to investigate. He was shocked to find his two companions fighting what appeared to be a vampire.

Syrena, having no knowledge that these were friends of his, implored that they leave immediately. Orval did not listen and charged right in.

"The more the merrier," Nestor taunted. "I will feast well tonight."

Prince Orval rushed in with several quick strikes.

Nestor dodged the attacks but was too off-balance for any counters. The vampire quickly learned this was no common thief, like the other, who impersonated the King. Orval had received training from Stonewood's greatest swordsmen from the time he was able to lift a wooden sword. Although he had seen very little real combat, he was still in a league far above the average man.

Sparks flew as their swords clashed over and over, each man effectively blocking or dodging the other's attacks. Nestor finally found flesh, as he jabbed his blade into Orval's unarmored thigh. The prince grunted but swung with a back-handed counter that caught Nestor high on his chest. This wound did hurt the vampire as the prince's blade was enchanted, as well as blessed by Krestina.

Nestor stepped back, with a new appreciation for his new opponent. It had been decades since anyone had ever wounded him with a blade.

Syrena hung back, out of sight behind a tombstone, watching the battle play out. She was unsure why her new friend had insisted on helping these two strangers but it appeared he possessed a brave and noble heart. The sorceress recognized the man in the black coat and hat as a vampire immediately and knew that this was no easy opponent to defeat. She was impressed with Minas' skills with a sword. She had a feeling early on that he was a capable warrior and now her instincts proved true. Syrena also noticed the vampire recoil as he was struck with Minas' sword, telling her that he carried no ordinary blade. She was unsure of what to do, so for the time being, she chose to watch.

Krestina thought to blast the vampire again with her

holy light but he and the prince fought fiercely, twisting and turning, offering her no clear shot. Suddenly, the priestess was startled as someone grabbed her shoulder. She relaxed to find Harcourt, who had regained consciousness and now stood next to her, his head and neck bloodied. He stood on unsteady legs and used her shoulder for support.

"What is that thing?" he asked.

"A vampire," Krestina replied.

The thief had long ago gotten over the fact that monsters existed that he had thought were only part of stories. "How do you kill a vampire? Wood? A stake to the head or something?"

"A stake to the heart, if the books I have read speak true," she said. "Also your blessed daggers and my spells can harm him - he is an unholy creature."

That was all the thief needed to hear. He drew his two daggers from the back of his belt and joined the battle. Nestor only smiled as if he relished the challenge, which he did.

The vampiric swashbuckler side-stepped a swing from the prince, then parried a dagger from the thief, following up with a counter to Harcourt's left side. He dodged the second dagger, whirling about to parry Orval's sword. Nestor was fast, inhumanly so, and would not tire, as his mortal opponents were now showing such signs.

Prince Orval was slowing and took a strike to his chest, which thankfully did not penetrate his steel breastplate. The vampire ducked underneath his counter-attack, drawing blood with a slash to his forearm. Twisting his body at an impossible angle, Nestor avoided one of Harcourt's daggers, countering with a slash to his shoulder.

The vampire danced out of reach and smiled at his two frustrated opponents.

Krestina then prayed for a bold spell, one powerful enough that perhaps only First Priest Viktor and a handful of other elder members may have been capable of casting. She prayed that if she was chosen by God then she would need this spell to save her friends, which in turn would eventually save their city.

In answer to her prayer, there was a loud clap of thunder overhead, even though there were no clouds present. Suddenly, the sky lit up, as bright as day. For a few moments, and a few moments only, a miniature sun blazed above the cemetery. A few moments though, was all that was necessary.

Nestor let out an inhuman screech as his skin caught fire and began to burn. The vampire dropped his sword and fell to his knees; he had nowhere to hide. As the mini-sun winked out of existence, Nestor still lived but sat immobile on the ground, much of his pale skin charred black.

Harcourt approached the vampire, a thick branch in his hand from a nearby tree. He sharpened the end of the branch with his dagger, then without a word, drove it into the heart of Nestor Nightsbridge. The century-old vampire let out one last inhuman screech before collapsing to the ground, never to move again.

Prince Orval looked over to Krestina. The shocked look upon his face matched that of the priestess's own expression.

"We must be leaving now," the prince said, looking about for Syrena. "Surely that spell got the attention of the entire city."

"No arguing with you there, prince," Harcourt replied, grabbing Krestina's hand and gently pulling her along.

Prince? Did the dark-cloaked man just say prince? Syrena thought to herself, still out of sight. She could not believe what she had just witnessed. That priestess, and a powerful one at that, had just summoned a miniature sun to burn the vampire they battled. Amazing. Simply amazing.

But now Syrena got the strange feeling that she had seen this dark-cloaked man before. Then it hit her like a stone. He was the meddlesome thief that had attacked High Priest Sarvin during the throne room battle. Harcourt was his name, she believed. So then, if Harcourt referred to her new friend as 'prince,' that could mean Minas was.........oh my, she thought. Her life had just become so much more complicated.

# CHAPTER 11

Captain Frock pushed his way through the gathered soldiers to see what all the commotion was about. He eventually found a man wearing a dark green cloak, being escorted by two of General Zayne's personal guards.

"What is going on here? Who is this man?" the captain demanded to know.

"You must be Captain Frock. Stonewood is in peril!" the man replied, panic in his voice.

"Silence!" shouted one of the guards. "You will speak to General Zayne first and nobody else!"

"I beg your pardon, Geoffrey. I am second-in-command of this army. This man may tell me whatever message he brings," Frock said, angrily.

"Sorry Captain Frock, this was General Zayne's explicit orders. This man will speak with the General first, then you will be called for council," Geoffrey replied.

"The demon, Lucivenus, he is…" the man attempted to blurt out but Geoffrey clamped a hand over the man's mouth.

"I said silence, soldier! Save it for the General, first!"

With that, the man was escorted away, towards General Zayne's tent.

"What was that all about?" asked a soldier and friend, now standing behind Captain Frock.

"I know not, Darrick, but I fear something terrible may have happened," the captain responded.

"That man said something about a demon. Could the Cult have hatched some evil plot?" Darrick wondered.

"Anything is possible. I have had a strange feeling ever since we marched out this way. I could not quite understand it. But I mean to get to the bottom of this."

*   *   *   *

The half-demon warlock strode into the throne room and knelt before Lucivenus, who was seated in the throne. Beside the demon lord, in a less extravagant chair, sat High Priest Sarvin.

"Rise," Lucivenus commanded, in his deep booming voice. "What have you learned?"

"Nothing of value yet, my lord," Gryndall answered. "I have found blood and signs of battle within the cemetery, but I have yet to determine who was involved."

"Did we have any patrols in that area? Do we have any men missing?" the demon lord inquired.

"None of our men were in the cemetery, my lord. None patrol there after dark. Nearby patrols though, all witnessed the same event. All claim it was as if the sun itself hovered above the cemetery, for a few brief moments. Lit up that entire section of the city like it was daylight. By the time any of our men reached the graveyard, there was nobody around," Gryndall replied.

"What manner of sorcery is that? Cast by that old fool, Fezzdin?" Lucivenus wondered.

"But against who?" Gryndall questioned. "If it was that meddlesome wizard, who would he have been fighting?"

"Thieves, perhaps?" Lucivenus guessed.

"It was holy magic," Sarvin said.

"What?" the demon asked, turning to regard the High Priest.

"That was definitely the work of holy magic," Sarvin replied, with confidence.

"I thought you said the ancient First Priest from that temple of fools was killed? Along with most of the senior priests and priestesses? By my reckoning, that would have been one powerful spell," the demon lord reasoned.

"There must have been someone we have overlooked," the High Priest said thoughtfully.

"I cannot believe that with all of our resources, we cannot find where this King and his companions hide!" Lucivenus bellowed, standing to his full height. "Drag in his relatives, in chains! Someone must be hiding him!"

Sarvin was still focused on the holy magic that must have summoned that pseudo sun. He was beginning to wonder if that event had anything to do with the fact that he had heard nothing from Nestor Nightsbridge, as of late. Sarvin knew that Syrena spent most of her time down in that end of the city. Perhaps he would summon her, to find out what she might know.

*   *   *   *

"How many others have you told this news to?" questioned General Zayne.

The general sat at a large table full of maps, within his lavish tent. Across from him sat William, one of several soldiers who had escaped Stonewood, through Filbur's smuggling tunnel, to get word to the city's armies and allies. Zayne's two personal guards, Geoffrey and Frederic, stood guard inside the tent's entrance.

"Nobody, sir," William replied. "I rode with all haste to your camp, barely stopping at all. My horse nearly died of exhaustion. Once I arrived here in camp, your two men, there, met with me and brought me here."

"Good, good," the general said, standing, then pacing about the tent.

"But, sir, we need to inform everyone. We need to march your men back to the city," William implored.

General Zayne, walked around the table until he stood behind the much younger soldier. He placed his hands upon the man's shoulders. "We do not wish to cause mass panic amidst the men, now would we? We have to remain calm."

"I suppose so, sir. But I think we still need to leave as soon as possible. The King cannot wait much longer."

"Damn the King," General Zayne hissed, wrapping both hands tightly around William's throat.

"Sir??" William screeched, attempting to stand but he was forced to his knees, gasping for breath.

"Let him go!" shouted Captain Frock, who had just entered the tent.

Geoffrey and Federic both grabbed the captain, holding him in place. General Zayne, eased up on William, who choked and sputtered, trying to draw in air.

"This man is a deserter, Captain Frock. Fleeing from our southern army. Luckily, we intercepted him," Zayne lied.

"I heard everything, from outside the tent," Frock responded.

"How unfortunate," the general said, shaking his head. "Geoffrey, Frederic, kill the captain."

Before Frederic's sword could clear his scabbard, a spear found his throat. Darrick entered the tent and twisted the spear, forcing the guard to the floor, then drew his sword. Frock body-checked Geoffrey further into the tent, both men drawing their swords.

Taking advantage of the sudden chaos within the tent, William pulled a dagger free from his belt and stabbed the general in his unarmored left calf. Zayne howled with pain and struck William with a large fist, square in the face. The younger soldier's nose exploded and he fell back to the floor. Zayne grabbed his sword which rested against a nearby table and raised it to meet the oncoming charge of Captain Frock.

Darrick engaged Geoffrey, leaving Frock free to deal with Zayne. The blonde-haired Darrick stood a few inches shorter than his opponent and happily took up battle against him. Darrick always hated Geoffrey and Frederic, there was something odd about the two men. They never mingled with the other soldiers and believed themselves better than everyone else. They spent all their time with General Zayne, who was not well liked among the troops either. Now, Darrick and Frock learned the reasoning behind their uneasy feelings towards the three men. They were apparently in league with the Cult of Demon-Worshippers.

Geoffrey feinted with a thrusting jab but Darrick batted it aside with ease. The Cult soldier then fully committed to several attacks, which his opponent blocked and parried, before countering with his own offensive. Darrick worked the taller man into a corner within the tent, then disarmed him with a solid strike to his hand. Geoffrey's sword and two of his fingers fell to the floor.

The Cultist looked down in disbelief, then Darrick's sword found a gap in the man's armor, the blade driving into his belly.

General Zayne and Captain Frock fought furiously. Swords clanged against swords and armor alike. Frock could have felled the man three times by now but Zayne wore the best plate armor that gold could buy, and the captain had yet to pierce that armor.

Frock preferred the lighter chain mail armor and he wore his as a vest at the moment, his arms bare. Zayne drew a line of blood across the captain's left arm. Frock backed up and growled, then Darrick joined in the fight.

The general worked his sword frantically, trying to keep both men at bay. Several times their blades slipped through but so far his armor proved that it was worth every gold coin he had spent on it. Zayne skipped back, then grabbed the edge of the largest table within his tent, flipping it over to strike Frock, forcing the captain to stumble away.

Darrick saw an opening but before he could capitalize on it, General Zayne spoke an indecipherable word, his eyes glowed a deep red, then excruciating pain exploded within the soldier's head. Darrick dropped his sword, his body falling limp to the floor.

Zayne was not only a Cult warrior but an

accomplished warrior-priest. Captain Frock had knocked the table aside and out of the way but hesitated, as he watched his friend collapse from an apparent spell attack, from the general. Frock was a seasoned warrior, a veteran of many battles, but he had never once faced a spell-wielder.

Thankfully, help arrived in the form of a dagger blade, that slipped into the general's right side. William took advantage of the distracted cultist and had crawled his way around behind the man, then found a gap in his armor.

Zayne howled, attempting to reach around with his free hand to pull the blade free. Frock advanced and removed the general's head in one clean sweep. The captain nodded a silent thanks to William, then collapsed in the closest chair, to catch his breath from the fierce battle.

Darrick regained control of his body once more and stumbled over to stand next to his exhausted friend. "What now.....General Frock?"

"We leave for Stonewood immediately," the former second-in-command replied.

William smiled and let out a giant sigh of relief.

\* \* \* \*

Syrena planned to ignore the knocking at her shop door but it would not cease. She had placed a *closed* sign on her door and had been ignoring people for the better part of the day, even when she knew it was her new *friend* standing outside, earlier that morning.

The incessant knocking finally caused the sorceress to

rise and answer the door. Outside stood a bald man in a black robe, a Cult priest, backed up by ten armored cultists. Patrols in the south district now numbered ten men or more.

"I am closed. There will be no readings today, I am sorry," she said, annoyed.

"Lord Sarvin requests your presence on the morrow," Brother Lucek said softly, eyeing the sorceress from top to bottom.

"What for?"

"He did not say. Just be there," the priest replied, then turned to leave.

Syrena locked her door and returned to the bed she had in her back room. She had lain there since the incident in the cemetery, the previous night. The man who claimed to be Minas had walked her back to her shop, avoiding all the night-time patrols. It was then that Syrena confirmed her fear. The beard had thrown her off before but Minas was indeed Prince Orval Stonewood.

It was just her luck, she thought to herself. Syrena craved the companionship of someone whom she could respect, someone who could stimulate her. She was drawn to the aura of the prince immediately when he had entered her shop that first time. There was a spark there, as both their eyes met, an immediate attraction that she had never before felt.

Now, she learned the man turned out to be the enemy. The other man was definitely the thief, Harcourt. And from the description she had be given, the beautiful brown-haired priestess must have been Krestina, the one who escaped from her castle cell.

But, the sorceress wondered, were they her enemy, or

just the Cult's? Syrena viewed herself more as an employee of the Cult, as opposed to a member of the Cult. She sighed and closed her eyes, her head resting on her pillow.

What would she do? Did Lord Sarvin already know about the prince's visits to her shop? Is that why she was being summoned? She had an obligation to tell the High Priest, that was what she was paid for. And Syrena was paid quite well, in both gold and magical knowledge. That was not something she could easily pass up.

She also had to wonder, how far could a relationship with the Prince of Stonewood really go? The man would one day be King, if they proved successful, and she was a sorceress who worked with the Cult. How could she keep that a secret forever? She was even the reason Prince Orval's beloved brother went missing. Syrena had not actually killed the young prince but she had handed him over to Sarvin and Devi-Lynn, which essentially was a death sentence. If Orval ever found that out……

Oh, why was life so complicated? she asked herself. All she ever wanted was to be a powerful sorceress. She had let her greed guide her down a dark path, a very, dark path, from which there was no return.

# CHAPTER 12

Lord Eddenvale, the patriarch of a wealthy noble family, stopped in his tracks as he entered his wife's jewelry shop and recognized the man who had been standing there waiting for him. Even with the beard, he knew Prince Orval's face immediately, those piercing eyes, like his father's, unmistakable.

"I would ask how you have been, but I think I already know," the older nobleman said.

"Yes, these are dark times, Lord Eddenvale, and only getting darker," Prince Orval replied.

"Your father?"

"He is well and sends his regards."

"And to what do I owe the pleasure of this visit, my prince?" Eddenvale inquired.

"Lord Eddenvale, you have many men in your employ. A few minor wizards too, if I am not mistaken. The King requires your help in these dark times. We are attempting to assemble a considerable-sized force within the city, to aid the armies we hope will be returning soon."

"You have the support of other lords as well?" Eddenvale wondered.

"We do. Several others."

"Who? How many men do you have now?"

"Not nearly enough, I am afraid, but the number is growing. As for who, I have sworn to keep the identities of everyone secret. As I will with yours, if you choose to help us. And those who do will be rewarded when this is over."

"The armies are returning? Why did they leave the city unprotected in the first place?"

"That, my lord, is a long story. But God willing and with some added luck, yes, they should be returning."

"Yes, I believe my family can be of help to you and your father, of course. I may also be able to sway a few other lords, if you wish to return here tomorrow. I will speak with them this afternoon and plead your case."

"My thanks to you, Lord Eddenvale. Tomorrow, then." The prince pulled the hood of his cloak over his head and exited the shop.

\*　　\*　　\*　　\*

"Lord Lucivenus, Lord Sarvin," Phyzantiss said with a bow, "Lord Eddenvale is here to see you." The demonic knight motioned to the exquisitely-dressed nobleman he escorted into the throne room.

Eddenvale found that he was trembling inside. He had not been this close to the demon lord, or his lackeys before now. They were something straight out of a nightmare. Red skin. Pointed horns. Razor-sharp teeth. And the lord was not sure if he was sweating from nervousness or from the heat these creatures from the Abyss seemed to give off.

"If you have other business, I can return later?" said Syrena, who also stood in the throne room, having arrived only moments before.

"That won't be necessary, this shouldn't take long," Lucivenus addressed the sorceress, eyeing her hungrily. "You can wait right here."

"What brings you to the castle, Eddenvale?" High Priest Sarvin asked, purposely leaving out the title of lord. "Speak quickly, for we are busy with other matters."

"Something has come to my attention that I believe you will find most interesting," said the nobleman, a long-time supporter of the Cult.

"Yes? Speak!" Sarvin commanded.

"I was visited, early this morning, by Prince Orval. He was waiting for me at my wife's jewelry shop, in the upper east district."

Syrena's eyes widened but she fought to remain composed.

"How interesting indeed," Sarvin smiled. "Continue."

"It seems the prince is visiting wealthy lords, recruiting them and their security forces to help them fight back. He would not say, though, who the others were or exactly how many men-at-arms had swelled their ranks."

"Where is this upstart fool hiding?" boomed Lucivenus. "How does he move about the city?"

"I have no idea where they are hiding, but the prince wears a heavy, hooded cloak and now wears a thick beard. He would be difficult to recognize, only I have met with him personally, many times in the past."

Lucivenus growled and turned to Sarvin. "That man

must be found. Even if we have to stop every bearded man on the streets!"

"That won't be necessary, my lord," Eddenvale interrupted. "I have arranged to meet with the prince again tomorrow, at the same shop. I have told him I would recruit others to aid him. He appeared to come alone."

Lucivenus smiled, a wide toothy smile. And he rarely smiled. "Phyzantiss, you will personally oversee the capturing of the prince. Bring a considerable force, in case he does not come alone, but keep them out of sight. I will not tolerate failure here. I will stand on the castle battlements and feast on his flesh for all to see. That should flush out his cowardly father."

High Priest Sarvin did not appreciate being left out of the planning. He addressed Syrena, with hopes that one of his personal agents could also impress. "What news do you bring us Syrena, from the bowels of the city?"

"Umm," the sorceress stammered, caught off guard. "Nothing much, I am afraid. Umm, there has not been many attacks lately, our enemy seems to be laying low."

Sarvin was not happy. "What of that event that took place in the cemetery? What do you know of it?"

"I have heard no whispers of it, my lord. It was a mystery to all, I believe, and those that may know, are keeping tight-lipped."

The Cult sorceress opted to remain silent about what she knew, but she was conflicted about it. She now felt uncomfortable in the presence of the High Priest, and especially in the presence of the demon lord. She wanted to be far from this throne room and quickly. And now she was left to wonder, what would she do about the prince's predicament? She knew she should just forget about the prince and walk away from this situation entirely.

"Bah! You are dismissed," Lucivenus said angrily to the sorceress. "Though I may have a use for you later on," he added, licking his lips.

Syrena shuddered inside and quickly left the room.

\*     \*     \*     \*

Harcourt, wearing the face of Weldrick, took a rare moment and lay on a comfortable sofa, flipping through the pages of an old book of fairy tales. He was mostly just admiring the illustrations. He liked the pictures of dragons and wondered if they too, were also real. Many folk told tales of dragons but of course, the thief had never believed any of them. Now though, he had to wonder.

He lay in a quiet chamber, located in the heart of the Thieves Guild's headquarters. This room was populated with bookcases full of all kinds of books, with two sofas and two writing tables.

"You wanted to see me?" asked a feminine voice, just entering the room.

Harcourt looked up to regard Feylane, her hair dyed a fiery-red. He was a little nervous about meeting with her after she had kissed him in the sewer tunnel, but he needed to speak with her and oddly, the assassin was the only person he fully trusted within the Guild. She was the only one who knew about his magical mask and to his knowledge, had kept that to herself.

"Yes, I do. I am glad you received the message. I never know how to get ahold of you," the Guild leader replied.

"I like to keep things that way," she stated.

"Yes, well, have a seat."

Feylane seemed to wear a strange, uncomfortable expression on her flawlessly beautiful face. "Look, about the tunnel…..I…."

Harcourt cut her off. "I didn't come here to talk about that," he said and the assassin visibly relaxed. "Feylane, you are the only person here I really trust. Now, I am going into the castle soon to attempt to steal a book from Sarvin's office. Fezzdin has provided me with a magical escape plan, but I haven't always been the luckiest person around. So if anything happens to me, I need someone to know where the 'King' has been hiding out, in order to continue to work together to see this city freed. I have been the link between our two groups but anything could happen to me."

"You are a brave man," Feylane said, with respect.

"Or a fool," Harcourt chuckled. "Actually, more the fool I think."

The assassin smiled.

"You can usually find Dornell and Fezzdin at the Ogre's Den," the thief continued. "We have maintained the appearance of it being abandoned. There are several other hideouts but the other one of note is the big red warehouse on Oakley Street. So please, if anything happens to me, see to it that you continue your truce with them and continue to work with them."

"I will. But if anything happens to you, how will we collect our reward from the King? I can still see the look of absolute hatred for us on the face of Captain Dornell. I do not trust him."

"Dornell is a man of his word that, you can trust. So is Fezzdin for that matter. Don't worry that pretty little head of yours over that. If anything happens to the King, you will still be compensated for your aid. Providing of course, that you are all successful. But I do plan on coming back, so there will be no problems."

Feylane stood to leave, then turned back to gently touch the cheek of the thief. "See that you do come back."

Harcourt watched the gorgeous assassin leave the room, then moments later exhaled, not realizing that he had been holding his breath. She was a tough one to figure out. He knew a real woman lurked beneath her tough exterior but could never tell if she was playing along or truly being herself. Harcourt never imagined the beautiful assassin could have had any real interest in him. After all, the woman could literally have any man she chose. But Feylane trusted very few people and respected even fewer. Harcourt got the feeling that she both trusted and respected him and now wondered if that had led her to some deeper feelings. As beautiful as Feylane was, and she was beautiful, Harcourt was now committed to Krestina, much as he had been to Jalanna, years ago. Krestina was beautiful as well, a kind soul, very much like Jalanna. Feylane had a cruel streak that unnerved the thief. She had her reasons and Harcourt did not fault her for it but it was still there. She was a dangerous woman.

Harcourt rose to leave, truly hoping that the assassin was not falling for him. He tossed the book he had been looking at on the closest table and ran into someone as he turned to leave.

"I have been looking for you," said the skeletal thief, who was nearly knocked to the floor.

Weldrick growled, "Now is not a good time, Andil. And I told you to stay away from me."

"Yes, I know. But why? What have I done to you?" the skinny thief asked.

"You are a back-stabbing liar who can never be trusted! That's why!" Weldrick shouted in the man's face. "Be thankful I have allowed you to live!"

"Why do you say that? What have I done? That was not me who stole all of those jewels that got me locked away. I was set up by that merchant contact of yours. I did nothing wrong," Andil pleaded.

Weldrick closed the door to the room and pulled a sofa over to bar the entrance. He then grabbed Andil by the front of his shirt and threw him roughly into a bookcase. A rain of books fell atop the skeletal thief's head. With his left hand, Weldrick grabbed Andil by his scrawny neck and began to squeeze.

"I…..don't……understand….," Andil managed to gasp out.

"You are about to," Weldrick replied.

The Guild leader mumbled two words under his breath, then with his right hand, peeled off his magical mask. Andil's eyes went wide as Harcourt glared at him, hatred plainly written across the bigger thief's face.

Harcourt slammed the other thief's head into the bookcase, then let him go. Andil slumped dizzily to the floor, never once taking his eyes off the Guild leader. His jaw hung open in shock.

"Now do you understand, you conniving little wretch??" Harcourt shouted, with little regard as to who might hear him.

"How….how…did you do that?"

"This here, is a magical mask," Harcourt answered, holding up the now featureless mask. "I have been

Weldrick the entire time. I know all about your scheming with Trascar. So do not even think to lie to me. Jalanna trusted you as a friend! As did I! And you let that vile man murder her!"

"I had nothing to do with her death!" the skinny thief implored. "I had no idea Trascar was going to kill her. I swear to you that's the truth!"

"You allowed it to happen. And how many times was I sent to the dungeon because of you? Eh? How many times I wonder?"

"I have spent years consumed with guilt over that, believe me."

"Poor you!"

"Look, Harcourt, I am no fighter. I had to do what Trascar wanted, I would have been tortured and killed otherwise. And it was not just me. I never told you but I have a sister. We came to Stonewood together with that troupe of performers. Trascar was going to do horrible things to her as well, if I did not cooperate. I never knew you before, so yes, I placed my sister's well-being over yours, since you were a stranger to me."

"You are one hell of an actor. I really believed we were friends, you know that?"

"We were, that was no act. We were friends, believe me. I just had to look after my sister."

"I would have taken my chances with trying to cut Trascar's throat, before ever betraying a friend and allowing an innocent woman to be murdered."

"That's where we differ. You have always been brave and strong, I am not. The gods cursed me with a skeleton's body."

"You could have just told me then. I would have

taken care of things myself, as I ended up doing eventually anyways."

"The gods also cursed me for a fool," Andil said, bowing his head in shame.

"They certainly did," Harcourt agreed. "Now I am no murderer, like Trascar, that is why you still live. But keep away from me or I swear to you that will change."

Harcourt placed his mask to his face and willed his appearance back to that of Weldrick. He shoved the sofa aside and strode from the room, leaving Andil sitting on the floor. The skeletal thief wept.

# CHAPTER 13

Two armor-clad castle guards stood at attention outside the first floor chamber door. They nodded to Gervas as he approached and allowed him to enter. Once the elderly advisor had closed the door behind him, a woman inside the chamber rose angrily and shouted.

"What is the meaning of this? Is this how you treat guests in Stonewood?"

"I apologize, my lady," Gervas said, sincerely. "But, you should not have come here."

"Pardon me? I was invited months ago, by King Stonewood. He should be honored that we even acknowledged his request to talk, let alone make the trek all the way here."

The angry blonde woman with the pale, ivory skin was an ambassador from the kingdom of Ryor-Suul, far to the south and east of Stonewood. The kingdom was fairly isolated, cut off from much of the world by hostile jungles and therefore news out of the region was scarce. Trade was even scarcer. Ryor-Suul was ruled by women and while they produced many goods that were coveted by folk around the world, they rarely traded. Visitors were generally unwelcome, especially men who believed a kingdom ruled by women must be weak and easily exploited. It was those men, who soon found their heads decorating the city walls of the kingdom's capital.

Months ago, King Stonewood thought to open up trade negotiations with the isolated kingdom. He sent an emissary with a message and a gift. The kingdom's rulers accepted the gift and the invitation to talk further. The middle-aged ambassador, Emma Mink, was dispatched to Stonewood to meet with the King.

The ambassador was flanked by her personal guard, Naziya, a petite woman, with brownish skin and long dark hair. Her silver armor was two-piece, leaving her six-pack stomach exposed. She wore a curved sabre at her hip and despite her feminine beauty, she had the look of someone you would not wish to cross.

"Yes, my lady, I am aware that you were invited. After all, I wrote the message that our emissary carried. But things have changed here."

"Where are the others that travelled with me?" Emma inquired, referring to the other guards and personal attendants that had travelled with her.

"They are....detained, my lady," Gervas answered, thinking it best not to inform the woman that Lucivenus had already had them executed.

"I demand to see the King, immediately!" the ambassador shouted.

"How much do you know about recent events in Stonewood?" Gervas inquired.

"We only arrived a day ago. We found those…things

162

that surround the city, distasteful. We were not aware that Stonewood employed an inhuman army."

"Much has changed that you apparently are not aware of," the elderly man said with a sigh.

Before Gervas could explain further, the door to the chamber opened and in walked High Priest Sarvin.

Gervas bowed. "My lord, I was just greeting our guests, from Ryor-Suul. I present to you, Ambassador Emma Mink and Naziya."

"Who are you?" Emma asked, in a not so pleasant tone.

"You are no longer in your kingdom, ambassador. I am a man you will address with respect. Shortly, you will meet with Stonewood's new ruler and you had best leave this attitude here in this chamber. Now, come along, Gervas. Let us leave these ladies, for now," Sarvin said, pulling the elderly man outside the chamber along with him.

High Priest Sarvin knew that Ryor-Suul was a wealthy kingdom, which is why King Stonewood had elected to attempt trade negotiations. Sarvin now saw these two women as wonderful bargaining tools, as Lucivenus would soon wish to expand his domain.

\*　　\*　　\*　　\*

"Syrena!" a voice down the street shouted.

The sorceress quickly entered her shop and closed the door behind her, drawing the blind over the window.

"Syrena, it's Minas," shouted the man outside the shop door, as he began knocking. "Look, I saw you enter the shop. I know you are in there."

Syrena held her breath, not sure what to do. She had hoped to just avoid the prince altogether but it seemed that he would not be so easy to cut loose.

"I know you must still be in shock over what you saw in the cemetery that night but we should really talk about it. Please?"

Prince Orval heard the door unlock and open slightly. The beautiful fortune teller peeked through, then allowed the man to enter. Orval reached for her hand but the sorceress took her customary seat at her readings table. Orval took the seat opposite her.

Syrena's heart beat faster, as it did every time she was in the presence of the prince. She could not deny her attraction to the man, which had doubled since his display against the vampire. But this would be a doomed relationship.

"About the other night, I am sorry you had to witness that. It was pure chance that we happened upon a few friends of mine," said the prince.

"You keep powerful friends. That spell that burned the vampire was no small feat," the sorceress replied.

"Indeed, I do have some very special friends, I have to admit. Perhaps, I could introduce you to them, maybe tonight?"

"No, ummmm, sorry I have an appointment to keep tonight. That will not be possible."

"Another time then," the prince said.

"Why don't we do a reading?" the sorceress suggested.

"I am afraid I have not brought any coins with me this morning, sorry."

"Don't worry about that, Minas, this one is free,"

Syrena flashed him a smile.

The prince nodded. Syrena shuffled her deck of cards then placed it back onto the table. She turned over the top card to reveal the skull and crossbones, the exact one she wanted.

"Ummm, that does not look like a good sign," Orval said, worriedly.

"No, it is not. You are right, it is not good at all."

"What does the card tell you?"

"I see," the sorceress paused for a moment, "I see a meeting, sometime today."

"Yes?" the prince sat up straight, listening intently.

"This meeting does not go well for you. There is some sort of betrayal."

"Are you absolutely sure about this?" he asked.

"Yes, the cards do not lie. I see a wealthy man, a lord perhaps, and he will betray you."

She must have been referring to Lord Eddenvale, he thought to himself. It must have been true then, for this woman could have no knowledge of his secret meeting with the lord. Eddenvale must have been planning a trap and that is why he suggested that the prince return to the shop.

"I thank you very much for this information."

Syrena realized that she had begun to warn the prince before she could even think about it first. This changed everything. She had just ruined Lucivenus's and Sarvin's plan to capture the prince. Were they to find out......she shuddered at the thought.

\* \* \* \*

Ambassador Mink and her personal guard and friend, Naziya, minus her sword, were led into the castle's throne room by the intimidating demonic warlock. The sight of the tattooed half-demon put the two women on edge. Naziya, especially, was no stranger to monsters. The jungles surrounding their kingdom were teeming with unspeakable horrors, looking to make a meal of unfortunate adventurers. But a warrior from the Abyss, that was something entirely different.

If the sight of Gryndall unnerved the two women, then the sight of Lucivenus himself, sitting comfortably upon the throne, filled them with absolute dread. The eight-foot demon lord leered at the two guests, as Gryndall led them to stand before him. High Priest Sarvin, as usual, was seated beside the demon.

"Where is King Stonewood?" Emma Mink hazarded to ask, after finding her voice.

"The King of Stonewood is no more. I am now king of this city," Lucivenus answered in his booming voice. "Your kingdom will now deal with me."

"We do not deal with creatures from the Abyss," the ambassador said defiantly, but the expression on the demon lord's face made her regret her comment.

The room seemed to grow warmer, much warmer. The angrier the demon lord got, the more heat his body gave off. He growled at the ambassador. "Your pathetic kingdom, where weak mortal women rule, will bow their knees and pay allegiance to me, in time."

"Never!" shouted Naziya.

"Oh, they will," Lucivenus replied, with a toothy grin. "They will, if they ever want to see their precious daughters again."

Emma had known there was something wrong as soon as her group had spotted the spindly, albino creatures that surrounded the city of Stonewood. She never could have guessed just how wrong things had gotten. The ambassador had travelled to many parts of the known world and had seen many strange things, but the sight of an actual demon from the Abyss beat them all. King Stonewood must indeed be dead, she thought to herself. She gave a silent prayer to the goddess Mia to keep them safe.

Just then, Phyzantiss strode purposely into the throne room, drawing the demon lord's attention. He proceeded until he stood directly beside the throne and whispered into his lord's pointed ear.

"NOOOO!" Lucivenus bellowed, smashing his massive fists into the arms of the throne. Phyzantiss backed off. "I was to feast on the prince's flesh this evening!"

"My lord, he just simply did not show," the demonic knight said.

"He must have been tipped off by something. You and your men must have been seen!" the demon lord accused.

"No, my lord, that is impossible. We were there hours before the appointed meeting. Myself, and my men, were not visible, I assure you. It must have been something else."

Lucivenus was beyond angry. Time and time again, this foolish king and his companions slipped through their grasp. Prince Orval should have been standing before him at this very moment, groveling for his pathetic life. Of course, it would have done him no good. The demon lord had planned to eat the prince and in so doing, enrage the King into a foolish retaliation. He had his mind set on human flesh this day. Well, he was not about to be denied.

In a murderous rage, Lucivenus rose and advanced on the ambassador. Emma's face paled as she shrank back, arms raised in a feeble defense. Naziya attempted to step in front of her mistress but Gryndall held her firmly in his grasp and pulled her further away.

"What are you doing? We need that one alive," implored High Priest Sarvin.

Lucivenus was not listening and grabbed the ambassador in his vice-like grip, sinking his teeth into her shoulder. Emma let out a blood-curdling scream as the demon lord began to feast. As her screams ceased, Naziya had to look away, disgusted, bile rising in her throat. She was no coward, but trembled at the thought that her fate would be the same.

Sarvin fumed. That ambassador was the perfect bargaining chip to use against Ryor-Suul. Now she was gone, in a fit of rage.

Lucivenus held what was left of the late ambassador, spitting a bone onto the floor. "That armor will not do," the demon lord said, motioning to the brown-skinned warrior. "Get her something more appropriate to wear, when she joins me for dinner later."

\*     \*     \*     \*

"So William, how many men are left, loyal to the King?" inquired Alexander Frock, the new general of Stonewood's northern army.

"The numbers are unknown, sir," William replied.

"Many guards have turned out to be traitors. The King surrounds himself with only a few trusted followers and Prince Orval is trying to recruit as many men as he can, from the private forces of the nobles."

General Frock, along with William and Darrick, rode out of earshot from the bulk of the army, as they marched back towards Stonewood. They kept the death of General Zayne a secret, not knowing how many others may have been allied with the traitorous general. The story was that the general had fallen ill and was now resting in an enclosed wagon. None were to disturb him.

"General, even when we reach Stonewood, we are still outnumbered two to one, if William's estimations are correct," commented Darrick.

"Our men are worth five of those filthy wraggoth but yes, I understand. That is why I have dispatched one hundred riders to get word to our southern army to meet us at Stonewood," the general said.

"I fear our southern army may be under control of the Cult, much like we were, until recently," Darrick pondered.

"I have known General Dalemont for many years, he is a good man," said Frock. "Now, Captain Kenny was only promoted to that position a year ago. Him, I do not know. That is why I have sent one hundred men to relay our message. They are to convince the general to march back to the city at all costs."

"When I left Stonewood on my mission to find you, another also left for the southern army. But he could have met the same end that Zayne had planned for me," William added.

Their conversation was suddenly interrupted by

another rider approaching. "Captain Frock, a message has just arrived," the soldier said, holding a rolled piece of parchment, a messenger pigeon perched upon his shoulder.

"Have you read it?" Frock asked.

"No sir, it is still sealed with the mark of the Chief Magistrate. With General Zayne indisposed, I brought it directly to you," the soldier replied, handing the parchment to the captain.

Frock accepted the message. "Very good, my thanks. You are dismissed. If a reply is required, I will call for you."

The man nodded, then rode off to join with the rest of the army.

"What does it say?" wondered a curious Darrick.

Frock broke the wax seal and read over the contents. "It would appear the Cult leader wishes Zayne to keep the army away from the city until the King is found and disposed of."

"I would like to see his face then, when ten thousand men return to the city," Darrick mused.

"We have to be cautious still," Frock said. "We will need to remain out of sight until we can formulate some plan and get word to the King inside the city. There is also the matter of a demon that we need to worry about."

"The wizard, Fezzdin, is working to solve that issue," William added.

"Also," Frock continued, reading the last part of the message, "This Lord Sarvin requests a reply."

"What will we do?" Darrick wondered.

"How good are your forgery skills, my old friend?" the new general inquired.

# CHAPTER 14

The bobbing lantern light chased away the shadows that brooded over the rarely-used sewer tunnel. A cautious Na'Jala took the lead, sword in one hand, a lantern in the other. Directly behind the former gladiator and guiding him, hobbled the now two-legged Kan.

"Yes, yes, I remember, I remember. To the right, turn right," Kan implored excitedly, as they reached a fork in the narrow tunnel.

Harcourt, wearing his own face, followed closely behind the pair, along with Dornell and Evonne. The petite bounty hunter brought up the rear with another lantern, glancing nervously into the darkness that followed them.

The group had decided to let Old Kan in on their secret about the King. The man had been more than eager to help and save the city that he too, called home. He also owed a huge debt to Harcourt for changing his life, though none knew just exactly how the thief had achieved that.

The sound of rushing water from the darkness ahead

caused the former beggar to hop up and down, smiling all the way. "That's it! That's it! The waterfall is just up ahead, around the next bend!"

"Keep it down up there," Evonne said, just loud enough to be heard. "You want everyone to know we are here?"

Moments later the tunnel curved to the right, then opened up into a large chamber, where the sound of a rushing waterfall was almost deafening. The water rained down from the darkness above and fed an underwater river that sped off through an opening in the chamber wall. No other tunnels led into, or out of, this particular chamber.

"Great, a dead end," Evonne commented, as she followed the rest of the group inside.

"No, not a dead end. Only a dead end to those who don't know better!" replied Kan.

Kan took the lantern from Na'Jala, then hobbled his way over to the waterfall, as close as one could get. "See? A narrow ledge here, hard to notice. It goes behind the waterfall, to the secret door into the castle."

Kan dared not risk the slick ledge, having only one real leg, and pointed it out once Harcourt stood next to him. The thief would not even consider it a ledge but it was enough to cross, if one was very careful. The water flowed swiftly from the chamber so a tumble from the ledge could prove to be certain doom.

"I still do not like this idea," Dornell said again, trying to be heard over the sound of rushing water.

"Noted, my friend," Harcourt replied. "But we are short on options at present."

The thief lay a large sack, which hung from his belt,

onto the floor and removed a heavy backpack that he slung over one shoulder. From within the backpack, he pulled out a steel breastplate with the symbol of Stonewood painted thereon. They had acquired a castle guard uniform that would fit the thief and he now put it on.

"Wearing that armor will make it more difficult to cross," Dornell noted.

"Better to be wearing it, than to be carrying it. And I do not wish to risk tossing the backpack across. If we lost it in the water, we would be delayed far too long in finding another suitable uniform," Harcourt replied.

"What a pity that would be," Dornell mumbled.

"Don't worry so much, Captain," Evonne said to Dornell. "The man is good at what he does. And that mask is remarkable. He'll get that book and use the wizard's ring to return in no time. You'll see."

Dornell wished he shared the bounty hunter's confidence. He knew Harcourt was a skilled thief, stealth being a specialty of his. But he also remembered how many times the thief had been sent to the dungeon for failed attempts. Failure this time was no trip to the dungeon but certain death, and a horrible one at that. The former captain also had to wonder what chance they would have of retaking the city, if the thief and his magical mask were lost to them.

With the uniform now donned, Harcourt was ready to risk the ledge. A strong hand grabbed his left arm.

"May the gods smile on you, my friend, and see you through this mission. We shall be waiting for you at the Den," Na'Jala said to his friend.

"Hey. Tell Lucivenus that Vrawg and I say hello,"

Evonne said, flashing the thief a wink.

"Don't encourage him," scolded Dornell.

Harcourt laughed then stopped before the ledge, getting a good gauge on how best to cross without taking a plunge. The footing and the wall were very slick.

Kan touched the thief's shoulder. "I owe you my life," he said again for the umpteenth time. "I would go with you and fight this demon, if you but ask."

Harcourt turned to face the man and smiled. "I know you would. And you don't owe me anything, my old friend. You led me to this secret door, so consider your debt paid. And I won't be fighting any demon, with luck, just retrieving that book."

"I would give my life to help you," Kan said, tearing up.

"I know you would but let's hope it doesn't come to that, eh? Just watch over Krestina for me, will ya? Keep her safe, Captain Kanalandiros," the thief saluted the man.

Krestina had repeatedly insisted on accompanying Harcourt, in search of the secret door into the castle. The thief had told her she would be too much of a distraction, he needed to be concentrating on his job and not worrying about whether she would get safely back to the Den. He wanted to beg her to leave Stonewood if anything should happen to him but decided not to mention that, and just told her that he would see her soon. Fezzdin's magic ring was supposed to transport the thief instantly to the Ogre's Den once he activated it, by twisting the gemstone embedded therein.

Harcourt felt around one of his pockets to confirm the ring was still there, then took his first step onto the extremely narrow ledge. His fingers found the smallest of indents, to add more stability to his walk. It was about ten feet to reach the landing that was hidden behind the waterfall.

About the half-way mark, Harcourt's left boot slipped off the slick stone, giving everyone a start, but quickly he regained his balance and soon disappeared behind the waterfall. There he found a heavy, iron-bound wooden door, perfectly hidden from view. Without Kan's help, they would have never have discovered this entrance.

It did not take the master thief very long before he had picked the lock and opened the heavy door. It had probably not been used in roughly fifty years. The small room beyond was one of many store rooms located far below the castle. Prince Orval and Captain Gregor had made Harcourt a simple map to help him navigate his way into the castle proper. Then he just needed to reach Sarvin's office on the second floor of the east wing and hope the book was still kept in the same place.

Harcourt leaned around the waterfall and gave his friends the thumbs up, indicating the door was open and his mission was about to begin. He motioned to the odd sack that he had brought with him but had left on the floor of the chamber. Dornell would toss it over to him. It was not as important as the uniform, in the event that it fell into the water.

Dornell lifted the roundish sack and was surprised that it was a little heavier than he had expected. "What do you have in here?" he asked, as he carefully tossed it towards the thief.

Harcourt leaned out a little farther than he should have but managed to catch the sack and save it from dropping into the rushing water below. The thief smiled.

"It's just a little gift for the High Priest," he said, loud enough to be heard.

*   *   *   *

After several wrong turns, Harcourt finally ascended a stairwell that led to the castle proper. He wore the uniform of a castle guard but had the face of just some anonymous person he dreamed up. His heart began to race even more than it already was at the sound of jingling armor from up above.

The thief took a deep breath, then continued up the narrow spiral staircase until a guard, posted in front of a door, came into view.

"Eh? Who's there?" the guard said, suddenly realizing that someone was coming up the stairs. "Where did you come from?"

"I think the more important question is, what in the Abyss is that on the step next to you?" Harcourt replied, quickly narrowing the gap between them.

As the guard glanced down to the step, the thief was on him in a flash. Harcourt wrapped one hand around the man's mouth and stuck a poisoned needle in his neck with his free hand. The pair slumped to the cold stone steps. Harcourt was doing his best to hold the slightly bigger man in place and keep from tumbling down the stairs. It took only a few moments, before the sleep poison that Harcourt had perfected many years ago, kicked in.

The guard ceased his struggling and his eyes closed shut. Once satisfied that he was indeed unconscious, the thief dragged the man down to the bottom of the staircase. Harcourt stared at the man's face for several moments, before his own face began to shift and change, until it resembled the sleeping guard's face almost perfectly; complete with the birthmark above his lip.

Harcourt proceeded through the door at the top of the stairwell and took a right turn down a long hallway. His disguise was about to be put to the test as he approached two more guards.

"Hey Condor, what's in the bag?" asked one of the two guards, the one with the curly blonde hair.

"Some house cleaning," Harcourt replied, clearing his throat and sniffling, feigning a cold. "Found something that Lord Sarvin might be interested in seeing."

"Been in a foul mood lately, he has. It had better be something good or I would not risk bothering him at all."

"Oh, it's good alright," mumbled the thief, continuing past the guards.

Harcourt reached a fork in the hall and did his best to visualize the map he had been given. Inside the castle he could no longer tell north from south but remembered he was to take a left then another right, to reach the main hall, which led to the throne room. From there he could recall the way to the second floor office in the east wing.

Once he found the main hallway, there were more people about, not just guards but staff members going about their duties. Everyone wore the same type of expression, fear. The guards posted throughout the castle were definitely hand-picked and loyal to the demon lord. But the staff, Harcourt could tell, trod quietly as they went about their business, doing their best to not be noticed. They did not make eye contact with guards and moved about quite quickly.

Harcourt did his best to walk with confidence and

appear as though he belonged and had a purpose. So far, none paid him any close attention. Soon he walked the halls of the castle's east wing. Two cleaning women averted their eyes as he approached and gave him a wide birth. This confirmed to the thief that he was doing the right thing. He did not know any of these people and would most likely even be looked down upon by many of them. But they were all children of Stonewood, and Lucivenus and Sarvin needed to be dealt with.

Climbing a set of stairs, Harcourt now stood on the second level of the east wing. The long 'L' shaped hallway was dotted with office doors for many of the city's officials. The thief passed another pair of guards who thankfully paid him no heed.

Harcourt was about to turn the corner of the hall, when he paused a moment. The office was not too far away now and the thought struck the thief, what if Sarvin was in his office? He knew the High Priest was a very powerful individual. They had fought, briefly, during the throne room battle. It did not go well for the thief. He also remembered that Feylane, the Guild's best assassin, had met with the High Priest one on one in his office, and was easily defeated. Well, he figured, this was going to be a wasted effort if he ran into the High Priest. He may not get another one.

Harcourt rounded the corner and found a wiry, brown-haired man, dressed in fairly common clothes, standing in front of what he recalled should have been the office door for the Chief Magistrate. The thief approached the man cautiously.

Harcourt cleared his throat once he stood behind the man and he whirled around, startled.

"Oh! I didn't hear you approaching. Ahh, is there something I can help you with?" the man asked, nervously.

"What are you doing here? Isn't this the office of the Chief Magistrate?" Harcourt asked, noticing the sign missing from the door.

"Yes, why, yes it is. I am just replacing the sign, sir. These will soon be Chief Magistrate Matteus' quarters."

Harcourt had never heard of Magistrate Matteus before but he would definitely just be another puppet of the High Priest.

"The office then, it is empty?" the thief inquired.

"No, not as of yet. I believe Lord Sarvin is moving all of his stuff out tomorrow. He is too busy with meetings today I was told."

Harcourt breathed a sigh of relief at that news. "But wait a moment. You said Chief Magistrate Matteus? I had heard that Magistrate Toben was the one that was promoted," the thief lied, making up a name.

The man scratched his head. "Hmm, no I am fairly sure I was told that it was Matteus."

"Well, you had better go double check, before you go putting that new sign up. I am positive I heard Toben."

"I couldn't have made a mistake. Or could I have? Hmmm….," the man muttered to himself as he walked away, in search of someone to clarify things for him.

The moment the hallway was devoid of any activity, Harcourt went to work immediately on the door's lock. The High Priest felt safe within the castle and the quality of the lock reflected that. The thief was in within mere moments and locked the door again behind him.

Two lanterns illuminated the room which told Harcourt that someone might be planning to return soon.

The main office area was a touch on the dusty side, as if it was not getting much use. Aside from that, everything appeared just as it had the night of the King's birthday.

Harcourt wasted no time in sitting down in the Chief Magistrate's comfy black chair and trying the handle to the top drawer. The drawer was locked but the thief made short work of the lock and breathed a deep sigh of relief at the sight of a particular leather-bound black tome. He leafed through a few of the brittle, yellowed pages of the book just to confirm that it was indeed the same book he had seen before. It was. With luck, this book should have all the information that Fezzdin would need, in order for them to banish and imprison Lucivenus once again.

Removing the sack that hung from his belt, Harcourt placed it on top of the large oak desk and smiled. As he was about to pull out the magical ring, there was a loud knock at the office door.

"Lord Sarvin, are you in there? It's Brother Velkan. Lord Lucivenus says you are late for a briefing. He is waiting for you in the third floor council chamber. Hello? My lord?"

The man knocked several more times until his footsteps faded down the hall. So the demon lord was only on the floor above, the thief thought, and the High Priest should be joining him shortly. Harcourt picked up the sack from the desk. He had an idea.

\* \* \* \*

Lucivenus paced back and forth within the large council chamber. Two Cult priests, sat nervously at the circular table along with the half-demon knight,

Phyzantiss. The demon lord was waiting on High Priest Sarvin and Gryndall to give him a report on the rounding up of King Stonewood's closest relatives. Lucivenus figured one of them must have been hiding the King, along with his troublesome son and companions. He wished to be rid of the King as soon as possible so he could focus his thoughts on what came next. Lucivenus would never be satisfied with just Stonewood, he planned to rule this world of weak mortals.

Sarvin entered the chamber and drew the demon lord from his thoughts. "Where have you been?" Lucivenus questioned.

"You changed the meeting room last minute. I have been waiting in the throne room," Sarvin replied, taking a seat at the circular table.

"Where is Gryndall?" the demon asked Phyzantiss.

"I know not, my lord. But he knows where we are," the knight responded.

Lucivenus was about to ask Sarvin for a progress report when a curious, cloaked individual, standing in the chamber doorway, caught his attention. "Who are you?" he boomed.

The man, whose face was hidden within the hood of his cloak, replied, "A gift for you, my lords."

He tossed his weighted sack into the room, landing it on the table in front of Sarvin. The sack had opened and out rolled a severed head, the head of the vampire, Nestor Nightsbridge.

Sarvin's eyes went wide and he rose from his seat and roared, "Who dares??"

"I dare," Harcourt replied, pulling back his hood to reveal the face of King Stonewood. "This is my home and now you know that I can get to you. Sleep with one eye open, you fools, for I will be back soon."

"YOU!!" Lucivenus bellowed with rage, his flaming sword appearing in his massive hand. "You will not leave here with your life, foolish human. Get him!"

Phyzantiss rose and drew his great sword. Harcourt figured that now was a good time to leave and fumbled in his pocket to find Fezzdin's ring.

An explosion of intense heat struck the thief and he flew from the doorway to land several feet down the hallway. Momentarily dazed, he glanced up to spot the half-demon warlock, who had just blasted him with a fireball spell. Gryndall's look of shock at finding the King outside the council chamber, was now replaced with a wicked grin as he walked towards his prey.

Harcourt managed to recover quickly and scramble to his feet as Phyzantiss and Sarvin entered the hallway. Weighed down with armor, he barely dodged another fireball from the warlock before turning to run.

The High Priest mumbled the words to a spell and a razor-sharp knife appeared in mid-air, hovering in front of the evil priest. With a point of his finger, the knife raced through the air and penetrated the thief's armor, embedding itself in the back of Harcourt's left shoulder. The thief grunted with pain and dove around a corner.

Harcourt cursed his foolishness as he sprinted full speed down the corridor, the sounds of pursuit close behind. Blood flowed freely from his wound and his left arm was wracked with pain. He needed to find somewhere to stop, to give him time to reach the magical ring that was deep inside a pocket.

The thief rounded the corner to a particularly long

corridor and collided with a castle guard, who stood watch outside of a door. The pair tumbled to the floor and before the guard had time to realize who it was that ran into him, a fist smashed into his nose, blurring his vision. A strong hand grabbed his throat and his head was repeatedly smacked against the stone floor until he drifted into unconsciousness.

The corridor was long, too long. Harcourt knew he could not reach the end before his pursuers rounded the corner and hurled more deadly spells at him. He snatched a key that hung from the guard's belt and fumbled with the lock to the door that the man had been guarding.

The lock clicked open and Harcourt rushed inside the room, not knowing what, or who, he might find inside. He slammed the door shut but found no way to lock the door from the inside. Desperately he looked to some furniture close by. He stood inside a lavishly decorated bedroom, a large ornately carved dresser not too far from the room's only door.

With a grunt, Harcourt dragged the heavy wooden dresser in front of the door, which thankfully did swing inwards. Just in time too, as fists could be heard banging on the door from the outside. The thief pulled Sarvin's book out from under his tunic, where he had stashed it and placed it on the dresser while he dragged over a second, much taller, piece of furniture.

Someone was now kicking the door and shouting curses from the hallway beyond. Harcourt leaned against the dresser, allowing himself a moment to catch his breath. He gritted his teeth, then reached around and pulled the knife from the back of his shoulder. Cursing his foolishness once again, he dropped the bloodied blade to the floor.

"W-who are you?"

Harcourt spun in a panic, drawing his sword at the sound of someone's voice in the room behind him. In his desperation to block the door, the thief had not even noticed the petite woman standing next to the huge, four-poster bed, set against the far wall.

The woman, who was only wearing a tight-fitting, blue gown, was surprised to realize who the man was that stood before her. She had seen portraits of King Stonewood throughout the castle and this was definitely the King, injured and in a panic.

"Y-you are the King?" she stammered.

"I am. And you are?"

"I am Naziya Amoorsafala, warrior of Ryor-Suul and personal escort to the late ambassador, Emma Mink."

Harcourt quickly looked over the woman with the exotic brown skin, who had just proclaimed that she was a warrior. She looked nothing like a warrior in that blue dress. Her skin appeared soft and flawless and she was beautiful, head to toe. Naziya was petite but then so was Evonne, and Harcourt knew full well what the blonde bounty hunter was capable of.

"Well, Naziya Amoorsafala, I am afraid I have brought doom upon us both by seeking a moment's refuge in this chamber," Harcourt said, as the pounding on the room's door continued.

"I was already doomed, my lord. That vile demon ate my mistress right in front of me and I believe I am on the menu for tonight."

Harcourt was disgusted. He had heard rumors that Lucivenus enjoyed eating people but was hoping that was just some scare-tactic employed by the Cult. The thief ran to the only window in the room and looked down to the long three-story drop, to the courtyard below.

"We were told that you were no more, my lord. I assumed you met your end from the demon as well. You have been hiding in this castle all this time?"

"No, I snuck back this evening, to fetch a certain book only."

"You did not have an escape plan?"

"I did but you just complicated things."

\*    \*    \*    \*

Krestina sat at a corner table within the Ogre's Den's main taproom. She had her head down but was trying to remain awake. The priestess was fearful that if she fell asleep, she would have some horrible dream or vision of Harcourt. The man she loved was currently inside Castle Stonewood, right in the midst of their enemies and she was worried sick.

"You should really try and eat something," Evonne said, sitting down opposite the priestess. "You haven't had a bite all day."

"I just can't. I have no appetite but thank you for your concern," Krestina said in response.

"Harcourt will be back any time now. Fezzdin's ring will bring him right here to this very room. Any sign of danger and he can disappear immediately," the bounty hunter tried to assure the other woman.

Krestina smiled, appreciative of Evonne's support.

"Isn't that right, Fezz? He'll appear right here in this room?" Evonne called over to the wizard.

Fezzdin sat across the room, alone at another table, his face buried in a pile of books. He seemingly did not hear the bounty hunter, as he continually shoved Lex off of the book he was attempting to read. The orange cat kept insisting on laying down on top of the one opened book.

"You have this whole tavern to find somewhere to lay down, why must you insist on this book, at this time?" the old wizard scolded.

Suddenly and without warning, the room was ablaze with light and the air crackled with energy. In the middle of the room, now stood a bewildered looking woman, wearing a blue dress. Under her left arm, she carried pieces of bright silver armor, and in her right hand, she held a black, leather-bound book. She wavered dizzily on bare feet, disoriented by the magical travel.

As she became aware of her surroundings, Naziya noticed a petite blonde woman with a ponytail, aiming a crossbow at her face.

"Who are you? And where is Harcourt?" Evonne demanded to know.

# CHAPTER 15

Phyzantiss repeatedly kicked the door to the barred bedroom, with a powerful leg. The door still did not budge.

High Priest Sarvin kneeled next to the unconscious guard, who lay on the floor. "What is the use in having guards who cannot watch one single door?"

The High Priest drew his red-bladed dagger from within the folds of his dark robe and plunged it into the heart of the guard. The evil blade drank hungrily and drained the man of his life.

As Sarvin stood, they were joined by Gryndall and a thoroughly enraged Lucivenus. The demon lord, with his flaming sword blazing in one hand, shoved the demonic knight aside, as if he were a mere child. Lucivenus raised his free hand and spoke a single word. A blast of flames shot forth that was so hot, the door, and the furniture stacked against it, were instantly incinerated. Black ash on the lush, brown carpet, were all that remained.

Fortunately for Lucivenus, all of the castle's rooms

and corridors, were built with high ceilings, allowing the eight-foot demon lord to walk about unhindered. He marched into the bed chamber, sword raised and ready.

"EMPTY!" he barked, his voice rattling a mirror that hung on a wall.

Lucivenus then spied an open window and rushed over, sticking his head out for a view. It was a straight drop, three stories to the bottom. And while it was dark outside, he spotted no bodies littering the courtyard below.

His flaming sword winked out of existence as he grabbed the bed with both hands and flipped it over. There was nothing.

Gryndall sniffed the air of the chamber. "Magic was used here. Ancient magic."

"Fezzdin," Sarvin hissed through clenched teeth.

"This is your fault!" Lucivenus accused, pointing a finger at the High Priest.

"Mine? How so?"

"You had captured this wizard and imprisoned him, instead of killing him outright. Your foolishness continues to haunt us."

Sarvin was about to reply, then wisely held back. He should have killed Fezzdin when he had the chance. But instead, he wished to gloat over the wizard and prove to him that he himself, was indeed the more powerful of the two. He had gravely mistaken the resourcefulness of Fezzdin and his friends. They could not have the King coming and going from the castle as he pleased. Then there was the matter of Nestor Nightsbridge. The man was a formidable vampire, a century old. And now, his severed head lay on the council chamber table. From the burn marks on his face, Sarvin now wondered if the strange

event in the cemetery had anything to do with the
vampire's demise. He was willing to bet that it did.

"The King is wounded but not mortally, I fear,"
Phyzantiss remarked, picking up the bloodied knife that
Harcourt had discarded.

Lucivenus spun around, to regard the weapon. "That
knife, it wounded the King?"

"Yes, my lord," Sarvin replied. "A spell of mine. But,
it struck only the King's shoulder. As Phyzantiss stated,
not a mortal wound, unfortunately."

The demon lord's face brightened and his smile ran
from ear to pointed ear. He snatched the knife from the
half-demon's hand, holding it up before his face, watching
crimson droplets, fall to the carpeted floor. The weapon
seemed tiny in the massive hand of the large demon. He
then laughed, a deep, evil, laugh.

"The life of King Stonewood is soon to end,"
Lucivenus proclaimed. "His blood is all that I require to
bring a horrible doom upon him."

Demonic laughter reverberated around the room and
out through the window, to the night beyond.

\*     \*     \*     \*

Two castle guards made their routine patrol within an
inner courtyard. The night was a particularly dark one;
thick clouds blotted out the stars above. While patrols out
in the city were fraught with dangers, within the castle
walls, nothing ever happened. The battle that took place in
the castle's throne room during the King's birthday was
the one exception.

Dyson preferred to make many patrols, otherwise he

would fall asleep at his post. The guard gave a great big yawn, then shook his head in disgust as something wet had splashed onto his hand.

"What's wrong with you?" Ned asked.

"Something dripped onto my hand. Better not have been a bird."

"At this hour? Don't be a fool, birds are asleep. Some rain perhaps."

Dyson quickened his pace to stand below a torch that hung on the east wing wall, then inspected his hand. "It looks like blood."

"Blood? Is your nose bleeding?"

"No, it's not from me," Dyson replied, inspecting his face and neck.

"You're right though, that sure looks like blood," Ned remarked, looking at his partner's hand under the torch light.

The two guards looked up the side of the castle, looking for anything out of the ordinary. Several windows dotted the wall but the night was so dark, they could not make out anything of interest.

"You know, Lord Sarvin always said that when Lucivenus reclaimed Stonewood, the city would rain blood," Ned remembered.

"I thought that was just a figure of speech?" Dyson said.

"Suppose not, it just rained blood."

Dyson wiped his hand clean on a nearby shrub, then the pair set off again to finish their patrol.

*   *   *   *

Harcourt's hands trembled, his knuckles white, as he held on for his life. The thief clung to the castle wall, not too far above the window he had climbed out of. He had stashed his armor inside a drawer within the bed chamber, so it would not hinder him while climbing. His fingers were dug into two deep crevices, worn out by weather that had battered the stone wall over centuries.

The thief had entered the castle with the perfect escape plan, Fezzdin's magic ring. But upon finding the female prisoner, Harcourt's plans had to change. The innocent woman figured she was to be a meal for Lucivenus, so he could not just leave her to that fate. She could never have climbed the wall as he did, so that left only one option for her to escape. Harcourt gave Naziya the magical ring and the book to give to Fezzdin. At least the wizard would have the book, no matter what else happened.

When the woman vanished from sight, Harcourt stripped off his armor and went out the window and up the wall. Moments later, the demon lord's head poked out through the window and the thief's heart stopped. Lucivenus peered about but thankfully had not looked up.

Harcourt could hear muffled voices from inside the bed chamber but could not make out specific words. The demon lord suddenly could be heard laughing. Why would he be laughing? the thief wondered. He should have been enraged at losing the King and his female prisoner. But it was definitely laughter.

Soon after, all was silent. It sounded as if his pursuers had vacated the room below. Harcourt could not stay on the wall for long, his shoulder throbbed with immense pain and he could feel the blood dripping from his knife wound. His fingers were beginning to slip, so it was time to move.

Slowly and carefully, the master thief probed the wall for indents and made his way back down towards the window. Going up was always much easier than going down. One slip meant certain death, though he figured splattering on the courtyard below was probably more desirable than being tortured and then eaten by the demon.

Luck was with the often-unlucky thief and soon Harcourt was perched on the window ledge, inspecting the scene within the bed chamber he had so hastily vacated. To his surprise, nothing remained of the room's door and the furniture he had used to block it with. The bed was overturned and a mirror lay on the floor in a hundred pieces. Fortunately, there was nobody left inside.

With the grace of a cat, Harcourt slid back into the room, silently made his way to the door and peeked around the corner. He noticed the guard he struggled with earlier, lying dead in the corridor, an apparent wound to his heart. Sarvin, the thief figured.

Voices and booted feet could now be heard approaching, men that were most likely dispatched to remove this body and clean up this room, Harcourt thought. With a sigh, the thief exited once more through the window. It would not be easy but he guessed his best course was going down the wall to the courtyard below.

He willed his face to change to that of some anonymous creation and began his slow descent.

\* \* \* \*

Krestina's face was as pale as a ghost's and tears welled up in her beautiful brown eyes as the exotic-looking woman in the blue dress told the tale of her escape. Dornell, Na'Jala and Kan, who had been sleeping in the cellar below, had now joined the rest of their companions in the main taproom. There was a silence that hung in the room, as Naziya finished her tale.

"Your friend wanted to be sure that book got to you all, he said that was the most important thing," Naziya said, breaking the silence. "I had no idea what the ring would do. I would not have let your friend stand alone, against those monsters. I would have stayed and fought but he left me no choice."

"Nobody is blaming you, child," Fezzdin said, with a gentle voice.

"You said there was a window in this room?" Na'Jala asked the warrior-woman.

Naziya nodded. "Yes, but a sheer drop and three stories up. I had thought to escape from there myself but it was just too high."

"You do not know our friend, he can climb like a spider," Na'Jala said.

"So, we can assume that is what he has done. He has probably escaped," Evonne suggested, trying to remain positive.

Dornell was not so certain. "He was being pursued. He might not have gotten far before being discovered and captured."

"She says he was wearing the face of the King. If Lucivenus and Sarvin believe that they have captured the King, I don't think they would kill him quickly. They will most likely use him as a tool, to draw the rest of us in,"

Evonne reasoned.

"Then the decision is made for us," Dornell announced. "We use the secret entrance and storm the castle with everyone we have available and rescue Harcourt."

"We are not ready for that kind of assault, not yet," the blonde bounty hunter replied.

"Evonne is right, Captain," Fezzdin said. "I need time to study this book. An attack on the castle will be for naught, if we cannot defeat Lucivenus. We jeopardize everything we have worked for, if we succumb to impulsive decisions."

"Impulsive? Harcourt is our friend!" Dornell shouted in frustration.

"I am not saying that he isn't," the old wizard countered. "We cannot risk the lives of everyone by acting foolishly. Harcourt still has his mask and is one resourceful man. We cannot be certain that he was captured. Now, let us all keep cool heads and see what happens. I believe Evonne is correct. If Harcourt is captured, they will use him to bring the rest of us out of hiding. We still have time to think."

Dornell growled and threw an empty mug against the wall. A distraught Krestina descended the cellar stairs, weeping as she went.

\* \* \* \*

Harcourt moved from shadow to shadow, as silently as a ghost. So far, the Cult had felt secure within the castle and the thief had only a few guards to avoid within the dark courtyard. Clouds had effectively blocked the moon and stars this night, making it darker than usual.

He figured his best course of action was to get ahold of another guard uniform and get back inside the castle, possibly making for the secret entrance. Going back the way he came would most likely be easier than scaling the outer wall. Too many men patrolled the battlements of the castle, even at night.

Harcourt definitely needed a new shirt, the black one he wore was torn at the back and blood still flowed from his wound. He was looking for the best way back into the castle when a curious sight at the far end of the courtyard grabbed his attention. He decided to move in, for a closer look.

Set against one of the courtyard's walls was what appeared to be a makeshift prison camp. Bars had been erected and a padlocked door held, the thief estimated, about fifty or so men. Spotting no guards in the immediate vicinity, Harcourt crept up to the prison and prodded the closest man to the bars, who had been soundly asleep, like the others.

"Wha? Who's there?" the disoriented man, blurted.

"Shhhhhhh," Harcourt whispered. "Make no noise. Who are you and what is this prison?"

The man's eyes were wide with shock, that someone would risk skulking about in the dark. "I am Rydor, of the castle guard. We here, are loyal to King Stonewood and would not join with the vile demon and his Cult. We have been locked in this prison and another like it stands over near the west wing of the castle. Periodically men are taken from here and do not return."

Harcourt could only imagine what fate befell those men.

"Who are you, stranger?" Rydor asked.

"I am a friend of the King."

The man's face lit up. "What news of the King? How does he fare?"

"The King is well and continues to fight on. He and Prince Orval will take back this city and overthrow the demon lord."

"All praise to God."

"You men are too few to fight your way out. I will unlock this door for you but I believe you should keep up the appearances that you are still prisoners and wait for a better opportunity. Perhaps, when the King and his army begin the fight outside the walls, you can aid from within."

"There is an armory, just over there through that door. See it?" the guard pointed. "This night is extraordinarily dark, a few of us can secure some weapons and keep them out of sight."

"A fine plan. See to it that you are not caught," Harcourt said, while picking the padlock and opening it with ease. "Keep the lock, so it appears intact. Do not arouse suspicion. I go now and will inform the King that he still has loyal men within the castle. Good luck, Rydor."

The guard nodded and began to quietly rouse the others in the cell.

\*     \*     \*     \*

High Priest Sarvin stood on the balcony of his newest quarters, rooms that once belonged to Prince Orval, and stared out into the night. Of late, they had met with failure at every turn. Or rather, he had, according to Lucivenus. The demon lord blamed Sarvin every chance he got. For

Sarvin was only a mortal human, so therefore was predisposed to be a failure, in his opinion.

Sarvin had dreamed of ruling Stonewood, beside the demon lord, as equals, as they went forth and crushed the surrounding regions, expanding their domain together. Despite being a powerful high priest, and the one who freed Lucivenus, Sarvin was treated like a common lackey. A man, far beneath the demon and his half-demon associates, to be ground underfoot.

Lucivenus was nearly unstoppable. He could have descended to the streets and wiped out this pitiful rebellion himself, with ease. But the demon lord was lazy and commanded others to do the work for him, then scolded them for their failures. When the King had miraculously appeared in the council chamber, it was the first time Sarvin had witnessed Lucivenus move into action. And even then, everyone else was to blame for the King's escape.

The demon lord made foolish decisions, with little regard to running the city effectively. He saw nothing as a legitimate threat to him, so simply did not care what befell the city. Humans were here only to serve him and nothing more. As long as he sat comfortably on the throne, surrounded by wealth, all was good.

Sarvin did not wish to have thoughts such as these, but he had worked so hard to get to where he was now. He was a genius and a powerful priest and he was destined to be a ruler.

He sighed and wished that he still had the cunning and beautiful Devi-Lynn, plotting by his side.

# CHAPTER 16

The town of LongBridge sat nestled against the Lake of Stars. It was the largest town that resided within the region controlled by Stonewood. While Stonewood's army was still responsible in large part, for patrolling the area and keeping it free of brigands, LongBridge still employed a force of its own. One thousand horseman made up the town's militia and protected it from immediate threats.

LongBridge fell under the supreme rule of King Stonewood but still had its own ruler, one Lord Steffan Lark. Lord Lark was an ambitious man and immensely jealous of Stonewood's wealth. Lark ruled because generations of Larks before him had all ruled the town. He was a man in his late twenties, young for a ruler, but after the mysterious drowning death of his father, he was next in line. He was a womanizer, with a short temper and not very well liked by the populace.

Lord Lark had spent the last several days stewing over a certain problem. He had not wanted to make any hasty decisions but now, his mind was finally made up.

"Ummm, my lord, is that a wise decision?" one of Lark's advisors inquired.

"Away from me! I am not in the mood for your face right now. And do not question me again!" Lord Lark barked.

The black-haired and black-moustached lord, strode out of his keep, followed by five of his personal guards. The sun was high in the sky and the town bustled with activity. Folk wore surprised expressions and quickly scrambled out of the path of Lord Lark, as he marched with purpose through the town.

Witnessing Lark walking through the town was not the surprising part, for he often did so; it was what he held in his right hand that grabbed the attention of everyone on the streets this day. For Lord Lark, ruler of LongBridge, carried a severed head, holding it by its long brown hair.

Several days past, LongBridge was visited by a frantic soldier of Stonewood. He told the tale of the demon lord, Lucivenus, who had seized control of the city with the aid of a cult of demon-worshippers. He told how King Stonewood was forced into hiding but was fighting back to reclaim his city. The King was calling on all of his allies for aid.

Lord Lark was never very fond of King Stonewood and while he had no particular love for demons and cults, he did not see the King as being victorious this time. So, why join the losing side? the lord had thought to himself. Better to make a gesture of good faith to the new ruler of the region and keep him on their good side.

Lark decided to keep Stonewood's plight a secret, known only by his inner circle. He had the Stonewood soldier beheaded and now was going to display the head at the entrance into the town, a warning to all traitors. He ordered a message be sent to Stonewood, informing them that he had captured a fleeing soldier and that the matter had been properly dealt with.

Satisfied with his decision, the Lord smiled to himself as he strolled back through the town scanning the streets for someone to keep him company this night.

He turned to the guard on his right side. "Her, the blonde that just entered that shop. Have her sent by the keep tonight for dinner. I like the looks of her."

"Yes, my lord."

\*   \*   \*   \*

Thelvius the Great, former gladiator and now leader of his very own mercenary army, rode his horse to the base of a hill, before dismounting and joining his second in command at the top of that particular hill.

Jordann Vance saluted the arrival of his commander. The wide-shouldered warrior had bronze skin, much like Thelvius, after spending most of his life in the blazing sun of the south. The mostly-bald man was missing several teeth, two fingers on his left hand and his left eye. Jordann refused to wear a patch, displaying the gruesome hollowed eye socket. He found the grisly sight most often caused an opponent to pause, and it was in that pause that the fierce warrior reacted, making his opponent pay dearly.

The one-eyed warrior was the toughest man Thelvius knew and the most loyal. Many years ago Jordann had been captured and tortured, to reveal information about the mercenary army's movements and location of Thelvius. Even after his left eye had been removed, the man still spat in the face of his captors. Thelvius promoted Jordann and trusted him above all others.

"What's the situation?" the mercenary leader asked.

From this hill, the pair could see the city of Stonewood in the distance, along with the wraggoth army that still surrounded it.

"Still no sign of Stonewood's northern or southern army. There is a cavalry unit that comes and goes but they would be loyal to the demon ruler," Jordann answered.

"Twenty thousand wraggoth then?"

Jordann nodded. "Somewhere in that range, yes. Divided though, on the four sides of the city. So we are looking at possibly groups of five thousand."

"There is still nothing we can do, without the aid of Stonewood soldiers," Thelvius reasoned. "Though we cannot wait forever. Our supplies run low. If there is no sign of them soon, we must withdraw. It's a suicide mission otherwise."

Thelvius had already waited longer than he would have liked. But he knew the city was wealthy, very wealthy. Helping the King would earn them considerable profits. And that is what they lived for.

\*　　\*　　\*　　\*

William spurred his horse on until he regrouped with the bulk of the northern army and joined General Frock and Darrick.

"We are making excellent time, General. We should be close enough to assess the situation in Stonewood in just a matter of days," William commented.

"What then? What's our plan going to be?" Darrick

asked.

Frock thought for a moment then answered, "As I have said, we will have to keep the army back and out of sight. William, can you manage to get into the city unseen? We should really make contact with the King and try to coordinate something with those who are inside."

"With the cover of darkness, I may be able to reach the secret tunnel we used to exit the city. It won't be easy but it's not impossible," William said.

"If you are up to the task, then that should be our first course of action," the general reasoned.

"You bet I am!"

\*　　\*　　\*　　\*

Syrena lay in the arms of Prince Orval, the pair relaxed in the back room of the sorceress's shop. Her *closed* sign was placed on the front door. The prince had been under much stress since the events of the throne room battle but found the company of the fortune teller soothing and needed to steal moments for himself when he could.

"You get no feelings at all as to where my brother could be?" the prince asked.

Syrena froze for a moment, finding the topic extremely difficult. "No, Minas. The cards have revealed nothing, aside from the feeling I get that he is alive, somewhere," she lied.

"I miss him so. And I could really use his help right about now. My brother is quite clever, you know? Not a warrior, like me. He inherited all the brains."

"I am sure he is quite brave, just like you," she said,

and knew that to be the truth, as she recalled the struggle the young prince had put up as they attempted to capture him.

Even before meeting Prince Orval, that day had haunted the sorceress. She had been aiding the Cult for years but something about what she had done that day in particular, had gnawed at her insides. She had crossed a line. Now the dark gods mocked her by having her fall for the young prince's older brother.

"I get the feeling though, that you and your brother, are important people."

"We are…..successful merchants. And, his advice and help would be very welcomed at this time."

"With the demon now ruling this city, businesses will suffer. Your business will suffer. Maybe you should consider leaving Stonewood, set up someplace else? We can leave together," the sorceress suggested.

"My home is here. I would not be so quick to abandon this city, not yet. I feel there are changes coming. You wish to leave?"

"I live here but it is not my home. My home is far from Stonewood. Also, it is not easy to make a living here in the south district. Life is tough and dangers lurk everywhere."

"Soon, my dear Syrena, I will rescue you from the bowels of this city. Once I am finished….making a few business deals, you will leave the south district and stay with me, where you will be forever safe."

Syrena forced a smile. She was not so sure of that.

*   *   *   *

Feylane sat in the main hall of the Guild headquarters, sharpening a set of throwing knives. The beautiful assassin was getting restless. Even though Randar had stated that it did not matter who sat on the throne, that the Guild would endure and survive as it always had, she came to realize that that was not so.

The Guild operated at night, for obvious reasons, and now with the city-wide curfew, their activities and movements were hindered. Some thieves had thought to press their luck and take advantage of the mostly-deserted streets. Many were captured by groups of patrolling cultists and immediately executed. There were no more trials, no more dungeon time, just instant death.

The Guild would not survive this and Feylane was anxious to see this over. She held a personal grudge against the Cult, ever since her humiliating capture at the hands of Lord Mornay, a cultist in disguise. She would have met a horrible end, if not for the bravery of the renegade thief, Harcourt.

Ah, Harcourt. What an intriguing man, she thought. So different from anyone else she had ever met. He was kind and selfless, yet tough and rugged. He had a code that he lived by and stuck with it, no matter what, much like the assassin. They both had been molded by their environment but not completely altered from the people they were. They both possessed wills, forged of iron.

Feylane found that she enjoyed his company, when he was around, and felt a little anxiety over the thought that he went into that castle, among their enemies, alone. The thief had told her about the secret entrance hidden in the sewers. If anything happened to him, she would be tempted to find that entrance and exact revenge.

She recalled her last meeting with the evil High Priest in his private office. Feylane had thought the man, just a soft magistrate, an easy target. She had been wrong, very wrong. Within an instant, she had been immobilized with a spell. He could have ended her life then and there but he wanted information out of her. He promised to return later and get better acquainted with her. Again, she owed her life to Harcourt, who had shown up and saved her. Were she to face the High Priest again, she would have to be better prepared.

"Where is Weldrick? When are we going to begin to take back the south district?"

The voice, right behind her, caused the assassin to jump. It was no easy task, to catch Feylane off guard, but Zenod was a master of stealth, much like herself.

"Do that again at the risk of your life," she said, composing herself.

"My apologies, usually you can hear me coming."

"My mind was elsewhere."

"Clearly."

"I do not know where Weldrick is, I am not his sitter. He is probably off to meet with the King. We are supposed to begin our cleanup very soon. Just waiting on the cue from the King."

"Do you think we have a chance? Truly?"

"Weldrick thinks that we do and I trust in Weldrick. He has an uncanny ability in making the right decisions, even though he thinks he has terrible luck."

"He is a good leader, one of the best the Guild has had. Though I suppose, even a troll would have been an improvement after Trascar's rule."

"That I agree with. Trascar was selfish and evil to the

core. A heart as black as coal. The Guild and Stonewood alike, are much better off without his presence."

The two Guild members turned to regard the skeletal thief, Andil, as he shuffled through the room. He wore a long face with a vacant stare. He did not even acknowledge the presence of the others.

"Hey, what's eating you?" Feylane called over. "You look guilty of something."

The skinny thief kept going, leaving the room without a word.

"All of us here are guilty of something," Zenod remarked.

# CHAPTER 17

Na'Jala stood amidst the gathered crowd in the upper east district and watched the smoke rise from a north district villa. There were other black-skinned people that lived in Stonewood but they were not many. And there was only one who wore a permanent gladiator's mask, making him an easy mark. So Na'Jala took precautions whenever walking the streets of the city. Gloves to cover his hands and a dark hood, ever covering his face.

Concerned for his friend, Harcourt, Na'Jala had ventured to the gates of the north district, thinking that if the King had been captured, the demon lord would soon be making that announcement for all to hear. The demon would gloat for sure.

Now, the former gladiator watched as a raging fire engulfed a large villa located in the north district. It was impossible for Na'Jala to gain access to the district for a closer look, as the gates were always heavily guarded.

"I believe that's Horace Stonewood's house that burns," someone amid the crowd was heard saying.

"You are right, it is," another said.

"It doesn't pay to be a cousin of the King now, does it?"

"I heard the demon's men are searching all of the homes and businesses of anyone related to the King."

"We are surely doomed if they find him!"

"God save us all!"

Na'Jala had heard all he needed to hear and set off. If they did not act soon, all of Prince Orval's family, no matter how distant, would be put to death. This was not Na'Jala's home and he owed nothing to the King or the Prince. But despite the opportunities he had to leave, the former gladiator decided to stay and see this through, for good or ill.

Harcourt had saved his life, so he would do anything in his power to aid the man. This Cult that ruled the city now, also reminded Na'Jala of the lords and slave owners that ran the city of Gladenfar, where he had spent eight years as a prisoner and gladiator. And while those leaders in the southern city were very powerful and could not be overthrown, here in Stonewood, they had a chance to overthrow tyranny. To Na'Jala, that was at least one small victory for the good people of the world. He could not get revenge on those in Gladenfar, so he would take it out on the Cult here, or die trying.

Na'Jala crossed the bridge into the lower east district, trying carefully not to draw the attention of the guards posted at each end. Luckily there was much traffic, as people came and went from the market square and he managed to blend right in. Stonewood was an enormous city, larger than even Gladenfar, which was still considered a big city. So it was not surprising, that Na'Jala still got lost among the winding streets as he attempted to remember his way back to the south district. Harcourt had taught him to always use Fezzdin's tower as a marker, as it was the tallest structure in the city.

After several frustrating wrong turns, Na'Jala finally found the familiar dusty streets of the south district. During his short stay, he had become fairly familiar with the poorest district and cautioned on which streets he should try to avoid, but then, the entire district was just one bad neighborhood.

Na'Jala lowered his head as several mounted guards passed him by but paid him no heed. Then a whisper from an alley to his left drew his attention.

"Hey stranger, over here," a tall man, with messy blonde hair said, trying not to speak too loudly.

Na'Jala did not recognize the man but he could be one of the King's men. He cautiously entered the alley as the other man had bade him and found the man was not alone, there was two others with him.

"What do you want?" the former gladiator asked, with his unmistakable accent, which was not of Stonewood.

"Anything of value that you carry, stranger," the man replied, drawing a dagger from behind his back.

The two other men, one short and skinny, the other broad-shouldered and muscular, now held similar blades. All wore hungry grins. Na'Jala slowly reached towards the inside of his cloak.

"Whoa, whoa, easy, friend. No weapons," the messy-haired thug warned.

"I have a pouch of gold, it is all yours," Na'Jala responded.

The man nodded and Na'Jala's right hand disappeared inside his cloak, to find the hilt of his dagger. With blinding-speed, the former gladiator slashed the arm of the closest thug, sending that man's weapon to the ground. Na'Jala stepped in and kicked the skinniest man in the chest, forcing him back several feet before he stumbled. Before the strongest looking thug of the trio even had time to react, Na'Jala's blade was held firmly to his throat.

During the quick burst of action, Na'Jala's hood had fallen back to reveal his masked face and long braided hair. The largest thug dropped his dagger, wanting no more part of this strange, exotic warrior. Neither did the other two, as they ran down the alley and exited the opposite end, leaving their friend behind.

"You should reconsider the company you keep," Na'Jala told the thug, pushing him away in the direction of the others. "And the demon's men are your enemies in this city, not the citizens."

The man took off without a word. With the demon's curfew in effect, it appeared that thieves were becoming bolder during the daylight hours. Na'Jala could have easily sent these three men to the underworld but he thought they could have been members of the Thieves Guild, and therefore, they may be needed in the fight to come.

Soon, and without further incident, Na'Jala arrived back at the Ogre's Den tavern, which still appeared to have been abandoned. They used the back alley entrance to come and go, as the front doors and windows were boarded up.

Na'Jala turned into the alley and was greeted with the sight of a man in a bloodied cloak, limping towards the back door of the Den. The former gladiator's sword was out in a flash and he pressed the tip into the man's back.

"Where do you think you are going?" Na'Jala asked.

"I need a place to lay down. A drink would also be great, right about now," a very familiar voice replied.

\*     \*     \*     \*

A relieved Dornell helped Na'Jala get Harcourt down the stairs into the Den's cellar, where they laid him onto a bed. With tears of joy, Krestina was right there with them, begging them to be careful with him. His clothes were bloodied, he looked exhausted and she did not yet know the extent of his wounds. The rest of their companions now all gathered around, each shared that same feeling of great relief.

"See, I told ya he would make it out of there," Evonne said, confidently.

Fezzdin nodded and smiled. "A resourceful man indeed."

Naziya squeezed her way through to kneel next to the bed. "I am so glad you managed to escape. I could not have lived with myself if I had made it out and you had not."

"Think nothing of it," Harcourt replied, his voice weak. "But tell me, Fezzdin, that the book was useful?"

"Indeed it was, my boy, you were correct. You did a fine job. I will tell everyone what I have discovered as soon as you get some rest and feel a little better. Now come along everyone, let us go up and give him some room to breathe and let Sister Krestina see to his wounds," the wizard said.

The group, especially Dornell, was reluctant to leave, wishing to hear all about the thief's adventure, but did as they were told.

"You had me worried sick," Krestina said, once the pair was alone. "When that woman appeared, using the magic ring, and told us how you remained in that room with demons battering the door, well I didn't know what to think."

"All under control," the thief smiled.

"Oh really? And these?" the priestess pointed to several slash wounds, after she had removed his shirt.

"A couple of stubborn guards didn't want to let me go."

"Please don't do anything like that again."

The priestess prayed for spells of healing and her prayers were answered, as her hands began to glow with a silvery light. She touched each wound, one by one, and they all closed, returning a healthy color to the thief's skin. Strength and vigor returned to Harcourt's body and he looked up into the eyes of the woman he loved. But then, he noticed a change in the priestess. She was still her beautiful self but she looked......older somehow.

Not knowing exactly how to put that into words, without offending the woman, he simply said, "You look tired. I think you need some rest too."

Only Krestina had seen the way he looked at her, seen the way his expression had changed. "I look older, don't I?"

"I wouldn't say that, you just look, tired."

"No, I do look older, I feel older. Harcourt, each time I cast a healing spell, I age a little. I give some of my life force, to heal others."

"What?? How do you know?"

"Because, as I said, I see it and feel it. And Sister Tarrah has confirmed my suspicions. The other priests and priestesses feel that I am some special 'chosen one.' And, that is how I am able to cast such powerful spells well beyond my years of experience. Remember the sun in the cemetery? But my powers come at a cost. The more I help others, the faster I age."

"Then you will have to stop," the thief said, sitting up. "Let the other survivors of the temple help heal when needed. You cannot continue this way."

"Oh? So I should stop helping others, when you give your only escape route away to a strange woman, endangering your own life?"

"That was different."

"No, it was not. We are both trying to save this city and its people. And, we both know the risks in doing so. We know that we are going to do whatever it takes, to see this through to the end."

Harcourt could not argue with her. He knew she was right. He just wanted to make sure that Krestina stood with him, when all this was over with. "What do you mean, by 'chosen one'?"

"Well, Sister Tarrah was the temple's historian. Apparently, in times of great crisis, there have been cases of temple members performing amazing feats in order to save others. She, along with others, feel that I am God's chosen this time around, to aid in our current crisis. Sounds strange I know but I cannot explain how I have cast the spells that I have."

Harcourt knew nothing of the world of magic or religion, so would have to take the word of others. He did understand though that she had wielded some very powerful spells that should have been beyond her ability. Perhaps there was something to all this.

He pulled her over and they both lay down on the bed. Neither had any sleep in nearly two days. She laid her head on his now-healed chest and listened to his heartbeat.

The thief thought how alike the pair of them really were. Neither of them had ever had much of a childhood. Life seemed to pass them by much too quickly. They never seemed to have much time to just relax and enjoy life. Fortunately, for the priestess, she had the orphanage, for whatever it was worth, which gave her a roof over her head.

"What was it like? Living in the orphanage?" Harcourt asked.

"It was tough," Krestina said, after a moment of thought. "Dahleene is the sweetest and kindest woman in all of Stonewood but she is just as poor as the rest of us. She would read us stories from old books and feed us when she could. You were lucky if you had a blanket, because the rats liked to nibble if you were not covered up. But your kind donations did help quite a lot."

"There was no time to be a child, was there?"

"No, not at all. We were given chores to do and the older kids were always tasked with looking after the younger ones. Very little time for play. The same for you, I imagine?"

"Well, fortunately for me, I had only myself to look after," Harcourt replied. "But you are right, I had no time to play and be a child. I had to learn to steal and fight in the streets, if I was to survive. It was no fun."

"Life is strange, isn't it?" the priestess thought. "Who

would have guessed, that two south-side orphans would be one day helping to save the city?"

Harcourt laughed. "Yes, who would have thought?" They lay in silence for some time before he spoke again. "We are no longer poor, you and I. When this saving the city business is all over, is there anything you have always wanted, but never before had?"

"You mean, besides a stable, normal life, shared with someone I love?"

"Yes, aside from that. Is there anything you had always wanted? Some jewelry perhaps, or, some fancy clothing?"

"A doll."

"A doll?"

"Yes, a doll. I always wanted a doll when I was young and I never had one. I had seen other girls with dolls and I lay awake many a night, wishing I had one too. One with long brown hair, that I could brush, maybe a pretty pink dress, or different dresses I could clothe her in, for different occasions. I wanted one to hug at night, so I wouldn't feel so alone."

"I will have to get you a doll then."

"I doubt it would be the same, now we are no longer children. That time has passed us by."

No, we are not, the thief thought with a sigh, then the two drifted off to sleep.

\* \* \* \*

"So Fezzdin, tell us what you have found," Harcourt said, as he and Krestina rose from the cellar into the main taproom of the Ogre's Den.

The others were all present, even Prince Orval, sharing drinks and a meal while waiting for the thief and priestess to rest up.

"Gather round, all of you," the wizard sat on a table in the center of the room. He tried, unsuccessfully, to pull the book out from under his cat, Lex, who slept on top of it. He gave up, figuring he would not need it.

The companions of the King all grabbed chairs and sat around the wizard, like children preparing for story time in a school.

"Harcourt's assumptions were correct. This book outlined the process the Cult used to free Lucivenus from his extra-planar prison. It also, went into detail, about the process that was used to capture him in the first place."

"Finally," Prince Orval interrupted, with a sigh of relief. "The demon's doom is at hand."

"Not so quick, my young prince. Yes, I have knowledge of the process, but we lack the tools at present. Your ancestor's allies were armed with two items that we will need to find before we can defeat the demon lord. The wizards of the Circle of Three possessed an eldritch book of ancient magic. Contained within this book, was the powerful spell that opened a gate and imprisoned Lucivenus. But this spell is a complicated one to cast, requiring precious time, time that one does not normally have, with an angry demon standing before them. That is where the second item comes into play. The demi-god, Crystalmanthus, bestowed a great gift onto the-then, First Priest Ulanov. It was a mace, a holy relic, forged in the heavens above. Unholy creatures such as the undead, or those that dwell in the Abyss, become paralyzed, when struck with the holy weapon. This was how they were able to hold Lucivenus in place until the spell could be successfully cast."

"Great," Orval grumbled sadly. "I am guessing these items have been missing, for the last three hundred years? The Circle of Three have been dead for centuries, how would we ever find a book that was owned by them?"

"One yet exists," the wizard replied.

"How could one of them still be alive? That is impossible," the prince could not believe that claim.

"I said exists, I did not say alive. Our friends here have already met him."

"The Lich Lord of Morgaldrun," Harcourt blurted out, remembering their encounter with the undead wizard.

"Indeed," Fezzdin nodded. "The Lich Lord was once Mortimus Runefeld, a powerful necromancer and member of the Circle of Three. He was obsessed with the pursuit of immortality and found it, in the form of undeath. I am convinced that the lich would still be in possession of this book."

"That is no good to us then," Dornell commented. "The lich made it quite clear that he did not want any further visitors. One of the other men that was with us found out the hard way, what happens when you anger the wizard."

"That is why we must steal the book, from him. I have been in Morgaldrun, long before Mortimus made it his home. I recall where the library is located and believe that is where the book can be found," Fezzdin said, while looking towards the thief, Harcourt.

Krestina paled. " No, no, no! You cannot send Harcourt into that place, with an angry undead wizard! Can you not use your magic to retrieve the book?"

Fezzdin frowned. "I am afraid Mortimus would detect my presence as he is in tune, with all things magical. He is powerful, so I cannot advise us to attempt to take the book by force. This would require stealth, a great deal of it. I can draw a map to the library and one person may be able to get in and out, unnoticed."

Harcourt remembered well, the feeling of dread they all shared while in the presence of the Lich Lord. But, he also knew he was the only one qualified for the mission. "I will go, though I do not remember the way back to Morgaldrun."

"I will take him there, then," Dornell offered.

"And I insist on accompanying him too. He should not have to do this alone," Krestina said.

"We will find a suitable guide," Fezzdin responded. "But you two will be needed to retrieve the second item. The mace is said to be buried deep within the temple's crypts, inside the tomb of First Priest Ulanov. With Lucivenus defeated, members of the temple buried the weapon with the priest, thinking the crisis was over, forever. Only a member of the temple can handle the weapon. So you, my dear Sister Krestina, will have to be the one to retrieve it. We must hope that the entrance to the crypts are still accessible, since the damage sustained to the temple by the Cult."

"But Fezzdin, the crypts are locked. Only First Priest Viktor and two others, who were also killed during that first attack on the temple, possessed the keys. I believe those will be lost to us now," Krestina figured.

Harcourt scratched his head and recalled, many years back, his friend, Andil, had always wanted to try and rob the temple's crypts, saying that he had acquired a key to get inside. "I think I might have that problem solved, if this person I am thinking of was not lying. Which of course, he could have been."

"Excellent!" the wizard clapped his hands together. "Please look into that. We have much to do now, my friends. The path to victory is now laid before us but it will not be an easy path to follow. We must trust in each other and in our abilities to see this through."

"While they search for the book and mace, I believe we should begin our fight, starting with taking back the south district," Prince Orval suggested.

"I agree, my prince," Fezzdin replied. "The fate of Stonewood is soon to be decided."

Krestina wrapped Harcourt in a tight hug. She knew he was the only one who could get that book, so there would be no arguing the point. But that did not mean she had to like it. She was so relieved that he had escaped the castle but now he would be off on an equally dangerous mission. The priestess did not know how much more of this she could handle.

Sensing her thoughts, Harcourt returned the hug and kissed her forehead.

# CHAPTER 18

High Priest Sarvin entered the dimly-lit chamber and joined Lucivenus and Gryndall, who were waiting inside. The warlock stood against the stone wall, while Lucivenus sat in the center. Phyzantiss stood guard in the hall, as they were not to be disturbed, by anyone at all.

"Do not step inside the circle, you and I must stand outside of it. Only Lord Lucivenus will be able to control the being inside," the demonic warlock commanded.

Sarvin stopped short, before stepping over the boundary of the perfect circle that Lucivenus had drawn on the floor in what appeared to be blood. This chamber was large and empty, without any windows. The stone floor was featureless, save for the red circle that was now drawn upon it. Four torches dimly-lit the room, one on each wall, casting many shadows within.

The demon lord sat cross-legged in the center of the circle, holding the dagger that had wounded King Stonewood. A small ebony brazier burned directly in front of Lucivenus.

"What are you planning to do?" the High Priest wondered aloud.

"Who would you say was the greatest enemy of King Stonewood? Who would have hated him the most?"

Sarvin pondered the question for a few moments before hazarding a guess. "Possibly the barbarian king, Hrolfdar. He was ever jealous of King Stonewood's wealth and kingdom. Hrolfdar united many barbarian tribes of the north and surrounded the city. There was a great battle and King Stonewood himself challenged King Hrolfdar to single combat in front of both armies. The mighty barbarian king, as strong as he was, was humiliated and defeated that day, in a fierce fight. Beheaded before his army. It would be difficult to imagine anyone who would bear King Stonewood more hatred. But why do you ask?"

Lucivenus smiled, with his toothy grin. "With the blood of King Stonewood, I am going to summon forth a soul wraith. A powerful spirit of the netherworld that is fueled by hatred, hatred for the one whose blood is used in the summoning. It will stop at nothing, to destroy this person."

"Hrolfdar was a mighty warrior in life, luck alone saved King Stonewood that day. I can only imagine how powerful the barbarian king would be in undeath," Sarvin commented.

The demon lord was pleased to hear that and then proceeded with the summoning. Lucivenus closed his eyes and began chanting in a guttural, demonic language that was not meant for the ears of mortals. Intense heat from his huge, red-skinned hands, began to liquefy the dried blood of the dagger, which he held. As he continued to chant the words of the unholy spell, blood began to drip from the blade, into the fires of the brazier. Each drop caused the flames to blaze brighter, until Sarvin was forced to avert his eyes.

As the last drop of blood fell into the brazier, all of the flames in the room were suddenly extinguished and an ear-piercing, inhuman screech, echoed off the walls.

Sarvin flinched in the darkness as a slight breeze tickled his face, as if something had passed by only inches away. To his relief, the torches lining the walls soon flared back to life. The High Priest sucked in his breath as he noticed a dark form standing where the brazier had stood, only moments before.

The figure appeared real enough but it seemed to be made up of swirling shadows. It stood about six feet tall, with a slender build, not at all like that of the huge barbarian king, Hrolfdar. Sarvin shifted positions for a better look at the soul wraith's face. Despite the ever-flowing shadows that made up its body, the face of the creature did have typical human features, but again, it looked nothing like Hrolfdar. The High Priest could not imagine someone else holding a deeper hatred for King Stonewood.

Lucivenus too, thought the wraith before him looked nothing like a barbarian king. His casting of the spell had been flawless so this creature was linked to the owner of the blood and hated him above all others.

"I am Lord Lucivenus, your master, until your task is complete. What is your name?"

"Trascar," the soul wraith answered, in a horrible, skin-shivering, whispery voice.

The demon lord looked to Sarvin with a questioning glare but the High Priest was just as clueless. Trascar? Who in the Abyss was Trascar? Well, the creature should still hate the King and would still stop at nothing to destroy him.

"Whom is it that you hate the most?" Lucivenus asked, curiously.

"HARCOURT!" the wraith shrieked, with unbridled fury from beyond the grave.

\*   \*   \*   \*

"It is time to take the south district back," Weldrick said, to the gathered Guild members, seated in the meeting chamber.

"What's the plan, then?" inquired Randar, with a hint of venom in his voice.

"I am leaving that up to you."

"Me? But you are our leader."

"And I am going to have business elsewhere, for the next few days. So, Randar, do whatever must be done to run the Cult out of this district. The King and his men will begin tomorrow. Just stay out of their way and they will stay out of ours."

"What happens when the district is ours?" Patch wondered. "This Cult is not just going to sit idly by. My guess is they will be back in force. They do have an army of twenty thousand just outside the walls."

"Stonewood's armies are returning, if the messengers have done their jobs. We have Thelvius and his mercenary company camped just out of sight. The prince has gathered many soldiers from several lords and the King has loyal men stationed within the castle. The south district is just phase one, we are not stopping there. The wizard,

Fezzdin, has even discovered a way to defeat the demon lord. The end of the Cult is coming."

"If things turn sour, we retreat to the sewers, let the King take the fall. I will not be risking my neck for his," Randar stated.

"Fine. As I said, do as you must," Weldrick said, standing to leave. "I will be back in a day or so."

Feylane caught up to the Guild leader in the hall outside the meeting room. "I see you are in one piece. Your mission was a success then?"

"It was. It could have gone a little more smoothly than it did but still, I retrieved the book and Fezzdin found the information we needed."

"So, all this time there has been a secret way into the castle?"

"Yes, at the very north end of the sewers, there is a dead end with a waterfall. The door is hidden behind the waterfall. Very clever."

"Now where are you off to? Time to play King some more?"

"I wish it was that simple. I am off again, after yet another book. Only this time I need to steal it from an undead wizard."

The beautiful assassin fixed him with a quizzical stare.

"I know how it sounds but trust me, I have met him once before. I am not kidding about that."

Feylane stepped closer to the thief, too close. "You be careful, promise?"

"Ah, Weldrick? You wanted to see me after the meeting?"

Andil just saved him from an uncomfortable situation. "Yes, a moment in private," the Guild leader replied. "And, yes, I promise," he said to Feylane.

The assassin nodded, then reluctantly went back into the meeting room with the other members. Weldrick found a smaller room not too far away and the skeletal thief followed him in.

"Does Feylane know who you really are?" Andil asked.

"She does. Not by choice though but I do trust her."

"So, what did you want to see me about?"

Harcourt hated thinking back, to the time when the pair were *friends*. "Years ago, you talked about breaking into the temple's crypts, do you recall?"

"Aye. But they were too well guarded so I gave up on that idea."

"How would you have gotten in? A key?"

"Yeah, I had a key. Brother Pitor, our man on the inside, secured me one of the keys."

"Do you have it still?"

"Well, I buried it years ago but it should still be where I left it. Why? Now really isn't the time to be treasure hunting."

"We need something buried in those crypts to defeat that demon. So I am asking you to find that key and bring it by the Ogre's Den tavern tomorrow afternoon. I won't be there, so leave it with Captain Dornell. Will you do that for me?"

"Aye, of course I will, old friend."

"Don't call me that!" the Guild leader barked. "Just be there tomorrow."

Harcourt turned and left. He really wished things could have been as he had believed they were, between the two thieves. He could not get over Andil's betrayal. Just the sight of the skeletal thief stirred up too many emotions and very few good ones. Harcourt knew the man was trying to change, trying to make things up to him, but he did not think it would ever be the same.

Harcourt exited the Guild headquarters and began the long trek back to the Den. He wanted to get back before it got dark to try and sleep a few hours. He was planning to leave for Morgaldrun before dawn's first light.

*   *   *   *

It had taken a little bit of digging but High Priest Sarvin finally figured out that Trascar was the former leader of the Thieves Guild. The man was believed to have fled Stonewood, after his identity had been discovered. That was right around the time that the thief, Harcourt, was reportedly killed. But clearly Harcourt still lived, so the mystery deepened. Harcourt must somehow have been disguised as the King; that is how his blood got on the dagger. That would also explain the youthful reflexes and speed the King seems to possess.

Sarvin was willing to bet that the King did indeed die, on that night of the throne room battle. Harcourt has somehow been impersonating the King, Sarvin deduced, most likely with the help of Fezzdin. A good job though, they had fooled him.

"You think there is no King, then?" Lucivenus asked, drawing Sarvin out of his thoughts.

"That would be my guess. Trascar must not have fled the city as we believed. He must have been killed, by Harcourt, and therefore hates him above all others. The thief must have been disguised as the King using magic, I am sure."

"Then we waste time searching the homes of the King's relatives. We need to raze the south district. That is where all the thieves hide, is it not?"

"Indeed it is," Sarvin replied. "Your soul wraith should eliminate Harcourt but I believe his friends do hide in the south district, somewhere. That is where we will find Prince Orval."

Sarvin looked to the soul wraith, who stood motionless beside the demon lord. Though his body looked like swirling shadows, it was solid enough to wear clothing. They had outfitted the wraith with a set of clothes and a dark cloak, to move about the city without drawing attention to itself.

"Go forth," Lucivenus commanded. "Find this Harcourt and destroy him. Your soul will be freed when it is done."

The soul wraith hissed in reply and disappeared through the closest window. The creature did hate Harcourt immensely and set off to find his most hated enemy. And when looking for Harcourt, one should start with the Ogre's Den tavern.

\*     \*     \*     \*

Tomorrow was a big day, so all the companions at the Den had decided to turn in early and try to get some sleep, even Fezzdin, who rarely seemed to sleep. Harcourt tossed and turned, on the cellar floor, where most of them slept. The combined snoring of Dornell and Fezzdin was enough to wake the dead, and the thief could not sleep a wink.

Finally Harcourt rose and made for the cellar stairs, dragging his blanket behind him. He did not want to wake Krestina or the others, who miraculously ignored the noise, but stealth was not required, as the sounds of snoring drowned out the sound of his footsteps up the creaking stairs.

In the main taproom, the thief found old Kan, sound asleep across two chairs. With his fake leg, it was too difficult for him to use the cellar stairs and he opted to stay above. Evonne was slumped over a corner table, passed out and drooling from too much drink.

Harcourt did his best to move a few tables aside quietly, then lay on the floor with his blanket. Within mere moment's he drifted off to dreamland.

\*     \*     \*     \*

Later that night, Trascar, the soul wraith, stealthily made his way through the streets of the south district, easily avoiding all Cult patrols. In life, Trascar grew up on these streets and as Guild leader, he had owned these streets. The wraith possessed the soul of the thief along with his memories, and he remembered these streets well.

Most of all though, he remembered Harcourt. The low-life, renegade thief had not been the one who actually killed Trascar but he may as well have been, since it was his scheme that led to the Guild leader's death. The wretch had orchestrated a fight between Trascar and Zorfal, the traitorous guard captain. The two of them had butchered each other. But Trascar had hung onto life just long enough for Harcourt to reveal that he was behind the whole thing, gloating over the dying Guild leader. The wraith's hatred towards the other thief was beyond imagining.

Soon, what was once the former Guild leader stood in front of the Ogre's Den tavern. The creature sniffed the air and hissed. It could smell Harcourt's blood, the thief was close. It approached the boarded-up front doors and looked about curiously. It knew something was different about the tavern but could not comprehend the idea of it being abandoned. The memories of Trascar told the wraith that the tavern should have been open for business at this hour.

The undead thief placed both shadowy hands against the pieces of wood that were nailed into the door to bar the entrance. Immediately, the wood began to rot and fall away from the unholy touch of the soul wraith.

Moments later, Trascar silently opened the tavern's door and slipped inside without a sound.

\*     \*     \*     \*

Reginald Tarm should not have been out in the streets after dark but he knew the Guild operated mostly at night and wanted to speak with a certain Guild member. He was a thief of some skill and melted into the shadows each time a guard patrol passed him by. So far, luck was with him. Getting caught was certainly not an option.

Reginald had been a thief but not a Guild member. That, however, had not stopped him from thievery; he had to support his family somehow and he had fallen on tough times. He had robbed a few merchants from the market square and gained the attention of the Guild.

Reginald made his biggest mistake though, by

attempting to pawn some jewelry to a beautiful woman who had turned out to be a member of the Thieves Guild. He had a sack thrown over his head and was brought to some secret Guild location, under threat of death. And he knew this woman meant it.

The thief figured his life was over. The Guild would most likely torture him and then kill him. But strangely, that is not what happened next. A male Guild member entered the room where he was kept and showed him compassion and mercy. The man had stuffed several gold coins into his pocket and had let him go. He told Reginald to wait a month or so, then go by the Ogre's Den tavern and ask for Weldrick about a job.

Luckily for Reginald, his life shortly took a turn for the better. He was given a job in a busy butcher's shop, in the lower east district. The wages were good and he no longer resorted to thievery. The shop was less busy, due to Stonewood's current situation with the demon lord but with a little luck, the King would reclaim his throne and save the city.

Reginald did not need any help from the Guild but he wanted to thank this man, Weldrick, for saving his life and setting him on the right path. He would be forever grateful to this mysterious man.

Not wishing to draw any attention from patrols, the former thief decided to use the alley behind the tavern and try the back door. Tavern business was suffering from the current curfew and generally would be closed at this hour, but this tavern must have been a Guild hangout. Reginald was willing to bet that there would be someone inside.

The alley was dark and eerily silent. Reginald stopped in front of the tavern's back door and at first, listened. He could hear no voices or activity from within. The former thief knocked gently upon the door. With no response, he knocked more loudly the second time.

\*  \*  \*  \*

Harcourt's eyes shot open at the sound of someone knocking on the back door of the tavern. He shivered from an unnatural chill in the air, one he had now felt twice before. The thief's skin prickled and he thought he noticed some movement in the gloom above him.

Instinctively, he rolled to his right. From the darkness came a hiss, and there was a loud bang from the spot where he lain only a moment earlier. Something had struck the floor and hard, in an attempt to hit the thief.

Harcourt was wide awake and on his feet in a flash, a dagger in his right hand. He backed up behind a table and as his eyes adjusted to the gloom, a shadowy figure in a dark cloak made its way towards him.

"What's going on?" he heard a groggy Evonne shout, from the other side of the room.

"Intruder!" Harcourt yelled, hoping that everyone would hear him, even down to the cellar.

The thief heard the bounty hunter draw her sword, then it sounded as if she stumbled, knocking chairs aside, as she probably still felt the effects of all she had drunk only hours before.

Again, there was a knocking at the door and now Kan sat up, disoriented. The shadowy figure dove across the table at the thief and Harcourt just barely stepped back out of reach. The man appeared unarmed and had attempted to grab the thief. Strange, Harcourt thought.

"Who are you?" Harcourt asked. "Come at me again and you will regret it, this I promise."

The figure hissed in response, an inhuman hiss which set off warning signals in the thief. Did the Cult send another vampire after him? or was this some other unholy creature? he wondered.

Harcourt positioned another table between him and his attacker, only to have it smashed to pieces from the powerful blow of a shadowy fist. It rushed in and again reached for the thief. Harcourt slashed its arm with his dagger and was rewarded with an inhuman screech. Smoke rose from the spot on the creature's arm where he had slashed it. It was some unholy monster, the thief thought to himself, as the dagger he wielded had been blessed by Krestina.

The taproom partially lit up as Kan ignited a large lantern. Harcourt finally got a better look at the intruder as it shrieked from the sudden illumination. It was clothed but its face and hands were as black as coal, almost appearing to be made of shadows themselves. Harcourt found its white eyes, devoid of pupils, the most unnerving. Its shadowy face had human characteristics and for a moment, Harcourt actually felt he recognized the face, but did not have time to ponder that, as he was again diving away from outstretched arms.

He ducked under its arms and dove to the floor. The soul wraith whirled around with amazing dexterity and was nearly on top of him when a flying bar stool struck it square in the face. Evonne had regained her balance and did the only thing she could do while standing too far from the melee. Her crossbow leaned against a wall out of reach.

The attack did no harm to the wraith but bought Harcourt enough time to get back to his feet and put a little more distance between himself and the strange creature. But it did not cease its attacks. It came forward, scattering tables and chairs like pieces of kindling.

Bravely, or perhaps foolishly, Old Kan stepped between the wraith and its most hated enemy, holding an axe aloft, ready to strike.

"This is my friend you are attacking," the former beggar declared. "You will have to get through me first!"

"Kan, no!" Harcourt shouted.

The soul wraith hissed and dove at Kan with lightning-speed. Before he could bring his axe down in defense, cold, shadowy hands wrapped around his throat. Kan tried to scream but it was cut off as he was choked.

Harcourt hurdled a table in an attempt to reach the pair when he noticed Kan's skin suddenly turned as grey as ash. The former beggar's eyes went wide with horror and his mouth opened in a silent scream. In the mere moments that Harcourt paused at the gruesome spectacle, Kan's skin shriveled up into a dry husk and the wraith tossed his lifeless body aside. The thief was speechless.

Finally, Evonne reached her crossbow and fired a perfect shot into the creature's throat. Upon contact with its shadowy skin, the bolt immediately turned to dust and drifted to the floor. In the blink of an eye, she reloaded and fired again. The bolt found its forehead but the result was exactly the same.

The soul wraith ignored the petite bounty hunter and ran straight for the thief. Harcourt left it with another smoking wound on its shoulder, before tumbling under its reach and racing for the bar, leaping over.

Evonne tossed aside her crossbow and retrieved her sword, advancing towards the creature.

"No!" Harcourt shouted at her. "It only wants me. Do not get in its way!"

The trap door to the cellar then burst open and in rushed Dornell, followed closely by Na'Jala, swords in hand.

"What devilry is this?" Dornell asked, noticing the strange shadowy creature, then the dried-up husk of Old Kan, lying on the floor.

"Keep back, if you cherish your lives," Harcourt shouted, as the wraith moved towards the bar, seemingly unconcerned about the arrival of others.

The wraith leaped upon the bar and hissed at the thief. A bolt of lightning struck it in the back and sent the undead creature straight into a wall, its head smashing clean through. There it hung for a moment, dangling from its head, until it began to move again and struggle to get free.

"I think it is some undead creature but it only seems interested in me," Harcourt told the others.

"Indeed it is," Fezzdin replied, watching the wood around the creature's neck begin to rot away. "It is a wraith of some sort. Beware its touch, it will drain the life from your body."

"I will lead it far from here. Have Symm meet me shortly at our designated spot. I am off for Morgaldrun then," Harcourt said, making for the kitchen and the back door located there. "Good luck!"

"The wraith cannot move about in daylight," Fezzdin called to the thief, before he disappeared through the door.

"Wait! Harcourt!" Krestina shouted, as she bounded

up the stairs, but the thief was already gone.

Harcourt's assumptions of the wraith were correct. As soon as it freed itself from the wall, it paid no heed to the others in the room and quickly followed the thief through the door, intent on catching its prey.

Harcourt burst through the tavern's back door, startling Reginald, who still stood outside listening to the commotion inside. The thief did not pause to consider who the stranger in the back alley was and took off running.

As Reginald composed himself, another figure burst through the doorway and hissed at him, but passed him by in pursuit of the other man. Both vanished into the darkness of the night.

# CHAPTER 19

Harcourt dashed down the very long and narrow Street of Sorrow. He still had not gotten used to the feel of seeing the streets of the south district empty at night. This was usually the time the district became alive with activity. Folk hopping from tavern to tavern, thieves and thugs going about their shady business. Now, there was nothing but Cult patrols, enforcing the demon lord's curfew.

The thief risked a glance behind, before rounding the next corner and caught a glimpse of the shadowy creature that still pursued him. Why did its strange face seem so familiar to him? he wondered.

The wraith moved quickly and was gaining on him. As Harcourt approached the next fork in the road, the sounds of booted feet to the left caused him to take a right. The patrol was walking in the opposite direction, so their backs were facing the sprinting thief. Every once in awhile, luck was with him, he mused.

Harcourt ducked into the first alley after turning onto Sword Street. He pressed his back to the wall, blending

into the shadows and peered around the corner, watching
for his pursuer. His heart raced as he tried to catch his
breath. The thief waited and waited but the wraith never
rounded the corner. Perhaps he had lost it, or the sounds
of the patrol had scared it off. Either way, it gave the thief
a moment of respite.

Harcourt sheathed his dagger and inspected the sides
of the buildings that made up this narrow alley. It would
be safer for him to move about using the rooftops, so up
the wall he went, finding the smallest of grooves to help
his climb.

He did not get very far, before he heard a hissing
sound and a vice-like grip grabbed his right boot. With a
feeling of panic, Harcourt expected this leg to shrivel up
and fall off but it had not. Perhaps the wraith needed to
touch bare skin, to have its devastating effect.

The creature pulled the thief off the wall with little
effort and Harcourt crashed hard to the ground below.
The soul wraith leaped into the air, attempting to pounce
on top of his hated enemy. Harcourt reached for a nearby
piece of wood, what was left of a some long destroyed
crate. The wraith landed on top of him but the
outstretched piece of wood kept the creature's body and
snarling face momentarily at bay.

The wraith grabbed the wood with both hands and
leaned over to hiss again, at the thief. With its face only
inches from his, Harcourt finally got a good look at it.

"Trascar??" he managed to say.

Trascar? The wraith's face resembled that of the thief
and former Guild leader, Trascar. How was that possible?
Harcourt thought.

But there was no time to ponder, as the wood began

to rot from the wraith's grasp and within moments, crumbled to ash. Harcourt managed to buck the creature off with his all his strength and jump to his feet. The wraith recovered quickly and was again reaching for him, intense anger evident upon its shadowy face.

Harcourt had a dagger in each hand and slashed at its arms while backpedalling out of the alley and back onto Sword Street. Smoke rose from each wound but the wraith never slowed.

The thief backed into something solid and his heart sank as he realized he was suddenly in the midst of a Cult patrol. The ten guards were equally as surprised as the thief, at the sudden appearance of two individuals battling each other.

"The dark gods above, what is going on here?" one shouted.

"This filthy thief is trying to rob me!" Harcourt responded.

The thief took advantage of the stunned guards and shouldered his way through the group, taking off in a sprint once more.

"Get back here!" called the patrol captain. " Get him, do not let him escape!"

A scream drew the captain's attention back to the second of the two men. He now had his hands wrapped around another guard's throat. The group stood slack-jawed, as they watched the guard's skin turn grey and begin to shrivel up.

Forgetting about the fleeing man, the guards drew their weapons and rushed the dark figure who had just killed one of their own.

From two blocks away, Harcourt could hear multiple

screams of terror from the group of guards, and kept running.

*   *   *   *

Two hours later, Harcourt and a man named Symm, walked through the dark smuggler's tunnel, which led from the Last Stop Tavern to outside the city walls. Symm was about the same build as the thief but had been a member of Stonewood's cavalry unit and loyal supporter of the King.

After Harcourt's last trip outside the city to meet with the mercenaries, he had left his horse and wagon at a farm located just outside the perimeter of wraggoth. The idea was to sneak past the army, using the cover of darkness and get to the farm. From there, Symm would get them to the fortress of the Lich Lord.

Fezzdin had given the soldier a special magical elixir, for the horse. It would allow the steed to run much faster and not tire, making their journey much quicker. Time was running out for the group of companions. If they could not do something about the demon lord and the Cult soon, all would be lost.

And now, the thief had to worry about that wraith running around on the loose, searching for him. It had to have been sent by Sarvin or Lucivenus but why had it looked so much like Trascar? he had to wonder. Perhaps it was just some trick or illusion, used to try and unnerve the thief even more. And if that was the case, why was it sent after him, personally, and not the King? Too many mysteries, too many unanswered questions.

Before departing through the tunnel, Harcourt had

written a message to be delivered to Fezzdin, telling him that he had escaped the wraith and that the Den might no longer be a safe place. The wraith could return to search for the thief. He also mentioned the strange appearance of the undead creature, resembling the former Guild leader. Perhaps that meant something to the wise wizard.

Poor Old Kan, he then thought. He did not deserve a fate as gruesome as that was. He had died trying to help the thief. The man had a good heart and Kan's death was now just one more thing, added to the long list of things, that Sarvin and his Cult had to answer for.

Harcourt was also saddened that he did not get to say a proper good-bye to Krestina. Everything had happened so fast. He hoped that their search for the holy mace would be a lot easier than his quest for the spell book. He would have to trust in Dornell and Na'Jala to keep her safe. Or, after witnessing some of her special talents of late, perhaps she would keep them safe.

\* \* \* \*

Andil cautiously slid through the back door to the Ogre's Den tavern, which had, strangely, been left unlocked. The skinny thief slunk through the kitchen, before poking his head through the door to the main taproom. Suddenly, a crossbow was leveled at his head.

"I am a friend of Harcourt's," he said, entering the room with his hands held palms out, showing he was unarmed.

"Is that so?" Evonne answered, not convinced, as she had never seen the skinny, baby-faced thief before.

"He is," Fezzdin called over, looking up from

Harcourt's message, that he had just been reading.

Evonne slowly lowered her weapon but did not take her eyes off the man. She never knew just what the Cult would try next.

"I have the key," Andil said, addressing everyone in the room. "The key to the temple's crypts."

"Where did you acquire that, I wonder? You don't look like a priest," Dornell asked, approaching the thief.

"I did and that is all that matters."

Harcourt certainly kept strange friends, Andil thought. A former guard captain, a wizard, a priestess, bounty hunters. He was not the down-and-out, reclusive thief that Andil remembered.

"Do you know where the door to the crypts are located?" inquired Dornell.

"I was told where to find it, yes. That is, if the temple basement is even still accessible, after what the Cult has done to the building."

"Good, you are coming with us then."

"Huh? Why? I will give you the key. She can find the entrance," Andil pointed to Krestina.

"I wasn't a member of the temple for too long and I was never taken to the basement and shown the crypt entrance," the priestess replied.

"What about all the temple members who escaped? I heard about that. One of them would know!"

"Too dangerous. We do not know what to expect inside the temple. The Cult could have left men there waiting to see if any returned," Dornell reasoned. "So you are coming with us."

The skeletal thief let out a defeated sigh.

"We will need to abandon this place for the time

being anyway," Fezzdin spoke up, having finished reading the message. "Our undead friend could be paying another visit here tonight, in search of Harcourt."

"What was that thing?" Evonne wondered.

"My educated guess would be a soul wraith," thought the wizard. "It is a powerful undead creature of the netherworld, summoned into our world by foul magic. It is linked to its target and will stop at nothing to find and kill that person."

Krestina paled. "But why Harcourt?"

"I am thinking that Harcourt was not the intended target. Soul wraiths are summoned using the blood of the target individual. In this case, I believe the Cult thought they were sending the creature after King Stonewood, only the blood they had acquired was Harcourt's. In his message, he mentioned that the wraith resembled a man named Trascar, a man he had a history with."

"Trascar was the Guild leader, who was behind Jalanna's murder. Harcourt's revenge plot ended with Trascar's death," Dornell remembered.

"Then it all makes sense," the wizard rubbed his bearded chin. "A soul wraith possesses the soul of a hated enemy, your most hated. With Harcourt's blood, the Cult summoned the spirit of this man, Trascar, who wishes Harcourt's death above all others. It came here, to the tavern, remembering that this is a place that Harcourt frequented."

"How can we stop it, Fezzdin?" Krestina asked. "Surely it will keep coming."

"Soul wraiths are very powerful creatures. This may be a question best asked of your elders from the temple. It was the unholiest of magic that summoned it, so it may take the most holy of magic to be rid of it. Necromancy has never been my area of expertise, I am sorry to say. I will look into this matter while you retrieve the mace."

"What can I do to help?" asked Naziya, who had remained silent in a corner until now.

"We can provide you with a place to hide, until it is safe for you to leave the city and return home," replied Dornell.

"I do not wish to hide. I seek revenge for my mistress. I am a warrior of Ryor-Suul, top of the academy of Cyndol. I lend you my sword until this evil is dealt with."

Dornell nodded in approval. "Every sword helps. Go with Evonne, she will need all the help she can get." He turned to Krestina. "Now, Sister, let us find this mace."

*    *    *    *

Vrawg sat against the cellar wall, his head resting on his knees. The half-ogre bounty hunter had been deeply saddened, left in this building to look after the members of the temple who had been rescued. But he was just simply too big to move about the city without being noticed. He was wanted by the Cult and could bring doom upon his companions if he was ever seen and followed. He understood why it was necessary but was not happy about it all the same.

"If your face gets any longer, you are gonna be tripping over it when you walk," a familiar voice said.

Vrawg looked up to find his long-time friend and partner, Evonne, standing before him, hands on her hips. He was happy to see her but it did not help improve his mood.

"Remember how you used to lecture me on how much I worked? You used to tell me how important it was to take a break every now and then, just relax and recuperate? Remember that? Now you get a little break and all you do is mope about with that sad face."

"He has been a delight to have around," said Sister Aymee, the slender, red-headed priestess, who joined the two bounty hunters. "We feel so safe having him here and he is a fantastic story teller."

"Oh, I see how it is," Evonne smirked. "You chat and flirt with all the pretty priestesses, then put on your long face when I am around, huh?"

Vrawg just shrugged his huge shoulders.

"Well get up, you oaf. We are leaving," the blonde bounty kicked him in the shin.

He looked at his partner quizzically.

"We have Cult members to smash. Are you coming or not?"

Vrawg leaped to his feet with an enormous smile.

\*     \*     \*     \*

"Things are about to change in Stonewood, to get ugly," Prince Orval said, sipping on a mug of ale. "Or I guess I should say, get uglier."

"Oh? What do you know?" asked Syrena, as the pair shared a drink in her shop which was closed for the day.

"Sources tell me that there is going to be fighting in the streets, fierce fighting. The King is going to take back his city, one district at a time. I would like to offer you a safe place to hide until this is over. You may not be safe here."

Syrena sighed. She still did not believe the prince and his father could win this battle. Lucivenus and Sarvin were just too powerful. "Let's just leave here, we can go south, where I am from," she tried, one more time.

"I cannot abandon my business here. I have spent a lifetime building it. I know it is hard for you to understand but everything will be clear soon enough."

"No, no. I understand, believe me. I understand much more than you know."

"Then please, allow me to take you somewhere safe. I don't want anything to happen you. I can protect you."

Syrena smiled weakly. "I will be fine here. The Cult leaves me alone and the Guild has never bothered me either. It's bad luck to harm a fortune teller."

"If you wish to be stubborn, then at least promise me you will stay inside here. Keep your shop closed and your door locked. Alright?"

The sorceress nodded. She would wait 'til the prince was long gone before she slipped out. The High Priest had summoned her back to the castle for another meeting.

# CHAPTER 20

Harcourt's stomach was in knots as he again, looked upon the shadow-haunted fortress of Morgaldrun, home to the undead wizard, Mortimus Runefeld. He and Symm had been fortunate enough to slip passed the Cult-controlled wraggoth army, without incident. The elixir Fezzdin had provided worked like a charm and their horse ran like the wind. They made great time in arriving at the Black Peak mountains and now stopped at the foot of the mountain, closest to the fortress. Morgaldrun was in view but the pair sat a safe distance away.

The sun had set long ago and the full moon illuminated the valley where the dark fortress sat nestled between two mountains. A chill wind blew down from the rocky slopes causing both men to shiver slightly.

"You are going in there? You are braver than I thought," whispered Symm.

"Nah, just foolish. I don't possess enough sense to refuse."

Harcourt remembered how quickly the lich had killed

Garth when the repulsive man had angered him. They were told not to return and now that was exactly what the thief planned to do. And to steal a book from the undead wizard, no less.

The last time Harcourt and his companions had visited the fortress, the thief was forced to open the front gates for the others. That had made a terrible racket that could have wakened the dead, which it had apparently done. This time he could just go up and over the wall as silently as a ghost and creep though the halls as just another shadow. With luck, the lich would never know he was even there.

"This should only take a couple of hours at most," Harcourt said to the cavalryman. "If I am not out by dawn, leave and inform the others I failed." He pulled his magical mask, which was wrapped in a cloth, out of a saddlebag and handed it to the other man. "And give this to Fezzdin."

Symm nodded and the thief set off for the fortress walls. Harcourt had decided to travel light. He wore black leather armor with a black cloak overtop but left his sword with the horse. His two customary daggers were sheathed behind his back and he had one more smaller knife at the top of his boot, though he had no plans for any fighting. If confronted by the undead wizard, Harcourt figured his life was forfeit. Even Fezzdin referred to Mortimus as very powerful.

Arriving at the tall ebony wall, Harcourt went up the side like a spider, finding the smallest grooves in the stone to aid his ascent. He paused at the top of the wall to survey the courtyard beyond and found it dark and devoid of life, just as he remembered.

He dropped to the ground on the other side and crouched motionless, scanning the windows of the main keep. As before, there were no visible light sources. The fortress would appear abandoned, to anyone who did not know better. Though rumors that it was haunted kept bandits, and any others, effectively away.

Harcourt, virtually invisible in the shadows, found the front doors to the keep still unlocked. That told him that the lich had little fear of thieves or other intruders. He slipped inside the dark foyer and shivered as he was hit with that unnerving chill that permeated the entire fortress. It was the deep chill of death.

Moonlight trickled through the windows and as his eyes adjusted to the gloom, Harcourt tried to remember the route that Fezzdin had said would lead him to the library. The old wizard had mentioned visiting Morgaldrun, long before Mortimus claimed it as his. That would make Fezzdin quite old, unnaturally old. But that was a riddle for another time; now the thief needed to focus.

Unlike his last visit, this time Harcourt was equipped with his best lock picks. It was not long before he was putting them to use. The lich had guided them last time, leaving only certain doors unlocked. Now, the thief chose his own path and made short work of the lock to a door, which led to a winding stairwell.

Stealthily, he descended. The corridor at the bottom of the stairwell was pitch-dark, devoid of windows to let in the moonlight. Harcourt fumbled around with a pouch attached to his belt, producing a small stone that was covered with a phosphorescent moss. The glow from the moss was just enough to allow the thief to see where he was going. Down the corridor he crept, making not a sound as he went.

Harcourt counted three doors on the right side of the hall, then tried the handle of the third door. He placed his stone on the floor and out came his lock picks. The fortress was built well over a century ago and Harcourt found the locks were simple to defeat, for a master thief.

As he was rewarded with the successful clicking sound of the door now unlocked, another sound, from within what should be the library, caught his attention. It was faint at first but was growing louder, or closer rather. It was a shuffling sound, like someone walking who was too lazy to pick up their feet. Harcourt remembered these sounds from their visit but had been fortunate enough to avoid whatever was causing it. If he had followed Fezzdin's directions properly, then this was the library and he would have to go in.

The sound suddenly stopped and the thief sat for several tense moments, listening intently. Nothing. Harcourt took a deep breath and steeled himself. He cautiously opened the door a crack and peered in but could make out nothing in the darkness of the room.

Harcourt rolled the moss covered stone into the room and it stopped somewhere in the center as it hit what appeared to be a reading chair. This room was large, as the glow from the moss could not illuminate the room's walls. Strangely, the floor of this room did not have the layer of dust that was so common throughout the rest of the fortress. Well, wizards did love their libraries, the thief thought; this room may get much use. The air inside was cold but not as cold as it was in the presence of the Lich Lord. That gave the thief some small hope.

He could not find the source of the shuffling sound in the gloom, so he slipped into the library, quietly closing the door behind him. The thief was greeted with the familiar smell of musty old books and figured he must have found the right place.

In he went, despite the hairs on his neck which stood on end. Silently, he made his way towards his stone. He would need it, in order to locate a torch or lantern in the room, that he could use for more light. Otherwise it would take him forever to find anything in here.

Suddenly, out of the darkness, a hand reached out and grabbed the thief by his right arm. To his credit, Harcourt managed to stay silent and not cry out in alarm. He attempted to pull his arm free but he was caught in an iron grip.

With his left hand, Harcourt drew one of his daggers and plunged it into the arm that held him tight. To his surprise, there was no cry of pain and the hand did not let him go. He pulled the blade free and slashed out for the shoulder. The thief felt his weapon bite deep into flesh but still no reaction as the arm pulled him violently towards whatever owned it.

Harcourt dropped to the floor, using his weight to pull his attacker off balance and down to the floor with him. The pair crashed hard on the stone floor and the thief slipped from the grasping hand. Harcourt crawled across the floor towards the stone; he needed more light to see who, or what, was attacking him.

As he grabbed the stone, the hand grabbed his right ankle. There was an unnerving moaning sound coming from the owner of that strong grip. Harcourt twisted around, holding the stone before him and was greeted with a horrific sight. He recognized his attacker immediately, though he had changed, and not for the better. The bald, heavy-set man Harcourt had known as Garth, held the thief's leg, and pulled it towards his opened mouth.

Garth's flesh was pale and rotted in spots, hanging from his body, his eyes a milky white, devoid of life and intelligence. The prisoner who had escaped the Cult's mountain hideout with Harcourt and the others, was now some zombie-like creature bent on feasting and Harcourt was on the menu.

Harcourt had never liked Garth. There was something unpleasant about the man, but nobody deserved a fate such as this. It was one thing to be dead, another altogether to be brought back in some mockery of your living self. Strangely, the zombie did not smell of death. The thief figured whatever dark magic had raised the former prisoner had also kept it from smelling foul.

With all his strength, Harcourt kicked Garth in the face with his free foot, planting his boot heel squarely in the man's nose. Harcourt fought back the urge to vomit as Garth's nose was torn from his face and fell to the floor. Still, the zombie did not let go.

Harcourt remembered stories of zombies, stories told to children and tales told in taverns. It was one of the things that the people of Stonewood feared would rise up from the graveyard at night, to feast on those who lingered there after dark. But the thief did not recall hearing of how one went about killing a zombie. Killing it again, that is, since it was already dead. A vampire, as Harcourt had recently found out, required a wooden stake to the heart. Perhaps the heart was also the key here as well.

Harcourt rolled several feet to this left and thankfully,

the twisting motion broke Garth's grip. The thief jumped to his feet and dropped his stone, drawing his second dagger. Garth too, struggled to stand on rotting legs. The zombie was strong, inhumanly so, but slow, the thief realized.

As Garth stood to his full height, Harcourt raced in and sunk one of his daggers into what should have been the undead man's heart. If the zombie felt any pain, it never showed. Garth reached to grab the thief again but Harcourt ducked under his arms and slipped in behind him, slashing one of his calves. The wound was deep but had no effect as Garth turned, mouth open and moaning, intent on catching the thief.

Harcourt nearly tripped over the leg of a table, as he strayed too far from the light of the moss-covered stone. At least, he thought, the zombie did not make much noise aside from the moaning and shuffling, and with luck, the lich might never hear the struggle.

The thief darted in again, this time piercing the zombie's throat. Garth never slowed and managed to grab the front of Harcourt's armor. Desperately, the thief hacked at the zombie's arm, until to his surprise, he severed it.

Harcourt stumbled back, with the disembodied arm, still attached to his armor. Garth came shambling forward. Disgusted, the thief tried to break the grasp of the rotting arm but it held on firmly. In Harcourt's distraction, the zombie was on him again.

With his one good arm, Garth again held the thief and leaned in to take a bite out of his shoulder. Panic-stricken, Harcourt drove a dagger straight into Garth's forehead, burying it, hilt-deep.

The horrible moaning ceased and the zombie slumped to the floor. Ah, the brain, he mused, as he fought to catch his breath, must have been the brain. Harcourt desperately tried to rip the arm off the front of his leather breastplate and eventually did, severing several rotted fingers in the process. Again, he fought back the urge to vomit and did his best to compose himself.

Harcourt suspiciously watched Garth's body for several long moments, making sure it was not going to rise up again. Finally satisfied, he retrieved his stone and walked the perimeter of the library, which was lined with bookcases. He found four torches, one on each wall, and lit two of them, using some flint and tinder which he had brought with him. It was amazing how some light made the room less frightening, he mused. Well, except for the rotting corpse laying in the middle of the floor.

Now the thief could see that literally thousands of books occupied the library. Bookcases were overflowing along the four walls of the room. There were two long, ornately-carved wooden tables, along with several comfortable-looking reading chairs. The library was spotless, not a single cobweb, or speck of dust. Wizards sure did like their books, the thief figured.

An obsidian podium caught Harcourt's eye. It looked as though it was carved from stone, the same black stones that made up the fortress keep. But it was the book that lay on top of the podium that the thief found curious. He walked over for a closer inspection and could not believe his luck. There, laying in front of him, was the book that Fezzdin had described to him. Bound in red leather, with the sigil of the great wizard, Aspiron, etched into the cover. Harcourt was told that this book of ancient spells was penned over a thousand years ago by one of the most powerful wizards that ever lived. Few wizards alive today could even read the contents of the book; fewer still could cast the spells contained within.

Harcourt had thought the search here would be a tedious one, since there were thousands of books within the room. He even imagined that the lich might have had this book, and others of importance, locked away or even warded with protective spells. But here it sat, in plain view. The thief even wondered if perhaps Mortimus had been reading this particular book just recently. And then, what would happen when he noticed it missing? That was another problem that would have to wait.

Harcourt was never one to look a gift horse in the mouth, so picked up the ancient tome and stuffed it into a sack. He took one last glance at what was left of the man, Garth, shook his head, then traced his steps back to the courtyard, outside the keep. Since finding the book had been relatively simple, the fight with the zombie aside, Harcourt still had plenty of time, so as not to worry Symm. He hoped nothing had happened to the cavalryman, since he did not know how to ride a horse.

Harcourt smiled. He was proud of himself. He had accomplished his mission and now prayed that the others were successful with theirs. His thoughts went to Krestina and hoped she was safe. She would have Dornell and Na'Jala by her side and that gave the thief much comfort. A man could not ask for two better friends than them. They were real friends, genuine, not that farce that Andil had led him to believe for years.

Harcourt breathed in the cool night air and found that it had gotten much colder than when he had been in the courtyard earlier. Shivering slightly, he climbed the fortress' outer wall and left Morgaldrun behind.

\*    \*    \*    \*

Mortimus Runefeld, the Lich Lord of Morgaldrun, stood invisible, on one of the keep's battlements. He watched the curious thief climb the protective wall and vanish into the night. He remembered the rogue as one of the four men who passed through his home not long ago. Only three of them had left, though.

So, the lich mused to himself, the Cult had actually succeeded in freeing the demon lord, Lucivenus. Mortimus had not believed that possible. The High Priest in charge of the Cult must have been powerful indeed.

The lich did believe that the Cult should be stopped and the demon lord banished again, from this world. But Mortimus was not the one to do it. He could not be bothered to save Stonewood, and the world, a second time. Let others do all the work this time, he figured. He allowed the thief to think that he had stolen the book. Let him take the book to that young wizard, Fezzdin, and let them deal with Lucivenus.

But, he thought to himself, he would have that book back, when this was all done.

# CHAPTER 21

Na'Jala was first through the secret door, which led from Stonewood's sewers into the temple of the One True God. Since the Cult's last attack on the temple, it lay empty, abandoned and much of the architecture ruined. The former gladiator worried more about how structurally-sound the temple was and less about any cultists left behind to stand guard.

The skinny thief, Andil, was next, carrying a torch to light the way. Behind him was Krestina who held a small lantern. Her eyes teared up at the state of the temple and the memories of that first horrific attack by the Cult. She was not supposed to feel anger and hatred but she did. She wished revenge for all her fellow priests and priestesses who fell to Cult blades. Dornell followed the priestess, keeping a vigilant watch behind them as Andil guided Na'Jala, up ahead.

Carpets and furniture had been put to the torch. Statues and sculptures, toppled and destroyed. Many of the walls were crumbling, making some corridors impassable.

The Cult had really left their mark here. Thankfully, there did not appear to be any cultists left behind.

Andil had never actually been inside the temple before but remembered studying the map he was shown, some time ago. His memory was sharp, for soon they were descending the steps to the temple's basement. This area had not been spared the Cult's wrath either and each of them looked to the cracked ceiling, hoping they would not get buried alive.

The skinny thief pointed to a chamber, at the end of a particularly long corridor and found the room strewn with rubble from crumbling walls and a partially-collapsed ceiling.

"This is the room," Andil whispered.

"From the looks of it, the Cult knew the entrance to the crypts were here but could not get in. They have nearly destroyed the chamber," Dornell commented.

After some exploration, Andil called the others over to where he stood. Large chunks of stone, from the ceiling above, almost completely blocked a stone door, an ornately-carved cross etched into its surface.

"This is it, but the keyhole may be inaccessible," Andil said, climbing onto the rubble.

Na'Jala attempted to move some of the large stones, to no avail. They were simply too big and too heavy. Andil snaked his skeletal arm, down behind a gap. He struggled to reach the key hole and had his arm not been as skinny as it was, they would not have heard the click, as the key turned and the door unlocked.

Dornell rushed over and with all his strength, pushed on one of the exposed sections of the door. Reluctantly, it opened, blasting them with a wave of cool, stale air. The only problem now - the exposed gap to the crypts was quite small, almost too small. Dornell did his best to clear a section of rubble away but met with the same result as Na'Jala. The chunks of stone were too heavy.

"Wonderful, we find the temple unguarded, we open the door to the crypts, now we cannot get in," Dornell lamented.

"I think I can fit," Krestina said, climbing up on the stones to peer into the dark chamber beyond. "It's a tight fit but I can do it."

Before Dornell could object, the priestess was already wiggling through up to her waist. Na'Jala held her legs, keeping her from falling through to the other side. It was a tight fit, as she had said, and she suffered a few scrapes and bruises on her hips and legs, but eventually slid through to the other side.

She stood and dusted her robe off as best she could. "Pass me the torch," she said, poking her head through the gap, "I cannot see a thing in here."

"I do not like this," Dornell admitted. "We do not know what it is in there."

"We have no choice, Captain," she replied. "I need to find that mace."

"Get in there," Dornell turned to Andil and commanded.

"What?"

"Na'Jala and myself cannot fit through there but you can. She is not going in there alone. So get in there."

"I was only supposed to unlock the door, I am no warrior," the thief pleaded.

"And neither is she! I will not have her in there alone."

The look on Dornell's face told Andil that arguing was not going to help. The skinny thief passed his torch to Na'Jala and climbed effortlessly through the gap. The former gladiator then passed the torch back to the thief. He and Dornell needed the priestess's lantern so they would not be left in the dark.

"Be careful," Dornell said to the pair. "At the first sign of any trouble, come right back."

"We will be fine, everyone in here should already be dead," Krestina flashed a smile.

That was what he was worried about, considering the recent events with the vampire and the wraith, but kept those concerns to himself.

As Andil hesitated, Krestina snatched the torch from his grasp and crept forward. She put on a brave face but her heart raced. There should be nothing to be worried about, she tried to tell herself, but creeping about in a pitch-black crypt was more than just a little unnerving.

It was not long before the pair was descending down some steps, deeper into the underground chambers. They were now in a long corridor of upright tombs that lined both sides of the walls. Upon closer inspection, Krestina could see the names of those buried within and the dates they had died. Several dated back hundreds of years.

"Do not get too close to the coffins," whispered the thief, nervously.

"Why?"

"The dead do not like to be disturbed."

"Stop that," scolded the priestess. She was already scared and she did not need him adding fuel to her imagination.

But she took his advice and they continued down the

corridor. It seemed to stretch on forever, as they passed by easily a hundred tombs. Some names Krestina remembered from her studies. Folk who had done great things, in the name of God and in service to the temple and Stonewood.

Not just anyone was buried in the holy crypts and it had been quite some time since someone had, as was evident from the thick, undisturbed dust that covered the corridor's floor. Krestina did take some comfort in the fact that no footprints were visible. Andil too, took note of that and felt somewhat relieved.

Krestina broke the silence. "I remember you."

"Eh? Yeah, we were rescued from the same prison cells."

"No, before that. You were Harcourt's friend."

"Was."

"I remember seeing you both together, many times."

"Long ago," the skinny thief said, with a distant look. "But I don't recall you. We never hung around the temple."

"I didn't grow up in the temple. I grew up in the orphanage."

"Ah, then that makes sense but I still don't recall you. I usually remember all the pretty girls."

"I was very young then."

That puzzled the thief, since she looked to be at least as old as he was. Andil had a baby face but was in his thirties. The priestess, while still beautiful, appeared slightly older than that. He kept that opinion to himself, seeing as how women were sensitive about such things.

"Why did you say 'was'?" she inquired.

"Eh?"

"I said you were Harcourt's friend and you said 'was'."

"We were friends, kinda, but that was long ago."

"What happened?"

"Things."

"What kind of things?"

"Just things, alright?"

Krestina halted. "Look, I am a little scared in here, I admit it. Talking is keeping my mind from wandering."

Andil sighed. "Harcourt hates me. Why don't we just leave it at that?"

"Harcourt hardly hates anyone. You are clearly not a Cult member, so hate is probably the wrong word."

"No, he hates me."

"You must have done something terrible then."

"I did, that much I admit. I am no hero and I let him down."

"Did you betray him?"

"Something like that. Him and Jalanna."

Andil took note of the change in expression on the priestess's face at the mention of Harcourt's old lover. "You like him, don't you?" he asked.

"I love him. I always have."

Ah, that explains it then, he thought. "Are you two, together then?"

"As together as two people can be, during these times, yes."

"An odd pairing, a priestess and a thief. I wonder what your God thinks of that?"

"He is not a thief, not anymore."

Andil chuckled. "Oh? Just the leader of all the thieves, then?"

"That was for the betterment of this city and to deal with this Cult."

"I suppose."

"Harcourt couldn't have hated you too much, he still freed you from your cell that night."

"That's just who he is, that is typical Harcourt. He helps others." Then he muttered, "Unlike me."

"What was that?"

"Be good to him, he deserves that."

"Look," she said, "the corridor ends. Maybe that is the chamber of First Priest Ulanov, up ahead."

The torchlight cast spooky shadows which had both of them on edge as they crept cautiously into what turned out to be a very large, circular chamber. The room had a high, domed ceiling and was occupied by several stone coffins. Six of the coffins lay against the walls while a seventh large coffin sat in the center of the room. It was elaborately carved into the shape of a man, lying on his back. A tall cross made of solid gold rose up from the man's stomach. Four bright green emeralds were embedded at each end of the golden cross. Andil's eyes lit up at the sight of that priceless treasure.

Krestina jumped upon noticing another occupant of the chamber, then relaxed as she realized it was only a stone statue. It stood about seven feet tall and was rather featureless. The statue was carved into the likeness of a person in that it had legs, and arms and a head, but the face was smooth and without any detail.

"Oh, look," the priestess said, more to herself, "here lies First Priestess Leeanne. She was the first female to be named a first priestess. I have read all about her in the history books," then she frowned, remembering the temple's library had been torched by the Cult.

Andil did not seem to hear her, his attention glued to the golden cross. Krestina  moved to the center tomb, shifting her focus back to the mission.

"The tomb of First Priest Ulanov, it is beautiful," she commented.

"Indeed it is," the skinny thief replied but his observation was directed more at the jewel-laden cross.

Krestina ran her hands over the smooth stone coffin, wondering just how they would open it. And, not for the first time, she had to wonder if they even should. Was that not some terrible sin, to open a tomb and take something from inside? Especially a holy relic? But she had to remember the cause. They were not tomb raiders, this was necessary to save countless lives and restore order to this great city.

"You are a thief, how do we open this?" she asked, after inspecting most of the coffin.

Andil shook himself from his trance and joined the priestess. He passed the torch over top, leaning in close, going over every inch of the priest's final resting place. He stopped at the foot of the coffin, running his hand over a certain spot that he had noticed but Krestina had not.

"Let's give this a try," he said.

He pressed on the curious spot he found and the pair jumped back, as the sound of stone, grating against stone, echoed off the walls. The thick stone lid of the coffin began to slide over, until there was just enough space to expose the ancient occupant, contained within.

The priestess and thief stood frozen in place for several long moments after the noise had ceased, until Krestina's courage revived. She peered inside the tomb and made the sign of the cross over her chest, upon viewing the skeletal remains of First Priest Ulanov. There he lay, wearing a simple brown robe, his hands resting on his chest. Beside the priest lay the holy mace that they sought. The hammer-like weapon had a black handle, long enough for a two-handed grip, with a silver head.

The holy weapon appeared heavy but was actually as light as a feather, Krestina realized, when she got the courage to lift it from the tomb. She caught her breath, waiting for something terrible to happen, but nothing did. There was no booming of thunder and she was not struck down by a bolt of lightning.

She exhaled with relief. "That was somewhat simple. See if you can close the lid and let's get out of here." She leaned over the tomb one more time. "Thank you, First Priest. We will put this to good use and return it to you when we are finished."

Andil tried pushing on the same spot as before and they were rewarded, as the stone lid slid securely back into place.

"How did you know where to push? I didn't see anything out of the ordinary," Krestina inquired.

"You don't have the eyes of a thief," Andil replied, handing the torch to the priestess. "Lead the way, Dornell must be worried sick about you."

With the torch in one hand and the mace in the other, Krestina walked to the corridor that led back to the others. As her back turned, Andil darted towards the golden cross. With lightning-speed, he drew a knife and plucked an emerald from the treasure. Just as he stuffed the gem into a pocket, his heart sank, as motion caught the corner of his eye.

The stone statue, that had stood motionless against the wall, now began to move. As it took its first step forward, the loud boom, echoed off the walls, causing Krestina to whirl around with a yelp. Her face paled, watching the featureless statue walking towards the skinny thief.

If Krestina's face was pale, words could not describe the shade of color the thief's face was now. "A golem! RUN!" he shouted, panic evident in his voice.

Fear had rooted him in place until the golem swung a stony first at his head. Andil ducked underneath and ran for the exit, shoving Krestina along in front of him.

"What is a golem?" she asked, running as fast as she could.

"A magical construct, created to protect something."

"What do we do? It must want the mace back!" she figured.

That gave the thief an idea. "No, I don't think it is the mace it was protecting."

The thief stopped and pulled the emerald from his pocket, holding it out towards the pursuing, stone creature. He tossed it back towards the chamber and it rolled right passed the golem. To Andil's horror, it paid it no heed and still marched towards him. The golem meant to punish the thieves who had defiled the golden cross; that was its sole purpose.

Krestina glanced back just in time to witness Andil, throw the emerald. She gritted her teeth in anger; the greedy thief had brought this on. They were probably free to take the mace in time of great need, but to steal treasure was a punishable sin.

The golem was determined, but slow. They soon

outdistanced the magical creature and flew up the stairs with great speed. Krestina began shouting for Dornell, as they neared the rubble-blocked door to the crypts. She then realized, they could not squeeze through that gap in time. A quick glance back revealed the golem was now ascending the stairs, each step it took, a loud echoing boom.

Dornell's face was now in the small gap. "What is going on in there??"

"Golem!" Krestina answered frantically.

The former captain had heard of golems before, usually in reference to guarding the homes of wizards. Fezzdin would know how to deal with a golem, but Fezzdin was not here.

"Quickly then, lass, squeeze through," Dornell implored.

Dornell and Na'Jala renewed their efforts to clear some of the rubble away but still met with failure. Krestina was about to attempt to climb through, when she was nudged by Andil. She turned to find the golem nearly upon them.

"STOP!!" the priestess commanded, attempting a spell that would usually immobilize an opponent.

The spell had no effect and she found herself roughly shoved into the wall of the corridor, dropping the torch. The golem swung at her with a huge, stony fist but Andil knocked her aside at the last possible moment. It turned its attention to the skinny thief which allowed Krestina the chance to scramble away, back towards the stairs.

As Andil agilely ducked and dodged the golem's attacks, an idea struck the priestess. She steeled her courage and ran at the golem, striking it in the back with the holy mace. The weapon was designed to paralyze unholy beings and Krestina was saddened when the magic of the mace had no effect. The golem was not an unholy creature and had been created by one of the priests of the temple, therefore was immune to the mace. It was however, still a magical weapon and had chipped a piece off the golem's stony back. But, Krestina was simply not strong enough to do it any real damage and looking to the skinny thief, neither was he.

The golem swung its arm back and Krestina almost did not get out of the way in time. She found herself between the golem and the dead end, once again. Thinking herself doomed, she ran to the door of the crypt and tossed the holy mace through the gap.

"Make good use of that, Captain Dornell, rid this city of that demon filth," she said.

"You are going to see that day, along with me," Dornell countered. "Just keep away from that thing while we think. Run back the way you came."

Andil scooped up the fallen torch and kept the golem's attention while Krestina ran past, back towards the stairs. The skinny thief soon joined her and they sped down the stairs again, reaching the long corridor. To their surprise, the golem did not pursue.

"It's guarding the only exit," Andil surmised, trying to catch his breath.

"What??"

"It probably knows we have to go back that way in order to escape. It could stand there for eternity, ensuring we do not get passed it."

"I don't want to die in here," Krestina said, her eyes tearing up.

"And you won't," the skinny thief replied, pulling her back up the stairs. "I am going to hold its attention while you climb through and escape."

"No, we will think of something together," the priestess protested.

"No time for that. I got you into this, I will get you out. Time to be the hero, for once in my life. I owe this to Harcourt. I could not save Jalanna, so I will at least save you."

"Dornell could fetch Fezzdin, they could help us."

"No time for that," he repeated, shoving her along to the top of the steps. "Now, as soon as it rushes for me, get passed it and get out of here."

Before Krestina could argue further, the thief ran towards the golem, waving the torch in the air. "Here I am, I took the emerald, come get me."

The golem began marching towards Andil and swung its fists, looking to crush the thief. He dodged the attacks and Krestina ran past, finding her opening. The golem turned to regard her and Andil kicked the creature, drawing its attention back. The thief continued to backpedal, waving the torch in the golem's face.

Krestina scrambled up to the gap and stuck her head and arms through. From the other side, Na'Jala grabbed her arms. This was no time to be gentle, he thought, and pulled her through with all his strength.

The priestess cried out with pain as her hips and legs were once again scraped and bloodied by the jagged stones. But she was through and safe.

Andil led the golem as close to the stairs as it would go, before stopping again. With great speed, he lunged past his giant stone adversary and sprinted for the door. The thief was skinnier than Krestina and had less of a problem climbing through the gap, earlier. Andil reached through and Dornell grabbed his arms. The former captain pulled the thief halfway out, before his progress halted. It was now a tug-of-war over the skinny thief, and Dornell lost.

With a scream of horror, Andil vanished back through the gap. There was a sickening crunch of bones and then all was silent, save for the footsteps of the golem, returning to the burial chamber, its duty completed.

# CHAPTER 22

Two horses pulled a covered wagon towards one of the two checkpoints where the south district led to the lower east district. Fifteen guards loyal to the Cult, stood watch here day and night.

It was the middle of the morning, so there was plenty of traffic going to and from the market square. It was not uncommon for merchants to pass by, their wagons laden with goods.

"Halt," a burly guard commanded, stepping in front of one of the passing wagons and addressing the two cloaked drivers. "Where are you going and what's in the wagon?"

"We are taking some clothing, to sell in the market," a female voice said from within the hood of her dark cloak.

"Corvan, Rees, search the wagon," ordered the post commander.

"You do not want to do that," the woman remarked.

"Pardon me? We will do as we wish."

The guard named Corvan, approached the rear of the

wagon and pulled the cover off the top. Corvan did not even have time to get his sword free before a grey-skinned monstrosity rose up from the wagon and crushed his skull with a massive warhammer.

With the help of some friendly priestesses, Vrawg was fully healed and extremely angry. He had spent too long hiding away. Now, it was time to take out his anger on those who invoked it in the first place. With a roar, the half-ogre leaped from the wagon and brought his hammer down onto the head of Rees, crushing him like an insect.

"You were warned," Evonne said, grabbing her crossbow that was hidden beside her.

The blonde bounty hunter fired and caught the post commander, who stood rooted with shock, right in the throat. He fell to the dusty ground and died moments later. Taking advantage of the momentary confusion, Evonne quickly reloaded and felled a second guard before drawing her sabre and leaping from the wagon.

Naziya, the brown-skinned warrior of Ryor-Suul who sat next to Evonne on the wagon, followed suit, drawing a similar curved sword and leaping into battle.

Folk scrambled off the street, as far from the skirmish as possible, but turned to watch with amazement. It was terrifying for those who were just passing by, and yet exhilarating, all at the same time. As guards fell over each other, attempting to put distance between themselves and the giant bounty hunter, they were cut down by the blindingly-fast sword-arms of two women.

Evonne and Naziya fought well together. They were of similar size and while their fighting styles differed slightly, they were equally as effective. The guards who stood their ground found the women impossible to hit and if they were not felled by the women's blades, their bones were crushed by the half-ogre's hammer.

It was not long before the bodies of fourteen guards, littered the dirty street. The last guard had seen enough and ran for his life, towards the lower east district. Evonne raced to the wagon and reloaded her crossbow. She took aim and fired, the bolt lodging itself in the man's back. He fell and rolled about in pain, attempting to remove the bolt. Naziya strolled over to the guard and put an end to his suffering. The gathered crowd cheered.

*   *   *   *

Brother Delfin, a Cult priest, strode arrogantly through a south district street surrounded by ten guards. He liked the way people scrambled aside, allowing them passage through the crowded street, fear plainly visible upon their dirty faces. Before the take-over of Lucivenus, Brother Delfin had lived in the lower west district and had never before set foot in the south district. It was a dangerous place, controlled largely by the Thieves Guild. Now, though, the priest walked with confidence; the Cult ruled this city and people knew their place.

Near the mouth of a dark alley, someone caught Delfin's eye. It was a stunningly attractive woman, her hair blonde, with bright red streaks throughout. She was dressed as a common harlot, with little left to the imagination. She smiled at the priest and he figured a little distraction would be nice. It would be free too, if she knew what was good for her.

"Keep an eye on the street, I will be back momentarily," Delfin said with a sly smile, to one of his guards.

The guard watched jealously, as the priest exchanged a few words with the beautiful woman, then the pair disappeared into the alley. That one was a nice find, he thought to himself, since many of the women in this area were filthy and unhealthy looking. He would have to remember this street and see if he could find her, later that day.

That was quick, he chuckled, as the woman emerged from the alley. She casually walked back onto the street alone, then the guard's eyes went wide as he noticed her using her skirt to wipe blood from a dagger.

The guard was about to bellow a command when from the corner of his eye, he noticed a dark-cloaked man rush to his side. He saw a weasily-looking face within the cloak's hood, then a dagger penetrated his stomach.

As the guard fell to his knees, the crowd around them erupted into action. Some wielded swords, others clubs. The cultists were beaten down and slaughtered in the middle of the street. Feylane wore a wicked grin, while wiping the last of the blood from her dagger.

\* \* \* \*

Zordan Crow led his men to the front of the Belching Bard tavern. Zordan was a Cult warrior, fiercely loyal to Sarvin and Lucivenus. His cunning and battle prowess had led to his special assignment to root out the King and his supporters, within the south district. Finally, the cultist had received a valuable tip, that the King's son, Prince Orval himself, was using this tavern as a base of operations. If Zordan could capture the prince, it would bring the King out of hiding.

He motioned for the twelve men with him to draw swords, then kicked open the front door to the tavern. With the night time curfew in effect, taverns were now busiest during the day. The Belching Bard was packed to capacity this afternoon and all patrons turned to regard the cultists, as they stormed in.

Zordan shoved a path through the main taproom, scattering tables and patrons alike, 'til his men stood in the center.

"I will make this simple! Hand over Prince Orval Stonewood and the rest of your filthy lives will be spared," he shouted to the crowd.

As two men seated near the tavern's entrance rose and barred the door, the barkeep turned and put down the mug he had been drying. He was a tall, slender man, with a patch over one eye.

"I am afraid, it is not going to be as easy as that," replied Patch, the former bandit leader.

Several of the tavern's patrons pulled small, concealable crossbows from beneath their cloaks and fired. A handful of Zordan's men were dead before swords met swords, in the cramped quarters of the tavern.

The fighting was ferocious, for as long as it lasted. Zordan himself took down three of the patrons-turned-thugs, before losing his head to Patch.

\* \* \* \*

A savage battle took place in the street, at a checkpoint where the south district met the lower west. Word of fights breaking out had spread and Cult reinforcements had arrived.

A Cult priest spoke the words of a spell and his eyes glowed red for a moment, before a Guild thug dropped to his knees, paralyzed. A sword then found the immobilized man's chest and ran him through.

The priest turned his attention to another man but the words of his next spell did not reach his lips, as a sword now burst from his chest from behind.

With a growl, Randar kicked the priest in the back, freeing his sword before turning it on the next closest cultist. Four bodies lay around the Guild thug as he paused to survey the scene before him.

He and some other Guild members had control of the checkpoint, before others had arrived. One of the cultists managed to blow his horn, signaling for aid before Randar could get to him. They were now outnumbered and two more of the vile priests numbered among the reinforcements. As much as it bothered the thug, they would have to retreat until Patch or Feylane arrived with help.

One of the priests pointed to Randar and barked a command to the other cultists. The smug look on the priest's face vanished, as the shaft of an arrow suddenly protruded from his chest. With a quick glance upwards, Randar spotted an archer in a dark green cloak, perched on the roof of a building.

A war cry erupted from an alley and Prince Orval Stonewood, now clean-shaven and wearing his gleaming, silver plate armor, rushed the cultists, with many armed soldiers in tow. These men-at-arms were borrowed from several noble families who had pledged their support, though they did not wear their house insignias into battle.

Orval and thirty-five soldiers routed the cultists, then chased them down and slaughtered them, to the man.

"I will leave these men here, to hold this position. I have others on their way to help hold the other key location with the bounty hunters," the prince said to Randar, figuring he was the one in charge of the street thugs.

The prince despised working with the Guild but beggars could not be choosers, in these dark times of need. He screwed his face up in disgust as he watched the stocky, shaved-headed thug remove the heads of two priests and carry them past.

"What are you doing with those?" Orval demanded to know.

"I am going to display them here, as a warning," Randar replied, matter-of-factly.

"That is not how we do things in my city."

"It's not your city, not yet anyways."

*   *   *   *

Evonne ducked back behind the wall of a shop, as an arrow nearly took her nose off. She reloaded her crossbow and cursed inwardly, noticing she was almost out of ammunition. The petite bounty hunter had found herself in a shoot-out with some Cult reinforcements. So far she had managed to halt their advance on the checkpoint, killing any brave souls who attempted to rush their position. But they now had an archer to keep the deadly blonde marksman ducking for cover.

Vrawg stood behind a wall on the opposite side of the street, hurling pieces of a wagon whenever an opportunity presented itself. One cultist already lay dead, after taking a wagon wheel to the head.

Evonne knew the cultists held back mostly because they did not know how many people they were up against. They might be a little braver if they knew that only she, Vrawg and Naziya, were currently holding this checkpoint. With only a handful of bolts left, they would not be holding this spot for much longer, she figured.

Evonne spun and cursed at the sound of sword against sword, ringing behind her. Small battles were currently taking place all over the south district. Those Cult members who were lucky enough to flee had to head for either of the checkpoints, to make for the lower east or west districts.

Naziya was now engaged with one such deserter. The man had caught her by surprise and she was off-balance, attempting to get her footing. Evonne raised her crossbow and took aim but the exotic warrior drove her blade through the cultist's stomach before Evonne could fire.

A second deserter made the mistake of running towards Vrawg's position. The half-ogre swatted the man with his hammer, sending him several feet in the air to land bloodied and broken.

Something told Evonne to turn and she noticed two of the reinforcements boldly advancing down the middle of the street. She shot one in the face and as he fell, the second retreated back to where the others hid behind a building. Again, the archer had Evonne also ducking back for cover.

The sounds of jingling chain mail from a nearby alley made her heart sink. She could hear several men running closer and she worried that she and her companions might be sandwiched between two forces.

She reloaded but breathed a sigh of relief as many men, recruited by the prince, jogged around a corner and gave her a salute. Their weapons and armor were bloody, having met with battle already in the streets. But now, they were ready to bolster her position here.

The cultists, noting the arrival of more enemy soldiers, deemed it wise to retreat back further into the lower east district.

*     *     *     *

High Priest Sarvin marched down the castle corridor, flanked by two of his personal guards. Lucivenus had summoned him and made sure he knew it was important.

Sarvin had spent the last hour turning his old office upside down, searching for one particular book. He was clearing out the last of his personal effects to make room for the new Chief Magistrate, when he noticed the book missing. At first, he assumed it was merely misplaced, but now, he was sure that it was gone.

The High Priest deduced that that was the purpose of the break-in they suffered recently. The man had been disguised as King Stonewood but in fact, it had been the thief named Harcourt. He must have come to the castle to steal the book. And how he had pulled that off still remained a mystery. How he even knew about the book, was an even deeper mystery.

The book outlined the way that Lucivenus could be defeated and banished from this world again. But the tools needed to perform this task, Sarvin knew, would not be easy for Fezzdin and his companions to acquire.

Sarvin entered the room where Lucivenus gazed out at the city from a small balcony. The demon lord turned to face the High Priest. "The south district is revolting."

"Yes, it is a disgusting place," Sarvin replied, misunderstanding the importance of that revelation.

"No, you fool, the thieves and the King's supporters are fighting back," the demon lord's booming voice rattled portraits on the wall. "You have lost the district!"

"Me? How have I lost the district?"

"You have eyes in the district. Your raven-haired witch could not have informed us of this, before it began?"

Sarvin wanted to mention the two half-demons that Lucivenus liked to rely upon so much but held his tongue. "There have been skirmishes throughout the city ever since you took over. Nothing major."

"This is different! They have taken control of the south district. Our forces were decimated and forced to retreat. This is an embarrassment."

"What of the soul wraith?" Sarvin inquired.

"It still exists and still hunts its prey but that is all I know. But according to you, it hunts an insignificant thief. His death matters little to me. The King, or the prince, or whoever is in charge of this revolt, is the head that I want. How am I ever to expand my kingdom when we cannot even take this filthy city?" Lucivenus clenched his fists in rage. "I will bring wraggoth troops into the city. I want two thousand of the beasts to scour the sewers, searching for hideouts. They are subterranean creatures, they will be in their element. Another force will swarm the south district. I also want our cavalry, with wraggoth to back them up, to destroy those mercenaries that are camped nearby. They are up to something. They number two thousand only, so we will wipe them out."

"We have the numbers to obliterate them all. It will be done."

"See that it is, or I will have you flayed to the bone."

The High Priest seethed with fury at that threat as he left the room. He would not be spoken to like that.

"My lord?" one of his guards said.

"What?" Sarvin barked back.

"The sorceress, Syrena, awaits you in the council chamber."

Sarvin made for the chamber with all haste, dismissing his guards before entering, wishing a private meeting with the sorceress.

"What do you have to say for yourself?" he asked, finding Syrena, sitting comfortably at the circular council table. " The south district is in chaos and you come here after the fact, to tell me?"

"I barely escaped with my life, my lord. There was no hint of what was planned beforehand, I swear it."

"Some fortune teller you are."

Sarvin was angry but it was not Syrena's fault. He was going to need loyal servants he could trust in the coming days, and those were too few now. The attractive sorceress was sorely needed and he wondered if she might make a good replacement for Devi-Lynn. Syrena was beautiful and cunning, her magical powers growing stronger.

"Prince Orval, and King Stonewood, if he still lives, have my very special tome, that we used to free Lucivenus."

"That's bad, is it?" Syrena wondered.

"Not entirely," the High Priest replied in a hushed tone, and the sorceress stared at him, curiously. He continued. "If that foolish wizard Fezzdin were to figure out how to imprison Lucivenus once again, then I would be left to rule."

"Isn't that treasonous talk? Didn't you dedicate your life to freeing Lucivenus?"

"I did, yes. And along the way I got a taste for power. I have led our order for more years than you have even been alive. I will not be cast aside like a dog and treated like a foolish lackey. I deserve to rule, I should rule!"

To say that Syrena was shocked by the High Priest's words was an understatement. She knew he was a power-hungry man but never expected him to betray the demon lord.

"If Lucivenus were to be defeated outside the castle, I would remain within and could hold the castle. We have more than enough wraggoth troops and I am still in control of Stonewood's armies. I have received a message back from General Zayne, of the northern army. He is still in command and awaiting my orders. Syrena, we can easily squash this rebellion and rule Stonewood without Lucivenus. You and I."

The sorceress sat up at the last comment the High Priest made; *you and I*, he had said. And now he eyed her up and down.

"You will be my right hand, Syrena, my most trusted ally. None will dare stand against us."

Syrena was speechless, at a total loss for words.

"From now on, I want to keep you near," he added. "From the balcony of my new quarters, we could watch the potential downfall of Lucivenus and the rise of King Sarvin! But how to get Lucivenus outside, for us to test Fezzdin's resourcefulness?"

# CHAPTER 23

Word had spread throughout Stonewood quickly that the King and his allies had taken control of the south district. As darkness fell over the city, the folk of the poorest district rejoiced and walked the streets freely, as they once did. Most expected the demon lord to retaliate but for now, they enjoyed themselves.

The citizens of the other districts peered hopefully through windows, praying the King and his followers would soon sweep through their district and rid the city of the vile Cult and its demonic leader.

Behind a boarded up building, in a dirty south-side alley, a dark figure silently slipped through a door. He soon heard the conversations of those huddled around a fire, in the middle of a large empty room. Fezzdin was very recognizable in the gloom, with his long white beard and tall conical hat. Beside him, though, was a sight of great relief to the silent figure who had just entered the room, a beautiful, brown-haired woman, wearing the brown robes of a priestess.

"Who is supposed to be watching that back door?" the man said, revealing himself.

Those in the room spun in surprise, hands on weapons, until the priestess Krestina screamed and ran for the man, wrapping him in a tight embrace. She wept tears of joy, her head buried in Harcourt's chest. The thief returned her hug with equal enthusiasm. He had been worried about her too but was confident in her abilities.

When the priestess finally released him, Harcourt tossed the book he carried to the wizard. "Next time, give me a harder challenge."

Dornell, who had been sitting in the corner of the room, rose and slapped his friend on the back, smiling and nodding with approval. "No run-ins with the lich, then?"

"Thankfully, no. Just our old friend Garth was there to greet me."

Before Dornell could ask him to explain that curious remark, Fezzdin cut in, after glancing quickly through the tome. "Excellent, excellent. Sister Krestina was successful as well. We have the mace and now we have the spellbook. I will require a few hours at the least, to study the book and prepare myself."

"Andil was helpful, then?" Harcourt wondered.

The room was silent for a few moments before Krestina told the tale of her escape from the temple's crypt. She had decided to exclude the part concerning the skinny thief stealing the emerald; nobody needed to know that. She spoke only of his bravery and his sacrifice, that allowed her to escape the golem.

Surprisingly, Harcourt felt a pang of sorrow. He figured it was just a reaction to the memory of the man that he once believed Andil to be, and not who he really had been. He was a conniving, backstabbing, con-man. But he had apparently saved Krestina's life, unselfishly, so Harcourt was grateful and wished he could have thanked him in person. Andil was now gone though and they had other matters to deal with.

"What about the wraith? Any more trouble?"

Fezzdin frowned. "It did return to the Ogre's Den but fortunately we had all left. I remained nearby to watch for it. It even paid a visit to the orphanage, though nobody was harmed, as you were not about. This creature will not rest and will hunt you for eternity, unless you, or it, is destroyed."

"How can we destroy it?"

Fezzdin was about to answer, then stopped and walked away, looking through the spellbook. Dornell wore a pained expression, then he too, turned and took his seat back in the corner. Harcourt was about to repeat his question when Krestina spoke up. "Harcourt, let's go into another room."

Curious, the thief followed the beautiful priestess into another empty room. Lit with a lantern and smaller than the previous room, she shut the door behind them.

"What is this about?"

Krestina struggled, trying to find the right words to explain to her lover. "Fezzdin and I consulted with Sister Tarrah and Brother Brallo. Fortunately, there was a record of an encounter, long ago, with a soul wraith."

"And it was defeated?"

"Yes, it eventually was, after much death and destruction."

"Perfect, so we know how to defeat it?"

"Essentially, yes." Krestina paused, then continued.

"The soul wraith is a terrible creature summoned from the underworld, as you know. It is bound by the blood of the person it hates the most, which, of course, is you, in this instance. Unholy magic brought this creature into this world and as Fezzdin had thought, holy magic is required to defeat it. A summoning is required, to counter it. A being as equally good and holy as the wraith is evil and unholy. In this case, an angel."

Harcourt had long ago gotten over the fact that everything he believed to be fairy tales, actually existed. "Can it be done? Can you summon an angel?"

"It may be possible. That priest who did so before was also considered 'chosen' by God, as people believe I have been."

"Then let's try it. What do we have to lose?"

"Harcourt, the angel will be linked to the wraith, much like the wraith is linked to you. So the soul of the angel will be the one who despises the soul of the wraith the most." Harcourt still did not catch on to her meaning. "This angel will be someone who may have had their life taken prematurely, by this Trascar. Someone who had everything dear to them stripped away by this vile man."

Then it dawned on the thief and his face paled. "Jalanna?"

"That is a very distinct possibility. Trascar murdered her, when she was at her happiest time. He killed her on her wedding day. We feel it would be her soul that would hate the wraith the most."

"You…..you would be summoning, Jalanna? Sh-she would be coming back?"

The priestess could see the obvious pain written across the thief's face. "Not the way that you think.

Harcourt, it won't be Jalanna as you remember her. It will be a holy being from the heavens, whose actions will be controlled by the soul of Jalanna. It will only remain here in this world, until the wraith is defeated. Then it will return home."

Harcourt stood glassy-eyed in silence for several long moments, while the weight of the priestess's words sunk in. He struggled with many different emotions, all at once.

"Harcourt, my love, what do you want to do? The wraith will not stop until you are dead and will kill anyone who tries to prevent it. I can't lose you again. We have worked so hard to free this city so we can have our lives back. A life together. But this decision is yours alone."

Harcourt closed his eyes and exhaled. "Alright, let's do it."

*     *     *     *

"Thelvius! Thelvius!" the mercenary soldier shouted, as he burst into their leader's tent.

Jag, the gigantic, bluish-grey war dog, woke from a deep sleep and stood, growling. He could sense the panic in the soldier's voice.

Thelvius looked up from a map that was spread out on a table before him. "What is it, Milton?"

Milton leaned on the map table and gasped to catch his breath before continuing. "A large number of the wraggoth were seen entering the city not long ago. Thousands, perhaps. Then the city's cavalry rode out. They joined with several thousand wraggoth and are heading our way at great speed. They will be upon us within the hour."

Thelvius stood. "How did they know we were here?

Prepare the men. I am not leaving this world without putting up one hell of a last stand." The mercenary leader scratched the dog on the head. "You ready, boy? Those cavalry haven't seen anything like you before."

Jag barked in response.

\*　　\*　　\*　　\*

Darrick handed General Frock the spyglass as the pair lay on top of a hill, hidden from view. Frock cursed; things were beginning to happen.

"My guess would be that the cavalry and those beasts are headed towards the mercenary army. That is roughly the direction where William said they were camped. They are going to be gravely outnumbered," the general guessed.

"Should we begin marching?"

Frock growled. "I hope William made it to Prince Orval. I was hoping we would have some direction from the prince and have a better understanding of what we are up against. Ready the men. I will not stand by and let those soldiers get slaughtered."

"Without the southern army, even we will be outnumbered."

\*　　\*　　\*　　\*

Prince Orval rushed into the bedroom of a house they were using as a hideout. Laying on the bed was a soldier he knew as William, the sheets around him, bloody.

William had been one of the brave men who left Stonewood to carry word of the Cult's take-over. Orval was informed that William had reached the northern army and that they were now camped fairly close to the city, awaiting orders.

"It was as you guessed, my lord. The northern army was in control of the Cult," William said, his voice labored. "But Captain Frock saw the truth and slew General Zayne. They await your orders, behind the Rolling Hills."

The soldier began coughing, blood appearing on his lips. Prince Orval laid a gentle hand on the man's chest. William had made it past the wraggoth army, sneaking back into the city, using the smuggling tunnel. But on his way to find the prince, he ran afoul of a Cult patrol and fought bravely. He managed to escape and to elude the cultists but suffered severe injuries. They had no priests or priestesses anywhere in the area as they were tied up elsewhere. William was not expected to pull through.

"You did well, my friend." Orval said. "Rest now, you have earned it."

"We know nothing of the southern army, there has been no word," he coughed again.

"Easy, easy. That's ok, you have brought the northern army back and for that you will be hailed as a hero. Get some rest, you will need your energy for the fight to come."

William Hamdon smiled and died shortly after the prince left the chamber.

"My lord, someone is here to see you. A woman," said one of the prince's men.

Prince Orval suddenly worried that something had gone wrong. Sister Krestina and Evonne should have been busy elsewhere and nobody else knew that he was here, in this particular house.

He walked to the foyer and his eyes went wide. There

was no mistaking the figure of Syrena even before she pulled back the hood of her jet-black cloak. The prince waved away some soldiers who watched the woman closely with suspicious eyes. "She is ok."

Orval took the beautiful, southern fortune teller by the hand and led her to another room where they could speak privately. He closed the door behind them and kissed her passionately but she held back, a worried expression on her face.

"I suppose you know my secret now, I apologize for the deception. How did you find me?"

"I have ways," she smiled, and she did.

The sorceress had cast a spell using a strand of the prince's hair that she had found in her shop. The spell allowed her to locate the prince's whereabouts.

"It is not safe for you to be around, cultists may still be hiding in the south district and we expect retaliation soon. Syrena, I was to going to tell you who I really was, eventually. It was for your own safety that I kept it from you. As you know, I am a wanted man."

"I always knew there was more to you than you let on. I am not mad. When I realized you were a prince, I took it upon myself to consult with spirits, to see what I might learn. The spirits revealed much to me."

"What did you learn?"

"There is a division within the Cult. The High Priest that summoned Lucivenus, Sarvin I think is his name, is not happy with the demon lord and his half-demon allies. The High Priest knows about a book that was stolen and wants to encourage Lucivenus to leave the castle to confront you and your father. Sarvin secretly hopes that you have found a way to banish Lucivenus, so that he can rule the city himself. He plans to remain within the castle and watch this all unfold from the comfort of his personal quarters, which used to be yours."

Prince Orval was surprised. That was a lot of detail to come from these spirits. Syrena was more powerful than he first thought.

"Also," she continued, "the Cult has sent out their cavalry to join with some wraggoth and annihilate the mercenaries camped nearby. On top of that, thousands of wraggoth have entered the city to scour the sewers and assault the south district. You and your people are in grave danger."

"You are sure about all this?"

"The spirits cannot lie to me when summoned by my spell."

"Once again, my beautiful Syrena, you have been a great help. You are going to be a princess, when this is all over, I promise you."

She smiled weakly.

"Now, I need you to stay somewhere safe. I can have some men escort you to another place where you can wait for this all to be over. Ok?"

"My Prince, I….."

"Orval, my name is Orval."

"Orval, Lucivenus is powerful. Beyond the capabilities of your wizard friend, Fezzdin, I fear. I can get us out of here. Can we not just leave together and start a new life elsewhere? Why throw away your life needlessly?"

"Syrena, now that you know I am Prince Orval, you must also know why I cannot leave. This is my city and I will not abandon it and its people to the fate of this vile Cult. We have the means to defeat Lucivenus and our northern army has returned. Shortly, I am leaving the city to join with the army and lead it against these filthy wraggoth. Fezzdin and my friends will deal with things inside the city until I ride through those front gates, my army behind me. We will win this."

Syrena had to try that one last time but she knew the prince would never leave his city. And thus, her dreams of a wonderful life vanished. Stonewood was no place for her. Either Sarvin would win and she would be forced to serve him for the rest of her life, or Orval would win and all would be right with the city, only Syrena could not remain. She could not live in the castle with the guilt of Prince Denniz weighing upon her conscience. Also, it would only be a matter of time before someone recognized her as the Cult's sorceress. The old man, Gervas, had seen her come and go from meetings with Sarvin, as with other staff members.

Prince Orval kissed her one last time before opening the door and calling someone to escort her to another location.

"It is not necessary, my dear. I have a secret spot below my shop, I am safe there. Do not fear for me, I will be fine."

"I will come get you then, the moment this is over."

The sorceress pulled up the hood of her cloak as she stepped outside the house and back onto the street. Princess Syrena…she liked the sound of that. But it was not meant to be. Tears welled up in her eyes as she glanced back at the house and thought about the life that could have been. She had been party to much evil and she hoped that the information she gave the prince would help redeem her, in some small way at least.

She spoke the words of a spell and vanished. Syrena the fortune teller was never seen in Stonewood again.

# CHAPTER 24

Harcourt, wearing the face of Weldrick, stood in a council chamber located within the Guild's headquarters. In front of him stood Feylane, the stunning assassin, her hair jet black.

"Thousands of wraggoth will soon be storming the sewers, searching for this hideout," he told her.

She shrugged. "Many have tried before, we are well hidden."

"These wraggoth are not human, they are subterranean creatures. They are more adept underground and have keen vision in the dark. They may succeed where others have failed. I think it best if you evacuate this location."

"So you are really going through with this mad idea? You are going to wear the face of the King and call out Lucivenus to fight?"

"Yes, it may be our only chance. We possess the tools now, to defeat him. We just need him to leave the castle, to engage with us. Prince Orval received information that

293

Sarvin wants Lucivenus gone. I believe the High Priest will urge the demon lord to face us. Sarvin plans to remain in the safety of the prince's old quarters, convinced that he will be able to hold this city even with Lucivenus gone. He doesn't yet realize that the northern army has returned. Orval has left to join them."

"But the castle is well fortified. Sarvin could hold out in there for quite some time, even if his wraggoth army is defeated."

Harcourt smiled. "Remember that secret entrance into the castle I told you about? Captain Gregor, the former captain of the castle guard, is leading a small force through that entrance. They will meet up with many imprisoned soldiers, loyal to the King."

"Well, sounds like you have everything sorted out. I am impressed. The High Priest, is still a powerful adversary and won't just give up."

"You are right, he won't. But at least he will not aid in the fight with Lucivenus. Then, we can deal with Sarvin later, alone."

Feylane stepped closer to the thief. "Harcourt, when this is all over... I...."

"I cannot wait for this to be over," he cut her off. "I cannot wait to go back to a normal life. I am thinking of even leaving Stonewood, with the priestess, Krestina, whom I love."

Feylane was a master of deception but this time, she could not mask the expression on her face. Harcourt had a feeling about where she was going with this conversation and had wanted to cut her off, before she said something that might embarrass herself. He knew that the assassin was not used to expressing feelings to anyone, and did not wish her to say something she would regret.

"Yes, exactly what I was going to say. I will be happy when this Cult is finally defeated and things return to normal," she said, though disappointment was evident in her voice. "Well, I have things to do. Good luck with the demon. Sorry I cannot help. Fighting demons is not in my repertoire."

"I understand. Look after yourself."

The assassin nodded and kissed him on the cheek, then quickly left the room. If not for Krestina, the thief would have been proud to share a life with Feylane. She had come a long way, from the cold, heartless viper he had first met. He knew that she struggled with emotions she was not used to and was looking to make some changes in her life. Feylane was the ultimate survivor. He knew she would get through this and would eventually find someone worthy of her. It just could not be him.

As Harcourt was about to leave the headquarters, he ran into Randar. There was a tense moment, as the Guild leader and the Guild enforcer stood staring at one another.

Randar spoke first. "The King better uphold his end of the deal and see us rewarded for all the work we have done. Or he may never get the chance to sit on that throne again."

"He will. And our work is not yet finished. I have heard that the King plans to call out Lucivenus in one final battle for the city. Many will storm the south district."

"Then he and his are on their own. We took back the south district, as we agreed. We are not an army to fight in open warfare. We can sit back now and see how the rest unfolds."

Harcourt valued the sword of the enforcer; few men

in the city could fight like him. He would feel better if Randar's blade was there to aid them in the coming fight. The thief knew how to ensure that it would be.

"Maybe you are right," the Guild leader said. "That half-demon knight, Phyzantiss, will most likely be leading the Cult's force. Next to Lucivenus, he is the most feared in Stonewood and we would do well to stay clear of him."

Harcourt thought to play on the enforcer's ego. Randar had always been the most feared man in the streets and he liked that. He worked hard to maintain that aura of fear. The thief knew that it would eat away at the vicious thug, to think that someone else was more feared than he.

Harcourt wanted Randar's help but he also would not mind if the enforcer met his end before this was done. The thief had been angry at the news of Serdic and that Randar, most likely, had been the one that killed him. He also knew that Stonewood would be a much safer city, without Randar living in it.

"Well, I am off," Weldrick said, turning to leave. "Find somewhere safe to hide and keep your head down. You don't want to lose it to that demonic knight."

The Guild leader left the headquarters and hurried through the sewers. He was not looking forward to calling out the demon lord but it had to be done. His fate, and the fate of the city, was soon to be decided.

Shortly after Harcourt disappeared in the labyrinth of tunnels, a shadow slunk about the hidden entrance to the Guild's headquarters. Trascar, the soul wraith, sniffed the air and knew his prey had been here recently. He hissed and sped off down a tunnel.

*   *   *   *

With the liberation of the south district, it was alive with activity. The folk here did not know how long this freedom would last, so they enjoyed it while they could. The taverns were open and the ale was flowing. There was still a nervousness in the air though. The demon lord was sure to be planning a counter-attack and none knew if he was planning to wipe out the entire district to make a point.

Harcourt wore his own face and wove through crowds of people on the dirty streets. It was a rare night when it was safe to walk the south district. Thieves, thugs, assassins and citizens alike all had a common enemy for once. Differences were put aside and anger was directed at the Cult.

The thief paused outside an all-too-familiar alley. An empty tin cup still sat on the ground, Kan's old cup. Harcourt clenched his fists in anger. Old Kan was just another victim of one of the thief's choices. He would still be sitting in that alley, alive, had Harcourt not given him a drink of the magical elixir. Though, if he had not done so, they would not have had the means with which to defeat the demon lord. Sometimes, Dornell had told him, sacrifices were needed to advance the goal. That, however, did not make it easier to accept.

Harcourt continued down the street and vowed to make Kan's sacrifice worthwhile. He turned down several mugs of free ale and offers to join in some revelry. The thief had one more stop he had to make tonight.

Soon he stood outside the Ogre's Den tavern. The windows were still boarded up and the front door repaired where the wraith had entered. With the tavern abandoned, there was little activity in this section of the street. Harcourt closed his eyes and imagined the tavern as it once had been, bustling with activity, Wulfred's jolly laugh heard over the voices of many drunk patrons, the beautiful Jalanna, smiling and serving drinks.

The thief went around behind the tavern and entered through the back door. It was dark inside but his eyes soon adjusted to the gloom, as there was just enough moonlight trickling through some gaps in the boarded windows.

Again he closed his eyes and could almost hear voices within the main taproom. He almost thought he could smell Jalanna's perfume. Then suddenly, he smelled something else. It smelled like......death.

There was a hissing sound behind the thief and he spun around, drawing his daggers, to face the soul wraith. Its shadowy face twisted in anger, at the sight of the man it hated so much.

"Let there be light!" a female voice shouted, from the shadows.

The room was suddenly illuminated as if lit by a hundred torches. The wraith screeched and held an arm up in front of its face.

Vrawg rose from behind the bar and tossed a heavy net which enveloped the unholy creature. Its shadowy skin began to smoke and its screeches became louder. Krestina had blessed the net and soaked it in holy water for much of the day.

"The net will not hold it for long, I must begin the summoning now," the priestess said.

"Quickly then, lass," urged Fezzdin, who stood beside the priestess, his staff at the ready.

Harcourt motioned for Dornell and Na'Jala to keep

their distance. "Stay back. If it gets loose, it only wants me. It will not bother with you if you stay out of its way."

Krestina sat cross-legged on the floor, closing her eyes and praying. She prayed that God would hear her and send them an angel to help in their time of need. Dornell and Na'Jala positioned themselves in front of her, forming a protective wall, just in case.

As the remnants of the holy water evaporated from the net it began to fall apart from the rotting touch of the wraith. Moments later, Trascar stood to his full height, free of his holy restraints.

"Come on, girl," Dornell mouthed, under his breath.

Vrawg was about to vault the bar when Evonne held onto his belt, with all her strength. She shook her head *no*.

Trascar raced towards the thief and Harcourt kicked a table over between them. The wraith lifted the table with ease and it crumbled within its grasp, the wood rotting almost instantly.

Harcourt kicked the creature square in the chest but it did not move an inch. It lashed out with a clawed, shadowy hand and the thief barely backpedalled, out of reach. It did not stop and lunged again. Harcourt rolled underneath its arms and skipped away. His daggers had been blessed but he did not wish to remain close enough to use them.

Vrawg hurled a bar stool, hoping to distract the creature. It broke against the wraith's back, causing only a momentary pause. Evonne briefly considered her crossbow but then recalled that it would be of no use here.

The soul of Trascar hissed in frustration, its anger reaching the boiling point. It never wanted anything as much as it wanted to rend this thief's skin to shreds and break every bone in his pathetic body.

With inhuman speed it sprang forward, catching the thief by surprise. Harcourt tripped over a chair and was tackled by the wraith. He punched and kicked with desperation, trying to keep those deadly shadowy hands from touching any part of his skin.

Dornell could stand and watch no longer. He rushed over to the wrestling pair and kicked the wraith with all his might, with little effect. The unholy creature had Harcourt pinned beneath it and it would not allow itself to be distracted.

"No!" Evonne shouted, as her huge partner vaulted the bar, his warhammer in hand.

Before the half-ogre could reach the wraith, a loud crack of thunder boomed overhead, shaking the walls and ceiling of the tavern. It gave everyone pause, including Trascar.

Suddenly, a blinding light filled the taproom, causing all to cover their stinging eyes. Even Harcourt, desperate to get his unholy enemy off of him, was forced to shut his eyes. He clenched his teeth, bracing himself for the rotting touch of the wraith, hoping that it would not hurt as much as he believed it would.

Instead, the wraith gave an ear-piercing wail and Harcourt felt the weight of it gone. The thief managed to open his eyes in a squint and gasped out loud. He stopped breathing altogether as he beheld the source of the light, hovering just above the floor, in the center of the taproom.

Where the wraith's body appeared to be made up of swirling shadows, the angel's form appeared as swirling, silvery mists. It hovered in the air with sparkling silvery wings, the light from its body now not nearly as brilliant as when it appeared. Like the wraith, the mists of its face took on human features and the face of the angel was, unmistakably, that of Jalanna. God had answered Krestina's prayer and sent them an angel.

Tears formed in Harcourt's eyes. So entranced was he that he did not even notice the wraith, rushing towards him yet again. The thief was oblivious to the coming danger, kneeling on the floor and staring up at the face of Jalanna.

As Trascar attempted to wrap his shadowy hands around the neck of his enemy, another blinding ray of silver light, more powerful than the first, blew him back and straight through the tavern wall. He landed on the street beyond and Jalanna followed him out. Folk that had been loitering nearby scattered at the sight of the pair, certain that Lucivenus had sent minions to wipe them all out.

Trascar hissed and rose, and Jalanna flew straight at him. The two otherworldly beings grappled in a deadly dance of death. The touch of the angel burned the wraith and caused it to screech. But so too did the wraith's touch have an effect; the silver light of the angel's body dimmed and turned black wherever the shadowy hands made contact.

Jalanna tightened her grip on Trascar's left wrist and finally burned right through it. The shadows of the wraith's hand dissipated and blew away in the night breeze. The wraith growled and grabbed the angel by the throat with his right hand. Jalanna's silver eyes went wide as her neck went black, tendrils of shadow creeping their way up her face.

Harcourt, who watched from the hole in the tavern's

wall, had no idea what would happen, if those shadows enveloped her face and did not want to wait to find out. With a roar, the thief charged forward and dove at the wraith, sinking both of his daggers deep into the creature's shoulders. The blessed blades did cause the wraith much pain and it released Jalanna, with a howl.

The angel's hands began to glow brightly until they reached a brilliance where Harcourt needed to avert his gaze. With one final blast of silver light, the angel blew a hole clean through the wraith's chest.

Trascar stood motionless, a dumb-founded expression upon its shadowy face. It glanced down to the hole in its chest, then the shadows of its body blew away in all directions and the soul of the former Guild leader returned to the pits of the Abyss.

Teary-eyed, Harcourt fell to his knees, looking up into the face of the angel. "I am sorry," he finally managed to say. "I am sorry I could not protect you."

The angel folded her wings against her back and softly dropped to the ground to stand in front of the thief. There was a warm smile and she placed her hand on his head. "It was not your fault," she replied, with a soothing melodic voice that reminded the thief of tiny chiming bells. "Do not blame yourself. What is done cannot be undone."

"Are….are you ok? You yet live?"

"No, my love, I do not live as you know it. But yes, I am fine. Death is not the end. More I cannot say, for it would be beyond your understanding. You will see, one day, but not this day."

"I have missed you."

Jalanna smiled. "And I you. But you have a life to live, so live it, enjoy it and do not dwell on the past.

Please."

Harcourt glanced over to Krestina who now stood nearby and Jalanna noticed the expression on his face. She lifted the thief's chin and leaned in closer.

"She is beautiful and worthy of you. Do not feel guilt, my love, you have my blessing. Do not let her get away. You can be very happy together and you deserve that. Worry not about me. As I said, things are different after death and one day you will understand. Now, my duty is fulfilled, I am being called back. Good-bye, Harcourt."

"Please, don't leave!"

"I must. And you must focus your love on the priestess now, all of it. That is my wish. Now, Harcourt, I must go. Be careful in the coming days. Lucivenus is powerful, do not underestimate him."

Jalanna kissed him on the forehead and he could feel a surge of energy. He reached up to touch her face but then she was gone. Despite the soul-wrenching sadness he felt, a weight lifted from his shoulders. He looked over to Krestina and smiled. He mouthed the words, *thank you.*

# CHAPTER 25

Lucivenus stormed back into the room from the balcony
and punched a wall in rage, his massive fist leaving a dent
in the solid stone. He was furious over the ceaseless taunts
which he had been subject to for the better part of the day.
King Stonewood, or whoever it was that was disguised as
the King, shouted taunts and challenges for the demon
lord to meet him in battle.

The wizard Fezzdin, had employed a spell which
amplified the King's voice so that the entire city could hear
him. The fool stood somewhere in the south district,
calling Lucivenus a coward and afraid to meet him a
second time.

"The soul wraith failed to kill whoever that fool is,"
the demon lord growled.

"They have proven themselves resourceful, my lord,
but they are no match for you," High Priest Sarvin said
smoothly, standing in the room, along with Phyzantiss and
Gryndall. "You should go to him. Destroy him once and
for all, and fly over the city holding his head aloft for all to

see."

"I will do precisely that," the demon's voice boomed. "When darkness again falls over the city, his life and the lives of those loyal to him will come to an end. Phyzantiss, gather a force of wraggoth. You will lead the way. Kill everyone in that loathsome district but leave the one who plays King. He is mine."

The demon lord and his lackeys left the chamber, once again leaving the High Priest out of their plans, thinking him not worthy. So be it, he thought to himself. If the demon lord had not been so lazy, he could have ended this long ago. Now the fools who opposed him had a chance. A slim one, but a chance none the less. Oh well, Sarvin thought to himself, he still held the castle, with many cultists loyal to him.

\*    \*    \*    \*

Captain Gregor, captain of the castle guard before the Cult takeover, led a force of men into an underground chamber within the sewer system. The roar of the waterfall, which concealed the hidden entrance into the castle, drowned out all sound of their approach.

Four men carried a long plank of thick wood and positioned one end on the far ledge where the door lay hidden behind the falling water. One soldier, dressed in heavy plate armor, tested the makeshift bridge, crossing safely to the other side. He gave the thumbs up and Captain Gregor led the rest of his force across and into the castle. They had to quickly find his imprisoned comrades, who he had been informed were ready and waiting to take back the castle.

As the last of Gregor's soldiers disappeared into the castle, a figure that had stood hidden among the shadows of the dark chamber followed them inside.

*   *   *   *

A full moon sat high in the sky and illuminated the fields outside the walls of Stonewood with its silver glow. Thelvius the Great wore his gleaming set of bronze plate armor complete with a bronze helm that covered his face, similar to the one he wore in the gladiatorial arenas of the south. He was mounted upon a great, black stallion which also wore bronze armor.

Thelvius had no desire to engage the wraggoth army, not without the aid of Stonewood troops. He counted his men among the greatest of warriors but they numbered too few. Somehow, the Cult had discovered them and moved quickly. It was too late to pull back and retreat, so now, he meant to take as many of those ugly beasts as he could along to the underworld with him.

"We should have left this city long ago, Stonewood be damned," the one-eyed Jordann remarked, seated on his own horse, next to Thelvius.

"Don't tell me the mighty Jordann is afraid to die?"

The mercenary scoffed at the notion. "Nay, you know better than that. I just have more living left in me to do."

"You mean, you have that brunette lass in Glennbarden that you have to go back and visit."

"That too."

Another large mercenary, a great battle axe strapped to his back, jogged up to join the pair, his armor jingling. "Thelvius, what's the plan?"

"Take as many of them down as you can before you fall," the mercenary leader replied.

The dark-haired mercenary grimaced, not expecting that answer from their great leader.

"Kris, we cannot fall back and we are sorely outnumbered. There are no tactics that will save us this night. So fight hard."

The Cult's cavalry stood a short distance away from the mercenary army. They had triple the number of horsemen that Thelvius had, but, the former gladiator had ways of neutralizing an enemy's cavalry.

As the mounted cultists began to trot forward, Thelvius looked down to his right. "Ok Jag, you ready boy? Go get them!"

The huge war dog, covered in spiked armor, growled and took off, racing towards the enemy cavalry. Behind him, ran another thirty dogs, similarly armored.

The cultists did not know what to make of the charging dogs. These men would send dogs to fight their battle? As Jag ran into their midst, their purpose became quite clear. The huge dogs were none-the-less low enough to run underneath the horses, their spiked armor ripping open the animal's stomachs. As well, the dogs were too low to the ground for a mounted warrior to strike at them.

Within minutes, the battlefield was a bloody mess. Thelvius hated to kill horses. They were good animals and expensive, but they were left with no choice.

"Alright boys, let's give Jag a hand!" the mercenary leader shouted to his men.

\*   \*   \*   \*

A glimmer of hope resonated throughout the city of Stonewood. Their King's voice could be heard everywhere, as he called out taunts and challenges to the evil Lucivenus. His voice was gravelly but then he had survived a terrible throat injury. If the King was calling out the demon lord, then he must have a plan.

Thousands of citizens climbed onto the roofs of their homes and other buildings to catch a glimpse of their King. Others huddled indoors, offering silent prayers to a multitude of various gods and goddesses. And some others, very brave souls, took up weapons, whether sword or pitchfork, or even a broom handle, and waited patiently for the final battle to begin where they would do their part and help their King.

Harcourt, wearing the face of King Stonewood, stood on the roof of a two-story building, near the intersection where the south district met with the lower east. This area of the district had been given the nickname of Cabbageville. It was the point where the bulk of the Cult's army would march into the south district. They were already positioned a few blocks north.

Night had fallen and Harcourt's throat was sore. Fezzdin's spell amplified his voice so they were sure that Lucivenus would hear him. He had shouted taunts at the demon lord all day long but they had a feeling that Lucivenus, would not respond until nightfall; demons and wraggoth despised sunlight.

Their assumptions were correct. "He comes," Harcourt said, almost despairingly, to the white-haired wizard next to him.

Off in the distance, a large shadowy form flew off one of the castle's balconies. Great bat-like wings carried the demon lord high into the sky. He circled several times in front of the full moon for dramatic effect, before setting his sights on the south district.

"I must be mad," Harcourt mumbled, just loud enough to be heard by Fezzdin. "I was a thief. Since when did I take up challenging demons to fights?"

Fezzdin smiled as the thief grabbed a rope and slid down the side of the building to the dirty street below. His stomach was in knots, thinking about the confrontation to come. They did not have enough warriors to defeat the cultists and wraggoth. They were placing all their hopes on defeating and banishing Lucivenus, and praying that his followers would flee thereafter.

Prince Orval was now in command of the northern army and was about to assault the hosts of wraggoth that had the city surrounded. But they would be of little help to the thief and his friends here on the streets inside the city. It was here, that the real battle for Stonewood would be fought, and there were so precious few of them.

Harcourt looked up to a second floor window where he winked to Evonne. The blonde bounty hunter sat by a window, the room she was in filled with more bolts than she could probably fire with her crossbow. She would grow weary of shooting long before she ran out of ammunition.

Other archers were also seen in several windows and roofs. Barros, their best marksman, saluted the King, from the roof where he was perched. He, like almost everyone else here, believed Harcourt was the real King and he would gladly give his life in aid of his King and his city.

Vrawg placed the last of the wagons on top of a makeshift barrier in the street. He had piled as many wagons and barrels and anything else he could get his hands on to create a barricade that would slow the advance of their enemies. It would not hold them for long but any delay would help.

Harcourt nodded to Naziya. The exotic warrior leaned against the wall of a building, nervously waiting. Her silver, two-piece armor gleamed in the moonlight. They had again implored her to hide somewhere safe but she insisted on being here, standing with them to the end.

Krestina stepped out of a dark alley, worry clearly written on her beautiful face. Since the summoning of the angel, more lines had formed underneath her eyes, the spell having taken a toll. The priestess now wore a suit of plate armor in place of her usual brown robes. She was no warrior-priestess and walked awkwardly in the bulky armor.

Harcourt insisted she wear the armor. The holy mace that was needed to defeat the demon lord could only be wielded by the priestess. Even Vrawg, with all his strength, could not lift the weapon. So the duty fell to Krestina and she would need to strike Lucivenus with the mace. It was said that the mace had the power to paralyze the demon lord, and give Fezzdin the time he would need to read the spell of imprisonment that would again banish Lucivenus from this world.

Krestina would be in great danger, forced to get so close to the demon lord. So it was determined that Dornell and Na'Jala would remain by her side, offering as much protection as they could.

Dornell stood to her left side, once again wearing the uniform of the south district captain, the emblem of Stonewood displayed proudly on the tunic he wore, overtop his chain mail armor.

Na'Jala stood on her opposite side, looking ever like the menacing gladiator, with the armor and mask that were permanently grafted to his skin. He too, had been given one last chance to leave the city and go back to his home. Of course, the black-skinned warrior refused and planned to stand with his new friends, no matter what they faced.

Harcourt hugged the armored priestess and whispered in her ear. "I love you. You be careful."

Krestina smiled. She had felt a small measure of worry at how Harcourt would deal with the encounter with the angel. She was not sure if seeing Jalanna, or what was once the soul of Jalanna, would change their relationship. She had noticed a change in her lover but it was a good change. He seemed genuinely happy, like a burden had been lifted.

"I love you too," she replied. "And you be more careful. Lucivenus is coming here for you, after all."

Harcourt laughed and again, thought himself mad. Here he was, impersonating the King of Stonewood and challenging an eight-foot demon to a fight. A demon which now hovered over the street, leering angrily down at the King.

A crossbowman, hiding in the same room as Evonne, lifted his weapon and took aim at the demon lord. Evonne slapped the weapon down.

"Our bolts will not harm him. If you draw his attention to us, I will shoot you myself."

The man paled and backed away from the window.

"So, little King, I am here!" Lucivenus shouted, while still hovering, far above the street.

Harcourt stood in the center of the street, gazing

upwards at the flying nightmare. Approximately one hundred and thirty soldiers, loyal to the King, were positioned all around the intersection. Not nearly enough but they would have to do.

Harcourt wore his studded leather armor, opting to forgo the armor more befitting a warrior-king. His job was to keep Lucivenus focused on himself, allowing Krestina to strike her blow. Since his plan consisted of ducking and dodging and not actually fighting, he needed the light maneuverable armor that he was accustomed to wearing.

The disguised thief gripped a long sword with both hands and called to the hovering demon. "Come and face me again. This time it shall end differently, I promise you."

"You are right, it will. This time I will fly over the city with your head, for all to see," the demon lord thundered. "But first, allow me to invite some others to our little party."

Lucivenus, still hovering high above, extended his right arm and hurled a ball of fire at the barricade in the street. A wagon exploded and several others caught fire. The human cultists, along with wraggoth troops, cheered loudly and began to charge forward, storming the flaming barricade.

*It's begun*, the thief thought with a sigh. He wanted nothing more than to disappear down a dark alley but he had no choice in this matter.

The demon lord hurled two more fireballs which exploded and opened gaps in the makeshift barrier; enemy soldiers swarmed through. Arrows and crossbow bolts rained down on the cultists from windows and roofs. Many fell but more just climbed over top the bodies.

Evonne took aim from her window and fired. Her

target fell and she quickly reloaded, dropping a second. The bounty hunter was deadly accurate, having honed her skills on the bobbing deck of a ship. As the fifth cultist fell, she dropped down behind the ledge; an enemy archer had found her hiding place. An arrow was now lodged in the wall behind her.

Vrawg roared and planted his hammer in the chest of a charging cultist. Ribs were crushed as the man flew back, knocking several others down with him. The half-ogre swatted two more aside, when one of the albino, spindly-limbed wraggoth leaped up and sunk his teeth and claws into the bounty hunter's left arm. Another latched onto one of his thick legs, which were not armored. Vrawg growled and spun, trying to shake the pale creatures loose.

Naziya and the soldiers around her soon found themselves overwhelmed. The petite, brown-skinned warrior drove her curved blade through the stomach of a wraggoth, before spinning and impaling a human cultist. She took a nasty gash across her forearm as she tried to pull her sword free. The cultist reversed his attack, aiming this time for her neck. An arrow from Barros' bow found his throat first.

A section of the flaming barricade flew away as Phyzantiss, the half-demon knight, marched through, unconcerned about the flames that licked at his ebony plate armor. His demonic heritage made him immune to fire.

From a block away, Harcourt watched the huge knight cleave his way through a group of the King's men as though he was fighting mere children. A ball of fire exploded next to the thief, pulling his full attention back to the demon lord, who began to descend to the street.

Lucivenus paused midway down, a curious sight catching his attention. From this height, he could see over the city walls to the regions around Stonewood. A large force of men were charging the wraggoth army, whose attention was focused on the mercenaries they now battled. The demon lord was puzzled. The human priest, Sarvin, had assured him that Stonewood's armies were under their control and far from the city. The fool had failed. Lucivenus raged inside. He would destroy that army himself, as soon as he finished with this man who played King.

The ground beneath Harcourt rumbled as the huge demon lord touched down a few feet away, a flaming sword suddenly appearing in his right hand.

"You were a fool for calling me out but I admire your courage," Lucivenus taunted, advancing forward.

Harcourt did not even have time to form a response before he was ducking under the demon's sword, wincing from the intense heat that emanated from the flaming blade. The demon was much faster than the thief had counted on and before he could even think of countering, he was backpedalling away from a second and third attack.

The thief planned to distract Lucivenus himself, minimizing the danger to others but men loyal to the King, rushed to his aid. Harcourt wanted to order them back but in the blink of an eye, one of the soldiers lost his head. Then a second fell away, as a fireball exploded in his chest. Lucivenus laughed.

\*      \*      \*      \*

Jag, the war dog, was in a battle frenzy. He clamped

his jaws onto the arm of an unfortunate wraggoth and pulled it from its socket. A spear found the dog's back but was repelled by the bronze armor that it wore. All the attack accomplished was to focus Jag's attention on the wielder of the weapon. That wraggoth went down with a shriek, as over two hundred pounds of muscle and steel crashed into him.

The bodies piled high around Thelvius the Great. As a gladiator, the man had never been defeated, not once. Many lords of Gladenfar and neighboring cities sent their best warriors into the arena, with the goal of taking Thelvius's head. All failed and he won his freedom. But now, he was in the toughest fight of his life. He and his men were outnumbered by the thousands. His only goal - to take down as many of his enemies before he fell.

Thelvius wore the best armor that money could buy. The savage wraggoth did not possess the skills to battle the fierce gladiator, or possess the wits to seek the smallest of openings in his armor. They attacked him in waves and fell just the same. He could not do this forever though; already his arms were feeling heavy.

Beside him, the one-eyed Jordann, wielded an axe and a short sword like a madman. The crazed mercenary never wore heavy, bulky armor and now bled from a half dozen wounds. But he did not slow. He just roared and fought on. Thelvius smiled and was happy to fight one last time beside his closest friend.

Suddenly, a horn could be heard blasting above the sounds of the battle. Thelvius wondered if the Cult was about to spring another surprise on them.

\*　　\*　　\*　　\*

Prince Orval Stonewood rode an armored horse at the front of the northern army. He raised a horn to his lips and blew, signaling to his men that the time to attack was at hand.

He was flanked by General Frock and a soldier named Darrick. The prince gave one last momentary thought to his new friends within Stonewood, and prayed that they would be successful. Then he brought his focus to the battle that waged in front of them and spurred his horse into a charge.

\*     \*     \*     \*

Dornell winced as the demon's flaming sword nearly took Harcourt's head off. The thief possessed amazing agility and twisted out of reach at the last possible moment. The former guard captain had never been an advocate of this plan but did understand that they had no other choice.

He was so very proud of the thief that he now called friend. Earlier in his life, Harcourt was nothing but a lowlife criminal, locked in the dungeons for petty crimes. Now here he was, risking his life to save the city.

Harcourt darted around behind Lucivenus and the demon lord spun to follow him, now exposing his back to Dornell and the others. The former captain turned to Na'Jala and Krestina. "Ok, let's go. Krestina, stay behind Na'Jala and I. Strike true, when we get close enough."

The priestess nodded nervously, then the trio left their alley and advanced towards the demon.

*   *   *   *

Soon after the arrival of Phyzantiss, the allies around Naziya dwindled to only a handful. The demonic knight made short work of all who got in his way. Now he set his sights on the exotic, brown-skinned warrior. He immediately recognized her as the one that somehow escaped the castle.

His great sword descended in a downward chop, to split her skull in half. Naziya managed to deflect the weapon but the sheer power of the blow sent a sharp pain throughout her arm and knocked her off balance.

The half-demon shot her a wicked smile and swung with a mighty two-handed grip, taking her sword from her hand. Naziya stumbled back and crashed to the ground, tripping over the body of a dead wraggoth.

Phyzantiss stalked forward, then grunted in obvious pain as someone darted behind and slid a short sword through a gap in his ebony armor. Enraged, the knight spun, slicing the air behind him with his deadly blade. He did not recognize the stocky human in front of him with the patchwork of scars that covered his face and shaved head.

Randar wasted no time and rushed the half-demon again. The Guild enforcer had only ever fought humans before but showed no fear in the face of the much larger, half-demon. Fortunately for the thug, his sword was enchanted and could harm the demonic knight. Many years ago, Randar had taken the sword from a travelling mercenary who had made the mistake of crossing the Guild.

Randar's arm was a blur of movement. Two of his

three strikes passed the knight's guard and struck armor. Sparks flew but Phyzantiss was unharmed. The half-demon countered, looking to cut the thug in half at the waist. Like Harcourt, Randar wore black leather armor so as not to restrict his movements. He dove under the great sword and rolled passed the demonic knight.

The thug leaped back to his feet and pulled a silver knife from his boot, driving it into a gap in the half-demon's side. Phyzantiss roared with a mixture of anger and pain. He reached out with a gauntleted fist and struck the Guild enforcer, before Randar had time to slip away. The steel fist landed solidly on Randar's left eye, which immediately began to swell as a burst of lights filled his vision.

The thug staggered and Phyzantiss swung his mighty sword again. Randar brought his blade up just in time to block the lethal blow but the force sent his sword arm wide. The half-demon followed up with a second attack. Randar did not have time to bring his sword back to block, so he cursed as he held up his left arm, in a feeble defense.

Phyzantiss cut the enforcer's left hand off at the wrist. Randar dropped to his knees with a gasp. The demonic knight rushed forward but lost his balance as someone tackled his legs, tripping him.

Naziya may have been petite but used the half-demon's momentum against him. She held onto his legs tightly, until the demonic knight dropped face first to the dirty street.

Phyzantiss rose dizzily to his knees, just in time to watch and feel Randar drive his enchanted blade into his throat. The half-demon gurgled and choked on his own blood. A second attack removed his head.

"I had that under control," Randar said in obvious pain, as he dropped his sword to clutch his severed wrist.

"You are welcome," Naziya replied.

*   *   *   *

Harcourt body checked a soldier out of the way before Lucivenus could cut him in two. The thief stumbled while doing so and was struck by the second attack. The flaming sword bit deeply into his right shoulder and ignited a portion of his armor.

Harcourt yelped and did his best to scramble back out of reach from the next attack. But it never came, as the demon lord howled and spun around. Dornell's blessed blade had scored a painful hit.

Lucivenus swung his flaming sword to decapitate the former guard captain but the attack was deflected by Na'Jala's blade. Dornell, Na'Jala and Lucivenus battled with a furious pace. Sparks and flames alike flew as weapons met weapons. Lucivenus was slower than the two human warriors but much stronger. Even blocking took a toll on the smaller men's arms.

Krestina was close by, waiting for the right moment. As an opportunity presented itself, she steeled herself and raised the mace above her head, running forward. Lucivenus caught the movement from the corner of his eye and suddenly recognized that hated weapon that the woman held aloft. Remembering well what would happen if that mace touched his body, he raised his left hand and hurled a ball of fire at the priestess.

Dornell jumped in its path and the fireball exploded against his chest and sent him flying several feet away. At that same moment, Harcourt drew his two blessed daggers and leaped upon the demon lord's back, digging his blades in deep. The thief cried out as the demon's body was hot to the touch and burned through his armor. But Harcourt did not let go.

That distraction was enough to allow Krestina to get inside the demon lord's guard and she smashed the holy mace against the red skin of his sword arm. Arcs of electricity leaped from the head of the mace and danced their way up the demon's arm. They soon engulfed his entire body and Lucivenus fell to the ground, twitching and convulsing with pain, unable to do much else.

Harcourt had dropped off his back, before being crushed underneath him. Panting, the thief looked around desperately for Fezzdin. He had no clue how long the demon would remain immobile. Still wearing the face of the King, he watched a trio of wraggoth charge their position. Three consecutive shots from a second story window dropped all three of the albino creatures. A familiar blonde-headed woman with a ponytail peeked over the ledge, scanning for more targets.

Vrawg, Naziya and a handful of soldiers continued to battle ceaselessly against the Cult's forces, when Fezzdin appeared next to the paralyzed demon lord. The wizard held up the ancient book and began to read the spell of imprisonment.

The air around them crackled with energy as the wizard neared the completion of the spell. But his voice suddenly faltered and the wizard stumbled forward, the book falling from his grasp.

"Fezzdin!!!" Harcourt shouted, noticing the sharpened end of an ebony staff, sticking out through the wizard's chest. Behind Fezzdin holding the staff was the half-demon warlock, Gryndall. The tattooed warlock laughed evilly and twisted the staff; Fezzdin fell to his knees, blood dripping from his mouth.

*     *     *     *

High Priest Sarvin used magic to enhance his vision and he clenched his fists in rage as he watched the battle outside of Stonewood. From a balcony high up in the castle, he witnessed Prince Orval cutting down the wraggoth troops, along with the northern army. The prince had lost his horse but fought valiantly, cutting a path through to the mercenary army led by Thelvius.

Sarvin was led to believe that his man, General Zayne, still controlled the army. He had been mistaken. Just when the evil priest was about to take comfort that he still held the castle, the sounds of battle below drew his attention.

He directed his magical vision below and cursed aloud as he beheld Captain Gregor, with other soldiers, battling cultists in a courtyard. Sarvin's men were outmatched and soon butchered.

Everything was unravelling all at once. This was not how it was supposed to be. The fate of their order now rested in Lucivenus' hands. If the demon lord was defeated, Sarvin would be forced to flee Stonewood. If Lucivenus prevailed, he would have no trouble squashing the rebellious men within the castle.

The High Priest sent his magical eye in the direction of the south district battle, seeking an update on how it was proceeding.

*     *     *     *

Harcourt, who had been propped up on his elbows, collapsed onto his back, giving in to despair. Cult forces still swarmed onto the street and Fezzdin, the one man who could end all this, was impaled on the warlock's staff. The thief felt foolish for believing they could have pulled this off. The odds were stacked so heavily against them, right from the beginning.

He rolled over and looked for Krestina, finding the priestess on her knees, weeping at the sight of Fezzdin. Na'Jala however, leaped into action. His sword almost found the warlock's belly but met air instead. Gryndall had vanished, then reappeared behind the former gladiator, slamming the head of his staff into the back of Na'Jala's skull.

The black warrior recovered quickly and countered, drawing a line of blood along the side of the warlock's neck. Na'Jala turned sideways, as a ball of fire flew passed him to explode against a building wall. He jabbed forward and Gryndall managed to avoid the attack and touch the blade, while speaking the words of a spell.

Na'Jala grunted and was forced to throw his blade to the ground. The weapon began to heat up until the former gladiator could no longer keep a grip on it, his palm burned.

A silver ray of light struck the warlock in the chest and smoke rose from the wound. Krestina cried out and blasted him again and again, the holy energy burning holes in the half-demon's skin.

Taking advantage of the warlock's distraction, Na'Jala

tackled him and drove a blessed dagger into his black heart.

Before Lucivenus could rise again, Krestina slammed the mace into his body. She struck him several times, crying with frustration. His body continued to twitch and convulse but he was otherwise unharmed. Krestina however, did not know what else they could do. Fezzdin was down and most likely dead, so she continued to strike the demon lord, giving in to her anger.

The priestess suddenly shivered as the air around her grew chill, almost painfully so. Then she heard a voice from behind, a terrible raspy voice that raised goosebumps like fingers on a chalkboard.

"You can cease that now and step aside," the voice said.

Harcourt could not believe his eyes. There, behind Krestina, stood a skeletal figure wearing a black robe that shifted and shimmered with a dizzying swirl of patterns. His head was a skull with red pinpoints of light, set back within the two dark pits of his eye sockets.

Mortimus Runefeld, the Lich Lord of Morgaldrun, extended both his bony arms and sent waves of lightning bolts through the ranks of wraggoth and Cult warriors. Dozens upon dozens, fell in a smoking heap, giving a momentary reprieve to the bloodied Vrawg and Naziya.

With a mere motion of his skeletal right hand, the ancient spell book floated up and hovered in front of him, pages turning on their own until they stopped at the needed spell. Again, the air crackled with energy and the demon lord's eyes went wide, realizing his fate was sealed.

Krestina got out of the way and ran to the fallen Fezzdin, who coughed up blood but still clung to life.

Tears ran down her cheeks and fervently, she prayed to God to allow her to heal the old wizard. Once again, her prayers were answered and her hands began to glow with a blinding silvery light. She placed them over the wizard's wound until color returned to his skin and the wound closed before her eyes.

More lines formed under her eyes and more grey crept into her hair. Despite the changes which she felt immediately, she smiled as the wizard smiled back at her.

With all attention focused elsewhere, Harcourt removed his mask, forgoing the disguise of the King and walked over to the priestess, placing a hand on her shoulder as he was watched a swirling, golden portal open up above the prone demon lord.

Lucivenus gave one last howl of ultimate rage, before being sucked into the black void of the portal and disappearing from sight. There was a silence that hung over the Cabbageville section of the south district and all battle ceased, as everyone beheld the defeat of the demon lord. Then, as predicted, the Cult forces scattered, heading for the nearest city gates. They had no desire to keep fighting after witnessing the fate of the powerful Lucivenus.

Harcourt suddenly looked about in panic and then relaxed as Dornell approached them, clutching his burnt chest. He was wounded but alive and offered them a salute.

Harcourt turned to Mortimus. "Our thanks, my lord. Your help could not have come at a better time."

"Do not mistake my aid for kindness," the lich rasped. "You fools were incapable of success. A failure here would only mean that I would have to deal with the foul demon myself, eventually. Now it is done and he will not be returning."

"Still, whatever your motives, thank you," the thief said.

"My aid does not come without a cost. I will be taking that most curious mask, as compensation."

Mortimus held out a bony hand and Harcourt's magical mask was ripped from his grasp. It flew straight into the lich's waiting hand. "Think not to seek me out. None of you are welcome in Morgaldrun. Do so at your own peril. You have been warned."

With that, the lich vanished, along with the spellbook, and the chill in the air receded. Krestina jumped to her feet and hugged Harcourt in the tightest embrace possible. He winced from his wounded shoulder but returned the hug.

"We did it," she said.

"Not yet," Harcourt replied. "The High Priest still lives."

\*     \*     \*     \*

High Priest Sarvin stood on the balcony, unmoving, for quite some time. His mind was attempting to make sense of all he had just seen through the use of his magical vision. The prince's friends had failed and the Cult should have won. Then the lich, Mortimus, who had not been seen in a century, suddenly appeared and stole that victory away.,

The two half-demons were dead and Sarvin could not have cared any less about that. Sarvin had even been secretly hoping that Lucivenus would be defeated so that he could rule Stonewood, alone. But he had not counted on losing his armies outside the city, along with his forces inside. Things had really taken a turn for the worse and the High Priest figured he would need to leave. He was a patient man, most of the time, and he would plot his revenge, then return.

There had been no word from the sorceress, Syrena. Sarvin had attempted to contact her but it was as if she had just vanished. He would have liked to have left along with her and have someone he could trust by his side.

The evil priest gripped the railing of the balcony tightly and contemplated his next move. Perhaps he would first make for the town of LongBridge. Lord Lark had proven himself a loyal ally. He could hide out there before deciding his next course of action.

Sarvin called out to his two personal guards who were posted outside the door to his private quarters, but neither replied.

The priest turned and entered his quarters, stopping short, after noticing a pool of blood forming underneath the door to the hallway. A feminine voice, off to his right side, gave the usually composed priest, a start.

"Going somewhere?" the woman asked, stepping out from behind a cabinet.

Sarvin narrowed his eyes, then suddenly recognized the beautiful blonde in the tight leather outfit, standing before him.

"You again!"

"We have some unfinished business, you and I," stated Feylane.

"I would have thought you had learned your lesson, that last time we met."

"Yes I did, thank you. I learned a valuable lesson."

Sarvin relaxed and picked up an unfinished drink off a nearby table, showing little regard for the beautiful assassin.

"I have one question I would like to ask, before I take your life," Feylane said.

Sarvin chuckled, genuinely amused. "Ask away."

"As a magistrate, many years ago, were you not the one in charge of collecting taxes and owed debts from the outlying farmlands around the city?"

"It was one of my many duties, yes."

"Thank you, that is all."

"I have a question for you now."

Feylane nodded.

"How did you get into the castle and all the way to these quarters?"

The blonde assassin motioned to a small brown sack that hung from her belt. "You are not the only one with magic to aid you."

Feylane revealed a knife that she had concealed in her right hand, then ran straight for the evil priest. Sarvin calmly spoke the words of a spell and the assassin stopped in her tracks, frozen in place like a statue.

He casually approached her and pried the knife from her immobile hand, tossing it aside. "I thought you said you learned your lesson, you foolish wench? You are no match for me."

Beads of nervous sweat formed on Feylane's forehead. She was frozen in place but was fully aware of her surroundings. Her mind was clear, only her body would not respond.

"I will not make the same mistake as last time," Sarvin continued. "This time, your death will be quick.

First though, let's see what you have here."

The High Priest reached down and snatched the small sack made from thick burlap from the assassin's belt. Curiously, Sarvin untied the top and opened it up. Instantly, his hand stung and he jumped back, dropping the sack. He held up his hand to inspect it and found two small puncture wounds. Glancing down, his eyes went wide, spotting the distinctive patterns of a hag viper as the serpent slithered away to find someplace to hide.

The snake was the deadliest in this region of the world. It got its name from the fact that witches, used the viper's deadly venom for all kinds of nefarious concoctions. The poison paralyzed its victim, then death followed shortly.

Searing pain shot up the priest's arm and the room began to spin. "Y-you witch!" he stammered.

The muscles in Sarvin's legs contracted and he collapsed to the floor, his vision blurry. A white foam formed in his mouth and ran down the side of his face. Like the spell that he had used on the assassin, Sarvin was still conscious but his body would not respond to his commands.

The spell holding Feylane soon expired and the blonde assassin retrieved her knife and crouched over the Cult leader. "I told you I learned my lesson," she purred. "I never make the same mistake twice."

Without any further conversation, her blade found the priest's throat.

# CHAPTER 26

Prince Orval rode into the city through the western gate. Beside him rode Thelvius the Great. Crowds of people gathered and cheered. The sun had risen and a new day was upon Stonewood, a good day. The evil Lucivenus had been defeated and his armies scattered and broken. Word had quickly spread that the young prince had fought valiantly to liberate the city.

Rumors too, began to circulate that his father the King had succumbed to wounds suffered at the hands of the demon lord. That meant that Orval would now be King.

Orval rode through the city, making for the castle, with a mixture of Stonewood soldiers and mercenaries following closely behind. They were met with cheers and applause every street they turned down, and kept a cautious eye open for any straggling cultists.

As they approached the castle's front gates, the prince smiled, noticing some familiar faces. Dornell bowed as Prince Orval dismounted.

"Stand up straight, my friend," the prince said, shaking his head. "The heroes of Stonewood need not bow to me."

"It is good to see you alive and well, my lord," Fezzdin smiled, looking his normal self, showing no sign of the wound he had suffered from the warlock.

"And I, you, you old rascal."

Prince Orval saluted each of the others in turn, Harcourt, Krestina, Na'Jala, Naziya, Evonne and Vrawg. "This city would not have been saved if not for your bravery. This I will never forget. Now, what of that traitorous Chief Magistrate? Has he locked himself inside the castle?"

Harcourt and the others glanced upwards and the prince followed their lead, looking to the battlements overtop the front gate. There sat the head of High Priest Sarvin, mounted on the end of spear for all to see.

"Who do I have to thank for that?" Orval wondered.

The prince's allies all shrugged, puzzled, not knowing who the mystery assassin was though Harcourt had a pretty good idea. Someone had spotted a beautiful blonde woman mounting the head on the spear. The thief smiled to himself, hoping Feylane came away unharmed from that encounter.

"Come, my friends. Let us enter the castle together. You are all my guests of honor. The drinks will flow this night," the prince declared.

\*   \*   \*   \*

Krestina finally tore herself away from the window and the beautiful view of the city to join Harcourt on the luxurious bed within the guest quarters of the castle. The thief's eyes fluttered open, having slept away much of the afternoon. He was out the moment his head hit that plush, silken pillow. Sleep was something he had been sorely lacking of late. Krestina too, but she was too taken with the fact that she was inside Castle Stonewood and the excitement would not allow her any sleep.

"Can you believe it?" she asked, noticing that Harcourt had awakened. "Two south-side orphans, staying inside the castle?"

The thief smiled. "You look beautiful."

Krestina had changed out of her normal brown robes and wore a stunning white gown that had been provided for her at the prince's request.

"Thank you," she replied, kissing him. "But I don't feel beautiful. I feel…older."

While she remained beautiful, she did look much older than the woman she was before this all started. She looked older even, than Harcourt, himself.

"Our childhoods were stolen from us," she continued, "and it would seem that so has my adulthood."

"Nonsense, you are gorgeous. No more silly talk, promise me?" he said, pulling her in close.

"Sister Tarrah wants me to become the First Priestess for the temple. They have already begun rebuilding."

"That is quite an honor. What do you think about that?"

"I am flattered. Beyond flattered. I would be the second woman to hold that title, after First Priestess Leeanne. But….."

"But?"

"But I declined. I don't want that responsibility."

"What do you want, then?"

"I want to be with you. Just you and I. We have served our purpose here. Let's just enjoy our lives together, without any more responsibility. I think we have earned that, no?"

"Yeah, I would say we have. Krestina, I want you to come on an adventure with me. Are you willing?"

"What kind of adventure?"

"It is going to be hard to explain at first but I need to know if you are willing to join me?"

"I will go anywhere that you go. I know you will keep me safe and always look after me. Yes, I am willing. Now, what adventure do you have in mind?"

\* \* \* \*

"Harcourt, I need good men like you, men I can trust. Can I not convince you to work for me?" Prince Orval asked.

"I appreciate the offer, my lord, really I do. But I am going away for awhile. Krestina and I will be leaving in a few days."

The prince sighed. "Very well, I cannot force you to stay. But please tell me you will not miss my crowning. I want you and Krestina to attend. That crown would not be mine if not for the two of you. We will also be holding a formal funeral for my father and brother with a special honoring of Captain Kanalandiros."

"We will be there, you have my word. Besides, Krestina would not let me miss it. She is beside herself with excitement at attending a real royal party."

"Excellent! And that will give me a few more days to

try convincing you to stay. There are many cultists and those who were loyal to Sarvin still on the loose and hiding. I need help in rooting them out and bringing them to justice."

Harcourt rubbed his chin in deep thought. "I think I have the perfect candidate in mind, if you were willing to hire her."

"Any friend of yours….."

"Great, I will see if I can find her and introduce you both."

"Harcourt, I cannot thank you enough for what you have done for this city. No reward is too great. I only wish my father was here to thank you himself."

"Think nothing of it, my lord. Stonewood is my home too. This was personal, for all of us."

"You made a good King."

Harcourt smiled and Orval watched the thief walk away. The prince approached a window and gazed out at the city. He wondered where Syrena had gone and if she was safe. Her shop was abandoned and there had been no sign of her since before the battle.

The prince was without his closest family members and had felt very alone these last few days. He knew now that his younger brother Denniz was not coming back. The Cult must have been behind his disappearance. He wished that he had the beautiful fortune teller, to be here by his side. He would not give up searching for her.

"My lord, there are ambassadors and dignitaries, awaiting your presence in the throne room."

Orval turned to regard Gervas, his father's advisor and his father's father's advisor. He smiled, realizing he did have some familiar faces left. Gervas may not have been blood but he was as loyal as they got.

"Ok Gervas, let us go then. I guess I need to get used to these kingly duties."

*   *   *   *

Harcourt led Dornell to the front entrance of the Ogre's Den tavern. The trip took them longer than expected as they were stopped by many citizens wishing to shake their hands and thank them for the role they played in saving the city. Harcourt was finding it difficult, adjusting to this new level of fame. He still felt like that same old, good-for-nothing thief he had been for most of his life. Now he was deemed a hero.

"Looks good, doesn't it?" the thief asked his friend, referring to the new sign that hung over the new doors.

Evonne and Vrawg had bought the tavern and had done a little restoring. Who better to own the new Ogre's Den than an actual ogre? Or half-ogre, in this case, but close enough.

"Does look good, amazing what a fresh coat of paint can do," Dornell commented.

"Have a drink with me," Harcourt offered.

"I don't drink."

"Well I am afraid you are going to have one with me. In fact, I insist," the thief replied, pushing the former guard captain, through the front door.

The pair was greeted by Evonne and saluted by Vrawg who stood behind the bar, giving it a good polish. The Den was not yet open to the public but one table was occupied by Na'Jala and Naziya. They had done their part in helping the bounty hunters with some renovations and now relaxed, enjoying a few drinks.

Harcourt told the former gladiator that they would join them shortly and pulled Dornell along to take a seat at the bar. The pair sat together, out of ear shot of the others.

"Krestina and I are leaving for some time. I just wanted you to know, my friend."

"Leaving? Leaving where?"

"Just leaving. A little adventure in search of something we have lost. We will be back at some point. I will miss you, you know."

Deep down, Dornell was a sentimental man but fought hard to conceal that part of himself. He cleared his throat and attempted to appear unconcerned.

"Yeah well, I will miss you too, I suppose. You kept me busy, for most of my life, trying to catch you and lock you up."

Harcourt laughed at the jest and saw it for the cover up that it was. "We will see each other again. I know not when but we shall."

In a surprising move, Dornell stood and pulled the thief in, giving him a giant hug and nearly crushing his ribs. "You better promise that you will be coming back, or I will hunt you down, I will," he whispered into the thief's ear.

"Let us have that drink now," Harcourt said, when Dornell finally let him go.

"I told you, I don't drink."

"You will like this one, trust me on that," the thief smiled, as he vaulted the bar to stand on the other side.

Harcourt grabbed two glasses and a bottle of very expensive, eastern liquor. He poured them both a drink and then using his sleight-of-hand skills, added a liquid to Dornell's glass. It was a sparkling golden liquid that dissolved when mixed with the liquor.

Harcourt clinked his glass against his friend's and they both took a sip. Immediately, Dornell felt invigorated. He felt a tingling sensation over his entire body. He took another sip and the feeling increased. He nodded to the thief in agreement; this was good. He gulped down the rest of his glass and he swore he felt years younger.

"What is in this?" he inquired.

"A secret ingredient," Harcourt smiled. "Now let's join the others. So Evonne, you both have decided to stay?"

The blonde bounty hunter shook her head. "Not quite. We have had our fill of your city, no offense."

"None taken."

"We own the tavern but we are gonna turn it over to those girls who used to work here, to run it for us. I am sure we will be back from time to time but I miss the sea. I may even buy a ship. Vrawg here keeps talking about it. He has always wanted to be a first mate. Haven't you, you big oaf?"

Harcourt and Dornell curiously turned to regard the half-orge, wondering if he was going to finally say something. The huge bounty hunter just shrugged his shoulders.

"And you, Naziya? Will you stay?" the thief wondered. "The new King is looking for people he can trust. You have definitely proven yourself."

"Thank you, but no. I will return but first I must travel home and deliver news of what has transpired here. I will be suggesting to our leaders that we open trade with Stonewood and its new King. I have been most impressed with the kindness and courage shown in the people here.

Especially you, Harcourt. I owe you my life."

"I did not do anything that anyone else in this room, would not have done in my place."

Naziya raised a toast to the thief and all took a drink. Even Dornell, who had received a refill, from Evonne. Though this time, the drink did not have the same effect as the one before it.

Dornell turned to address Na'Jala. "Will you be going home now?"

"I will. I am honored to have met you all and to call you all my friends. But I have been away from home for far too long. I am eager to see my children. Prince Orval was quite generous with his reward. I could probably even buy my own ship to get home," the former gladiator chuckled.

Harcourt stood and placed a hand on Na'Jala's shoulder. "I know you have already done more than anyone could have ever expected from you, but I was wondering if I could trouble you with one more favor, my friend?"

"Anything, just name it."

\* \* \* \*

Harcourt left the tower of Fezzdin the Fantastic and breathed in the cool night air. It was a nice feeling, to be able to walk the city streets again at night and not have to worry about the Cult-imposed curfew. It was also a strange feeling to walk the streets of the north district unescorted. Harcourt was hailed as one of the heroes of Stonewood and was given free access to any part of the city, including the castle.

He had been invited to live in the castle and work for Prince Orval, who was soon to be crowned King Stonewood VIII. But that was not the life for Harcourt, as tempting as it was. Harcourt was a simple man with simple tastes. He did not crave the pampered life of a royal or a noble. The thief had wealth enough now to sustain himself and he had a beautiful companion, in Krestina. He could not ask for more than that.

Harcourt felt at peace for the first time since losing Jalanna. Getting the chance to speak with her was exactly what he needed to be able to properly move on. And he had to admire Krestina for going ahead with the summoning, not knowing how it was going to affect their relationship. But she did it anyway, to save him. He was blessed to have had two women like them in his life.

As the thief casually made his way back towards the castle where he had been staying, his thoughts drifted to his magical mask. Surprisingly, he found that he was not sad that it was now gone and far beyond his reach. Surely he could not have accomplished all that he had without it. But now that the city was saved and he no longer needed to live the life of a thief, it was of no further use. Another chapter of his life was closed and a new one was about to begin.

Harcourt was nervous about the days to come and the adventure he had planned for himself and Krestina. They would be stepping into the unknown and it was not without danger. But, after a lengthy discussion, both decided to go ahead with the plan.

Stonewood would be safe in the capable hands of the new King and the watchful eyes of Fezzdin. The Thieves Guild was no more and hopefully the south district would get a makeover, making it a safe place for people to live. Orval had promised to invest in the district and help make it a better place.

A contented Harcourt entered the castle in search of Krestina.

# EPILOGUE

Dornell walked the east wing of the castle, feeling like a
new man. His body no longer ached or felt as stiff when
he awoke in the mornings. He had no idea what Harcourt
had mixed into his drink that evening but for the last
several days, he had felt great.

A wave of sadness came over him then, as he thought
of the thief, or former thief, he figured he should say now.
He was truly going to miss his friend. Harcourt had been
quite cryptic when mentioning that he and Krestina would
be leaving for a time. Dornell did not wish to pry into their
business but hoped they would be ok. He knew that
Harcourt had never done any travelling outside the region
around Stonewood. The world could be a dangerous place.
Krestina would look after him, he mused.

Dornell pressed himself against the wall of the
hallway, making room for some of the castle's soldiers
who were dragging a struggling older man bound in chains.

"You are making a terrible mistake!" the prisoner
shouted. "I am innocent here!"

The man had been one of the city's magistrates. King Stonewood had begun the hunt for all those who were loyal to or aided the Cult in any fashion. Dornell had spent many years of his life attempting to track down Cult members and it was no easy task. The King had his work cut out for him but now, the Cult did not have their evil leader to save them or guide them.

And Dornell planned to continue to do his part in cleaning up the city, his city. His role had changed now. He was no longer a city guard or a member of the Investigations Unit, but his skills and knowledge of the laws would not go to waste.

Gervas, the elderly advisor to the King and the overseer to all the goings-on within the castle, approached Dornell and gave a short bow.

"Good morning, Chief Magistrate. Shall I show you to your new office?"

"Lead on," Dornell replied.

\*     \*     \*     \*

Lord Lark of LongBridge strolled through the streets of his town, surrounded by his usual entourage. He had been surprised that the demon lord, Lucivenus, and the Cult members, had been so quickly deposed. Not that he cared overly much. He was not very fond of the Stonewood family but he supposed they were still better than some demon-worshipping cult. Lark figured he should send a message to the new King of Stonewood, congratulating him on his victory and inviting him to the town for a celebratory dinner.

First though, he had other things on his mind. Lord

Lark spotted a beautiful blonde woman exiting a clothing shop across the street. She was easily the most beautiful woman he had ever seen and wondered how she had escaped his notice 'til today. He motioned to one of his men then continued down the street, back to his keep.

"Excuse me, my lady," Lark's man said to the woman. "Lord Lark wishes to invite you to a private dinner this evening, at the keep. Would you be free to attend?"

"I am so flattered," Feylane answered. "I would be honored to meet Lord Lark in person. You can tell him that I will be there, this evening."

\*     \*     \*     \*

Zenod sat in a far corner of the main taproom in the Lonely Traveller inn and tavern. It was the busiest and most successful inn of Stonewood, located near the eastern gate to the city. The master thief was pleased with his investment, having bought the inn from Serdic's widow. Serdic would have been happy, knowing that his friend would look after the business that he had built and of which he had been so proud.

Zenod had never been involved with a legitimate, legal business and wondered how long he could fight off the urges to return to a life of thievery. The weasily-looking man was wealthy, he did not need to steal but he enjoyed the thrill and loved a challenge.

\*     \*     \*     \*

A heavily-laden wagon, rolled out of Stonewood

through the western gate. Two large horses pulled the wagon filled with supplies, along with the two drivers.

The bounty hunters, Evonne and Vrawg, were eager to get away from the city and get back to the western coast. They would miss their new friends though Evonne would never admit that. Vrawg was supposed to be the one with the soft heart but his sentiment had been rubbing off on his petite partner.

Evonne propped her feet up and laid her head back onto a sack of salt. "Now Vrawg, it's a long way to the coast. I don't want to put up with any of your long rants or boring lectures. Got it? Let's just try to enjoy the scenery and keep the chatter to a minimum."

The half-orge, who seldom spoke, just shrugged his massive shoulders.

*     *     *     *

Thelvius the Great rode ahead of his marching mercenary army, the giant dog, Jag, running alongside. Days earlier, he and his men had liberated Stonewood's southern army from the control of Captain Kenny, who, as believed, had been an agent of the Cult.

Now the mercenaries pushed west, towards the Black Peak mountains, chasing any remaining wraggoth back to their mountain home. The King had paid them well, extremely well. Thelvius had made the right choice in sticking around and aiding the battle for Stonewood.

*     *     *     *

Night had fallen over Stonewood and the south

district, as usual, became alive with activity. King
Stonewood had increased patrols and did his best to keep
the streets safe for folk to walk about at any time. But the
south district was vast and still filled with many
undesirable types; it was impossible to control completely.
After the defeat of Lucivenus, things had quieted down for
awhile. But over time, life in the south began to revert
back to the way they had been.

A young man exited a busy tavern, counting the coins
he had left after enjoying several drinks. Two men stepped
out of the shadows to block his path and one produced a
dagger.

"Hand over those coins, if you value your life."

The young man paled and was about to do just that
when suddenly a blade protruded out from the dagger-
wielding thug's throat. His partner reached for a weapon
but was advised against that course of action.

"No, no, you don't want to do that," a man said,
kicking the dying thug to the ground.

The young man with the handful of coins, threw
them at the men and turned to run. They let him go.

The thug locked stares with this murderer and found
his eyes cold and calculating. There was a confidence
about the man, that he found unnerving. Scars crisscrossed
the man's face and shaved head. His left arm ended with
razor-sharp blade, where a hand should have been.

"Who the hell are you?" the would-be robber dared
to ask.

"I own these streets now and you would do well to
remember that," Randar threatened, as another man
wearing a patch over one eye, stepped out of the shadows
to join him.

# The King of Stonewood

Fezzdin the Fantastic leaned back in his chair and gave up on attempting to read the book that lay before him. Lex had decided to lay down on top of the tome and get comfortable, and now the orange cat was sound asleep.

The wizard was happy to be back in his tower and was surprised at how everything had worked out so well. Evil was punished and good had prevailed. He blamed himself, somewhat, for the Cult rising to the level that they had. Fezzdin had been lax in his duties to keep an eye on the realm. But that would change. King Orval Stonewood would need all the help he could get, restoring order to the city and then maintaining it.

Fezzdin was also more than a little concerned by the fact that the lich, Mortimus Runefeld, was now in possession of Harcourt's magical mask. The undead wizard was dangerous enough as it was, but now with the remarkable mask, he warranted watching.

*Ahhhh*, Fezzdin sighed, a wizard's work was never done.

*     *     *     *

The air around this part of Suldarn was salty. The wind blew in from the ocean to buffet the bluffs of the beautiful coastal city. The climate was always warm in this region of the world, which well suited the man, who climbed the steps to the front gate of a marvelous-looking estate.

The visitor to the city pulled a rope, to ring the bell

and alert someone inside of a guest at the gate. A skinny servant, his skin bronzed from the southern sun, approached the gate and jumped back at the sight of the visitor. It was not what he had been expecting.

"I am here to see your master," the visitor said. "I sent a message, ahead of my arrival."

"Ah yes, of course, of course. The master of the house is waiting."

The front gate was unlocked and the pair made their way through the lovely gardens that surrounded the estate. They passed several more servants before entering a back door, which led to a wonderful glass room overlooking the ocean.

"The master of the house has been in poor health, lately. He will not be able entertain you for long. So please be quick."

The visitor nodded and was directed towards a large comfy chair, where sat a frail, elderly man. A few wisps of white hair were visible on his otherwise bald head. The man did indeed look ill, his eyes glossy. He did, however, notice the arrival of the stranger and did his best to sit up straight.

"Who are you, if I may ask? You have the look of a gladiator, if my eyes do not fail me."

"They do not fail you. My name is Na'Jala and I was once a gladiator."

"What can I do for you, Na'Jala?"

"I have traveled all the way from Stonewood. I come bearing a gift from an old friend, Harcourt."

"Harcourt? Harcourt?" Warden wondered aloud. Why did that name sound so familiar? he thought silently. Then it dawned on him and he remembered the thief and his old magical mask. "Ah, yes, Harcourt. How is he doing?"

"Perhaps you should look at his gift, then we can discuss him further," Na'Jala said, placing a small package onto Warden's lap.

The former gladiator apologized when he realized the one-handed man would have trouble opening the package. Na'Jala opened it for him and handed the elderly thief a small flask that contained a sparking golden liquid. Warden accepted the flask with his one good hand, then held it up to inspect it.

"What is this?"

"Harcourt wanted to thank you for the wonderful gift that you had given him. He asked me to deliver this flask to you and said that you would enjoy the taste, very much."

Warden had been a connoisseur of fine drinks and could not imagine there being something that he had yet to try. But, he would try it anyways. He pulled the stopper out with his teeth and downed the golden liquid in one gulp. The results were almost instant. Na'Jala knew what the effects would be but that still did not prepare him for witnessing it in person.

Warden jumped to his feet, feeling about twenty years younger. "Remarkable!" he shouted. "Incredible! Amazing! I cannot believe this!"

For the last year, Warden had felt like a prisoner inside his failing body. Age had caught up with him and there was nothing that all his wealth could do to stop that. Now though, Harcourt had repaid the older thief's kindness by giving him back years of his life.

Na'Jala smiled. Harcourt had offered him a drink of

the magical liquid as well but Na'Jala had turned it down, thinking it unnatural. It certainly was amazing, that much he agreed with. He wondered what the thief had planned to do with the rest, that was left over.

A jubilant Warden hopped all over the room shouting for joy. The retired thief insisted that Na'Jala spend the night so that he could hear all about the adventures in Stonewood.

Na'Jala agreed and the pair spoke long into the night and into the next morning. Warden heard all about Harcourt and the Cult and his old mask. He was pleased to hear that his gift had helped save the city that he once had called home. It was good to know that he had made the right decision to give the mask to the down-and-out thief all those years ago. Warden was distraught by the news of Jalanna but happy to hear about Krestina and that Harcourt was content.

Na'Jala left the next afternoon and headed down towards the harbor. He had already booked passage on a ship before visiting the home of Warden.

As the former gladiator approached the docked ship, he suddenly felt more nervous than he had ever felt, before any battle in any arena. He was finally going home.

\* \* \* \*

Dahleene Edgewood had run the orphanage in the south district for most of her adult life. She was a poor woman herself and relied mostly on the donations of others to keep a roof over the children's heads and food in their bellies. Much of those donations had come from either Harcourt or Krestina. She tried for years to get funding from the city but it had been a losing battle.

Since the defeat of Lucivenus though, things had changed. Not only was she now getting full funding from King Stonewood but he also had a school built in the south district, in her honor. It was named the Edgewood Public School. On top of running the orphanage, she taught full time at the school and received a salary from the city.

Oh how she cried when Harcourt and Krestina broke the news to her about the King's backing. She had them to thank for everything. The two of them would have made wonderful teachers and mentors to the children at the school but they had both decided to leave Stonewood. She was happy to see the two of them together though. Dahleene knew of nobody else as kind and caring as they were. They were a perfect match.

The short, round woman with the short, curly black hair hurried down a hall within the school. She did not want to be late for class. She needed to be an example for the children, after all. And this was one of her most favorite classes, story time. It was her favorite, since it was always the children's favorite. She loved to see the excitement on their faces as they sat on the floor, listening intently to every word.

Every once in awhile, she would ask for volunteers and have the children tell different parts of the stories. It helped with their memorization skills and they were always encouraged to get up and act out parts of the story, which was another favorite activity for the kids. Dahleene figured she would have them do that today. She had already told the children the story of *King Stonewood and the Demon* once, so today she would test them, to see how much of it they retained.

Dahleene entered her class and found most of the children already present, sitting on the floor and eager for story time. She quickly counted heads and found only two were missing.

As the bell tolled the beginning of classes, Dahleene could hear two little pairs of feet, running desperately down the hall. A boy and a girl skidded around the corner of the door and quickly took a seat on the floor, eager for today's story.

Dahleene smiled; they were a cute pair and they were inseparable. They arrived at the orphanage together, not long ago, but were not brother and sister. She had not been able to get much information about where they had come from but she had suspected abuse. The young boy had messy brown hair that he liked to keep short and many scars were visible on his face, head, hands and arms. She had never seen so many scars on a boy before and many looked as though were caused by blades. He had refused to talk about them though. Strangely, for a child of abuse, the boy named Harry, was always smiling and in a cheerful mood.

The little girl, Kristen, was always in high spirits as well. She was a tall skinny girl with long beautiful brown hair. Everywhere the girl went she carried with her a doll, with the same long brown hair clothed in a pink dress. Krestin held onto that doll tightly, as if it meant the world to her. Often she could be seen brushing the doll's hair so lovingly.

"Alright, children," Dahleene addressed the class as she sat in her chair. "Today we're going to hear the story of King Stonewood and the Demon again, only this time, I am going to ask for volunteers to tell the story. And don't be shy to act out any of the parts."

"YAY!" the children cheered in unison. They loved this story; it was one they had all lived through as well and knew it to be true.

"Now I know you have only heard the story here once, so if any of you get stuck on any parts, I am here to help you. Would anyone like to start us off?"

A few of the children shot up their arms, waving them in the air for attention but Harry seemed to have gotten his up first.

"Ok, Harry, how about you start us off today. And remember, if you get stuck, I will help you along."

Harry stood up and began telling the story. He acted out scenes, he did perfect voices. He retold the story with such detail and such enthusiasm. The boy never got stuck once. So impressed was Dahleene that she let him continue. His memory was uncanny. He told the story almost as if he had been there and seen all of it himself.

On the floor, Krestin hugged her doll tightly and hung on every word the boy said. She did not even blink, so enthralled she was by the story.

Dahleene thought it was so cute, there was so much love in the young girl's eyes. Again, she thought it so strange, how two children from apparently rough upbringings, could be so happy.

# ABOUT THE AUTHOR

Jeremy was born in Scarborough, Ontario, Canada. He started creating his own characters and writing his own stories by the age of 9. He is a boxing fanatic, having been an amateur boxer and is now a professional boxing judge. In his spare time when not watching boxing, or reruns of Lost in Space and Rocket Robin Hood, Jeremy tries to find time to write some of the many stories floating around in his head.

ed

9 780991 864249